Other Books by John Dunning

The Holland Suggestions
Tune in Yesterday: The Ultimate Encyclopedia of Old-time Radio
Looking for Ginger North

DENVER

JOHN DUNNING

Scribner
A Division of Simon & Schuster, Inc.
1230 Avenue of the Americas
New York, NY 10020

Originally published in hardcover by Times Books

First Scribner trade paperback edition October 2010

SCRIBNER and design are registered trademarks of The Gale Group, Inc.,
used under license by Simon & Schuster, Inc., the publisher of this work.

For information about special discounts for bulk purchases,
please contact Simon & Schuster Special Sales at
1-866-506-1949 or business@simonandschuster.com.

The Simon & Schuster Speakers Bureau can bring authors to your
live event. For more information or to book an event contact the
Simon & Schuster Speakers Bureau at 1-866-248-3049 or visit our
website at www.simonspeakers.com.

Manufactured in the United States of America

1   3   5   7   9   10   8   6   4   2

Library of Congress Control Number: 79019306

ISBN 978-1-4516-2613-1
ISBN 978-1-4516-2618-6 (ebook)

For Jim and Katie, and again for Helen.

CAST OF CHARACTERS

TOM HASTINGS, a reporter for the *Denver Post.*

NELL CLEMENT HASTINGS, his wife.

MARVEL MILLETTE, a reporter for the *Rocky Mountain News.*

DAVID WALDO, a printer.

ANNA KOHL, Tom's half-sister.

TERESA HASTINGS KOHL, Tom's mother.

SAMMY KOHL, Tom's stepfather.

GREGORY CLEMENT, Nell's father.

ALBERTA CLEMENT, her mother.

ABE KOHL, Tom's half-brother.

GABRIEL KOHL, Anna's illegitimate son.

JACOB HOWE, a blacksmith.

EMILY HOWE, Jacob's wife.

JULIA HOWE, their daughter.

JORDAN ABBOTT, a drifter.

JESSIE ABBOTT, his daughter.

PAUL | The sons of
MICHAEL | Tom and Nell.

ALICE WILDER, an artist at the *Denver Post.*

FRED BONFILS | co-owners of
 | the *Denver*
HARRY TAMMEN | *Post.*

JOHN GALEN LOCKE, Grand Dragon, Colorado Ku Klux Klan.

WILLIAM BROWN, president of Mountain States Coal, a rising politician.

SHAUGHNESSY, the fighting coach.

MRS. SHAUGHNESSY

ETHAN KOHL, Tom's stepbrother.

GENE FOWLER, former *Post* reporter, gone on to better things.

CARL GOODWIN, a *Post* photographer.

OLLIE BOOKER, a reporter for the *Denver Times.*

ARTHUR McCANTLESS, a young *Post* reporter.

BARNEY GALLAGHER, a reporter for the *Denver Express.*

SIDNEY WHIPPLE, editor of the *Denver Express.*

BEN STAPLETON, mayor of Denver.

CLARENCE MORLEY, governor of Colorado.

VIRGIL JOSEPH MORAN, a policeman.

RUBE HENRY, a lawyer, later a District Court judge.

ORRIN JAMES, handyman and chauffeur, employed by Gregory Clement.

MALLOY, a reporter for the *Denver Post*.

PRESTON PORTER, a gandy dancer for the railroad, murder suspect.

WILLIAM L. KERR, *Denver Post* reporter assigned to the Porter story.

LOUISE FROST, child murder victim.

ROBERT FROST, her father.

MRS. FROST, her mother.

MAN IN THE WHITE HAT, leader of the lynch mob.

GEORGEANN JOHANSSEN, a maid on Capitol Hill.

ELVIN PIKE ⎫ Klan
NATE NEWTON ⎭ strongmen.

GAIL JAFFE OWENS, wife of a senator.

SENATOR PHILIP OWENS.

MR. JAFFE ⎫ Gail's parents.
MRS. JAFFE ⎭

SENATOR ELI EAKER, leader of the conservative coalition.

PAT EAKER, his wife.

SAUL REISMANN, Klan attorney.

MR. JONAS, the landlord.

MRS. WASSERMANN, the neighborhood gossip.

LAURIE THE HOOKER

WILLIAM CANDLISH, chief of police, Denver.

BUFFIE, a maid working for Gregory Clement.

WOODROW, a butler working for Gregory Clement.

HANS, a grounds man working for Gregory Clement.

AIMEE SEMPLE McPHERSON, an evangelist.

MRS. MADGE REYNOLDS, a philanthropist.

SENATOR THOMAS PATTERSON, owner of the *Rocky Mountain News*.

VIRGIL, a boy in the *Post* camp.

BOY ON THE COT.

SHERIFF WHEELER, sheriff of Lincoln County.

HARVEY SETTLE, a landlord.

D.C. STEPHENSON, Grand Dragon, Ku Klux Klan of Indiana.

HIRAM WESLEY EVANS, Texas Klansman, soon to be Imperial Wizard.

HOTEL CLERK

JOEL CREGAR, a Denver businessman.

MILLER, owner of a speakeasy in Denver.

EDDIE O'REILLY, an assistant city editor at the *Denver Post*.

EDDIE DAY, city editor, *Rocky Mountain News*.

THURMAN HAYES, the rape judge.

MR. SANDERS, owner of a Denver market.

COLLINS, a cop.

A SERGEANT

A POLICEMAN

THE FIRE INVESTIGATOR

JOHN ROBERTS, a supervisor at the *Denver Post*.

THE DOCTOR, at the asylum.

MIRANDA JAMES, an inmate of the asylum.

MISS BERGER, a chaperone.

ERNESTINA HAMMOND, a girl on the train.

CALVIN COOLIDGE

MRS. GRACE COOLIDGE, the First Lady.

SCOTT HAMILTON, an etiquette tutor.

JON TAKETA, owner of the Silvercliff Hotel.

THREE MEN, hotel drifters.

WARREN POTTER, a lawyer.

THE WARDEN, Colorado State Penitentiary.

BOOK ONE

BOOK
OF
TOM

On the staff of the *Post*, as on the Hearst papers later, he was the embodiment of the Nothing-Sacred school of newspapering that flourished in his time. The newspapermen of Fowler's day were, in cold fact, much as newspapermen were pictured on stage and screen—hard-drinking, irreverent, girl-goosing, iconoclastic young men wearing snap-brim hats, with cigarettes dangling from their whiskey-wet lips and bent upon insulting any and all individuals who stood in their paths, no matter how celebrated or sacrosanct. There were some who complained at times about this popular depiction, insisting that it was not a true portrait, that the gin-soaked reprobates were few in number. They lied in their teeth. Ben Hecht and Charlie MacArthur had it right.
                              —H. Allen Smith,
                                 The Life and Legend of Gene Fowler

CHAPTER ONE

1

The President died on their eighth wedding anniversary. It was the fatal flaw in a day that had been carefully planned to exclude all flaws. The mistake was hers: She would come to know that in the days that followed, but by then the thing was done. People couldn't plan for the death of a president, or for acts of God, so, Nell Hastings came to think, it was useless to plan at all. The President died in a San Francisco hotel room, 1,200 miles away, not knowing or caring that his death would change lives in Denver as well as in Washington.

Nell had been planning the day for weeks: a few hours free of children and work, telephones and radio, free of all outside noise. The thought of it sustained her, made her heart beat faster. At times it was like being a bride again—that tremendous inner turmoil. Rejuvenation, a new beginning: time for touching and talking and making love in the sun. That was her program, that and precious little else. It left numberless exotic avenues open to investigation.

That morning she was up before dawn. She drew herself a deep bath of hot water and added a dash of oil. She hung the kerosene lamp on its nail above the tub and stepped tenderly into the water, sliding down to her neck and loving it as the heat seeped into her pores. She touched her pink skin with her fingertips, down to her knees, up again, down, up, giggling then like a silly child. A smile, brilliant and involuntary, came to her lips. Her fingers walked down from her navel and buried themselves in the thick, wiry triangle. She blushed at her own wickedness, then laughed softly and dismissed it from her mind. She was thirty years old, married many years, and all her Victorian inhibitions—well, at least most of them—were deep in her past. If she'd been a virgin at marriage, and of course she had, she and Tom had made up for it since then. An average of at least three times a week, fifty-two weeks a year, minus twelve for her monthly disability—forty weeks times eight years. They had made up for it nine hundred and sixty times.

When the water had chilled, she got out of the tub, dried herself with a rough towel, and waited, listening. Outside, the first purple light had come to the foothills. The house was still dark, and Tom and the boys slept deeply. She walked naked into the hall, enjoying her young body and the sense of adventure she felt. If one of her sons had blundered suddenly into the hall, she would have been mortified.

When daylight did come, it came fast. With it came the sounds of the outside world: the horse's feet as the milk wagon came by; the cries of paperboys; the smooth clatter of the Denver trolley as it swayed past, half a block away. She eased back into the bathroom, picking up her robe, slipping her arms inside and drawing the robe tight around her waist. Again she moved through the gloomy house, crossing the living room to the front door. And she waited there, watching the gravel road that ran along the foothills and dipped into the trees for its twelve-mile run to Denver.

"Come on," she said softly. "God, God, don't be late today."

The sun was just breaking over the eastern plains when she saw it: the green Packard limousine coming along the road in a swirl of dust. Orrin, as always, was driving. Her father would be sitting in the back seat like a monarch. She resented him the moment the car came over the rise, the instant she could see that he was in it. At least he'd come personally, without making her tell him why she'd been so insistent. She didn't like the boys being alone with the ghoulish Orrin, even for the brief drive back to the estate.

The Packard pulled into the front yard and idled near the front steps. The men inside it waited, as she knew they would. Gregory Clement would not come into her house, had come in only once during the entire eight years of her marriage to Tom. That was two years ago, when Tom was out of town on assignment. She had coaxed and urged, and had finally persuaded him to come inside for a cup of afternoon tea. But he didn't drink the tea that she put before him; he just sat at the kitchen table, letting his eyes roam around the plain room. After a while he said, "How do you stand it?" She smiled bravely and said it was easy; she loved it. Then the old man got up and strolled through, looking into the bathroom that still, after all these years, didn't have an electric light, pursing his lips in distaste before moving on to the boys' room. He stood for a long time, staring into the bedroom that she and Tom shared, sucking his tongue in disgust at the centrally placed bed with its opaque wireglass skylight and the obscene ceiling fan. He walked out without saying another word. He hadn't been back since, and she hadn't invited him.

So now she walked the length of the hallway again, went into the boys' room and woke them gently. First Paul, who stirred silently and understood at once; then Michael, who protested loudly until she shushed him with a dangerous look. "Up now, and be quick about it," she said. "Into your clothes and not another word out of you. I want you out of here in two minutes."

They struggled into their clothes and she herded them out through the front door. Paul tapped his way down the stairs, probing with his cane.

Leaving his throne in the back seat, Gregory Clement opened the door and the boys climbed in. His eyes met hers briefly, without expression, but somehow the emotions that passed between them were accusation and guilt. The guilt of authority defied. She had tried it once as an adolescent and he had committed her to a hospital for treatment. Only much later had she made her escape, drawing on Tom's strength to boost her own, and Gregory Clement had never quite forgiven them for slipping out of his grasp. It was always there in his eyes, that coldness, but she did not waver. She closed the door and stood with her back against it, breathing heavily. At last. Yes, at last, but not quite. She stood at the east window until the Packard had dropped out of sight and the dust had begun to settle over the road to Denver.

Done. She let out her breath again and clutched her robe against her neck. It was a perfect moment: exquisite, flawless. Anticipation brought a shiver up her spine. She went into the bathroom and carefully inserted her diaphragm. The floor creaked as she came into the bedroom. Already the skylight, facing east, was ablaze with morning. Only the top of Tom's tousled head was visible on the pillow. She stood over him, determined not to move, to stand there for as long as it might take. She waited until she couldn't stand it, then she leaned over and gently folded down the sheet. His eyes were wide open and he was grinning. He looked at her smooth flesh, then reached out and touched her. "Yummy," he said. She laughed and threw back the sheet.

She knew well enough how to please him. The best way, always, was by letting him know how much he pleased her. Gone were their days of groping love in the dark while her body lay stiff and enduring. Victorian. It had become her favorite word. How Victorian, how silly. She had been brought up that way, told about male lust and the duties of a wife by her Victorian mother in furtive whispers at home. When they married she had insisted that the shutters be drawn and drapes closed over the skylight. She had made him retire to the bathroom while she changed into a floor-length nightie, but he was patient. Gently he lifted the nightie in the dark and eased himself beneath it. She endured. Six weeks later she had her first orgasm, and she began to see the silliness of the old ways. Their sex life began on that day and had grown consistently better. Now they lay clutching each other in white heat and white light as the sun settled into the center of the skylight and blew up the room with the brilliance of a magnifying glass. She wanted to burst against him. "Ah God, sweet Jesus, dear Tom . . ." She thrust herself upward and thought, if she could think anything in that last moment, that it was, yes, nine hundred and sixty . . . *one*. She collapsed, drained and spent. "Lovely," she said. She had long since discarded her reluctance to tell him how much she enjoyed sex. She knew he liked to hear it. Her lips were against his ear; both of them were slippery with sweat, hot and steamy the way she liked it. Even the fan didn't help until five minutes later, when suddenly the room went chilly and they dove for the sheets.

Their first interruption came at noon, for the iceman. She tiptoed through the living room and told him she was sick and couldn't open the door. By the time she got back to bed her head was beginning to pound. When they remembered the ice, another hour had passed. Tom put on his pants and went out to retrieve it. The fifty pounds had become thirty and a steady pool of water was running off the porch. He clumsily carried the block in, shoved it in the icebox, and came back to bed.

So far so good. Nell hadn't mentioned his job and Tom hadn't mentioned her father. A fair stand-off. Banish those two elements from their lives and they might live happily ever after, like characters in a storybook. It was the first Thursday in August, the first weekday he'd had off since the war, and he was soaking up the luxury of just loafing. He enjoyed that as much as she enjoyed the frantic bursts of love. She had really become a sexual person; possibly, he suspected,

6

because she had no other interests. The kids were in school, the vote was won, the suffrage movement was now history, and she hadn't found anything serious to take its place.

Sometime after noon they got up for a light lunch—cheese and dark bread and bootleg wine. They finished off the whole bottle—which was a big one—and for most of the next hour she felt tipsy. They sat in the living room, separated by the width of it, and after a while the thought crossed her mind that perhaps he was getting bored. He got up and walked to the window at the west end of the house, where they had a clear view of the mountains. Then she heard it, the constant drone of cars outside. She came and stood beside him, her bare skin touching his. The shutter was cracked open, just enough for them to see without being seen. The procession of cars was unending; one came past every thirty seconds like clockwork. Most were Fords or Studebakers, cars of the common man, intermingled with an occasional Chrysler or Peerless. "There's a Klan meeting on the mountain tonight," he said. "I'd forgotten."

She shivered and drew the shutters tight, but he continued watching, peering between the slats. "Must be some big deal for them to come up in the middle of the week."

"I don't care." She was angry that the noise had penetrated their haven. "Who cares what they do?"

"A lot of people must care. Otherwise why have all these cars coming past our house at two o'clock in the afternoon?"

"Oh please, please, don't start that."

"Start what?"

"Being a reporter again." She regretted saying it at once. It was like the iceman, his sudden disinterest, her building headache: a taint on the day. She knew she should have dropped it then and there, but she said, "If you do, I'll scream."

"Don't scream." He put his arm around her shoulders and kissed the top of her head. And they stood for a while longer, watching the cars.

"They frighten me," she said.

"Now isn't that silly? You're exactly the kind of white womanhood they like to protect."

"I don't want their protection. I just want them to leave me alone."

He shook his head. "Crazy bastards." After a thoughtful silence, he asked her whether her fear was caused by the fact that his stepfather was a Jew. She only shook her head. A moment later she said, "I really don't want to hear any more of that. Not today. Those people just give me the shivers. Come on, let's go back to bed."

But he stood a while longer, fascinated by the clockwork procession of cars.

"To-om!"

"I'm sorry. You're really lovely today."

"Just today?"

"Especially today." He came toward her, remembering that it was her time and nothing was to spoil it. They still had two hours before the boys were due home. She lay in a yellow beam of sunlight, afternoon yellow, more mellow and romantic than the brilliant white heat of early morning. Her skin seemed to have a different hue, Oriental almost, and her appetites were more subdued, almost tender. It was like being in bed with different women, morning and afternoon. They moved slowly until they were locked together and her hot blood began to churn. She was moaning, rocking back and forth, when she heard the car door slam. She stiffened, unwinding her legs from his. "Tom! Jesus, Tom, the kids are home!"

But he was lost in her, floating in those final seconds when nothing matters. "Tom!" she cried. "For God's sake, the bedroom door's wide open! Get . . . *up!*" She heaved and he rolled over, angry and frustrated. From the hall they heard the front door open.

"Mommy? . . . Dad?"

It was Paul, calling cautiously from the front porch. They heard the tapping of his cane, then Michael's angry voice shouting, "Get out of the way, Paul!" Nell flushed; her Victorian sense of guilt came washing over her, and suddenly she was a *lady,* caught doing something dirty. She ran on her tiptoes to the door, closed it gently and called, "We're back here, dear!" Michael came storming up the hallway. He banged on the door and screamed. Paul had called him a name. "Just a minute, Mike!" She raced around the bed, gathering her things and foolishly trying to hide her nakedness. With an irritated gesture she motioned to Tom to get dressed and she disappeared into the bathroom.

He lay on his back, staring at the clock. Three o'clock it said, and wasn't it just like the old man to bring them home an hour early? Yes, as if he could see what was happening and took special delight in messing it up. Honestly, if he had had the old man there at the moment, he'd have punched his face in. Just thinking about it pushed him over the edge, and for a moment he lost control. He jerked on his pants, opened the bedroom door with a bang, and rushed past his screaming son. From the bathroom, he heard Nell call out, "Tom, don't start anything . . . Tom!" He ran out onto the porch, shirtless, steaming, and leaped down the stairs into the front yard. The green Packard was just pulling out into the gravel road. The chauffeur turned toward Denver and in the back seat Gregory Clement rode majestically, without once looking back at the half-naked figure of his raging son-in-law.

He picked up a rock and threw it, missing widely.

"Son of a bitch!" He walked slowly back to the house. Paul was standing at the edge of the porch, his blank eyes fastened on Tom's face. Tom climbed the five steps and put an arm over the boy's shoulder, squeezing softly.

Inside, Michael had wound up the Victrola and had dropped the needle down in midchorus of "Yes, We Have No Bananas." Sometimes Tom wondered if he'd outlive that goddamn record, or if it would drive him slowly out of his mind in the months and years to come. "Turn it down, Mike," he said as he came through the room. But if Michael turned it down, he couldn't tell from the bedroom.

Nell was still in the bathroom. Water poured and the toilet flushed. When at last she came out, she was still hot and beet-red. Her eyes were as frustrated and angry as his, but she blushed anew as Paul came tapping past the open door. Tom stood alone near the window that looked north toward Table Mountain. She came to him and touched his fingers.

"Sorry."

He shrugged.

"We can make it up later, after the boys go to bed."

But Tom didn't want to commit himself. What he did was have a drink, a stiff shot of straight gin from his flask. "I'd rather you didn't start that," she said. But it tasted so good he had another, refilling the flask from an illicit, unlabeled bottle hidden away under the sink.

He took the flask with him into the front room, where Michael was starting "Yes, We Have No Bananas" for at least the fifth time. "Play something else, will you, Mike?" When Michael showed no interest in changing the record, Tom lifted the needle, enjoying the loud *zip* as the point cut across the grooves. He fought off the urge to drop the disc edge-down on the hardwood floor. Instead he put it in its brown slipcase and replaced it on the Victrola with a Paul Whiteman thing called "Whispering." In the kitchen, Nell began to sing sweetly, rattling her pans and drifting away into falsetto humming whenever the words wouldn't come.

Tom Hastings sat in his chair at the head of the room and surveyed his world. It was an old house, rented, in the town of Golden at the foot of the Rocky Mountains. The floors needed varnish and they creaked when you walked on them. The walls needed a touch of paint, but were probably okay for another year. There was an unstoppable drip from the kitchen—the roof sometimes leaked and water dribbled in around the window in the boys' room, forcing Nell to stuff rags into the sash when it rained. But it didn't rain much here. Denver had three hundred days of sunshine a year. They had good furniture. The sofa was brand-new, but that was a gift from her mother, last year, before the old lady died. The Victrola, the china cabinet, the table his feet rested on, had all come from the old man— gifts to her and the boys, it was carefully pointed out. Nell hadn't wanted him to know that, but Michael told him. On the table were books: Fitzgerald's *Beautiful and the Damned* and Sinclair Lewis' *Babbitt:* gifts to Nell from one of her intellectual friends of suffrage days. On the far corner of the table, *Tom Swift and His Motor Cycle,* a gift to Paul from his Grandpa, still opened to the middle where Nell had stopped reading to him last night. The hell with gifts. The old man always made him do this, always made him feel like the scum of the earth. He had bought some of the things himself, plenty of things. The china that went in the cabinet was not as fine as he'd have liked for her, but not bad either. The kitchen table from a secondhand furniture store on Larimer Street, downtown. The beds in both bedrooms, the dressing sets, the chiffarobe. That was the extent of it; that was the kingdom. The material acquisitions of ten years' labor and eight years' marriage.

But they had love and good food, and in wintertime he dressed them warmly without any help from her goddamned father. Those things counted too, even if the king didn't think so. In his mind he could see Gregory Clement's stern face, saying nothing, condemning with his silence. Love? Tell it to the bill collector.

He took another drink. Good smells were coming from the kitchen, meat smells and red rice and mixed vegetables that Nell bought from an old colored lady at the end of the lane. He heard the rattle of the silverware (he'd bought that too) and the clink of glasses (her mom again), and he realized suddenly that he had been sitting there, drinking and dreaming, for a long time. "Whispering" was long finished, the needle scraping against the record label. The clock over the mantel said a quarter to six. He got up and went into the back of the house to find Paul.

He found his son near the window in the bedroom, enjoying the evening breeze. The cane rested against the table near his radio. Paul had built the radio himself from an oatmeal box. Seven years old and the kid had built himself a radio. Tom watched him do it, five nights running. He watched, fascinated, from a corner of the room, wanting to help but resisting it, letting Paul grope through his darkness for lost tools, lost pieces, shellac. He had the fingers of a surgeon. He shellacked the oatmeal box, then wound the copper wire around it, shellacked that, attached the tracks and sliders, put on the aerial and earphones. Finally, he fixed the crystal with its cat whisker to the base of the set, touching the whisker to the crystal and easing the slider down the track in search of a station. His head jerked up. "Dad! I got something in Chicago!" But by the time Tom rushed across the room and put on the earphones, Chicago had faded to a fuzzy hum.

In the following days Paul got Pittsburgh and Kansas City. One fine, clear night he got a burst of Spanish, which Nell told him was Radio Havana.

Now Tom picked up his son and carried him through the hall. Darkness had come as they sat down to eat. Nell said grace and they passed the steaming plates around the table.

And afterward, sitting alone again in his living-room chair, his mind drifted back over the eight years and he wondered how he was letting his life slip away. He was thirty-five years old and he had never written his book, which had once seemed so inevitable that he was almost shocked to realize how much time had passed since he had last seen it. He had figured it as a two-year project, writing part-time in the two hours before work each morning. He had his material, a grisly little lynching that had really happened. He would fictionalize it, yes, but not so much that people would forget or miss the point. He had his material and his theme—justice. He had some rough preliminary notes, and some outlines for characters. He had another drink.

He hadn't looked at it in years. Yet once he had been serious enough to write a series of prospective dedications. It would be for Nell, of course, but how he would say it would be the trick. Writers who slobbered over their wives in flowery dedications made him sick. He had toyed with, then slaved over, the words. *For Nell, who has . . . who . . . whose . . .* Christ! Now he remembered that he had settled on simplicity. *For Nell,* period. It was enough. She would know from that how important she was. Only now she might never know, because he hadn't touched the notes in six years, and if she should stumble onto his pitiful chicken scratches and find her name there, it would be more embarrassing than complimentary. Maybe he should burn it, just in case. In case he died tonight.

But he couldn't do that either, couldn't even burn the lone page with her name on it. Somehow that would refute the whole thing, expose it as a charade. It would be an admission to himself that he had truly given up, had turned his back on it and would write no more. An invitation to the walking death. He saw it every day at the *Post,* walking dead men who must have wanted to write something good (otherwise why be a journalist?), but had given it up and become paper-shuffling vegetables. It worried him, especially in moments like this, when he could almost convince himself that he wasn't good enough, didn't have the discipline, that even his skills as a reporter were eroding. He hadn't had a good story in weeks.

In fact, months had passed since his last good "writer's story." The hard-edged, sensitive, or emotional kind that he did better than

11

anyone alive. Maybe he was drinking too much again. Maybe Nell was right. Maybe alcohol rotted the brain.

He tipped up the flask and found it empty. When he stood, the room reeled. Outside a horn blew, then another. Darkness had come; her day was done. He hoped she had liked it, in spite of the iceman and the Ku Klux Klan, whose cars were still streaming past on the way to Table Mountain; in spite of her goddamn father, and her stupid husband, and his booze, and the kids. He was sorry it hadn't been perfect. He just hoped it had been good enough.

The telephone rang.

She hurried in from the kitchen. She was wearing that old green dress he had always liked, and had brushed her hair back until it shone in the dim light. "Don't answer it," she said.

He looked at her, bleary-eyed and unsteady. "You know I can't do that."

"Just make like we're not here. That seems simple enough to me. We're not here, we're out somewhere for a drive. We're over at Lakeside seeing the lights. I don't see what's so hard about that."

She seemed to be holding her breath while he looked at her and then at the telephone. He lifted the receiver, said hello, and listened while someone talked for a minute. Whatever it was, the news sobered him. She could see his eyes beginning to clear while he stood there. He hung up and looked at her.

"Harding is dead."

She drew in her breath. "My God, how?"

"Nobody's sure yet. It just happened. He took sick in San Francisco and died. That's all anybody knows right now."

He went into the kitchen, bent over the sink, and refilled his flask. She came in behind him and stood for a moment, staring off into space. Absorbing the shock. Two minutes for that, then she looked around for him. He was gone, back to their bedroom, to change shirts.

She stood in the bedroom doorway. "What are you doing?"

"Changing. I've got to get down to the office."

"Why?"

He looked at her strangely, surprised that she should ask such a silly question.

"Why, I said, why? Why, Tom? Why you?"

"Not just me. Everybody."

"Why? I mean, that's what I'm trying to find out. Someone dies a thousand miles away and they reach in here and take you away from me."

"Not somebody. The President died, and tomorrow there won't be anything else in the whole newspaper. That's why. Everybody in town will be doing local reaction tonight."

It didn't mean anything to her. The shock of the President's passing was already somewhere in the past, along with all the other nights he had gone out and left her alone. He brushed past her, giving an apologetic smile as he hurried out the front door. She followed helplessly, down the porch steps to the garage. He had turned on the light, a harsh bulb that hung from a frayed cord, and had climbed into the Model T to set the spark and throttle. He got out to crank, pulling the choke wire with one hand and cranking with the other. The crank whipped around and cracked him hard against the wrist. He doubled over, groaning to Jesus from the pain of it. But his pain felt good to her as she stood behind him and wondered how, short of murder, she could impress upon him what he was doing to her.

He tackled the crank again and the car rumbled into life. He leaped inside, and reset the spark and throttle, then eased the car out into the dark yard.

The mistake he made was going back. But the sight of her, framed in the garage doorway, looked tiny and fragile and tragic, finally got to him. He let the car idle, got out and went to her. She turned her back. He tried to take her shoulders and nuzzle her neck, but suddenly she whirled and slapped him hard across the mouth.

"Get away from me."

He looked at her in disbelief. It was the first violence that had ever occurred between them.

"You stupid *ape!*" Then for a full ten seconds then she was speechless. "You're everything my father ever said. You and your stupid red headlines and your filthy cheap job!" She burst into tears. "Now look what you've done! You've ruined everything!"

"Your lousy old man did that without any help from me."

"Shut up!" She clasped her hands to her ears. "Shut up, shut up, shut up!" She struck out at him and missed. She bent over, her hand tightening immediately around a stone, and rose swinging it hard, hitting him above the right eye.

He grabbed at her shoulder. The pain almost brought him to his knees. But now she was angry beyond caring. She pushed him away. "I don't care what you do," she said. "Just go away and leave me alone."

He left her. He didn't look back. Her rage was mindless and tangible, like a third person in the yard with them, a manifestation of all her years of frustration and inability to communicate.

He turned into traffic, his own anger rising and falling like a tide of water. Klan cars came at him in an unbroken line. Cars without end, all full of crazy people. Line up all the crazy people and you'd have a line from New York to Tokyo.

He held the wheel with one hand and fished out his flask with the other. He unscrewed the top with his teeth, tipping it back and loving the burn as the gin flowed free. Damn. God damn. God damn the world and everything in it. God damn people and bigots and dead presidents. Damn misunderstandings, because that's all it was. Someday they would laugh about it. He took another gulp, unconcerned about the job ahead of him. He could turn out better copy drunk than anyone in town could do sober. Some people said he wrote better drunk. He screwed on the top and hit the gas, peaking at thirty miles an hour, kidding himself that he was anxious for the long night to end, so he could go home to his wife and children.

2

A fiery cross, thirty feet high and fifteen feet wide, lit up the night above Golden. People stood in groups around houses and stores downtown, in tiny family knots on back porches and in vacant lots, watching. Children hung out of open second-story windows, laughing across the gaps between houses or windows. It was nervous laughter, the way kids do in the middle of a ghost story. On the street, some people stood alone, happy if they were white Protestants and grimly silent if they weren't, but watching, fascinated, in any case. On downtown streets no Negroes were to be seen. Throughout the week, the people had heard about the Klan meeting on "Kastle Mountain." An important Goblin was to be in town, coming all the way from Atlanta, Georgia. He would be here for one night only, and the Grand Dragon wanted a turnout, even though it was midweek and a work night. A mailing went out to all Klansmen, drawn from the Dragon's secret list, and on Monday the posters went up, nailed to telephone poles from Denver to Brighton.

The posters were written in that strange Klan language—full of mysterious words like Klakom Klukom and panther–anther, and were written in verse.

Throughout the town small boys had been memorizing the verse all week. In the Hastings house, Michael had come home chanting it. He was sitting at the window, watching the fire on the mountain. He was transfixed. Paul had gone to their room to play with the radio, which was okay because he couldn't see the flames anyway. Paul had always been blind, so he and Michael had their separate worlds. Michael knew that these were exciting times, that something exciting was happening tonight. The Kluxers were like great white gods. He had seen them parading in Denver, one day when he and his mother were shopping. He had asked her who they were, but she hadn't answered him. Later he asked a friend, Freddie Barton, and Freddie had scowled and said, "Boy, are you dumb. They're the Kluxers. They want to make the race pure." Freddie was two years older than Paul, and knew a lot. "My dad is one," he said softly, sharing a secret. The thought of Freddie's dad marching with the Kluxers in a sheet and hood was exciting. Freddie's dad was fifty. He was fat and bald-headed. He talked slowly and worked as a mechanic in a Golden garage. He seemed pretty dumb to Michael; not an exciting man like Michael's dad. But Michael never looked at Freddie's dad in quite the same way again, because now he knew that on Friday nights Freddie's dad changed his greasy pants and flannel shirt for the sheet and hood of a Kluxer. Later he asked Freddie Barton what Kluxers did. *What does it mean, to make the race pure?* "To get rid of the niggers and kikes," Freddie said. Michael looked grave. *You mean kill them?* His mouth dropped open. He could imagine Kluxers killing people, torturing them in weird ceremonies on the mountain. Pulling their fuzzy black heads off, like he sometimes did with bugs. But Freddie only looked exasperated. "Of course not, stupid. Just run them out of the country, back to Africa or anywhere else that'll take them."

Tonight he'd planned to ask his dad why he hadn't joined, but his dad had gone off to work again and now his mother was in the bedroom crying. She had been back there for a long time. When she did come out, her eyes were puffy and red. She came to him and hugged him hard, as though the hurt was in him, and when he finally wriggled free and tried to watch the burning crosses she seemed to get angry. She closed the shutters and made him move away from the window.

"The Kluxers are bad people," she said.

Neither of them spoke for a while. When he looked at her again, his eyes seemed to burn into hers. "If they're bad people, there must be a lot of bad people around here."

"I suppose there are."

"Thousands."

When she didn't answer that, he said, "Millions, maybe. What if they decided to take over the world?"

She just shook her head.

"If they decided to kill all the niggers and Jews, nobody could do anything about it."

"Michael! I'll wash your mouth out with soap if I hear that again. If that's what you're picking up from Freddie Barton you'd better find yourself another playmate."

"Why, if it's true?"

"It isn't true. How many times have I told you that? There's nothing wrong with colored people or Jewish people."

"Some people don't believe that."

"*You'd* better believe it, mister. Why, your own grandfather is Jewish."

"He's not my real grandfather."

"He certainly is."

Michael shook his head. "I asked Dad once and he told me. Grandpa Sammy isn't his real father."

"That's right, but still . . ."

"I like my other Grandpa better."

"That's because you've had more time to spend with him. We haven't been over to see Grandpa Sammy in a long time." She looked at her son and felt the guilt starting again.

After a while Michael got tired of staring at the closed shutters. He moved back into the bedroom to see what Paul was doing. That was when he saw the suitcases, three large ones, laced tight and standing in the hall. "Are we going somewhere, Mom?"

"Yes, dear. We're going to Grandpa Gregory's for the night." Maybe, she thought, for a few days, until they could get things straight between them.

Her father had been delighted, as she had known he would be. The car would be by for them within the hour. It sent her into a frenzy of packing. Later, when she was finished, she was amazed at how little there was: so few things of real value that she would want to take with her. For a while she sat on the bed, uncertain, not sure she was doing the right thing. Then sure, then not sure. Back and forth for long minutes. She had called her father in one of her strong moments, when she was absolutely sure. She had had a vision, clear and straight: Let Tom have a taste of the loneliness she had lived with for eight years. Let him know it for one night and he'd do anything to get her back. Then the uncertainty, the doubt. He wasn't the kind of man you fooled with that way. She had made a mistake; she would call her father and tell him not to come, she had changed her mind. But she didn't call, not then or later, when doubt became even stronger than the anger. A new factor, obstinacy, had entered the game. Let him suffer.

Faced with the imminent arrival of her father, she walked through the creaky old house and looked around. Her inspection was critical, her judgment harsh. The walls were a disgrace. They should have been painted five years ago. The drip in the kitchen drove her crazy; the leaky roof was a sin before God. Everything they had that was any good had come from her parents. The furniture that Tom had bought with his miserable sixty dollars a week was laughable, Victorian, only most of the time she felt like crying, not laughing. Every time she saw her father, that unspoken thing was there. You left home for *this?* The words were as clear as if he'd said them.

Their bed was an embarrassment. It squeaked so badly that some mornings she was ashamed to face her sons. This week one of the handles had come off the cheap bureau drawer. The chiffarobe he had bought was a ramshackle; even paint wouldn't help that. She would have thrown it out long ago but for two things: He'd have been hurt and she did need the storage space. The rooms had a hollow, empty sound, even filled with their things. Their skylight was the lone reminder that it had been elegant, a studio used by an artist who wanted to paint the mountains. Forty years ago. It had been eight years for them, and just now she couldn't recall a single night that hadn't been spent here, in this room, in that bed. And tonight she would sleep at home, in her old fourposter by the window, with a view of the lawn and the pool and the trees beyond the fence. Sleep lightly, uneasily, without her man beside her for the first time since 1915.

There would be some problems going home, but she knew them and thought she could handle them. Her father's damned Victorian manners, his possessiveness that bordered on tyranny. How would she handle that now? Again she saw the white walls of the hospital where he had placed her, and she shivered and drew her wrap around her neck. It had been done in love, he had insisted, to teach her manners, to help her grow up properly; but it had contributed to the nervous state that had plagued her ever since. Another scene, fully drawn, jumped into her mind. She and Tom had been seeing each other for six weeks, meeting clandestinely in restaurants, in City Park, at the Elitch ballroom. It was scandalous behavior for a lady of 1915—exciting, wicked fun. He drove her home, but this time, instead of leaving her at the gate, he drove past the guardhouse and pulled up in front of the mansion. She protested frantically, but he got out and opened the door, taking her arm, leading her up the stone steps to the front door. There a butler told them that Mr. and Mrs. Clement were at poolside, around back. Gregory and Alberta Clement were lounging in easy chairs, sipping from tall glasses and watching the day die in bored silence. He shattered their boredom in an instant. Suspicion crossed the old man's face as he recognized Tom: that reporter who covered our party. That snot-kid reporter with the chip on his shoulder.

"Father, Mother, this is Mister Hastings."

"We remember."

"He brought me home."

"That's not entirely correct, sir," Tom said. "I did bring her home, but I did something else. I fell in love with her."

"Indeed."

"I'm going to marry her."

Mrs. Clement almost dropped her glass. Even Nell couldn't suppress a gasp.

But the old man remained icy and calm. "Not only are you not going to marry her, you're not even going to see her again."

Tom met his eyes. "You can bet me on that. Sir."

Mom?

She blinked.

"Mom?" Michael had come into the room. "A car just pulled up in front."

Then she heard it: the click of the car door, the clump of heavy shoes on the front porch. Michael raced for the door. "Michael! Just you wait a minute, mister. You know we don't just throw open the door when your father's away." Especially, she thought, with those maniacs meeting on the mountain. She went to the door and peeped through the curtain. A square frame of light fell on the yellow face of Orrin. She looked beyond him, to the empty car, disappointed that Gregory Clement hadn't seen fit to come himself. Disappointed and, yes, as she always was around Orrin, a little afraid.

She opened the door. "Where's Father?"

Orrin gave a stiff half-bow and looked into the room. "Mister Clement had a guest when you called. A business guest, I believe, from the plant in St. Louis. They should be finished by the time we get there." His eyes continued to pan the room, as if he too disapproved. It infuriated her, but before she could tell him so, he spied her bags at the end of the hall. He moved past her and swept them into his arms. He was incredibly strong for such a light man.

He brushed past her again, so close that she could see the tiny cuts in his skin where he had shaved that morning. At least, she thought, real blood flowed in his veins. His mouth was pinched tight, a tiny ball like the vampire's; his hair was cropped short, almost to the skull. He wore a cap. He never smiled, because his teeth were going bad, perhaps, or just because there was no humor in him. He went outside, stashing the bags in the front seat, and held the back door for her and the children. So. The time had come, and she was either to go or stay. Michael and Paul came out and climbed into the car, while she walked through the house one more time, touching things, turning out lights. She turned out the light in their bedroom, touched the cool sheet and remembered the nine hundred and sixty days and nights. Then she walked straightaway to the car, locking the front door and throwing her shawl around her shoulders.

She had never ridden in her father's car. It was lush and modern, a businessman's car. She remembered that he even motored to St.

Louis occasionally, when business at his luggage factory took him there. Glass separated the driver from the passengers. There was a sliding glass panel, which she left closed. They had left everything, even Paul's radio, convinced that they would be home by tomorrow.

The Klan cars had stopped coming. Everyone who was going to the mountain was there. Orrin handled the car expertly and they made good time, working their way down through west Denver. They burst out of a tunnel of trees and into West Colfax Avenue, hitting the paved part, beginning at Hooker, with a bump. They had whisked past the Jewish area near Cheltenham School so fast that she hadn't had time to notice, to see if the area around Osceola Street, where Tom's family lived, had changed since she'd seen it last. Six years ago; that damned disastrous picnic and never again. Incompatibility. Worlds apart, of different ethics and instincts and organic makeup. Like people from Mars, trying to marry and socialize with people from Earth, and the confusion later, as if no one could remember who were the Martians and who the Earthmen.

They crossed Denver and soon the estate loomed up on the right. Elms grew down close to the road and willow trees hugged the ground just inside the gate. The guardhouse was dark and empty. Orrin got out, opened the padlock, and let the gate swing in. Even from there it was a long drive to the front door. The graveled drive made a picturesque turn around the garden. The house looked awesome, even to her. It had been built in the eighties by a silver king, an illiterate millionaire who had made his fortune in the hills above Leadville. His wife had wanted a little place in the country. And it had been country then: Nell had seen the pictures. There had been no fence, few trees, and Denver was an adventurous drive by buckboard. Seeing it for the first time in years, she didn't wonder that people were intimidated by it, and by the thin man with the white hair who lived here now.

Lights blazed from both floors. The front door stood open, with only an ornate screen closed against the insects of the warm summer night. Orrin held her door. She stepped out and waited like royalty for him to grapple with the bags and lead her up the sloping stone steps. Amazing, she thought, how quickly old habits return. Her back was somehow stiffer, her head higher: She carried herself with more grace and dignity than she had in years. The children followed at her heels. Buffie the maid came out, curtsied, and held open the screen door. Woodrow the butler, who had worked for her family almost as long as Orrin had, took her shawl and said how happy he was to see her. The grounds man, Hans, welcomed her in that deep Scandinavian-English brogue. Then came her father, King Gregory, down from the upper floors. He stopped at the foot of the steps and seemed to inspect her critically. Orrin, still holding the bags, stepped forward. "I've fetched her home for you, sir."

The remark infuriated her. "Orrin," she said, her voice full of anger. But before she could say another word, Gregory Clement crossed the ten-foot gap between them. He bent, still stiff and formal, to kiss her cheek. "My dear . . . it's so good to have you home again. Woodrow, please show Miss Nell to her old room."

3

A black Farmers truck rattled over the Colfax viaduct and dumped off three huge stacks of the *Rocky Mountain News* at the corner of Colfax and Hooker. Two raggy kids, not yet in their teens, jumped out and tore at the strings that bound the papers together. In a bed in an upstairs room half a block away, David Waldo heard the voices and thumps of the papers hitting the dirt street. He gave up his fight against insomnia and sat up on the edge of his bed.

His window was open wide. A light breeze ruffled the curtains. He moved carefully, so as not to disturb the young woman sleeping at his side. Not much danger of that. If the papers announced the end of the world, and preceded the event by five minutes, Jessie would sleep through it all, peaceful, content. David slipped into his pants and crossed the room, climbing down the narrow wooden circular staircase to his print shop. It was very dark; a streetlight fifty yards away provided the only light until he fired up a lantern and put it high on a mantel near the front door. The light revealed huge, disorganized piles of books and papers, all in disarray. There was a counter near the front door, where orders were taken, but now it too was cluttered with junk.

He went outside and walked up toward the hustling newsboys and their voices drifted back to him.

"Goddammit, Eddie, hurry up. Goddamn *Post*'ll be here in a minute."

But the smaller one was having his troubles. "I'm working as fast as I can. Jesus Christ!" He sat on the street in tears as he lost a grip on his papers and they began to billow away in the breeze.

David came upon them suddenly. "What's going on, boys?"

They looked at him in surprise and some fear. He was a huge man, forty years old, with bushy hair and a thick black beard. Stepping out of the night like that, he must have put the fear into their little black

20

hearts, but the big boy faced him bravely. "The President's croaked, sir."

He whistled. "Yes, please." He paid his nickel and stared at the cold headline. He had never liked Harding, had never liked any politician. He believed that there had been no good presidents since Lincoln. Still it was a shock, and his first instinct was to reject it. He walked the fifty yards back to the store. Inside, he blew out the lantern and turned on a small electric light over the round table, huddling there to read. Nobody knew, or was saying at that point, what had brought about the President's death. In fact, the story under the headline was only one paragraph, in bulletin form, made up and inserted above what was basically yesterday's paper. He had been cheated, really, suckered in by the old newsboy's con. He came to his door and watched them work their trade. They went through the street, baying the headline, and all along the block, lights came on. People tossed out nickels, then padded downstairs in robes and slippers to fetch the papers on their doorsteps. And they were shocked, and some of them probably grieved. None felt cheated.

Upstairs, Jessie stirred and came awake. He didn't answer when she called his name softly. He hoped she'd roll over and go back to sleep. Just now he wanted time alone. Thinking time. He enjoyed pushing the pieces of life around, especially at midnight when his brain worked best. Tonight, more than any night in a long time, he wanted to be alone. But she got up, calling him again. "I'm down here," he said softly.

He reached up and turned out the light, and in another moment she was standing in the darkness at his elbow. "The President died," he said.

"Oh," she said. Just *oh*. Another minute passed, and she said, "Come back to bed."

"You go. I can't sleep anyway."

She touched his cheek. "Come back anyway."

He didn't want to do that either. If she sensed the rebuff she didn't show it. She never did. She only showed her feelings when she felt happy. Jessie lived within herself, and people didn't get to her. "You want to talk?"

"No." But he found himself talking anyway. He talked about economics, which had become his self-taught specialty, and about history and the false prosperity that the country was having, about the economic depression that was sure to come because things usually happened that way. He told her that Harding hadn't been a particularly bright man, and why Coolidge wouldn't be any better, and she sat there without caring or understanding, or caring that she didn't understand. A lovely human sounding board who nodded and said "Mmm" at regular intervals. If all people were like Jessie Abbott, being a benevolent dictator would be a cinch. But who would need one?

Her father was Jordan Abbott, a drunk who lived in a tarpaper shack overlooking the valley. Once he had played vaudeville with a drama troupe. He had reached New York and got within shouting range of the Palace before his luck began to turn. He had played Shakespeare in Boston and Kansas City, and now he begged for a living, drank cheap wine, and in wintertime burned old tires to keep warm. Sometimes he disappeared for days. David knew he was in jail, drying out, but he never told Jessie. He just said, "He'll be back," and she believed it, like she believed everything he said. Someday, he knew, Jordan Abbott wouldn't be back, but he didn't have the heart to tell her that. She was so innocent, so naive. Her mother had died when she was a child, and Abbott's drinking had become progressively worse. They moved around, father and daughter, seeing everything, going everywhere. She lived in hobo jungles, slept in abandoned railroad cars, ate beans out of a can. The men had never touched her. Jordan Abbott had seen to that. He could be extremely dangerous, and people knew it. So she became the honor code of the rails, someone they enjoyed and laughed with and maybe dreamed about, but never touched. She had never gone to school.

She was lovely. Her body was flawless and wild, tough and strong. She could work with any man. Her blond hair had grown in its own way, getting washed in streams and seldom feeling the caress of a comb. She never complained. She loved everyone with the same ignorance of human nature that a child has.

David had met them two winters before. He was downtown and had lost his wallet. His pockets were empty; he didn't even have the six cents for trolley fare. So he had to walk across the valley to the West Side. On Fourteenth Street the snow began, one of those unexpected early winter storms. A pre-dusk pall fell over the city and hung on through the last hours of daylight. At five o'clock, David could see that the storm was settling in for the night.

He struck out into the valley, feeling the cold bite through his clothes. The wind cut through his pockets and numbed his fingers. By the time he reached the bottom of the valley, the snow had begun to drift. He slipped constantly in his good shoes as he tried to climb, falling, pushing himself out of the snow with his bare hands, falling again. His fingers began to freeze, his breath came harder, and for a time he actually seemed to be losing ground, sliding back down the bank into white oblivion. He had heard of men, sober and strong, who had been caught in these Colorado snows and had just frozen, sometimes within a few feet of help. When he saw the shack, he stopped and blinked, like a desert traveler facing a mirage. It sat at the top of the bank, rickety and abandoned. It had been a storage shack, used by the railroad for more than twenty years. He clawed his way up the last few yards, found the door, and pushed it open. A burst of heat almost knocked him backward. He smelled the stench of whiskey and old vomit. There was no light. His eyes, after the harsh white snow, took a moment to adjust. The old man sat behind the table, a long butcher knife in his hand. The girl was on the bunk. There was absolutely no fear on her face. Within the eyes of the old man were all the fears and furies of human experience. In a corner of the room, a tiny blue flame licked around some old tires. A crude piece of pipe jutted through the ceiling, carrying away much of the smoke, but what was left burned the skin and eyes. David made a gesture of apology. "I'm sorry . . . I thought this shack was deserted." Gesturing with the knife, the old man said, "Don't let the warm out, mister. Come in or go out, one thing or the other."

"Come in," the girl said.

Her voice lured him: sweet and polite, and that angelic face, framed in blond. He stepped inside and closed the door. "Just a minute," he said, still breathing hard. "I'm sorry to bother you. I got caught in the storm."

The old man grunted. It sounded like contempt. They stayed that way, motionless, speechless, for perhaps a minute. Then the girl said, "I'm sorry, mister. We don't have anything."

He didn't know what to say to that. Did they think he was a robber, demanding money? Then he understood: She was explaining why they couldn't offer him hospitality. They literally didn't have anything. His eyes moved over the room and he saw their possessions: a battered mouth organ on the table; a tiny red handkerchief knotted hobo-style at the end of a stick; assorted loose ends; the clothes on their backs. His eyes returned to her, and he realized that another minute had passed and he hadn't acknowledged her apology. He cleared his throat. "Thank you for the thought, miss. Just a few minutes more, to warm my hands, and I'll be off."

"How far are you going?"

"Not far now. The worst is behind me."

"My name is Jessie."

"Jessie." He liked the wild sound of it.

"This is my father, Mister Jordan Abbott. He is an actor."

Abbott cursed, a vile and violent oath, and threw the knife into the wall. He was forty-five years old, David later learned, though he looked sixty. His hair and beard were streaked with gray and his eyes had a blank, dead look that David had seen before. It came with drink and hard living, and too many years on the road. Jessie watched him with cool eyes, making no apology for their home or clothes. He was standing there dumbly; he still hadn't told them his name.

"I'm called David."

She accepted it without comment, with no change of expression, no hint of what she was thinking. When he finally made ready to leave, she said, "There's a path, if you can find it in the snow. It leads down through the trees to the street."

She got up and came to the door to show him. The smell of the shack had saturated her clothes. He smelled smoke from the tires in her hair. She took his hand, as if they'd always been friends, and led him through a snowbank. Beneath her shirt she wore nothing, yet she never shivered or cringed in the wind. "Through there," she said, pointing. "It takes you down to the street."

He thanked her again and struck off across a meadow. At the edge of the trees he turned to look, and he caught a brief flash of her before she disappeared into the shack. She was leaping snowdrifts, like some wild creature left to raise itself in the forest. He stood for a moment watching the shack, hoping she might reappear. When she didn't, he moved on. But he thought about her all the way up West Colfax Avenue to the store. She was like another wild girl he had known vicariously in his youth. She was like Rima, the jungle goddess in his favorite book. Alone that night in his apartment above the store, he rummaged through his things until he found the book, a first edition *Green Mansions*. He stayed up all night reading it, seeing himself as Abel and her as Rima. It was fine until he came to the part where Rima dies in the fire. Knowing it as well as he did, he put it aside and created his own, happier, ending.

In the morning he left the store closed and slept till noon. He knew only that he had to see her again, today, before she and the old man drifted away and lost themselves in the railroad jungle below the bank. He found a bottle of whiskey, given him by a customer who couldn't pay. He rarely drank, so the seal was still unbroken. In his ice chest he found a ham, too large for one. He cooked it with great care, seasoning with expertise. When it was ready he wrapped it, took three cans of beans from his cupboard and threw in a jar of applesauce. He grabbed the bottle of whiskey and struck out toward the valley.

He took to the back streets, which were still snowpacked, and reached the shack in less than thirty minutes. It was deserted. He knocked on the door and pushed it open. A faint smell of last night lingered, of old booze and burnt tires. He crossed the room and felt the ashes, where a faint trace of warmth lingered.

It was a bitter disappointment, but he decided to wait and see if

24

they would return. He put the ham in a snowbank and sat in the old man's chair, falling asleep after a time. They came back just before dusk: Suddenly the door was jerked open and the old man was standing above him, brandishing the knife. "Get out of here," he said sharply. "This place is ours."

Abbott looked seven feet tall. In reality, David towered over him. The shock of cold air and the hostile voice brought him to his feet, but the old man showed no fear. "What do you want?" Abbott said.

"I wanted to thank you for yesterday. I was hoping we could share a meal."

"We ain't got a meal. Just enough for two, that's all there is."

Now he saw that Abbott carried a loaf of bread in his free hand. The girl had a melon and a can of something. "I brought the food," David said. He eased past the old man and fished the ham out of the snowbank. When he placed it on the table and folded back the wrappings, her eyes went wide.

Abbott nodded toward the fireplace. "Get a fire going, girl."

They ate out of cans and off sheets of waxed paper. As always, David was careful not to overeat, but the Abbotts ate until the last scrap and crumb had disappeared. There was no conversation during the meal. A few times he looked at her, always catching her eye, always being the first to look away. She had none of the modesty of the old generation, none of the insolence of the new.

When the last crumbs had gone, he brought out the bottle. He saw at once that it was a mistake. Abbott's eyes clouded with suspicion, yet he was clearly unable to refuse the drink. David hedged, then said, "Just enough for a little after-dinner drink." He looked at Jessie and for the first time saw a trace of annoyance in her face. There was much more than enough for a friendly drink, and David knew that, once Abbott got started, there would be no stopping him until the bottle was empty. Abbott drank deeply. He rubbed the neck against his coat sleeve and gave it back across the table. Now David felt obligated to drink his share. He took much more than he wanted, anxious for it to be gone. They sat there for thirty minutes, passing it back and forth like old friends over a campfire. They never offered it to her or looked her way while they drank, as if the mere suggestion would be obscene. Abbott finished off the last few drops. "Just enough to wet your whistle," he said agreeably.

Later they talked—the two of them talked and she listened. David found the old man's mind keen and challenging. They talked Darwin and Nietzsche and Marx. The girl drifted off into a world of her own. David told Abbott about his friendship with Jack London and how London had converted him to socialism. They talked about the Sacco-Vanzetti arrests, both feeling that the men were being railroaded. It must have been nearly midnight when David got up and moved to the door. He hoped she would walk out with him again, but she didn't move. This time it was Abbott who walked with him, until they were out of earshot of the shack.

"I know what you want," he said.

David looked at him in the moonlight, but the threat he expected wasn't there. It was simply a statement of fact. The alcohol had drained from Abbott's face and voice, and what was left was a wise, wrinkled man who had lived too long and not nearly long enough, who had done everything and heard all the words there were to hear.

"I've met a hundred men in the last four years and they all wanted the same thing," Abbott said. "The one thing that stopped 'em was me. They knew I wouldn't stop short of murder."

"Would you kill me?"

To a stranger watching them, the question might seem ridiculous, but it was not so to either of them. Size had nothing to do with them. Abbott looked at him hard, trying to see past the eyes to what was underneath. "Come again tomorrow," he said. "We'll talk some more."

They did. The next afternoon they walked down among the railroad tracks. Jessie did not appear, all that day or the day after, when they walked again. Both times they went down to a hobo jungle in the trees, where they sat around a pile of cans and argued socialism and capitalism and anarchy. Each time, near the end of the day, the old man brought up his daughter. For a week the print shop remained closed, and the routine varied only in the different ways they found to express themselves.

He ached to see her again, but that was something Abbott wasn't yet ready to permit. On the eighth day it snowed again. This time there was no philosophical buildup. Abbott just walked until he found a window to conversation. "I made a mistake," he said.

David stepped across steel rails and waited.

"I let her grow up wild," the old man said. "I thought it was the best way."

"She's turned out lovely."

"And totally unequipped to face the world. I don't know what might happen to her when I die. I've thought of that constantly these past few years. Christ, I've thought of nothing else."

"You may be around another twenty years."

"Stop talking. You don't have to be polite to me. I'm dying now; I know that. Every time I take a drink I die a little. My guts hurt all the time. I once went to pre-med school, so I know what raw booze does, especially the rotten swill you get today. It eats out your liver, corrodes your kidneys. I've been pissing blood off and on for six months. So this time next week, next year, two years from now. Sometime, and not too goddamn long. Maybe someday I'll just drink too much and fall asleep in the snow. I know it, you know it, Waldo. Only Jessie doesn't know it. She thinks I'll go on forever."

He paused, coughing up a yellow blob and spitting it into the snow. "She has . . . something missing . . . somewhere. She wasn't ever interested in the things I wanted her to have, knew she had to have, and I never found a way to make her understand. Then the drinking got worse, and then for a while that was all that mattered. It seemed like just the blink of an eye before she was grown and ready for the vultures. She's got no shame about her body: She'd walk naked in front of a dozen men without thinking twice. No idea what that does to a man, even to her father, you know? No idea what some men would do to her, given half a chance. She'd play with dolls if I let her. She could entertain herself all day long like that. She doesn't know how to do anything but sit around looking beautiful."

"To some men, that's enough."

Abbott turned then, and David saw such pain in the old man's face that he wanted to weep. He touched Abbott's shoulder and some of it seemed to go away, as if he'd pulled open a drain. "I'm taking a hell of a chance on you," Abbott said. "You understand that."

There was another pause, then Abbott said, "If you want her, then okay."

The words thrilled and frightened him at the same time.

"Okay," Abbott said again. "She likes you."

"She told you that?"

"She don't have to tell me, I know her. She might have a kid's brain, but she's got a woman's emotions. I've seen her watch men when she don't know I'm watching. It's the look of a woman, not a child. A hunger. We all know about that, men and women alike, we all know that feeling. She's ready for something more than looking and she knows it. She's ready and she ought to have it." He turned gradually until they were headed back along the western base of the valley. "Look, all I'm asking is that you find some way to help her come to grips with life. I tried and failed. If you try and fail too, I can't ask any more than that. But you've got to try. And that's all there is. The only condition. Take it or leave it."

They didn't say anything more. They walked up the slope for another ten minutes, until the shack rose above the rim. Abbott stopped at the top, where the breeze stirred the brown grass as it stuck up through the snow. He waited for David's answer before approaching the shack. And David knew then that there were a dozen problems that hadn't been covered in the simplicity of Abbott's incredible offer, and that he could not voice any of them. There could be no bargaining without somehow cheapening it, robbing it of its nobility. "I'll try," David said. Abbott nodded. "Just one more thing, and I'll never mention it again. All I ask from you is what's right. Just try, that's all. No man could ask for more than that. If you don't, there'll be something to settle between you and me."

He wrenched open the door. She was sitting on the bed wearing a white dress. Where she got it God only knew. Her hair hung down her back to her waist. It was parted evenly and tied with a ribbon. Her cheeks shone red from scrubbing and her eyes revealed an excitement that he had not seen in her. "Come here, girl," Abbott said. He led her out into the light, his most prized possession. She smelled fresh and sweet. "Take her," Abbott said. The old man disappeared over the rim, walking east toward the railroad, rubbing his eyes as he went.

David watched him for a long moment. The girl never looked back. Together they walked across the meadow toward Colfax Avenue, and the start of her new life.

4

They were still sitting in the dark print shop when the police came. She seemed, as always, content simply to be with him, to wait for him to come out of his mood, take her upstairs, read to her and finally, perhaps, impale her against the cool sheet. Now the night was still. The paperboys were gone, the lights along the street had gone out and people across town were coming to grips with a president's passing. On the table beside them lay an old copy of *Wuthering Heights*, cracked open about midway. It was the fourth time he had read it to her. Four times for that, three for *Little Women*, three each for *Jane Eyre* and *Lorna Doone*, and countless times for *Green Mansions*. Her tastes ran to exotic, faraway love, and after a while she excluded everything that didn't conform. When he hadn't read a favorite in some time, she would thrust it at him as though she had just discovered it, saying, "Here, David, read me this." She knew the books by the colors of their covers. He had tried to teach her to read for herself, but she had never learned. He made some notable tries at variety. Once he tried her on *David Copperfield*, but the cruelty in that upset her and she asked him to stop. He gambled on *Romeo and Juliet*. It was her kind of tale, but the language was beyond her. He tried to explain it but she wasn't interested. Shakespeare hadn't given her enough to grasp and cling to. So they fell into a rut. They read the same books and had the same talks, and made love four and five times a week. It fulfilled her and was enough.

But for David the days of the second year had become long and exasperating. He had seen a great deal of progress in her first few weeks, and after that, nothing. She relied on him completely. He had his work, business was steady, and once a month his round table meeting, when many of the west side's self-proclaimed intellectuals gathered in the shop to discuss theories of life. He found himself looking forward to the meetings. They gave him an escape hatch from Jessie. He could count on her to disappear for those few hours every third Saturday of the month. Now she gave him this time without any complaint. She could let him have his one Saturday afternoon a month and still be content, as long as she could command the rest of his time. He was living in a bottle and she was the keeper of the cork.

The problem was deepened by the fact that he loved her. What Abbott had hoped would happen had happened. David couldn't imagine living without her. Losing her would be like losing a daughter, yet she was so much more than that. So much more and at the same time less. And that was why, on this August night, he could sit with her and feel absolutely alone. He was thinking about their time together and how much he loved her when the police car pulled up outside.

For a moment his mind went blank. He stared through the open storefront and saw black shadows move in the car. There were at least three of them, maybe four. He felt, as he always did when they came, the faint beginnings of fear. It seemed like a long time that they sat like that, the police outside, the man and the girl inside. Then one of the cops opened a car door and stepped out, throwing a cigarette into the street. David stiffened. His fingers closed around her arm. "Go upstairs," he said. His voice was soft but urgent. "Go upstairs and get dressed."

She obeyed at once. It was an old story for both of them. Now the other cops got out and came around toward his door, forming a small knot of moving darkness. There were four of them. The pounding began, steady, insistent. When he knew Jessie was out of sight, he turned on the light and went to the door. At the threshold was Joe Moran, a lieutenant. The others were patrol cops from the cut of their clothes. The routine varied only in the number that came after him. He stepped back from the doorway and Moran came in. The others stood back in his shadow. Moran's eyes swept the entire shop, lingering on the circular staircase.

"Well," David said, "what this time?"

"Just a few questions, *Mister* Waldo. That okay with you, Mister Waldo?"

"It's pretty late, Moran, even for you."

"I don't tell things when to happen, Mister Waldo. I'd like to know your whereabouts tonight."

"What things? You think maybe I had something to do with the President's death?"

"I'd like you to answer the question, if you don't mind."

"All right. What time tonight?"

"All night."

"I was here mostly."

"How about when you weren't here?"

"Took a walk. Around the lake."

"It's a big lake. Must take at least an hour. Maybe two."

"Took us two. We stopped and sat for a while."

"Who's we?"

"I went with a friend."

"What's his name?"

"Her name, Lieutenant, is Jessie Abbott. As you well know."

The floor creaked upstairs. Moran cut his eyes up.

"Not much of an alibi, is she?"

"Why should I need an alibi?"

"What time did you take this walk?"

"Around seven o'clock."

"That'd put you back here around what, nine o'clock?"

"More or less."

"Well, was it or wasn't it?"

"I told you, more or less. I don't carry a watch."

Again Moran looked at the ceiling. "Anybody see you at the lake?"

"Not that I know."

"Anybody visit you here, either before you left or after you got back?"

"No."

"Uh-huh." Moran crossed the room, looking up the staircase into the black apartment. ". . . I think we'd better continue this talk downtown. That okay with you?"

"No, it's not okay with me. What are you doing, making my store a monthly beat?"

"I think you'd better get your shirt. *Mister* Waldo."

He sighed and moved over to the staircase.

"Tell her to bring it," Moran said. "And come down with it."

Her feet were still bare. She had dressed in jeans and a pullover sweatshirt. The jeans were skin-tight, showing up every curve and crack. Moran and his men exchanged looks, and one of the cops cleared his throat. She held his shirt for him, and that seemed to amuse them. Soft snickers went around the room. He slipped his arms in and squeezed her shoulder lightly. Out on the street, one of the men pushed him toward the car. He sat in the back seat, wedged between two of them. The driver slipped under the wheel, but Moran paused on the sidewalk as if lost in a second thought. He went back to the shop and looked in at Jessie.

He spoke to her, trying for a balance between sympathy and authority. "You ought to know it if you don't already. You're keeping bad company."

She just looked at him.

"This man is a known agitator. He's a communist, an anarchist. He's a subversive." Softer, then: "Do you know what that means, Jessie?"

She shook her head, so slightly. No. No, of course not.

"We've been keeping an eye on him ever since he came to town."

Her lips didn't move, but her eyes asked why.

"We do that with known radicals. These are dangerous times." He paused, then said, "If you're smart, you'll find yourself another friend." He let the thought hang there for a moment, then he turned and walked briskly out of the shop.

"What did you say to her?" David said.

"It's not important."

"I want to know what you said."

"I told her not to wait up. We may be a while."

They released him about an hour before dawn. They had taken their time about everything, beginning with the ride into Denver. The driver zigzagged and backtracked, through the colored areas east of town, through Curtis Street where the theaters and lights and speakeasies were, up Champa Street past the *Denver Post* building which tonight, even this late, was busy and blazing with light. It was after two o'clock when they arrived on Larimer Street and parked at City Hall. They ushered him around the corner toward the Police Department side, on Fourteenth Street. The cop who liked to push people pushed him through the doorway and he stumbled down a short flight of stairs into the office. The cop pushed him ahead, through a dark hallway, until they came to a small, windowless room. There was nothing in the room but chairs and a table. David was pushed toward a chair in the corner. The cops rolled smokes and soon the air was blue.

Moran did the questioning. For most of the first hour, David was not told why he had been brought in. Later he learned that someone had held up a grocery store on the west side, about ten blocks from his print shop. The questioning zeroed in on his whereabouts at approximately ten-fifteen when, he remembered vividly, he and Jessie had been in bed. He told Moran that they had been talking then. Moran carried a short piece of stiff garden hose, which he slapped in his hand as he paced before David's chair and went through the same questions. After a while Moran slipped the hose into an inside pocket and David knew the interrogation was over. But Moran didn't let him go yet. He stood near the door—watching, running something through his mind that had been there before, many times. "Tell me something, Waldo, what's that little piece like in bed?" he said. David just looked at him. "She's so quiet on the outside, I bet she's all fire between the sheets. That right, Waldo? That what you were doing during the stickup? Did she like it, Waldo? Does it make her shiver and squeal?" Moran jerked open the door, letting in cool air and the sound of typewriters. "Get out of here, Waldo," he said. "Just remember, when you do slip up, I'll be right behind you."

The bells were tolling four o'clock as he walked out into the fresh air of Larimer Street. He looked up the empty trolley track and, not knowing how long he might have to wait, he began to walk. He was about two blocks from City Hall when he heard the sounds behind him. He stopped short, and for two or three seconds the sounds of running footsteps echoed through the empty street. It sounded like several men running. He squinted into the streetlight, but saw no one behind him. He listened for another moment, then he pushed ahead toward the viaduct and the valley.

The steps came again, much closer now. He stopped and turned and saw nothing. He came to a corner, one block up from the viaduct, and he stopped there and watched. He heard something: a few clicks, grinding, like a man trying to be quiet walking across broken glass.

Abruptly he turned off course, heading north along a street that dead-ended into a fenced junkyard. Beyond it were the railroad yards, the broad spaces broken by bunches of open freight cars waiting to be coupled up. An alley ran along the outside of the fence. A sharp noise brought him around and now he saw them, three shadows about fifty yards away. They had come into the street and were moving toward him, fanned out, to minimize his chance of getting past them. He heard a snap, saw a gleam of metal, heard a bottle go spinning into a gutter.

He turned and walked quickly into the alley, not east toward the police station, but west, toward the dark underbelly of the viaduct. Behind him came the sounds of running feet. He stepped around some garbage cans, stopped and pulled them out into the middle of the alley. Then he whirled and ran blindly toward the street.

He heard the clatter as the men hit the cans, and now for the first time he heard their voices. He slipped under the viaduct and flattened himself against one of the huge concrete pillars.

The best thing now was simply be still. If they were robbers, they'd search briefly under the viaduct, give it up as a bad job, and leave. If they were cops . . . He held his breath. A vision of Moran returning alone to his shop danced through his mind. The sounds of footsteps came again, and light pierced the darkness. The man in the middle held it as they came, playing the beam back and forth, stopping on any hiding place. His foot touched something heavy and round: a heavy iron construction rod, cut off about five feet long. He bent his knees and lowered his body. He gripped the bar with his right hand and, just as slowly, straightened his knees until he was standing again.

The one with the flashlight was perhaps ten yards away now; the others fanned out perhaps another ten yards either way. They came steadily, until the hand holding the light began appearing around the column. David raised the iron rod and swung at the light, hit something, and heard the light drop, still shining to the ground. He smashed it under his boot and in the same movement whirled, swinging the iron rod in a complete circle. He swung hard, vicious chops that might have taken a man's head off. But he hit nothing, and soon he dropped low, near the ground, and waited for their next move. No one moved and none of them talked. After a while he knew he was alone under the viaduct. He stood slowly, still cautious, and moved out to the west. He walked until the viaduct dropped away and he saw the reassuring sky over the railroad tracks.

He pushed on to the west, past Jordan Abbott's shack, and into the side streets above West Colfax, where the houses were few and he could walk under cover of trees and heavy undergrowth. From here out to Sheridan, nothing was paved. Colfax, the main drag east and west, was lined with houses and ramshackle stores, but the streets around it were little more than old farmlands marked off in squares. Beyond Cheltenham School the houses diminished in number and the streets became rougher, muddier, harder to travel. He walked in the bushes, pausing occasionally to watch and listen behind him. No one came. He walked to Osceola Street, several blocks beyond his store, and sat there under an elm tree, to watch the road in all directions for a long time.

He thought about Jessie. The heat in Moran's eyes whenever he looked at Jessie had not been lost on David, and he thought now that perhaps Abbott should be consulted before it went any further. There was a danger there: Abbott might decide to pack her off to Florida. He had talked about it often enough, and a problem with the police might be enough to push him on. It was a painful thought. Yet it filled him with a nostalgic feeling for the days before Jessie, when he could think and read for himself. He wanted that freedom, and wanted her at the same time. Either way, the toll was great.

He had realized quite suddenly that his romance with Jessie had begun to pale. He had, in fact, become interested in another woman, though they had never met and he didn't know her name. She was lovely, dark where Jessie was fair, and he imagined her to be witty and full of interesting talk. She lived on Osceola Street. There it was, then—the reason why he had walked past his store instead of returning to his love's bed. The woman in the window.

The thought of her brought him to his feet, and he started up the road toward her house. Theirs was the only house on the west side of the block. It was a two-story frame house surrounded by trees. The family name was Kohl. The father ran a grocery store on Colfax, two blocks from David's shop. The son was a cripple who had lost both legs in the war. David knew these things: He had seen the son being pushed along Colfax in his wheelchair by Julia Howe, one of the young intellectuals who came to his round table. He had intended to ask her about the Kohls, many times, but somehow the subject had never come up. Instead, he picked up neighborhood scuttlebutt. They were Jews; as most families in this neighborhood were. The mother was eccentric. The father was a widely respected neighborhood sage. There were brothers in addition to the one without legs. One was still a child, no more than ten years old; the other was grown and moved away, living somewhere with his own wife and family. David had heard that he worked for the *Denver Post*. The sister, that lovely woman of the window, was a recluse. Perhaps that was what first attracted him to her: that air of mystery. People gossiped about her, but no one seemed to *know* anything. David had only seen her five or six times, always standing in her upper-floor room by the oval window.

He came past the trees at the front of her house, and saw that her light was on. It often was on at odd hours. David knew, because that was when he did most of his walking. He drew abreast of the house, and through the oval window he could see her dark head. She was sitting by a lamp reading a book.

He stood there for a long time, hoping she would stand. His right arm for a glimpse of the woman in the window; his soul for a chance to talk to her. But she didn't move. At last, afraid of being discovered, he moved away down the street. He turned into Colfax just in time to see Moran's police car pulling away from the front of his shop.

5

Inside the house on Osceola Street, the woman of the window was leafing through a leatherbound scrapbook. Her name written in beautiful Victorian script inside the front cover: Anna Kohl. The scrapbook was divided into two sections, one much fatter than the other. In the hours since one o'clock she had gone through the slender section and half of the other. At least twice a year she read the book, lingering over scraps and cuttings.

The first section of the book was labeled WBIII, the initials of William Brown III. The great love of her life, who had risen from the poor west side to become one of the state's political powers. There were cuttings from three papers. She insisted that her father take them all, *News, Post, Times*. It was one of the few things she had asked of anyone. Many of the stories she had saved were different treatments of the same event. There were business stories: WBIII elected officer of this or that club, Brown getting the presidency of Mountain States Coal, becoming, at thirty-one, the youngest man ever to hold that post. There was political material: Brown meeting the President, shaking Harding's hand in the White House garden. There was a very long interview about Willie Brown becoming one of the state's great silent powers, a man behind men, a political wizard whose instincts were considered flawless. And there were society cuttings, for Willie Brown had married into society, twice. There were chatty pieces about the Browns attending opening nights, being invited to prominent weddings, and of course that brief item about their divorce. Then, another brief on his second marriage, still another on *their* separation and divorce just this year. William Brown III had had two children with two wives and in his thirties had attained more than most men get in a lifetime. None of it had made him happy, and in all Denver only Anna Kohl knew why.

The second section of the scrapbook was much larger. Its clippings had outgrown the book, and many lay loosely between the last page and the cover. This part was labeled "Bonfils."

She didn't remember how old she'd been when she began collecting material on Bonfils. The most recent cutting had come from last week's *Post;* the earliest were undated, but were yellow with age. She might have been as young as six, which would put them around 1900, 1901. She remembered going to school then, being on a summer break the first time she'd seen him. She had made friends with a child named Gail Jaffe, who had married a powerful state senator and, she supposed, would still be her friend. They hadn't seen each other in many years. Gail's parents were rich Jews from New York. Her father had made a lot of money in imports, and was very liberal. He seemed to enjoy having his daughter play with someone of Anna's deprived background. The Jaffees had bought a mansion near Cheesman Park. They also owned a cabin at Sloan's Lake, and that was how the girls had met. Sometimes during the summers Anna would stay down overnight, soaking up the luxury of lace and silk and a private room with an adjoining bath. Her window overlooked a hedge into Bonfils' yard. That first summer she had seen Bonfils at a distance, and then only occasionally as he left his mansion early in the morning. He was a dapper man who wore loud clothes and stepped lively. He was trim; not an inch of fat anywhere. He had thick, dark hair and a moustache. She hardly noticed him at all until Gail began telling her about the scandals one night. From then on, Bonfils' name was linked in her mind with all the characters of mystery and adventure that she knew from books. Bonfils was a rogue, and Anna Kohl always had a soft place in her heart for rogues.

He must have been in his late thirties then. One morning at breakfast, Gail mentioned his name and her father calmly folded his *News* and silenced her with an icy stare. "Just what have you been hearing about Mister Bonfils?" he asked. He always pronounced it Bon-fills, as it was spelled, instead of the correct Bon-fees.

Gail said she hadn't heard anything.

"Mister Bonfils," her father said, "is a liar and a thief."

Mrs. Jaffe blanched, but her husband said, "They're not too young to hear words like that. They should know there are people like Bonfils in the world. They'll be poor samples of womanhood if they grow up sheltered and protected."

Gail didn't say anything. Anna said, "Why do you say that about Mister Bonfils? What's he done?"

"He publishes a sheet of scandal and sensationalism that disguises itself as a daily newspaper. Actually it's a vile piece of trash."

It was the first reference Anna heard to Bonfils' line of work. Later she heard, also from Mr. Jaffe, that Bonfils had been a land swindler somewhere back east, in Kansas or Oklahoma, and that he'd been involved in other shady deals before he teamed up with Harry Tammen to buy the *Post*. Tammen lived half a block away, and Mr. Jaffe said he was even worse. He had met Tammen, and found him to be coarse and vulgar. Mr. Jaffe would not pass the time of day with either Bonfils or Tammen if they met on the street. The *Denver Post* itself was the biggest scandal in town, to Mr. Jaffe's thinking. Bonfils and Tammen were constantly rocking Denver with screaming red headlines, exposing everything in sight. That too, Mr. Jaffe said, was a sham. It was an established fact that Bonfils and Tammen used their newspaper purely and simply to extort money from people. It was known by everyone in town that *Post* pressure had been applied to advertising holdouts. Bonfils and Tammen had run a series on sweatshops, which stopped as soon as the department stores fell into line. Mr. Jaffe said he should know: He had a fifty percent interest in one store downtown, and he knew most of the merchants by their first names. Throughout Denver, people agreed: Bonfils and Tammen were poison, the worst extortionists in the state.

She had always been a romantic, and now she dreamed about the intriguingly wicked Mr. Bonfils. Whenever she stayed at the Jaffe mansion, she got up early and posted a chair near her bedroom window. She caught little glimpses of him as he flashed past. Then, dissatisfied with that, she crept downstairs and outside, standing at a corner of the hedge where she could not be noticed. He came out at once, causing her to catch her breath. He was magnificent. He wore a Derby hat, tweeds, and a vest. His erect posture and brisk step suggested nobility, and made him a giant in her eyes. She was amazed to learn that he worked Saturdays and sometimes even Sundays. It was on a Saturday morning that he first saw her. She was waiting behind the hedge, shifting her weight for a better look and breaking a stick under her foot. Bonfils fixed those dark, liquid eyes on her. She stared at her feet until his shadow fell over her. When she finally did look up, he was directly above her, separated from her by the hedge. He said hello, softly and kindly, and his voice was like velvet, exactly as she'd imagined it. "You're a pretty little girl," he said. "Come over here and I'll give you something."

She shook her head.

"You don't have to be afraid of me. I've got two girls myself. They're not home now. Come." He held out his hand but made no move toward her.

"I can't," she said.

"Why not?"

"I'm not allowed to cross the hedge."

"Not even for some candy?"

"No, sir."

"Then I guess you'll have to miss it." He looked up at Jaffe's window. "You see, I'm not allowed to cross the hedge either."

She was to see Bonfils again, many times. When she was alone, he always nodded to her. Sometimes he spoke, though never if adults were present. She read his paper ravenously in her own home, where it was more welcome. She was fascinated by the gallery of human freaks portrayed there. Even more interesting were the *Post*'s editorial stands. By the time she was nine, she had as much journalistic knowledge as the average adult. She understood that the *Post* had no formal editorial page, didn't need one, because its views were expressed up front, in its Page One news stories. Sometimes Bonfils himself signed the editorials, which also ran on page one.

By the fifth summer of her friendship with Gail Jaffe, she had become almost a permanent weekend guest. Gail was an introvert with few friends, and the Jaffes were grateful that Anna was willing to spend so much time there. They didn't know that she dressed each day before dawn, slipped out of the house through a side door, went down into the garden, and exchanged a few words with Bonfils. Even on the occasional Sunday when he didn't go to work, he was up early and around. He would come outside for his newspaper, fully and properly dressed, and would stroll casually around the house. He always seemed surprised to see her. "Hello, little girl," he said. He never learned her name, never asked. He must have thought she belonged to the Jaffes. "Still can't come through the hedge?" When she shook her head, he shook his, but he seldom smiled. Sometimes he passed a few more words with her. "Nice day," he would say. "Good day to go fishing. Have you ever been fishing, little girl? No? You'll have to get your father to take you sometime." His dark eyes would grip hers and hold them for a moment, and she would stand as if hypnotized.

At home, her Bonfils lore grew. He really was a rogue. Seldom did a week pass when he was not personally attacked in the *Rocky Mountain News* or the *Denver Times*. The *News* and *Times* were owned by an ex-senator named Thomas M. Patterson, then in his sixties, who apparently shared Mr. Jaffe's opinion of Bonfils. Patterson ran vicious attacks on Bonfils and the *Post,* questioning his character and calling down his journalistic practices. One of Patterson's papers—she had forgotten which one and had foolishly cut away the banner—had run an editorial cartoon depicting Bonfils as Captain Kidd, plundering the merchants and citizens of Denver. That had started the biggest scandal in her scrapbook. The cartoon had run near Christmas, 1907. A few days later, Patterson was walking to his office when Bonfils suddenly appeared behind him. "Good morning," Bonfils said. The senator turned and Bonfils knocked him down with one punch, breaking open a rubber plate inside his mouth and slicing open his gums. Patterson stared in disbelief at the figure hovering over him. "You dirty old son of a bitch," Bonfils said. "If my name ever appears again in your papers I'll shoot you down like a dog." It had all come out at the trial. That afternoon Patterson swore out a complaint and a warrant was issued for Bonfils' arrest. The papers had given it their usual treatment, the *News* portraying Patterson as an elderly gentleman, brutalized by a younger ruffian, while the *Post* showed Bonfils as a man among men, defending his honor against the vicious, libelous assaults of a jealous competitor.

She skimmed through the stories of the trial, which Bonfils had escaped with a fifty dollar fine and a stern lecture from the judge, and soon she came to a small clipping from the *News*. It was the early edition, dated February 22, 1908, and the headline said MRS. REYNOLDS DIES. She might not have cut that at all, might never have known of Bonfils' connection with the story, but by then a strange new step in their relationship had developed. By the summer of 1907, she was in her early teens. She still visited the Jaffes a few times each summer, and the magic was always there. She was still captivated by that lush wealth, and by the gross excesses that the Jaffes showered upon their daughter and her friends. From her room she watched the Bonfils house. She had heard that Bonfils had no friends, was despised by the community as a whole, was hated by his employees and family alike. She seldom saw the Bonfils girls. The only people she saw regularly were two men, who she later learned were paid bodyguards. Looking at the dark house, it was easy to believe that he was sitting there with his lights off, alone and friendless, just beyond the windows. On this night, the first of the new summer, she didn't watch long. She walked up the street in the half-light and turned into Cheesman Park. She was halfway across the park when she saw the erect, familiar figure coming toward her. It was uncanny, almost as if he'd known that she would be here, and for a moment it gave her the shakes. She felt a brief urge to run toward the dark row of trees that ringed the park, but she kept walking slowly toward him. He stopped when they were about ten feet apart, studying her face, genuinely surprised to see her. At last he said, "Little girl."

She forced herself to be brave. "Not so little anymore."

"That's the truth. Where are you off to this early in the morning?"

"I always walk in the park."

"Would you like to walk with me?"

"I don't know."

"It's not safe walking by yourself. Especially this early."

"It's not safe walking with strangers either. My father told me that."

"Especially this stranger, eh, little girl?"

She was afraid she had hurt him. Very prim, very formal now, she said, "You may accompany me once around the park if you like."

He actually smiled at that. It was one of the few times she ever saw a smile cross his lips. They circled the perimeter of the park, strolled along Eighth Avenue, where the dust from a passing car was still settling, and started across the open grass. In all that time not a word passed between them. At the edge of the park she thanked him; and they went their separate ways.

They met again, apparently by accident, a month later. This time Bonfils talked a bit more, but she still said nothing. She was determined to be a good listener, and after their third walk she decided that she had found her proper role with him: quiet, ladylike, appreciative. Sometimes he talked freely now, if she didn't interrupt. He was her secret.

He told her about Mrs. Reynolds on two successive days, the last weekend of her 1907 summer holiday. They walked and his words came tumbling out. Anna could see at once that he was a man in love, and it was just as clear that his love was this lady, this Mrs. Reynolds. She felt a stab of jealousy, but she listened intently. He had been seeing Mrs. Reynolds for about four years. She was a rich lady of Denver society, a philanthropist, in her mid-thirties. One day in 1903 she had walked into his life, appearing in the editorial offices of the *Denver Post* with a cause to plead. There was a man, young and good, who had come to her attention. He was in the state penitentiary and had been there for more than a dozen years, a murder convict. Mrs. Reynolds had met the man and had been drawn into a lengthy correspondence; now she was his passionate defender. He had done this thing as a child and had lived most of his life among hardened criminals. Bonfils took up the sword, announcing to his staff that *he* would free Antone Woode as a present to this lovely lady. The editorial attack began that week, and four years later Antone Woode was freed.

Through the long fight, Bonfils and Mrs. Reynolds met frequently in the *Post* Red Room, and with the passing months their relationship warmed from Mrs. Reynolds and Mr. Bonfils to Madge and Frederick. He began to call at her home on Logan Street, and they went horseback riding together in the high Rockies.

Her home was a salon of Denver's rich and powerful. Her most intimate friends were Bonfils' violent enemies. They included Senator Patterson, top corporation lawyers, the highest-ranking officers of the city's public utilities, and the rich magnates of Denver's Tramway system. All had been attacked in print or in person by Bonfils and Tammen; all considered him beneath contempt; none would share a room with him, even in the home of the respected Mrs. Reynolds. So Bonfils went alone to her home, on days when the friends were not there. Intense affection grew between them, and she tried to change his roughhouse ways. She closed her doors to him for several weeks after his brutal attack on Senator Patterson; she chided and scolded and in the end she relented. Through the fall and winter of 1907–1908 they drew closer, until Bonfils began considering marriage.

That February they went riding in the mountains, an outing that he had planned as the turning point in their relationship. He would ask for her hand in a do-or-die drama on the mountaintop. But she paled in the high altitude: Her head felt light and once she almost fainted. Late that afternoon they returned to Denver. Bonfils went home to his mansion to sit alone and plan his next move. Mrs. Reynolds went to her home to die. She bathed, changed her clothes, and collapsed.

Anna saw the story in the *News* the next morning. She called her friend Gail Jaffe and got herself invited for the night. That evening after dinner, she sat in a corner of the living room and watched

Bonfils' house. A faint light burned in an upper-floor window. Her heart went out to him. "You poor, poor man," she said. She looked up, shocked that she had said the words aloud. The entire Jaffe family was watching her curiously. As usual, the eyes of Mr. Jaffe were hard and cold. "Don't pity that man," he said. "He's got just what he wants."

Uncontrollable anger grew inside her and burst out. "What do you know about it?" she said. "What do you know about anything?"

Gail's mouth dropped open in horror. Mr. Jaffe sat up. "Now see here . . ."

But she didn't wait for the rest of the lecture. She walked out of the room and went upstairs. In the morning she slipped away without saying good-bye, and she never went back.

She did return to the park the following weekend. She felt a need to see Bonfils once more. She told her mother that she was going to the Jaffes', but instead she raided her bank and spent the night in an old hotel on East Colfax. It was a major adventure in her life. In the morning she walked to Cheesman Park before sunup and found him sitting alone near a grove of trees. She walked up and sat beside him. For a long time he took no notice of her. He seemed to be in shock. When at last he did talk, the words were rambling and disjointed.

He had gone to her funeral. It was in Fairmount, a cemetery in south Denver. He drew up unnoticed in the throng of carriages and cars outside the main gate. He walked into the cemetery and came up through the trees. Far outside the ring of mourners, he stopped. His old enemy, Senator Patterson, stood by the casket. Other enemies were grouped around the hole. Flowers were everywhere: In the midst of them all was a huge blanket of roses that he had sent. The pallbearers moved in, Senator Patterson among them, and gently lifted the casket. As the body was lowered into the earth, Bonfils stepped out of the shadows. A murmur rippled through the ranks, and the people parted to let him pass. He walked to the grave, and no one tried to stop him. His fingers touched the blanket and pulled out a rose. He dropped it on the casket and walked away.

The knock on her door brought her back to the present. She was still far from finished, but light had come to the Osceola Street window. Softly the knock came again. She recognized that reluctant insistence as her father's. She stood and closed her book of cuttings, tied it with a string and slipped it under her bed.

She opened the door and found him already dressed for his day in the store. He was an old man, nearing seventy now, with snowy hair, a large nose, and rimless glasses. He looked at her and his eyes disapproved, and suddenly she realized that she was still wearing yesterday's dress. He came in and looked down from her window into Osceola Street.

"This isn't healthy, Anna. What you're doing will ruin your health."

"I get plenty of sleep, Papa. Only sometimes, at night . . ."

"Sometimes at night." He shook his head. "You're not sleeping, you're not eating right. You never get out of this house."

"I'm happy."

"How can you be happy? Look at you, you're pale as a sheet. You can't be happy leading the kind of life you lead. How can I make you get out of here? Sometimes I don't know who I worry about more, you or Abe."

"Save it for Abe, Papa. He needs it more." Then, to ease the harshness of her voice, she went to him and touched his shoulder.

"At least the little one seems well," the old man said. She turned away. She didn't want to talk about the little one.

But Sammy Kohl wasn't ready to be dismissed. He seldom bothered her, hardly ever lectured, rarely gave advice without being asked. Whenever he talked like this, it was out of accumulated worry. He nodded toward a framed picture on the wall above her bed. The woman in it glared out with intense eyes. The inscription said, "To Anna Kohl, Yours in Christ, Aimee Semple McPherson."

"Since you went to see that woman it's become worse. You're more withdrawn than ever."

She waved him away, becoming impatient. "Nothing's worse. If anything, my life's taken on a deeper meaning. Listen, Papa, I know that's hard for you to accept, and I'm sorry. That's how I feel."

"It's not how you were brought up."

"I can't help it, and I'm sorry if it hurts you. I'm happy with my life now. At least I'm content, and God knows that's got to be an improvement. This woman has helped me through a very bad time. Naturally, if you're not happy with me, with what I do here . . ."

He raised his hands in his best perish-the-thought gesture. "We all know how hard you work, what with the house and garden. If what I said even makes you think that, well . . ." He paused and finished weakly, "Perish the thought."

Sammy looked at her for another moment, his sad eyes unconvinced. He moved to the door. He looked back once, then went out, closing the door so softly that she didn't hear him leave.

He went past Gabriel's room, past Abe's room, past the room at the head of the stairs that he and Teresa had shared for so many years. He paused for a listen—listening to the house where the family slept—then he went downstairs without disturbing anyone.

In the kitchen he had his usual breakfast: a full glass of milk and a cinnamon roll. He sat on a stool and thought about his family. The troubled brood. Just now he was the most troubled of all, because he had two secrets that he hadn't been able to share. He left the glass in the sink and went to his old desk in a corner of the living room. In the top drawer, which he had never locked until recently, he pushed aside his bankbook and found the letter he had begun last night. A letter to his first son, Ethan, whom he hadn't seen in more than twenty years. He turned on a desk lamp and opened the letter. Just another few lines and he could mail it. He began to write.

> It hurts me to tell you this. It hurts always to deny any of my children. I would send the money if I could. The fact of the matter is that I am not well, and I can't leave my family unprovided for. The money I sent you a few months back was exactly one-half of everything in our bank account. Beyond that I cannot go. I hope you'll understand that and find it in your heart to forgive me for not being a better provider. I pray God smiles on you and brings you through your troubles. Come see us if you can.
>
> Love,
> Papa

A look into his bankbook strengthened him. The $2,000 withdrawal in May was sobering. He had, as he'd told Ethan, responsibilities to his family. He had given Ethan seven years' savings. It had to end somewhere.

That was half of Sammy Kohl's secret. The other half was the lump he had discovered under his left arm two weeks ago. It had grown until it was now the size of a golf ball. It didn't hurt, but he slept on it at night, so Teresa wouldn't discover it if she touched him. He hadn't been to a doctor and wouldn't go until he had to. He knew well enough what it was. It was what his father had died of, and there was nothing to be done.

Images appeared before him. Anna, lovely and brilliant, tragic and alone. Teresa, strong on the outside, vulnerable within. Crippled Abe. Gabriel, the little one. And Tom. Thank God, at least, for Tom. Well married, good home, fine job, lovely children. Beautiful grandsons, even if they didn't carry his name or blood. Thank God for Tom. Nobody would have to take care of him.

6

A few hours earlier, across town in the newsroom of the *Denver Post*, Tom had finished his last assignment on the Harding death. It was an interview with Dr. John Galen Locke, Grand Dragon of the Ku Klux

Klan. Inspired by a Klan promoter, assistant city editor Eddie O'Reilly had sent him to Locke's office on Glenarm Place. The caller had said that Locke had known the dead President personally, and might have some exclusive reflections for *Post* readers. O'Reilly said, "First time I can remember when Locke's asked to be interviewed." Tom walked over at midnight, accompanied by a photographer named Carl Goodwin. At the door they were stopped by a figure still wearing a hood and sheet. They waited while word was carried in to Locke, and the response brought back that the reporter might enter but the photographer must wait outside. They protested, but finally Tom went in alone. No reporter Tom knew had ever seen Locke's office. It was a combined medical office and Klan stronghold. There was an operating room, and in a room beneath street level, a door that opened into Locke's secret Klan chamber.

Locke was a man of medium height. He wore a goatee and moustache, flawlessly trimmed, and was decked out in full Klan costume, as if he had just come down from the mountain. At the head of the room was a thone, with a set of crisscrossed pistols on the wall above it. Locke was sitting in the chair as Tom was shown in. At Locke's feet was a perfectly spotted Dalmation. Two Great Danes stood guard beside the chair, both tensed as if ready to leap at the slightest indication from the master. To Tom's left was a fireplace; above it, a gold reproduction of the United States seal. Directly across from that was a painting of Christ's agony, topped by another gun, a muzzle-loader of another era. Locke did not invite him to sit, though there was an empty chair facing the throne. He didn't offer his hand, ask Tom's name, or grant hospitality. He looked like a feudal lord, giving reluctant audience to a peasant. Reporters in Denver knew how to deal with that. With equal reluctance, in a flat tone that was almost dead bordeom, Tom said, "I'm told you have a statement about the President."

"I knew him," Locke said.

Tom waited. When Locke held his peace, Tom said, "And?"

Locke studied him. "I must say, young man, you're not a very good interviewer. Do you want to do this or not?"

"Sir, if you have a statement, I'd like to hear it. Something interesting, perhaps, touching on what kind of man Mr. Harding was."

"He'll be missed," Locke said.

Tom shook his head. "Look, I just interviewed the governor by phone. He said the President will be missed. The mayor said he'll be missed. The attorney general said his kind won't be seen again. The D.A. said he was a shining light among politicians. Two U.S. senators used almost identical words to describe him as a giant among men.

You get the picture now, sir? I was told to come over here, that you knew him and maybe had something different to add. That's why I'm here."

"Your arrogance is incredible. I grant you the interview for one reason only. Mr. Harding deserves better than you're obviously prepared to give him. So ask your questions and get out."

"Fair enough. How well did you know him?"

"Not well, but perhaps well enough. We met twice, in Washington, last year. We had breakfast one morning in the White House. Let's say we established an understanding quickly, and let it go at that."

"President Harding never took a position on the Klan."

Locke shook his head. "I don't want to get into that."

"But Klan chiefs from here to Georgia were always lavish in their praise of the President."

"I said . . ."

"The question, sir, is, was he a Klan President?"

"You mean was he a member?" Locke smiled. "Don't be absurd."

"What does that mean?"

"It means your question is absurd. I won't dignify it with an answer."

"What about Coolidge?"

"What about him?"

"Same question."

"Same answer, then." Locke shifted in his chair, indicating that he might terminate the interview. But he said, "In the first place, if you know anything about the Ku Klux Klan, you know that our membership rosters are secret information. And if you know anything about national politics, which seems doubtful, you'd know that the President couldn't afford to be tied to an organization . . ."

"Like yours?"

"Any kind of militant organization. America doesn't work that way."

"Can we say, then, that the late President was sympathetic?"

"You can't say anything, attributed to me, that doesn't come out of my own mouth."

"No offense, sir, but nothing's come out of your mouth yet."

Locke smiled and his eyes narrowed. His hostility was everywhere in the room. "Perhaps you're asking the wrong questions."

"Such as?"

"Anything about us. You weren't invited here to pry into my affairs. You're here to get my impression of the fallen President."

"I wasn't told there were ground rules."

"Consider yourself told now."

"Then we're back to first base." Tom waited, but Locke offered nothing. At last he said, "Let's try another approach, then. You just tell me what you know about the President, and we'll see if it fits in the paper."

Even that offended Locke. "What do you mean, if it fits?"

"Just that there's a lot of reaction in tomorrow's paper."

"Are you telling me that this might not even make the paper?"

"Unless you give me more than you have so far, I'd say there's an excellent chance of it."

"I knew this was a mistake. I told them so." Locke stood, and the two Great Danes got to their feet, their eyes fastened on Tom. "I think we can end this so-called interview here and now." He stepped down from the throne and the dogs walked at his side. Locke smiled. "One word from me and they'd tear you to pieces, newspaperman. That's how well-trained they are."

"Maybe sometime you could invite me back, I could do a piece on that. How the Grand Dragon trains his dogs. I think people would be interested in that."

Locke followed him through the outer office and upstairs. As they passed through the medical office, he said, "I never did get your name."

"Hastings."

Locke stopped and scribbled it in a notebook. "I make it a point of knowing who our enemies are."

"I try not to be anybody's enemy."

"But you don't try very hard in our case." They had reached the outer door, and Locke stopped. "Let me tell you something, newspaperman, and then you go home and sleep on it. There's a new day coming to this country. The good people, white people who were raised to fear God and live decently, are getting fed up with this tide of radicalism and excess that we've been going through. We are the majority and we will call the tune. It will come, Mr. Hastings. And when it does, all the liberal boot-lickers from Congress on down will fall in line. You people will be standing five deep waiting to join our ranks. Just remember, the Ku Klux Klan is an exclusive organization. It's a lot easier to be kept out than it is to get in."

"I thought all it took was ten bucks."

"Don't believe everything you hear." Locke turned and disappeared back into the darkness. A door closed and the hooded figure emerged from the shadows to escort him up to the street. Goodwin, waiting on the sidewalk, asked if he had gotten anything good.

"Hell," Tom said. "The man's a goddamn maniac."

For this, he thought, I pissed off my wife so badly she'll be a month getting over it.

The *Denver Post* was in the 1500 block of Champa Street. The building was four stories high and had a wrought-iron balcony that overlooked the street from the offices of its two owners. At street level was the press room, glass-fronted so people passing by could look in and see the most interesting part of the show—the papers rolling off the presses. Wire service bulletins were taped to the inside of the glass, giving shoppers small snatches of breaking news. Today all of them would be about Harding, Coolidge, and the power shift in Washington. From the balcony, flags would hang at half-staff over the street, giving the place an air of store-bought dignity. It was definitely not your run-of-the-mill workday, when Bonfils might appear suddenly on the balcony, scattering handfuls of pennies to children in the streets, then laughing quietly as fistfights erupted under his feet. Today there would be no circus acts or wailking sirens, no human flies scaling the Foster Building across the street: none of the things that had made Bonfils and Tammen famous and the *Post* notorious. But the day was just beginning, and Bonfils was probably working on it. If a way could be found to turn a president's passing into a *Post* promotion, dignity and discretion would be the losers. The sirens would sound, the whistles would blow, and freaks would be paraded along the sidewalk. *Hurry, hurry, hurry, guess the exact minute the body goes in the ground and win a ton of* Denver Post *coal.* In fact, nothing that Bonfils and Tammen did surprised him. Anyone who grew up with the *Post*, as he had, assumed that its ways were the ways of journalists everywhere. Now he knew better. In the arena of the wild and woolly, only Chicago could hold a light to Denver.

Bonfils and Tammen were showmen, not journalists. Nearly thirty years had passed since they had bought the paper, using Bonfils' money and Tammen's brass, and in that time they had become millionaires many times over. Tom couldn't remember a time when Sammy and every other merchant on the west side hadn't read the *Denver Post*. Tammen had built the *Post* on flair and daring, on the premise that a dogfight on Curtis Street is more important than a war in Europe. Gone were the narrow, conservative columns with their tiny headlines. In were screaming banners, eight columns across, in flaming red ink. A mass of front-page stories, sometimes as many as twenty, confronted the reader, and Tammen had compounded the collage by ordering each set in a different typeface. Professors of journalism offered the *Denver Post* to their students as a newspaper-man's nightmare. Tammen didn't give a damn. He scorned schools of journalism and seldom hired their graduates. His reporters pecked out their stories with two fingers and spelled by the dictionary. Often Tammen watched them, drifting through the newsroom and coming to roost over the desk of a favored staffer. There he could play the father role he loved.

Sometimes he took the story out of a reporter's machine and composed his own headline. Even when the grammar was off and the point strayed, the headlines sang. When the explorer Stanley died, Tammen wrote a headline that read STANLEY GOES TO FIND LIVINGSTONE AGAIN. He turned Champa Street into Denver's hub of free entertainment. The *Post* bought the Empress Theater and brought over a parade of dancing girls to perform on the street. Tammen bought the Sells Brothers Circus and ordered a cage of lions pushed past the *Post*'s front doors, drawing 2,000 people into Champa Street and creating a midday traffic jam for blocks around. Later he had a circus elephant stuffed and mounted in glass and placed in the newspaper's lobby.

The partners created a constant public stir. When coal prices doubled, Bonfils and Tammen declared war on the "coal trust." They bought a coal mine and undercut prices, running huge ads and contests for *"Denver Post* coal." They sponsored an annual jackrabbit hunt at Christmas, and each year up to 7,000 rabbits were shot and clubbed on the plains east of Denver, then shipped by train to the *Post,* where the meat was distributed to the poor. They called the *Post* the people's Big Brother, and they never missed a chance at a visiting celebrity. Tom was still carrying the *Post* as a newsboy the day his idol Harry Houdini was hung by the heels from the *Post* balcony to escape from a strait jacket, while thousands watched and cheered.

The building itself was Victorian and drab. From Champa Street the door opened into a white tiled lobby. Painted above the door was a motto from Bonfils: *O justice, when expelled from other habitations, make this thy dwelling place.* Inside to the right was the want-ad counter. Straight ahead, a black iron staircase went up to editorial chambers. The staircase went up beyond a mezzanine to the newsroom, a dark, creaky world of wooden floors, heavy wood desks and chairs, telephones, and typewriters. Sometimes in the morning Tammen stood at the top of the stairs, watch in hand, clocking in his reporters as they passed through the door. One of the joys of working all night, Tom thought as he and Goodwin climbed past the mezzanine, was the certainty of not finding Tammen waiting at the top of the stairs.

He sat at his desk and wrote. There wasn't much worth writing, a few graphs at most. It took him less than three minutes.

> Dr. John Galen Locke, Grand Dragon of Colorado's Ku Klux Klan, heard of the President's death while officiating at a Klan meeting on Lookout Mountain in Golden.
> Locke reacted to the news with sorrow. "He will be missed," Locke said.
> Locke said he knew the President, though not well.

48

He had breakfasted with Harding at the White House on one occasion last year, Locke said, and "we established understanding quickly."

Locke refused to comment on what this "understanding" entailed, or on Harding's true feeling about the controversial Klan. He also refused to speculate on how the Klan might be received by Calvin Coolidge, who this morning became the nation's thirtieth president.

Neither Harding nor Coolidge has ever gone on record on the Klan question, which has mushroomed into a national sensation and a hot political issue since election of the Republican ticket in 1920.

He tossed the single page in the basket on city desk. O'Reilly brought it back to him. "Is this all?"

"The man's not worth a story. I'd give you that as a possible ad somewhere."

"Jesus Christ." He dropped the page in the waste basket and walked away.

So he could write off the last two hours at least as a waste of time. Now the long night was almost over. Over on the copy desk, the dim, green-shaded lamp still burned, and the tiny group of old men still huddled over the steady flow of copy that poured across. The reporters sat like Tom, drained and exhausted. Many had worked two straight shifts without a break. Most were still coming down from that emotional high that always came with fast work. Gradually they drifted out; a few went back to the lounge behind the photographers' darkrooms, where they knew they could get a drink and relax. The thought of it made him realize that, Jesus, he had almost sobered up.

A small group had gathered in the studio. Tom pushed back the curtains of Goodwin's darkroom, opened the drawer and found the unmarked bottle of brown liquid. There was a glass jar, half-full of nickels and handwritten IOUs. Even at bootleg prices, the son of a bitch was making a good buck a bottle. Tom tossed in a dime and poured two shot glasses into a paper cup. He leaned against the wall, like the rest of them, almost too tired to think. A few other people drifted in, a copy boy, a sportswriter who thought the night's baseball scores were at least as important as the death of a president, a young girl from the art department.

The girl was Alice Wilder. She was twenty-two and had been with the *Post* since graduating from high school. She drew the scrolls and curlicues that adorned society pictures, and painted in dotted lines running from the bank into the street to show which way the robbers had gone. She had always had a wild crush on Tom. Everyone on the paper knew it; it was so obvious that even Tom knew it. He had always dismissed it as her love affair with the image. She had come along after Damon Runyon and Gene Fowler deserted Denver for the bigger game of New York, but in time to see Tom at his best. There was a year, and he thought of it now, when he could do no wrong. Some staffers still referred to it cynically as the "Year of Hastings." Denver was like a big red grape, waiting to be picked. Vice and corruption ran free, still did, only his inclination to break it open wasn't as strong these days. Denver's roots were sunk deep in its frontier heritage: Characters packing guns still walked the streets, and almost every weekend there were sensational shootings, stabbings, and ax murders. It was the beginning of the crime age, when almost every good killing rated Tammen's full treatment and reporters raced cops for clues. Working alone, Tom cracked the Halifax case in Colorado Springs, breaking it on page one while the cops were stonewalled. When little Mary Wolfe disappeared from her backyard, Tom found her body in a shallow grave in the woods about half a mile from her home. He found the killer too, a demented gardener who worked weekends for a neighbor. He covered the trial and was in Canon City the night of the hanging. One of his most sensational stories came late that year, when he followed an anonymous tip to a summer camp in the mountains, run by a minister, where children were being brutalized and sexually assaulted.

Alice Wilder had been among the impressed. She was the new breed of womanhood—free, slightly reckless, and, some said, sexually liberated. Her skirts were fashionably (or scandalously, depending on whom you talked to) short, and she wore her hair bobbed, with what men vulgarly called spitcurls hugging her ears. She wore light red lipstick, slick silk blouses, knickers, and beige silk stockings. Her body was slim; she had small, firm breasts, again very much in style, and she gave off an undercurrent of sex. People Tom knew claimed to have been with her. She was big on exercise, took ballet, went to a women's gym three times a week. She could touch either toe with either hand, do a backbend and hold herself like that forever. Alice liked dancing in the dark, hayrides and horseback riding in the mountains. A very young *Post* reporter named Arthur McCantless had encountered her once at a petting party. He told people about it, then made the mistake of falling in love with her. She wouldn't give him the time of day. Now he was sitting across from her, swallowing whiskey like a man.

A reporter named Malloy started the talk. It was all small talk, shop talk, plain and boring. The *Rocky Mountain News* had hired a hotshot reporter this week, some dame from back east. Alice nodded and said she knew her. "We went to high school together. She was three grades ahead of me, so she didn't really know me. But I remember her."

"Friend of mine told me she's from back east," Malloy said.

"She's from here. She worked at the *News* during the war, but I guess she had to leave town to get a break. Now she's come home in glory, and nobody remembers."

"I sure don't," Malloy said. "Marvel Millette. Jesus, what a handle. I know I'd never forget a name like that. Marvel. What a great by-line. I wonder if she's any good."

"She won prizes in Cleveland," Tom said. "That's just what I read in the trade press." He withdrew into the darkroom and poured himself another drink. This time he made it a triple, feeding the kitty fifteen cents. When he came out, Malloy was still turning the name over his tongue. "Marvel Milette. Jesus. I wonder if she'd come to work for us."

"She hasn't even done her first piece for the *News* yet," Tom said. "Why not wait and see if she's any good before you get hot and bothered about it."

For a brief instant Tom regretted his words. Malloy was just lonely. His wife had died last year, and he didn't function well as a single.

"If she won prizes in Cleveland, she must be pretty good."

"Yeah, well, you know how that is," Tom said. "We can all win prizes in Cleveland. Doesn't mean a damn thing when you get to Denver." He turned and walked out. He had seen a dozen hotshots, male and female, come and go at both papers. He had once been a hotshot himself. It was all so temporary, and he found talking about it small and boring.

He sat at his desk, took a long drag on the bourbon, and stared at his telephone. The clock on the wall said five after four. Alice came out of the studio, slightly unsteady on her feet, looking rather deliberately bored. Her desk was directly behind his, in a long row of desks used by three *Post* artists. He could almost feel her eyes on his back; she would be sitting there, legs spread just an inch, watching him. It would be so simple to make her. Just a quick turn of the head, a "Hi, Alice," a few words of buildup because no girl wants to feel cheap. A few friendly laughs, a sip of booze, and then the pitch. Within the hour they would be in some hotel room; he knew that beyond a doubt, but knowing made it somehow harder to do. He had never been unfaithful to his wife.

He drained the last of his drink, stood unsteadily and looked around for the door. The room reeled. He took a few shaky steps, then walked in a straight line to the door. He could hear her moving behind him, gathering her pocketbook in her arms, pushing her chair under her desk. She followed him down the stairs to the first floor. When he stopped again to get his balance, just inside the lobby, she came even with him and took his arm. "Here," she said. Her voice was tense, obviously nervous. "You can walk me to my car."

They pushed out into the warm morning air, and suddenly he felt lighthearted and silly. "Miss Wilder . . ." He broke off abruptly, snickered, and they both doubled over in laughter. "Miss Wilder . . ."

"Yeeess?"

Again they fell into fits of laughter. Tom drew himself erect and faced the building. He raised his hand as though saluting. "Madame, the great American press functioned at its best tonight." He looked upward and began to quote from the building. "O justice, when . . ." He stopped short. From the balcony the dark eyes of Bonfils met his. He tipped his hat, determined not to back off, and finished the sentence. "Mr. Bonfils, sir, your humble servants have done your bidding." He made a half bow.

Alice, again clutching his arm, tried to draw him away. "Mr. Hastings," Bonfils said, peering over the railing. "It seems we've been indulging ourselves tonight."

"You too, sir?"

Bonfils was not a man for drinking or for jokes. He did not smile. "My suggestion to you is that you get off the street. In case you hadn't heard, this is a day of national mourning."

"Good morning to you too, sir."

Alice burst into a fit of giggling, which continued all the way down the block. It was a strange walk, filled with alternating mirth and terror. "My God, he'll probably fire us both tomorrow," she said. And they laughed about that.

Her car was in a vacant lot half a block away; his, in another lot two blocks across. She clutched him all the way, as if he might break away and escape. At the lot, she seemed to sober up. "I seem to be in better condition than you are. You're in no condition to drive, you know. My place is just a few minutes away. I could fix you some coffee."

They had come up to the moment of truth, now or never, yes or no. He stood erect and took a deep breath. She looked so small and delectable. Trying for his serious face, he said, "I don't think that's too smart. Do you?"

"I think it's brilliant."

"I mean . . ."

"I know what you mean. And it doesn't matter." She put her finger to his lips. "Don't say anything, just come or go."

"Then I'd better go."

Now she relented; her eyes pleaded with his. "No complications. No problems," she said.

"I'd still better go." He shook his head, breathing in the fresh air. "Look, something happened tonight . . ."

"No, no." Again she touched his lips. "No complications, no talk. Goodnight, Mr. Hastings."

She started her car and drove away without looking back. Now, feeling fully sober, he walked to his car. As he set the spark and throttle, he noticed that someone had printed something in the dust of his windshield. It was carefully done, with all the letters written backward so he could read it from the inside. It said I LOVE YOU. A.W. When he got out to crank, he rubbed it off.

On the road he felt better. His head cleared and the breeze that poured in through the window helped him face the ordeal of home. He made good time. The house was dark as he pulled into the yard, but he could imagine her lying awake, staring at the ceiling, as full of turmoil as he was. Whatever the night had been for him, it must have been hell for her. She would be worrying about him, as she always did. She would be sorry and embarrassed and, no question about it, still angry on top of it all. He would have to work to overcome the anger and hurt, but time had passed, the heat of the moment was gone, and that would work for him.

He knew he was afraid. He leaned against the car and put off going in, as if more time would smooth it over and heal it. The house had an air of emptiness about it, as if no people had lived there for a long time. The morning was absolutely quiet. The memories of the night swept over him. He had interviewed a governor and helped put a president to rest, and he had turned down a lovely girl who wanted to tempt him away from his wife. If after that he had been the wrong man to interview Locke, so be it. The Ku Klux Klan deserved what it would get, which was nothing. He would tell his wife that and she would be proud. Perhaps he would even tell her why he hated people like Locke, and always had. Maybe tonight he could tell her at last about the Preston Porter thing.

The thought of it made him shiver. He took a deep breath and went inside.

CHAPTER
TWO

1

The days of Tom's youth were full of love and strife. His father had given him a shaky start, abandoning them before his second birthday, but he wouldn't remember any of that. He did remember a brief series of faceless men, and then Sammy Kohl had come out of nowhere to become his new father. It was an unlikely match. Sammy was a quiet little Jew from New York. He was fifteen years older than Teresa, a widower with a son who himself was nearly a man. Sammy's first wife had died in a cholera epidemic and he had raised the boy, whose name was Ethan, alone.

People who knew Teresa before her marriage predicted disaster. She was young and good-looking, and she had an animal instinct for survival. In her youth she was wild and rebellious, roughhousing with boys in alleys and back lots, and the idea of her marrying this mild Jewish merchant from the east was slightly ridiculous. But in Sammy she had found a stability that she had never known, and now, in her middle age, she had assumed a mantle of dignity that had all but blotted out her tempestuous youth. Sammy Kohl took in her son as if Tom were his own blood.

Teresa went to Sammy's temple on Saturdays, but she had never given up the Presbyterian faith and sometimes she went to Sunday services as well. Tom grew up with a smattering of each religion and finally dropped both. When Teresa protested, Sammy calmed her fears. "Leave him be," Tom heard him say. "When the boy needs religion, he'll know which way to turn. We've given him that, you and I, so what else can we do?" He listened from the attic. There were tiny cracks in the ceiling, and he could look down into the parents' room, and into the room next to it that he shared with Ethan. He heard many things. When he was five, he heard them talking about changing his name. Teresa wanted him to be called Thomas Kohl. She wanted to go to court and get it done legally, with papers to prove it. She thought this would make Sammy proud, but he recoiled at once. "You can't steal a boy's name, Teresa, no matter what you feel about his father. A boy has nothing if you take away his name." She never raised the subject again.

2

In the early years of their marriage, Sammy and Teresa were poor and they moved often. First they lived on the east side, south of Colfax, in a series of walk-up apartments. Once they were evicted by a new landlord who didn't like Jews. Tom was in the second grade then, and he'd come home early with the flu. A heavy snow was falling, and a stiff wind blew in from the mountains. As he turned a corner he saw men carrying their furniture out and piling it in the snow on the front lawn. Teresa wasn't there. When the movers had arrived, she'd walked across town in the snow, carrying Anna in her arms, to the store where Sammy worked as a clerk and accountant. They returned to find Tom huddled in terror, half frozen under a snowdrift on the sofa. Sammy took the boy in his arms and rubbed him all over until his skin tingled and he was warm again. Then they waited for Ethan to come home from school, and Sammy spent half of his first week's pay on a hotel for the night.

In the winter of 1896 they moved into the country on the west end, on what would become Osceola Street. Sammy opened a store of his own, and they were poor but happy. Only Ethan resented their poverty. He saw anti-Semitism everywhere: on every streetcorner, on the trolley, in every pair of lingering eyes. He fought constantly at school, using his fists and his boots on his enemies, devastating them with vicious attacks. A rumor was out that Ethan had killed a boy back east, and it was a story Ethan didn't deny. Tom found that being his stepbrother had certain advantages. Even the big boys backed away if he threatened to have Ethan come after them. In truth, Ethan was a stranger to him. In age they were nine years apart. He knew Ethan resented him, resented especially having to share his bedroom. His interests were different, his life a mystery. While Tom was delivering newspapers, Ethan was fighting and pursuing girls.

At first he pursued them with his eyes. In his early high school years, Ethan would stand on corners near the school and watch with hot eyes as young mothers and older sisters came to pick up the children. Ethan liked older women, and some of the mothers complained about the dirty looks he gave them. His eyes were always fastened in one particular place, though none of them could tell the principal that. They simply said his staring was annoying, and when a warning from the school didn't work, someone called the police. Ethan abandoned the streetcorners for Denver's red-light district, where he could stand for hours and watch the whores go by.

There was a strong chemistry between Teresa and Ethan. Tom saw the looks Ethan gave her when Sammy wasn't home; hot and unhealthy. Teresa defied him, staring him down, but after a while she began avoiding his eyes. She found excuses to be out of the house during the day, when Ethan might come in unexpectedly and catch her there alone. Often she didn't return until the hour before Sammy closed the store and came home for dinner. They had, in effect, given Ethan the house for the afternoon, and Tom had his circle of friends and often wasn't home until dinner.

One afternoon he came in early. He climbed into the attic and lay there dreaming. Soon he heard noises below. He crawled over to the crack above his bedroom, and what he saw shocked him. Ethan and a girl he had never seen were sitting on the bed. Ethan was stripping away her clothes while she giggled and tried to help. He ripped her dress and she slapped him, though there was no attempt to stop him. The girl, now fully nude, stepped around the bed, flopped down, and spread herself wide. Tom watched, fascinated, as Ethan crawled over her, dropped down, and in a series of quick thrusts drained himself into her in less than a minute. They dressed just as quickly, the girl looking disappointed and unfulfilled. Tom shifted in the attic and his shoe thumped against the sloping ceiling-wall.

For perhaps thirty seconds there was no sound at all. A moment later, Tom heard footsteps on the attic steps. Terrified, he crawled

56

across the room, pushed open the attic window and climbed out onto the roof. He squirmed along the edge until he came to the gutter, then dropped his legs over the side and began to slide down. As he reached the ground, Ethan looked out and saw him. Tom leaped the fence and ran toward Sloan's Lake. He looked back once and saw Ethan in furious pursuit, carrying a short piece of rope in his hand. Tom sprinted along the eastern edge of the lake and up the wooded hill above it, breaking through the trees and underbrush. He moved carefully through the trees until he found a small thicket, where the ground was covered with autumn leaves. He crawled into the thicket and pulled the leaves over his body.

Soon Ethan came up through the woods. He crouched, tightening the rope in his hands like an Indian stalking a deadly enemy. Tom didn't breathe. He waited until Ethan had moved past and out of sight. Already the sun was low over the mountains west of town. The woods grew darker, and far away, perhaps as far as Colfax, a horse whinnied.

At last he pushed back the blanket of leaves and lay listening for a moment. He struck out through the trees toward the lake. He was hurrying now, fighting down the urge to run. The sun had settled, leaving long fingers of silver on the water. The ground began to slope down, and he had just broken into a trot when a movement brought him up short. Ethan stepped from behind a tree.

Now they were separated by no more than ten yards, and Ethan was coming toward him, twisting the rope. "Eth . . ." He lost his breath, fought for it and blurted out, "It was a mistake, Ethan, honest. I didn't mean it, didn't mean to spy on you." He backed away, then tripped and sat down hard in the leaves.

"It was a mistake," he said again. "You know I won't tell anybody."

"I know you won't." Ethan loomed over him. "You know how I know?"

All he could do was shake his head.

"Because I'm going to kill you."

Ethan kicked him hard in the ribs, and he doubled over. He tried to roll away but Ethan gripped him from behind and looped the rope over his neck. He felt the rope go tight, felt his air cut off with terrifying abruptness, lashed out with his feet. The rope began biting his skin, and he tried to scream. Ethan was serious. Ethan was killing him.

Red streaks flashed before him; the world was spinning. Somewhere far away he heard a voice: a man, shouting up the hill. *Hey! What the hell's going on up there?* The rope went slack and Ethan sat on his chest. *Just playing, mister.* Ethan rolled over, and in a moment Tom's vision began coming back. He sucked in air in huge gulps.

Far down the slope a man was watching them. He had a dog on a leash. "That don't look like playing to me."

"Tell him," Ethan said softly. "Tell him, God damn you, or I'll kill you both."

Ethan pushed him down and looked at the man in defiance. "All right, then, remember this," he said through his teeth. "You ever tell anybody about this and I'll finish the job. I'll get you, brother, even if they string me up for doing it."

The burns on his neck were the main points of dinnertime talk. Ethan watched him across the table. Tom told them he had been running through Jacob Howe's backyard and had run full-speed into a clothesline. Teresa started to scold, and then something changed her mind. Her eyes went from Tom to Ethan and back again. In the morning Tom saw her talking to Emily Howe. He watched from a vantage point above the lake, where Ethan had almost killed him. The Howe farm was just visible across the end of the lake, but he could see their heads above the picket fence that ringed the Howes' backyard. He knew Teresa would be wondering how a boy not yet five feet tall had gotten whiplashed by a six-foot clothesline. But she never asked.

3

The new century had dawned. In 1900, Ethan was twenty-one, Teresa twenty-nine, and Tom was twelve.

Teresa had been talking with Sammy about getting Ethan to move out on his own. From his perch in the attic, Tom heard them talking about it. Teresa argued that Ethan was a grown man, working in his own job, and he should have his own place. Sammy agreed to talk to Ethan. But he made it clear that this was Ethan's house too, and he wouldn't be forced out.

Ethan showed no interest in moving. He did seem to withdraw, and became more a loner than ever. He seldom went out nights. He had little to do with people of either sex. Tom wondered if women were as much afraid of Ethan as men were. Ethan got a vicarious pleasure from his reading. He read strange books with long words that Tom didn't understand. Once Tom mentioned them to Teresa and she told him he must never look at them. She didn't try to govern Ethan's reading, but she rode herd on Anna and the boys.

That changed quite suddenly one afternoon. School had let out early for a teacher's conference downtown, and he came in just after noon. Ethan worked in a livery; he worked early and came home early, so there was no telling when he might be here. But today the house was deserted. Tom changed his clothes and in the bedroom he looked for his baseball. He was on his hands and knees, looking through the closet floor, when he saw the envelope. It had been tucked into the springs of Ethan's bed, but carelessly, so that one corner hung down. Tom pulled it out, lifted the flap and looked inside. His first reaction was shock, then that mixed thrill that all adolescents feel at their first peep into the adult world. There were perhaps a dozen eight-by-ten pictures, mostly engravings, showing people in various stages of sexual intercourse. The detail was fantastic. The last two were actual photographs of a couple "doing" each other with their mouths. He put them back under the bed, careful to leave the flap hanging down, just as it had been. But the images of that man and woman hung in the forefront of his mind and his heart beat furiously at the thought of it. He couldn't resist one more quick look. He had the envelope open and the pictures spread out on Ethan's bed when the front door opened and footsteps came up the stairs toward him.

He grabbed at the pictures and tried desperately to get them into the envelope. One tore down the middle. His hands shook and he dropped the whole package there on the bed. He hurried to the closet and got inside, pulling the door closed behind him.

"Thomas?"

It was Teresa, home with the children. She came toward Tom's room, opened the door and stood there. He heard her footsteps come into the room, and then came a sharp rustle of paper. He heard a soft gasp, then more paper rustling as she tied the envelope together.

She moved down the hall, then down the stairs. Tom crept to the top of the stairs and listened. From the kitchen, he heard his mother's voice. "Children, I want you to go over to the Howes' till suppertime. Anna, take this note to Mrs. Howe; tell her I'm sorry to do this but something's come up. I'll send Thomas for you when you're to come back."

She didn't have long to wait for Ethan. He came about five minutes later, coming straight to his room. Tom stood in the dark closet, holding his breath. He heard Ethan sit on his bed, then a slight scuffle as Ethan got down on his hands and knees and looked under the bed. Ethan banged out of the room and stalked down the hall like some rogue beast on the rampage. Tom was terrified. He pushed open the closet and went into the hall. Their voices drifted up clearly from the kitchen.

"Is that what you call literature?" Teresa said. He could almost see her down the stairwell. If he stretched his neck far enough, he could just see the brown envelope on the table between her hands.

Ethan moved slowly into the room. "What business is it of yours?"

"Everything that happens in this house is my business."

"So that gives you the right to snoop through my things?"

"When you leave trash like this on your bed, I take the right."

"I didn't leave it. The kid must have been into it."

"Then Thomas saw this filth, is what you're telling me?"

"I'm telling you what I'm telling you. And I'm not putting up with any inquisition."

For perhaps a minute neither of them spoke. Then Teresa said, "I want you out of this house. Tonight," she said.

"And what will you tell the old man?"

"He's not an old man, and the question is what *you'll* tell him. That's your problem, so make up something. I only know I won't have you sleeping with my boy any longer."

"You and your goddamned boy!"

"And I won't listen to that kind of talk."

Ethan moved into the room, looming over her. "I won't be forced out, not by you or anybody else. I pay my share."

"You can keep your money. We got along before you went to work. I just want you out of here."

"You've always hated me. Come on, tell the truth. There's nobody here but you and me now. Nobody to hear how you've always looked down your high-and-mighty nose."

"God knows how Sammy raised a monster like you."

"Listen to you. So much hate. You think I didn't know that? Right from that first day . . ."

"That's not true."

"Not true? Who do you think you're kidding? I knew all along what was between you and me, and I knew what it was doing to you. Only you're such a pious bitch, you'd never admit that, so you twisted it until it became hate. Isn't that why you used to look at me that way, with those lovely black eyes and that luscious mouth . . ."

Tom heard the sound of his mother's open palm striking Ethan's face. Ethan pushed her against the wall and held her there.

"Get away from me." Her voice was wild and full of rage. "Get away before I kill you."

"I'll get away. After I've done this."

There was absolute silence. It stretched past fifteen seconds while Tom stood in the hallway, terrified. Their breathing came again, angry and frenzied, and there were bumps as she struggled between Ethan and the wall. Ethan broke the kiss and stepped back, and

60

Teresa hurled a stream of curse words at him that Tom had never heard her use before or since. She came at him like an animal, raking his face both ways with her nails. He gripped her wrist and threw her to the floor. Then he was down upon her. She gasped as his hand felt under her dress, up along her bare leg. "You . . . *pig!*" For a moment she pulled her hand free, enough to slap him twice, and then he pinned her down again. At that instant Tom leaped into the room. He gripped Ethan's head, but was brushed off with one arm. He fell against the kitchen cabinet, jerked open the drawer, and got the butcher knife. He jumped on Ethan's back, plunging the knife into Ethan's side. Ethan bucked Tom off and rolled over on his back, gasping for air. Teresa took the knife out of Tom's hands, and clutched him tight against her, in the folds of her skirt.

She was holding the knife high, threatening with the blade. "Now you get out of here." Slowly Ethan pulled himself to his feet. He moved to the cabinet under the sink, where Teresa kept her rags. He stuffed the rags into his shirt, then went back to his room and threw his clothes into a traveling bag. He was gone in five minutes.

They stood on the porch and watched him go. Teresa held Tom's head against her breast until they both stopped trembling. "You wash that knife," she said at last. "Wash it good, in boiling hot water, and mop the mess up off the kitchen floor. I've got some papers to burn before your father gets home."

4

In the spring of 1900 Tom graduated from grammar school and announced to Sammy and Teresa that he wouldn't be going on. He didn't tell them yet, but he had heard of a new school, run by Bonfils and Tammen of the *Denver Post*. Here, he had heard, newsboys from poor families were taught some of the finer points of the newspaper business. He thought he might like to be a reporter, and in September, 1900 he boarded a train at Union Station for the two-hour trip east. Everyone thought it strange that the *Post* school was so far out of the way. It was located in an old two-story farmhouse south of Limon. The town, on the plains sixty miles from Denver, was little more than a main street and a few ramshackle buildings. Its dusty street still had wooden walks and hitching posts for horses and buckboards, and most of the businesses were clustered around the one saloon. He arrived on a Friday afternoon, when hands from the surrounding ranches were pouring into town from both ends.

Laughter rang out along the street, following him as he walked past the black doorways of the open stores.

The sun was low in the western sky when he found the road and began the four-mile walk to the *Post* ranch. On the plains he saw a buckboard, full of boys, most a year or two older than himself. The driver was a thin boy who looked to be the oldest of the lot. The buckboard slowed as it passed him, and fifteen pairs of unfriendly eyes followed him past. No one spoke. The house was old, perhaps built before there had been a town. Victorian gingerbread stretched like wooden lace around the porch, and gables jutted into the evening sky from all four sides. Behind it was a crumbling windmill, one blade broken and hanging. He came into the yard, which was full of sagebrush and tumbleweeds. The weather was still warm, so the front door was open. He looked into the dark hall, knocked softly, and almost immediately a tremendous, fat woman with a fierce face came out of a side room and walked toward him. The first thing he noticed was the blood on her hands.

Later he learned that she had butchered a hog and was cutting the meat for a meal. But that first impression, of cold eyes and jowls, a mouth that turned down at the corners, and blood everywhere, would remain with him always. She came close and looked down at him. "So you're another one." Her voice boomed down the empty hall. "Well? Cat got your tongue, sonny?" At last he got out some kind of answer. She led him through the hall, past rooms dim and dark, to a door at the foot of a staircase. "It's first-come, first-served here. All the rooms upstairs is taken. All that's left is a bed in the basement." She jerked open the door, revealing a narrow set of stairs, railed with flimsy boards on each side. There were no lights. He swallowed hard and looked at the woman; she jerked her head toward the stairs and he started down. The woman slammed the door, jarring him with the force of it. His first reaction was terror and panic. Then he saw a faint light below. The light became brighter and soon he reached the floor. The basement was no more than an unfinished hole in the ground. The earth around it was shored up by heavy boards. The floor was wood planks, and it squished when he walked on it, as if water had seeped in just below. The place had a dank, stale smell. Pushed over against the far wall were three double-decker bunk beds. A kerosene lamp hung from a nail in the wall.

A boy, perhaps a year younger than he was, lay still on the bottom half of one of the bunks. His eyes were wide and unmoving. Tom sat on one of the adjacent beds. "Is it okay if I take this one?"

Without looking at him, the boy said, "Take any one you want. I don't care what you do."

About three hours later he heard the movement of many feet through the house, and guessed that the buckboard had returned. The movement was orderly and disciplined, as the kids marched through the hallway and up the stairs. Soon he heard a bell, the basement door opened, and the woman yelled "Supper!" The boy on the opposite bunk didn't move. Tom sat up on his bed. "They're calling us to supper."

Still the kid didn't move. After a while Tom got up and climbed the stairs. The dining room was a long, drab chamber, lighted by wall lanterns. Outside, the plains were dark. All of the boys had taken their seats and were eating when he arrived. He sat at a vacant place near the end of the table, and waited until the old woman came through. "Supper call was fifteen minutes ago," she said. "Go without tonight and learn to be on time tomorrow."

After supper, the boys all retired to their beds upstairs and Tom returned to the basement. The small kid was still staring up at nothing. Tom lay on his bunk and listened to the quiet. Soon he heard tiny scurrying noises, as a rat dashed across the floor.

A new arrival came in around nine o'clock. He was a larger boy than any Tom had yet seen. He must have been nearly sixteen. Stubble grew from his chin and his clothes were two sizes too tight. His eyes were primitive, small and beady, set deep into his skull. He came to the foot of Tom's bed and dropped an old suitcase on the floor.

"Get up. I'm taking this bed."

Tom looked across the room. "There's another lower over there."

"I'm taking this one."

He got up and moved without comment, settling into the third bed slowly. Half an hour later the woman opened the door and yelled, "Lights out!"

The new kid looked at Tom. "You turn it out." And Tom got up, blew out the lantern, and settled back for the long night.

In the morning he learned what the school was about. After breakfast the boys were assembled in a huge room on the ground floor. There were some desks and even some books, but these were obviously for show. Soon a muscular, heavy-set man came in. He was about the same age as the woman, and Tom guessed that he would be her husband. Both arms were tattooed with anchors and ships. He smoked a black cigar. He stood for a moment looking at the boys, then he shook his head.

"What a sorry goddamn lot of trash." He walked around them, making a full circle, until he faced the entire group again. "God lord

Christamighty, it's incredible the likes of what they're sendin' me. Simperin' kids, and they expect me to make you over into men. Well, there's no helpin' what you are, only what you can be."

He paused like an old actor, sure of his timing, then began again. "You call me Shaughnessy. Not sir, not mister, just Shaughnessy. The missus in there's Missus Shaughnessy. You're all newsboys, are ye not? All work for the *Denver Post,* do ye not? Now it's come to the attention of Messrs Bonfils and Tammen that some of you're gettin' pushed off the streets by tough kids carryin' the rival newspaper. We can't stand for that; won't stand for it. It costs the *Post* its much-needed circulation and costs your families cash that might be used for worthy projects.

"What, you say, dast we do about it? That's why you're here, to learn just such as that, and I'm the one to show you. Who amongst you carries the heaviest clout?"

When no one stepped forward, Shaughnessy said, "Come, come, who amongst you feels he can whip the pack?"

Another moment passed while the boys looked face to face. Then the bully boy who had taken over Tom's bed got to his feet. Shaughnessy broke into a huge grin. Ah, yes. There was always one in every crowd. "Come up here, laddie."

The boy went to the front of the room, swaggering a little. Shaughnessy clapped a hand over his back. "Ya look big an' strong, lad, tough as a mule's kick. Now, boy, I want you to make believe for a minute. What's your name?"

The boy glowed. "Virgil."

"Thas a good lad. All right, then, make believe I'm the *News* carrier. We've just bumped into each other on the street downtown. I've told you to get out of my block. What do you do?"

"I punch you in the gut."

A titter of laughter went around the room. Shaughnessy laughed too. Virgil was pleased by his sudden rise in status. Shaughnessy let his gut, swollen by years of beer-drinking, hang over his belt.

"Go ahead, then, have at it. Let's see how you'd do it."

"You mean hit you?"

"Aye, just like you'd do to that *News* kid. Make it hard, now; don't hold anything back. We all want to see how much stuff you've got in you."

Virgil cocked his fist and swung hard at Shaughnessy's belt. But Shaughnessy wasn't there. He grabbed Virgil's wrist and jerked him off balance, stiff-arming him in the nose with the free hand. Blood poured down Virgil's face. Shaughnessy stepped hard on his foot. Virgil jerked up and Shaughnessy kneed him between the legs,

64

doubling him over again. The boy sank to the floor sobbing and gagging.

Shaughnessy helped him up and clapped his shoulder. "Nay, lad, don't cry. Take yourself into the kitchen and tell the missus I sez fix your nose up. And stop that guddamn snifflin'. That was just the first lesson."

5

Shaughnessy drilled them daily in the fine art of brutality. He was an ex-Rough Rider and a fistics expert. When he wasn't working, he drank. He disappeared into his den each night after supper, to return, red-eyed and ready to go, in the morning. Shaughnessy taught them to butt and nut-kick. He told them about the element of surprise, how sometimes a dash of sand in the face could turn even an impossible battle around.

Tom listened intently. He felt that Shaughnessy was talking directly to him. By the end of the second week, he looked forward to the long afternoon drills in the field behind the house. There was no pretense that the Bon-Tam school was anything other than what it was: a seminar on guerilla tactics for the street. The schoolbooks lay untouched in the house, and that was fine with all of them. Tom suspected that neither of the Shaughnessys could read anyway. Sometimes he wondered what would happen if some state senator dropped in unexpectedly, to give the place a once-over. Knowing Shaughnessy, he probably had that covered too.

He came to enjoy sweating in the sun. He liked the feeling of competition. Most of all he liked the physical contact. Sometimes he wondered, as the autumn chill drifted over the plains, what the basic differences were between himself and his lost brother Ethan.

In October he and half a dozen kids from the school were sent into Denver for a couple of days to try their new tactics on the street. He went into Welton Street and within minutes he met an old tormentor. Tom flattened him with two hard kicks to the groin and a backhand to the nose. Then he grabbed him by the hair and held his face down in the Sixteenth Street drinking fountain, in the lower bowl that the city had put at street level for thirsty dogs.

6

Later that month he met Louise Frost. He walked into Limon feeling tough and sassy, and hoping for a letter from home. The post office was inside the mercantile company, and as he approached he saw a small buggy hitched out front. She came out at once, a small girl with blond curls. She wore a long gingham dress and a sunbonnet tied under her chin. Her cheeks were red from the chilly air. She gave him a quick look. In her hands were three letters. She shifted them and climbed into her buggy, driving away along the road out of town. He followed her with his eyes until she disappeared on the plains.

Inside, he picked up his mail, a short note from his mother. Anna was down with a cold; otherwise, the family was fine. He read it through, then turned back to the window and asked the postmaster about the girl.

"Her name's Louise Frost. She comes in here every afternoon this time, picks up the mail after school."

"Where's she live?"

"Her dad's Bob Frost. They've got a ranch a few miles from town."

The next day he waited again outside the mercantile company in the late afternoon. She seemed determined to play her icy role, to keep her nose up and brush past as if he had smallpox. He said hello as she whisked by. She didn't speak and didn't turn her head. He felt crushed and embarrassed; most of all, he felt angry. He followed her to the edge of the boardwalk, then stepped down into the street and took her horse's reins.

"Miss, I spoke to you back there. Twice."

She just looked at him. Icy. Calm.

He quaked inside. But he said, "All right, be like that. I come from a big city where people don't talk to other people much. They're either too uppity or scared, I don't know which. I always heard it was different in the country, but I guess I was wrong. People are snobs all over."

Her face remained cool, in control. She said, "Even in these parts, sir, a gentleman waits until he is introduced."

So it was ladies and gentlemen, even at twelve. Later he would learn that she really wasn't like that, wasn't ever formal except with boys she liked. It was one of the few things he learned about her in the two weeks he was to know her. Now he smiled, trying to act devilish and worldly. "That's fine, miss, only I'm new here. I don't know anybody who might introduce us."

"Is it important that we meet?"

"To me it is."

"Then it might be proper to present yourself to my father." She clicked her tongue and turned her horse away from him. The buggy went off slowly, not with the rapid pace of yesterday, and for a moment he didn't know what she expected of him. At the end of the street, she stopped and turned in her seat, peeping around the canvas top at him. He took off after her at a run.

It was a long run and she never quite let him catch her. The road was like all prairie roads: two simple ruts in the land. It wound through gulches and ravines, and across long stretches of flat grazing land. Sometimes, by cutting across country, he could almost reach her, and then she clicked her tongue and pushed the horse ahead faster. He ran the entire three miles to the ranch. It was a simple one-story house, with a fence along its front edge and a windmill behind. She had already tied her buggy and gone inside, leaving him to his own courage and ingenuity. He wished for a spring of water so he could splash his face. Having none, he brushed back his hair with his hands, walked straight to the door and knocked. A moment later a woman opened it.

"Ma'am, my name's Tom Hastings. I was wondering if I could call on your daughter."

A flicker of a smile began around the edges of her mouth, hardened, and became sadness, as if the mother suddenly realized that some future she had been dreading had finally come to call. She opened the door, letting him into a snug room, nicely furnished. Mrs. Frost (he never learned her first name) called out to her daughter and a moment later she appeared. She had changed her dress, and was now wearing a yellow summer frock. Her hair had been brushed back and her cheeks held a touch of red that the chill hadn't put there. "Louise," her mother said, "do you know Mr. Tom Hastings?"

"We have met."

"Fine. Your father will be home in an hour, so don't wander. Dinner is on. You'll stay and eat with us?"

"Thank you, ma'am."

They walked through the dusk, around the perimeter of the ranch yard. As they talked, formality dropped away. She told him that her family had come west a few years ago, and her father had 4,000 sheep. Then the father came: Tom found him to be a tall, slightly forbidding man with quick, intelligent eyes. He would always remember Mr. Robert Frost's eyes; that and cornbread, a feeling of warmth, a tightness and love that circled the dinner table and drew them together like an invisible lasso. Afterward, he and Louise were allowed to sit together on the front porch. They sat and talked, looking through the front window at the fire roaring in the hearth. The Frosts had come to Colorado from Nebraska. For a while, her father had run a stable in Hugo, the county seat, fifteen miles away. Louise was born in 1888, as Tom was. There had been a younger sister, Fay, who had died horribly last year. She had choked to death on a bean.

Night was full by the time he struck out for Limon. He walked alone across the starlit plains, following the ruts and thinking about being in love. It was late when he got back to town, and the first person he saw coming toward him out of the darkness of the railroad depot was Ethan.

7

Tom bent over and picked up a rock. Ethan paused, looking more amused than worried. "Little brother, preparing for battle," he said.

"How'd you find me?"

"I got ways. Ways of finding you, ways of getting to you, if I want to."

Tom didn't say anything.

Ethan moved closer. "I need some money."

"I haven't got any."

"No? Well, the old man has. He'd send it if you asked."

"Ask him yourself."

"A hundred dollars would get me out of your hair for good. I want to go back east."

"I don't care where you go."

"Then do this favor for me."

He didn't answer. He moved past Ethan and walked away.

The next day Ethan stood in the black mouth of the saloon and watched as Tom walked past beside Louise Frost's buggy. He was there the day after that, watching. And that night, when Tom came through town on his way home from the Frost ranch, Ethan was standing in the shadows waiting for him.

This time Ethan walked with him out of town toward Shaughnessy's. He walked at a distance, well off the road and just out of reach. "I'm getting tired of fooling with you, little brother," he said loudly. "Your attitude is starting to get to me."

"Then why don't you get out of here?"

"Get that money for me and I will."

"Get it yourself. Whatever happened to your job, anyway?"

"Just say I'm between things."

"I'll bet. Probably got fired for feeling the boss's daughter."

68

If the words angered him, Tom couldn't tell. That dark rage against all mankind was always in Ethan's face. It made even his smile seem cruel, like a deformed arm. "Speaking of feeling up," Ethan said, "that's quite a little piece you've got now."

"You leave her out of this."

"All I said . . ."

"I know what you said, and I'm telling you, Ethan, shut your goddamn mouth before I bounce this rock off your head."

"You forget what happened that day by the lake?"

"That was a long time ago."

"Not so long. I could still kill you."

"Just you try it."

Ethan shifted his weight, leaning on one foot. "I always did like young pussy. How old is she, little brother, twelve? Thirteen? Just right—green, but coming to ripe."

"You touch her and I swear to God *I'll* kill *you.*"

Ethan's eyes narrowed. He watched Tom for another moment, then his lips drew back in a sneer of contempt. "I do believe little brother's gone and fell in love. That's too bad." He kicked the ground and a swirl of dust settled over Tom's shoes. Then he spat on the ground between Tom's feet. Without another word, he turned and started back toward town.

8

Ethan's appearance was like an omen. Every afternoon he watched as Tom met Louise Frost at the mercantile post office and walked with her across the plains. They had their first quarrel, a silly thing that just started, grew, and burst out of control. He tried to apologize and kiss her; she pushed him away and slapped his face. She told him she never wanted to see him again, and the following afternoon she circled the town and bypassed the post office completely. Ethan stood in the doorway of the saloon and watched as Tom walked out of town alone. That night at Shaughnessy's he sank into despair, crying silently into his pillow. In the morning, Shaughnessy walked with him on the plains, away from the house and the prying eyes of the kids.

"I know how it is, laddie," Shaughnessy said. "You've got all the looks of a man smitten and scorned."

The tears came again, and Shaughnessy threw an arm over his shoulder. "Listen to the old man and let me tell you something about the ladies. Every manchild goes through exactly what you're goin' through this minute. Every one of us with red blood and a man's eye for skirts and fluff. You think you're goin' to die, and that first time's always the worst there is because you've got nothin' in your past to tell you it'll get better. The only way to handle this is to be a man about it. It'll be hard, but stay away from her. Let *her* sweat it out, damn her hussy's heart. If you take your raw broken heart now and lay it before her, she'll tear it to pieces. They all do that. It's the she-devil in 'em, and it's part of what makes us love 'em like we do. Give her a week, ten days maybe, then just appear suddenly like nothin' ever happened. Be nonchalant and gay. Talk about your trip to Denver, even if you never went, and how good it was to see all your old friends. You don't have to say ladyfriends. She'll get the message."

"But, Shaughnessy, what if she still doesn't care?"

"Then you've lost, lad. But you'll have the satisfaction of knowin' that you gave it your best shot and you'd have lost anyway. Remember this: No man ever had a decent affair with a lady if it's built on simperin' and whinin' and cowtowin'."

The days at the ranch dragged.

On the seventh day, Tom stood in the yard and watched the boys go into town. Shaughnessy was sitting on the porch, drinking from a warm glass of beer.

"Do you think . . . ?"

"Nay, lad, she's not had enough stewin' time yet. Give her another few days. What's today, Thursday? Let her stew over the weekend and go down Monday."

He suffered silently through the night. In the morning some men came to the house, rousing Shaughnessy out of his hangover and talking to him for a long time on the front porch. When they had gone, Shaughnessy came inside. His face was pale, his eyes red and moody. He stared at the eating boys, and at last his eyes came to rest upon Tom. That morning he worked them mercilessly—full contact in the fighting drills, double counts in calisthenics. Throughout the morning, Tom found Shaughnessy giving him those troubled looks. It made him nervous and apprehensive.

Just after noon Shaughnessy pulled him out of the group and they walked down into a tiny glade of dwarfed trees. Now it was Shaughnessy who was nervous, fidgety, as if he couldn't find the words for what he had to tell. "It's a good thing, lad, a good thing you stayed at the ranch yesterday." He told Tom the rest quickly. The day before, Louise Frost had been intercepted by some unknown man on the road from Limon to her father's ranch. She was raped and stabbed

70

and robbed of fifty-three cents. Her throat was cut and the marks of the killer's boots were still on her forehead.

9

He walked alone to the ranchhouse and lay on his bed in the dark. There, overcome by the terrible reality of it, he cried again, but it was like a fishbone stuck in his windpipe; something that wouldn't go up or down. Much later, when the sun was low in the sky, he got up and struck out for town.

Dusk had come by the time he arrived in Limon. Lights blazed from every building, and men gathered in ugly knots and talked of lynching. The afternoon trains had brought reporters from all four Denver dailies, and the late edition of the *Post* contained the open suggestion that the killer should be tracked down and lynched without mercy. The story was boxed on the right side of page one. Tom read every word, sitting on the boardwalk under the light that spilled through the general store window. The details etched themselves in his mind forever. Her skull had been fractured, the forehead caved in by the force of the killer's boots. Both eyes were black from bludgeoning, and the coroner had found another fracture behind her ear. The knife had been plunged into her breast many times, and then had been used to hack at her neck. The papers cited it as the brand of lawlessness that comes when the death penalty is abolished, as Colorado had done three years before. Bonfils and Tammen stood on the sidelines and cheered as the people of Limon prepared to take law into their own hands.

They had sent one William L. Kerr to report from the scene. Kerr mingled with people along the main street, picking up the most volatile snatches of dialogue he could find. Tom saw him scribbling furiously as one cowboy described what he would do to the killer when he was found. "All I want to do is put out his eyes with this spike, then cut his ears and tongue off. After that, you people can have him." A rumble moved along the dusty street, a living pulse of insanity, magnifying as it went. The popping of photographers' lights brought his attention to the man from the *Republican*. Farther along, reporters from the *News* and *Times* blended out of one mob and into another, crossed the street, and drifted along toward the telegraph office.

When he had read every account of the murder, he headed out of town toward the Frost ranch. It was important that her parents know he cared. He memorized a speech, but now he didn't know if he could do it without breaking down. In the end he didn't do anything. He stood off from the house and watched the lights come on in the front room, and a growing feeling of responsibility added to his grief. If he'd been with her it wouldn't have happened. He couldn't have stood having Mr. Robert Frost's eyes on him after that.

Only later, as he drifted aimlessly back toward Limon did he think of Ethan. The thought hit him with such power that it stopped him cold for five full minutes.

Ethan.

Jesus Mother. He was almost as much appalled that he had been so slow to think of Ethan as he was that Ethan might be the killer. Might be? It was as inescapable as death itself. Or was it? Even Ethan couldn't have done this. Still, someone had done it, someone brutal and half-human, and Ethan was the most brutal man he knew. He was still thinking about it when a sheriff's posse rumbled out of a ravine toward the Frost ranch. The horses surrounded him and two men jumped down and jostled him roughly. He saw a rope dangling from a saddle horn. Its end had been made over into a hanging noose. He had a moment of real fear, then one of the men said, "He's from Shaughnessy's. We were out there this morning. Shaughnessy alibis him." The two men mounted, the horses whipped around, and they were gone. One rider did not go. Mr. Frost got down from his horse and came toward him until he was close enough to touch. He put his hand on Tom's shoulder. "I know, son," he said softly. "We're all feeling the same thing. But we'll get him." Tom was so glad he couldn't see those eyes. Mr. Frost squeezed gently, then turned and mounted. As he rode away to his house, Tom began to walk the other way, tears stinging his cheeks. Ethan had become too large a burden for him to carry alone.

He began his search on the east end of Limon, working along both sides of the street. For a Friday night, the town was dead. The mobs had dissolved and the saloon had closed. In his walk across town he saw only one man, the reporter Kerr, coming out of the telegraph office. Finally, he staggered back to Shaughnessy's. He was followed all the way by the old emotions of shock and grief, and now by the new one of guilt.

10

Sheriff John Freeman came to Shaughnessy's again in the morning. He and Shaughnessy talked on the front porch while a dozen armed men waited in the yard. When they left, Shaughnessy addressed the boys as a group. "Lads, we're bein' pressed into service. All of us are asked to join a search party lookin' for the killer of the Frost girl. The sheriff wants every nook an' cranny searched for miles around. We're lookin' for her purse, an' handkerchief, an' also for anybody suspicious we might be seeing. There's one bit of new evidence that might be of help. We're probably huntin' a nigger."

Tom looked up. "How do you know that?"

"A young lad told the sheriff he'd seen a nigger running away from the murder scene just about dark Thursday. So keep your eyes peeled, lads."

They fanned out and combed the plains. By mid-morning Tom had begun to feel better. The shock had passed, and the word that the killer was a black had lanced and drained his guilt like a needle thrust into a boil. Ethan had not done it, and he could think of little else. They searched all day, twice encountering bands of roving men from town. Afterward Tom hiked into Limon to see if there was any news. Again he read every word. And the editorial heat continued. The story had moved up to banner status in the *Post,* with the eight-column head BLOODHOUNDS FIND THE TRAIL OF THE LIMON FIEND. They had worked the rape angle in, very high, with the veiled hint that the killer's "crime was not confined to murder alone." The *Republican* warned that "the assailant of the little girl may expect nothing but death by lynching when found."

The telegraph office was running overtime. Reporters crowded in, filing their day's copy. The saloon remained closed. Tom moved through the crowds lining the street, still searching the faces for Ethan. By eight o'clock the people had left the street and returned to their homes, and Limon was like a ghost town. A scare story, begun late yesterday, had resurfaced, sending the men rushing to their women and children. The newest speculation was that the killing of Louise Frost had been a vengeance murder, not the work of a Negro at all. Mr. Frost had served in a posse some months before, and had helped track down a gang of train robbers. Two of the robbers had been killed and the others had vowed vengeance upon each member of the posse. People went home to lock doors and load shotguns, and by nine o'clock the telegraph office was the only lighted window along the street.

He would always remember the fear, and that strange feeling of an entire town gone crazy. More than that, he would remember the press: the dandy reporters in derby hats, pressing the people for one more drop of emotion, one more vicious quote. They were the barkers for this circus, calling up the masses through paper megaphones. The *Post* led the charge, speculating in one of its earliest stories that "the murderer wouldn't live ten minutes after being taken back to Limon." And on the third day, when a young black suspect was arrested in Denver, the *Post* story left little doubt that the killer had been found.

His name was Preston John Porter, Junior. He was sixteen years old and a runaway from Limon, where he had been seen as recently as Thursday morning. He was a gandy dancer with the Union Pacific. He had been caught in Denver, with his father and his brother Arthur. Tom stopped looking for Ethan. He drifted around town, picking up the emotional tempo as lynch talk began anew. That night's *Post* convicted Porter in the first paragraph.

> "John Porter is the murderer of Louise Frost," says Sheriff Freeman of Lincoln County, who has been working day and night on the case.
> John Porter is in the (Denver) jail, a badly frightened Negro. His father, Preston Porter, and his brother, Arthur Porter, are also in jail, but the sheriff will ask for the release of the other two men. He will take John Porter back to Hugo, the county seat of Lincoln County, and make an effort to land him in the jail at that place. It is thought that the sheriff's efforts in this respect will be useless, for angry mobs are waiting at Hugo and Limon ready to wreak vengeance on the murderer of Louise Frost.
> The evidence against John Porter is circumstantial, and, the sheriff says, very damaging.
> Yesterday, when the houses were searched, a pair of shoes, which were the property of John Porter, were found. These shoes were taken to the gulch by which the murderer made his escape, leaving his tracks in the sand, and the sheriff says they fitted the tracks exactly.
> "We've got the murderer of Louise Frost and you can gamble on it," was the way Sheriff Freeman expressed himself this morning. "I'm sure Porter is the murderer. Yes, I'll take him to Hugo and put him in the jail there. I will resist to the bitter end all efforts of the mob to take him away, and if the mob gets him it will be after the members have killed me."

In the morning, the Limon paper openly advocated lynching. "The crowd is waiting to see the Negro, and when it does, the lynching is the next order of business. Just what punishment will be meted out to the murderer cannot be told at this time, but it is safe to say that he will be tortured in a most horrible manner." The call was repeated by the afternoon *Post,* as Bonfils and Tammen crusaded for the return of capital punishment. The article bore the flair and style of Bonfils, saying that "there are times when nothing short of the death penalty will satisfy the demands of justice." The *Post* columnist, Winifred Black, wrote an endorsement of capital punishment and concluded that, "if he is guilty, I hope he will be lynched." Tom breathed newsprint, consuming every line and syllable, and re-reading it all many times over. He ran messages back and forth between the sheriff's office and Western Union, earning fifty cents from the *Post* and a quarter from the *News,* and he was there when word came from Denver that Porter had confessed.

It struck the town like an earthquake. One cowboy with a drooping moustache went from group to group telling everyone, and soon the street was alive with it. "He's confessed. The nigger confessed." It gave them new life, fanned the fires into white heat. Once again the town began filling with men as word spread to the nearby ranches. Tom carried Kerr's dispatches to the telegraph office, reading them as he hurried along. The reporter had tried to dramatize the atmosphere in Limon, putting in numerous blind quotes, some that Tom had overheard himself. "In all directions can be seen the dust of horsemen as they hurry to take part in the lynching," Kerr wrote. He followed that with the quote from the cowboy, uttered days earlier, before Porter had been arrested or identified. "All I want to do is punch his eyes out with this spike, cut his ears, nose, and tongue off." There was speculation in all the dispatches about what strategy the sheriff would use to keep his prisoner out of the hands of the mob. Kerr suggested that Freeman might take a roundabout route, driving across the plains with Porter to get him into the Hugo jail. "Then, if he gets him in jail, goes home to see his family and the mob breaks down the jail, it is no fault of his." There followed a quote from an unnamed man, reportedly well posted on the politics of Lincoln County: "If he doesn't bring him through here, he'll never serve another term as sheriff."

Tom was amazed at how all this information, sent piecemeal, came out in such coherent form in the newspaper. That night's *Post* had all the details of the confession as well as the dispatches from the scene. Porter had confessed suddenly, in the presence of several witnesses. Yes, he had intercepted Louise Frost, had taken her purse, had stabbed her. But he had stabbed her only once. "Before God, I cut that girl only once. If she was cut more, someone else did it." The quote was buried in the story, ignored by the mob. In that same issue was a piece headlined A PSYCHOLOGICAL STUDY OF THE PRISONER, written by a *Post* reporter who had visited Porter at city jail. The first sentence read, "John Porter is pure brute. That he has even human form is astonishing to one who knows of his horrid deed and watches him while he talks of it." The articles noted that Porter talked of his crime arrogantly, and even Tom, as he read them, found himself thirsting for Porter's blood. The specter of Ethan Kohl paled and vanished, and his bitterness and hatred were directed at a young black man he had never seen, who waited alone in a Denver cell for his delivery to a pack of madmen on the plains.

11

And now impatience swept the mob. Fed by rumor and by newsprint, mobs formed at every station along the Denver–Limon run, awaiting the attempt of Sheriff Freeman to get Porter to Hugo. Reporters had come from all over the state, and some from outside the state, to witness the lynching of Preston John Porter. The last official act, a flat refusal by the governor to bring out troops to help Sheriff Freeman protect Porter, sealed the boy's doom. The mob was whipped into a frenzy by the repeated statements of Sheriff Freeman, that Porter would be put in the Hugo jail alive. Mr. Robert Frost erupted in anger. "I tell you, I'll have that nigger," he told the men at the railroad depot. "I'll have that brute. You all know me. You know I've always stood for law and order. But if the sheriff tries to stand between me and the nigger, let it be said here and now that he's less than a man, he's a spineless coward, and I'll have his hide too." Reporter Kerr hung over the fringes of the mob, writing in his notebook. Then a new excitement rippled up the street. Someone had burst out of the sheriff's office and was working his way along, shouting into each knot of men. In Denver, the *Post* had just hit the street, with an eight-column banner reading PORTER WILL BE TAKEN BACK TO LIMON TONIGHT. A great cheer went up. The man who had spread the word, a stout man wearing a broad-brimmed white hat, said, "Now, boys, let's do this neat and orderly. We'll form a committee of ten men. One'll bring the rope, one provide the buckboard. Nobody'll do any out-and-out lynching, but everybody'll provide one tiny piece of it. We'll string the bastard up from the railroad bridge where it crosses the Big Sandy."

"Rip his belly open and tear his guts out," another said.

The men retired to the saloon to select the committee. Tom watched from the boardwalk out front, peeping in through the swinging door. The committee was selected and lots drawn, and within fifteen minutes the mob had gathered again at the depot to await the arrival of the Denver trains. The first train in was a Rock Island Line special. The committee boarded it and searched through each coach, while the mob, some two hundred strong, waited outside. "He ain't there," the stout man yelled, and a collective sigh swept over the mob. There were some laughs and nervous talk. No one expected the sheriff to bring Porter on the Rock Island Line, but it had to be searched anyway. A Union Pacific came through in the early afternoon, and the men fairly leaped up into the coaches, half-running from one to the other in the heat of the search. Nothing. A new mood—frustration—set in. It compounded the anger and made the men moody and sullen. Throughout the day and into the night the committee boarded the trains, searching the coaches thoroughly before letting them go through. And with each passing hour the mood of the mob became uglier.

By morning it was apparent that Freeman had not brought Porter back despite the *Post* story, and most of the men had gone home for a few hours' rest. A band of runners was organized, to spread the word in case the prisoner should arrive suddenly, without warning. Shortly after noon, the papers brought out more news, and the results were telegraphed to Limon. PORTER IS NOW ON HIS WAY, said the *Post*, TAKEN FROM JAIL, DRIVEN TO 40TH STREET, PUT ON THE REGULAR TRAIN, WHICH LEFT DENVER AT 1:10 P.M. Beneath it, a subhead: PORTER WILL REACH LIMON AT 3:45 O'CLOCK THIS AFTERNOON: LIMON MOB HAS THE HANGMAN'S NOOSE READY FOR PORTER. Again, led by the stout man in the wide-brimmed hat, the committee and its accompanying mob engulfed the depot and waited through the afternoon. Standing far back from the crowd, the boys from Shaughnessy's watched in awe.

At four o'clock, the Union Pacific bound for Kansas City rolled into the tiny station. The committee, tipped off in advance, mounted the end coach, an empty being pulled back to Missouri, and found Freeman and Porter sitting there alone. "Now boys," the sheriff said. The men marched up the aisle, gripped Freeman around the head, and wrestled him down in the seat. A noose was dropped over Preston Porter's head and jerked tight around the neck. He was pushed out into the dust, losing his derby hat under the feet of the mob. A great roar went up. Porter was jerked to his feet and led by the rope, down the track toward the ravine where Louise Frost had been murdered.

Clutched in his hand was a Bible. He read from it as he walked. Two men preceded him, one leading him by the rope around his neck.

If Porter understood what was happening, if he knew that his death was moments away, he showed no evidence of panic. Someone asked for a page from the Bible as a souvenir, and Porter tore it out and gave it to him. Soon everyone wanted one, and Porter, smiling now, tore the leaves out as fast as his fingers could grip them. They reached the wagon road and turned left toward the ravine. Discussion broke out as to the manner of his death. Should he be castrated first? Should he be burned? At the ravine they stopped. Louise Frost's blood still stained the earth a few feet away. The sight of it seemed to enrage Mr. Frost, and he talked with the committee while Porter continued passing out pages from his Bible. The stout man said, "The girl's father wants him burned," and again the men cheered. "Send somebody to town for wood and a stake," the stout man said. The wagon roared off toward Limon.

By the time it returned, Porter's Bible was in ruins. Darkness had come, and a few photographers were still at work, taking time exposures of Porter at the death scene. The wagon, piled high with wood, was backed into the ravine, and a long railroad iron was driven into the ground about fifteen feet from the blood-soaked earth. The wood was unloaded and piled around the stake, and Porter walked up and leaned his back against it.

Still so confident, still no fear. Two cowboys chained Porter to the stake and tied his hands behind him. Wood was heaped around him and soaked with coal oil. Now for the first time a hint of fear crossed Preston Porter's face. His head hung low and his chin touched his chest. The stout man—he would be called the "master of ceremonies" in tomorrow's *Post*—stepped up close to the stake and faced the mob.

"Gentlemen, everything is ready. Mr. Frost, the father of the murdered girl, has been accorded the privilege of setting fire to this pile."

Frost stepped out of the crowd. His eyes danced from face to face, but avoided the face of Porter, chained before him. "Gentlemen," he said, "I touch off this pile without a tremor of the hand." He struck a match, revealing a face gone pale in its glow. He bent and touched it to the wood.

It went out. Quickly now, moving with some impatience, Mr. Frost struck another one, bent and watched the flame catch. He stood, keeping his eyes away from Porter's face. "Now, gentlemen, I leave him to you." He blended back into the crowd, and again the stout man came forward. "All right, boys," he said, "Let's get the fire going in lots of places, get him going good and warm."

Two men hurried forward.

"Not too fast," the stout man said. "We don't want to burn him too quick. Give it time. It'll get to him."

Porter's eyes dropped to his feet, where red fingers of flame were

78

crackling around his shoes. The fire curled upward between his legs.

"What time is it?" the stout man said. "Let's see how long he'll last."

"Six twenty-three."

The stout man looked toward the western sky, where only a trace of pink remained.

Suddenly the flame leaped to Porter's waist. His shoes began to crisp. His pants caught and began to burn, and he screamed. Such a scream, such a scream. Tom had never in his life heard a human voice scream like that.

The stout man laughed. "So you know how it is, huh, nigger. You know what it feels like now. Holler—holler, you black-hearted bastard."

"God almighty," said Porter, looking at his tormentor. "Lord God have mercy."

"What mercy'd you show, nigger?"

"Oh, God pity me, God forgive me. Sweet Jesus, let me in. Jesus tell them . . . tell the newspapermen, tell them Jesus, tell my father and brother I'm going to heaven tonight. Oh, God, forgive these men, God forgive them."

The flames had reached his neck. His flesh had begun burning, his juices sizzling down into the coals. With a heave, Porter pulled his hands loose. "Oh, men, stop this! Stop it, please, men. Mister, stop it and I'll tell you something else! Please . . ."

"Stop nothing. Come on, blackie, holler louder, so's we all know you're cooking right." A wave of laughter, broken by sporadic cheering, swept over the crowd. Porter lurched forward and the chain slipped over his shoulder. Still chained by his feet, he fell across the fire, twitching, dancing like a drop of water on a griddle. More cheering, more laughter. "Please!" Porter screamed, "please, mister, stand me up again so I can die fast. Please, mister."

"Take all the time you want, nigger."

"Oh, my head. Jesus, somebody shoot me. Please shoot me, mister. My God, my legs . . ."

He had no legs. The fire had engulfed his lower body and was sucked upward by the draft. The stout man piled more wood upon the writhing mass of fire, devoid now of all but head and arms and voice. That voice kept on beyond anything they thought possible. Porter shrieked and pleaded. His face flopped over and over, its flesh melting away, until it was nothing more than a disembodied voice. The voice moaned on, with less force each second until, at the end, there was a great sigh and another cheer from the people. Porter's last audible words were again framed around a prayer to his god. "God, oh, God, have mercy on these men and on the little girl, and on her father."

"What time is it?"

"Six thirty-five."

"And he only took twelve minutes to die?"

"That's what it took."

"Well, it wouldn't have taken that long if he hadn't tumbled over. It was a lucky thing he fell."

The fire had begun to die now, and one of the men had probed through the coals with a stick. "Here's his head. Looks like he's done real good." Some of the men, including Mr. Frost, had stepped close to look. Porter's skull, bare and white, lay face-down in the ashes.

"Turn him over."

Flesh still hung to Porter's face. Mr. Frost seemed to recoil, as if the probing stick had uncovered something evil, and contagious.

"Burn every bone in his body," he said. "Don't let a vestige of him remain to poison the coyotes. The wind will scatter his ashes as they ought to be scattered, and then he'll be off the face of the earth forever."

There was more fire now, heaps of planks and railroad ties, half-burned faggots piled again into the burning heap. Mr. Frost stood hunched over near the fire, trying to warm away the cold feeling they all felt so suddenly. Only Tom knew the feeling would not warm away, not ever. Preston Porter's screams echoed in his soul. His words rose up in a sea of newspapers. *Before God, I cut that girl only once. If she was cut more, someone else did it.* Dear God. Dear Jesus.

God have mercy.

He would not go back to Shaughnessy's. In the morning, dry-eyed and pale, he bought the papers, reading compulsively every ghastly detail of the burning of Preston Porter. He would read too of the coroner's inquest on Saturday, when the bones and teeth were taken to Limon for identification and study. The jury would find that Porter's death came "at the hands of parties unknown." Two days later, he boarded the Denver train and left Limon. As it pulled out of the station, his eyes scanned the faces of people waiting under the snowshed. Nestled in among them, standing perfectly still, was Ethan.

Their eyes met, then he flicked out of sight.

12

He was halfway back to Denver when he thought, the papers killed that boy. As surely as if they'd lit the fire under the stake, Bonfils and Tammen, Senator Patterson, the man who owned the *Republican*—all of them had murdered Preston Porter. He didn't know it then, but he was just a step away from a career in journalism. He came home full of the need for change, convinced of his new calling. He hit the streets with a new vigor, and he began to save his money.

In his late teens, he was closer to Anna than anyone. As his star rose, she became a cheering section of one. She was sixteen then, the prettiest girl in west Denver, and still in love with Willie Brown III. After supper she talked with Tom. They walked in the garden, and sometimes around Sloan's Lake, sharing their deepest thoughts. He thought Anna was a candidate for sainthood. She was quiet, respectful, beautiful, and religious, and her mind was brilliant. She understood everything she read and made top grades in school without having to study. She delighted in his success. It had come late: He was nineteen before he made the jump from the streets into the newsroom, and another three years had passed before he began to get any play with his stories. Anna was ecstatic. He had moved out of the family home and she had begun coming by his apartment after school. They would sit together under an umbrella on the sundeck overlooking Arapahoe Street, talking, sipping cold tea, dreaming about the future.

His future was looking ever brighter. He had met Damon Runyon before Runyon left for New York, and was on a first-name basis with Gene Fowler. Fowler was then a star reporter for the *News*. One night in the Denver Press Club, Fowler cornered Tom and drew him aside. "Do you have your own tools yet?" Tom just blinked. "Burglar tools," Fowler said. "You'll need 'em working for those thieves, and I know a guy who wants to unload a set."

Fowler was a great one for kidding. But soon he learned that Fowler hadn't been kidding, that everyone broke into everything, that police reporters had no more honesty than the criminals they covered. He learned that his best friends broke and entered if a story depended on it. They broke into hospitals for medical records, into the City Hall storeroom to steal cases of confiscated liquor, into the homes of murder victims for pictures. In one of those crazy, early assignments, Tom had gotten the story, but Fowler got the pictures for the *News*. Tammen called him on the carpet. "How come we didn't have them goddamn pictures?" Tom shrugged and said he didn't know how Fowler had gotten them. And Tammen had said, "Find out. And when you do find out, remember it. Don't ever let yourself get beat like that again."

Nothing was ever said in Tammen's presence, and certainly not around Bonfils, about burglary. Everyone from copyboy up knew what was expected, just as they knew what would and would not make print, just as editors knew which politicians and social figures were on Bonfils' ban list and should not appear in the paper. It was Bonfils' way of punishing people who had been unpleasant: Their names simply did not appear in his newspaper. To Fowler it was all an amusing game. He had an arrogance and an irreverence for all formal structures and social mores. One day he just quit the *News*, walked into the *Post* city room and, without bothering with the usual formalities of applying for work, took his coat off and began pounding out his first *Post* story. Tom watched, amazed, from across the newsroom. To have that much brass; it was a gift that couldn't be learned. He attached himself to Fowler like a lost pup. They went to poker games in the Press Club, on binges in Park Hill, on roaring drunks to Cheyenne during Frontier Days. They went into seedy bars on the lowers in quest of the flesh scattered by George Creel's whorehouse raids. They were exactly the same age, but Fowler seemed older, and he loved the role of mentor. One night Fowler told him the secret. "Tommy, you've got to change your whole way of looking at the world. Reach out for things, don't be afraid to touch silk, and read like a son of a bitch. Learning intimidates people, and that's the name of the game we're in. The intimidation business. Even your bosses—if they think you're smarter than they are, they'll back off. The kind of people we deal with respect intellect a hell of a lot more than muscle. They are actually afraid of it. In their alleged minds there's nothing worse than getting shown up for the mental midgets they are. If you can do that, you've got them by the balls and they leave you alone. If you're good enough and you learn enough, you might even become a goddamn legend in your own time. Now don't that make you want to puke?"

When Fowler wasn't drinking or whoring or writing copy for the next edition, he was reading. "Read Shakespeare," Fowler told him. "God damn it, there's more real poop in there than you'll find in the drivel of a thousand self-inflated philosophers. Jesus Christ, I love words. Sometimes they keep working for centuries after you're dead. Look at Shakespeare's words—still moving people after three hundred goddamn years. What we do on newspapers is Neanderthalism alongside that. But it's still important, still working with words, still leaving behind something that wasn't there before. Don't let the pricks tell you the newspaper is dead tomorrow, or it's just something to wrap a fish in. The hell with that. The next goddamn Shakespeare might be reading *us* a hundred years from now, just to get one tiny fragment, maybe a mood, for *his Julius Caesar*. Think of it like that and it helps, Tommy, it honest to Christ does. Whenever the bastards start getting to me, I think, what if I'd been some hack writer in Caesar's time, and some little thing I'd written gave Shakespeare a few lines for his play. And that's enough."

Fowler gave him a list of books to read. "Try to find these in secondhand stores, so you'll have 'em at home. You'll find yourself going back to them all your life. And try to read something about Egypt, and the kind of civilization they had all those years ago. It'll give you a sense of your own insignificance, help you understand what bullshit everything else is. People say I've got brass balls, but if you want to know where they came from, I got 'em from the old pharaohs."

His breakthrough into Fowler's world came a few months later. He was working the Saturday night police beat when a call came in on a shooting on Grant Street. Tom recognized the address as midway up Millionaire's Row; a big, big story on the face of it. Anything combining high society and death was certain front page. He got to the scene just before the cops arrived. The victim, he learned later, was Howard Bonner. The body was still lying by the piano in the den, its blood blotting the expensive Persian rug.

The place was crawling with people. Nobody knew who Bonner was or what he was doing here. The house belonged to Mr. and Mrs. Wilbur Jackson, country club patrons, contributors to charities, cornerstones of society. Mrs. Jackson was sitting in a vestibule, being distraught. The gun, a Smith and Wesson, lay at Bonner's feet, about three feet away. Mr. Jackson was comforting his wife. Her brother, a man named Arthur Pomeroy, had taken charge. He met Tom at the door.

"Who're you?"

"Hastings, *Denver Post*."

"Sorry, we're not releasing this to the press." He slammed the door.

The police arrived. Then the coroner came, then Booker from the *Times,* and in the third wave of cars, Goodwin arrived with his camera. Tom told Goodwin what the man had said and Goodwin let out a bellow that could be heard for two blocks. *"Not releasing this to the press!* What the hell does he think this is, one of their goddamn tea parties? Hey! Hey, goddammit, open up in there!" He pounded the door until a uniformed cop came. "Sorry, Carl," the cop said. "You boys'll have to wait a while. The loo-tenant'll have a statement when we get through in here."

"Well, what about pictures, Mickey? What the hell am I supposed to do, take a picture of the loooo-tenant standing here reading a goddamn statement?"

The cop shrugged and closed the door.

"Watch what happens," Booker said. "These sons of bitches think they can buy anything with money. They're trying to turn this into a two-inch filler for the back pages."

An hour later the covered body of Howard Bonner was brought out on a stretcher. The attendants stopped reluctantly while the photographers set up and shot by flashlight. A few minutes later the lieutenant came out and gave his statement. Bonner was an "old friend" of Mrs. Jackson. He had been staying with the Jacksons as their houseguest. He was from St. Louis, Missouri. He was thirty-eight years old. He had been shot once in the upper chest by a Smith and Wesson weapon owned by Mr. Jackson. He was killed at once. Bonner had been drinking and had become belligerent. Mr. Jackson had produced the gun and Bonner had attacked. In the struggle he had been shot once. There were some loose ends, which would have to wait until morning. No, they had not booked anyone. Allowing for the reputations and social standing of the Jacksons, they were being allowed to come in on their own in the morning for more detailed statements.

That was it. The cops rolled in their awnings, the meat wagon departed, and the reporters milled around, grumbling. "Goddamn millionaires," Booker said. "Sons of bitches can buy their way out of anything." At the *Post*, O'Reilly told him they were set up for a Page One lead piece, with headshots of the Jacksons from the *Post* morgue and whatever Goodwin had as art. "We need a headshot of the victim," O'Reilly said. "The page is gonna look funny as hell with pictures of everybody but the victim."

Tom shook his head. "There's no way that Pomeroy will let anybody in there again. It's a tough one, Ed, especially since the guy wasn't from here."

"You just better be damn sure the other side doesn't come up with one. Cover your ass, as the little boss says."

By midnight he had worked up a state of near paranoia, and then Fowler came into the newsroom. He was red-eyed and staggering. He sat at a desk and tried to write something, gave up with a loud "Jesus Christ," and slumped over the typewriter. Suddenly, as if by telepathy, Fowler sat upright and fastened his eyes on Tom. "It's little Tommy Hastings, as I live and breathe. What troubles you so late, Tommy? Is it women? Or women?"

Tom sat with him and told him about it. Fowler nodded gravely.

"Tommy, you're *so* goddamn unimaginative and common. How many times must I tell you, in cases like this you've got to consider the impossible right along with the possible. Now what have we got? We got us a stiff, and he's from out of town. Only one picture in the city, if that, and the family's sitting on it. The main obstacle is an anal orifice, personified as the brother of the lady in the case. We've got no idea where in the house they might have this picture, or even if such exists. Is that an accurate assessment?"

"Pretty much."

"Okay, did you try bribing the prick?"

"Come on, Gene, these people are rich."

"Come on yourself; that's probably how they got that way. But never mind, forget that impossibility. You already missed it anyway. Let's do something else. Grab your photog and let's take us a ride."

Goodwin was just finished printing. The three of them tumbled downstairs and into Fowler's car. Fowler drove, weaving dangerously back and forth across the trolley tracks. Tom noticed that he was headed toward City Hall.

In the darkened hallway of the county morgue, a block from City Hall, Fowler opened his bag of picks and went to work on the lock. It took him eight minutes to open it and another three minutes to find the new file on Howard Bonner. He walked to the slab, pulled it out, and rolled down the sheet.

"There he is, boys. Carl, do your stuff."

"Hell," Goodwin said. "His eyes are closed."

"He's dead, isn't he? What the hell do you expect, dummy?"

"He's dead and he looks it," Goodwin said. "They'll never run that."

"Sure they will. Here." Fowler reached into his pocket and found a toothpick. He broke it into two pieces, leaned over the dead man, and gently propped open the eyelids. "I guess I've got to do all the goddamn thinking in this outfit."

"That's even worse," Goodwin said. "His eyes are rolled up. You can't even see the pupils. Christ, it's too goddamn morbid. A man without eyeballs." He shivered.

"We'll get the artist to give him some eyeballs," Fowler said. "Would you just get it moving before some son of a bitch walks in here and catches us? What do you want from him, a smile? Here, I'll give you a smile." He went to the attendant's desk and tore off two strips of white tape. He fastened each strip to a cheek and drew the face up into a grotesque grin.

"That don't look half bad, except for the tape," Goodwin said.

"We'll get the artist to paint out the tape when we give him his eyeballs. Now, would you shoot the goddamn thing so we can get out of here?"

The *Post* ran the touched-up picture of Howard Bonner in all editions the next day. The *News* and *Times* had nothing. That afternoon Tom dropped by Fowler's desk and thanked him, but Fowler just looked at him as if he didn't understand. "Funny," he said, "I don't remember any of that." A year later he was gone. He took the path of Damon Runyon, who had left the *Post* for New York seven years before. "You'll be next," Fowler said. "I'll see you in the big city." But Tom had no designs on the big city. Here a man with talent could be king of the world. But some of the fun went out of the *Post* when Fowler left, and Tom never quite filled his shoes. He was a better writer, yes, he was that, but there was never a place in his makeup for action without doubt. As long as he worked for the *Post,* he felt cheated of imagination and guts.

13

Sometimes, when he came home to his Arapahoe Street apartment from a long day at the *Post,* Anna was already there. He had begun leaving his key outside, under the floormat, and she would let herself in. At least once a week she prepared his dinner, something simple but nice, usually taken from Teresa's *Depression Era Cookbook* of 1897. She usually came on Thursdays, and he could smell her home cooking all the way up the stairwell. It was the summer of her graduation from high school, and she was floating through life with uncertainty and melancholia. Her four-year campaign to win the heart of William Brown III had apparently ended in failure. She didn't talk about it anymore, and Tom was happy to let William III slip away into the faceless past where he belonged. But Willie wouldn't stay there. Tom found that out in July. He and Goodwin were coming in from an assignment in Boulder. As they turned past Arapahoe Street, he looked up and saw Anna on the sundeck. She was there for only a second, but in that flash he'd seen someone with her, a large figure standing just beyond, near the door.

She had never come down on Tuesday, and seldom got to the apartment before three o'clock. "Pull over, will you, Carl? I think I'll eat lunch at my place and walk back to work afterward." He watched Goodwin drive away, then turned and started up the stairs. He stood outside his door for a long time, listening. For a moment he wondered if he'd imagined seeing her, if maybe the heat was getting to him. He lifted the floormat. The key was gone.

He made no noise as he slipped back downstairs. That evening after work he walked the streets for a long time before going home. All afternoon a faint suspicion had begun growing in his mind. It was insane, absurd; in that day and time an unspeakable horror. At the top of the stairs he found his key. She had replaced it carefully, exactly where he had left it that morning. The place, for all appearances, was just as he'd last seen it. The door leading from the bedroom to the sundeck was latched, as he'd left it, and the bed was rumpled and he'd left it that way too. He thought about her through the long night.

He stayed up late reading, and occasionally, involuntarily, his eyes would wander up from the printed page and zero in on the bed. "Be careful, sis," he said, closing the book.

Alone in the dark, he realized how much she meant to him. Her blood was his, and she was plotting a course for disaster. He would have to talk to her.

But he didn't, not the next day or the day after that. He didn't see her at all on Wednesday. He thought of going out to the family home, but he didn't. At two o'clock Wednesday, he wandered over from the *Post*, lifted his floormat, and stood there for a long moment, looking at the key. He didn't go in. On Thursday she came as usual. She cooked a spaghetti dish she loved. They didn't talk much; just sat on the sundeck and watched the sun slip behind the mountains. Later he walked her to the trolley and made one attempt to draw her out.

"I saw you the other day."

"Oh?" She kept walking. Her eyes were on her feet. "How could that be? Were you out our way?"

"Here, at the apartment. Thought I saw you on the sundeck."

"Couldn't have, love. When was I here last? Must have been a week ago today, wasn't it?"

"That's what I thought."

But she wouldn't look at him and he knew. Along with everything else, she had begun to lie.

Her visits became sporadic. She didn't come the following Thursday, then she did come, then she missed two weeks. When he visited home, she wouldn't sit with him in the garden, making an excuse to retire right after dinner. As Sammy noticed, she was off her feed. Teresa said she was having trouble sleeping too. "She's still in love," said Abe. "With that dumb William Brown the third."

On another Tuesday, two months to the day since he'd seen her on the sundeck, he climbed the stairs after work and was shocked to find his front door wide open. He lifted the floormat; the key was gone. He moved into the apartment, calling her name softly. Could they still be here? Had they lost track of the time? Or had she just been careless in her flight? He moved through the room, calling, but there was no answer. He peeped into the bedroom.

She wasn't there either, but the sundeck door was open. Quickly now he crossed the room and saw her, standing on a large wooden box above the railing, staring down at the street three floors below.

"Anna!"

She whirled and lost her balance. Her arms thrashed at the air and she began to tip over. Then he was beside her, grasping her around the waist. She went limp with a sigh. He carried her inside and put her on the bed, loosened her blouse at the neck, hurried into the kitchen for water. He chipped up the last of this morning's ice and brought it to her wrapped in a rag.

The cold compress made her stir. Her eyes fluttered open and she burst into tears. Her hands trembled. He took them in his and held them tightly until the trembling stopped.

"You know, don't you?" she said. "You know what's been going on?"

"I think I do."

"Oh, my God, what a mess. I can't believe this is happening to me. I can't believe it. The way I've let mother down. All of you."

"Nobody needs to know, sis."

"You still don't understand, do you? You still don't know the worst of it. My God, Tom, what am I going to do? How on earth can I go through with this? I can't live and I can't kill myself. I can't do anything right. Tom. Thomas . . ." She clasped his hand very tightly now and looked straight into his face. "I'm going to have a baby, Tom. Hadn't you figured that out yet?"

"Wow." He sank to the floor, running his fingers through his hair. His scalp felt gritty.

"Yes," she said. "Tom, what am I going to do? You know how that neighborhood is. Mother will never live it down. You've got to help me."

"How?" He had never felt quite so helpless or alone.

She looked at him for a while, then said quietly. "Yes, how? That was a stupid thing for me to say, wasn't it? How dumb of me. What can you do? What can anybody do?"

"Have you told him yet?"

"Who?"

"Him." He couldn't say the name. "The third."

"I can't get near him. Suddenly he's just not there anymore. He's out of touch, locked up tight somewhere in his mother's house." She began to tremble again. "Thomas, I'm scared. I'm out of my mind with it."

He looked at her and offered nothing.

"I can't handle it alone," she said. "Today I went there, to his mother's place. I needed to talk to somebody. It was the first time I had met her. She was horrid beyond belief. She called me some terrible things. Said I was Jewish trash. How can people be so terrible? Can you understand that?"

No, he said, he couldn't understand it either.

He rode the trolley with her that night, and walked her to the door of the family home. He didn't go in. Afterward, he went looking for William Brown III. He went to the Brown house, and a man there told him that Willie had gone to a party in Denver. He got the address and caught another trolley, getting off thirty minutes later on the fringes of Park Hill. The sounds of the party flowed down the block and met him. It had spilled over into the yard, where groups of boys and girls were talking loudly and laughing. On a table near the garage, someone had set up a Victrola and waltz records filled the night. Boys wearing coats and ties danced with girls in ankle-length dresses, gliding across the grass under a string of gas lamps. He asked for Willie Brown, but no one seemed to know where he had gone. He pushed his way through the party, looking at the faces, and finally he came upon Willie III and his new flame, standing in the darkness of the backyard, cuddled together near the alley. They didn't see him until he was very close.

"You Willie Brown?"

"That's right. Who're you?"

Tom came closer, close enough to see the sudden alarm on the face of Willie's pretty young woman.

"My name's Tom Hastings."

"So?"

"Anna Kohl is my sister."

Willie Brown didn't say anything.

"You want her to hear this?"

Willie cleared his throat. "Marjorie . . ."

No one had to draw her a picture. "I'll wait up front with the others," she said. "Don't be long."

When she was out of earshot, Brown said, "You can't make me marry her."

Tom dropped him with one punch. He felt the bridge of Willie's nose give under his knuckles. He grabbed Willie Brown by the hair and dragged him into the alley, past a long row of garbage cans. He pulled off a lid and pushed Willie face-down into the smell of rotten meat and sour milk.

"I'd kill her myself before I'd let her marry you, pig." He kicked Willie in the ribs, upsetting the can and scattering garbage across the alley. Willie got to his hands and knees and Tom kicked him in the face, breaking something, opening his lip, flattening him on his back. Then he walked along and poured each garbage can over Willie's body until he was covered under a mound of slime.

Tom stood over him. "You better teach your old lady some manners, pig. Next time she talks about Jewish trash, you remember this. Remember what happened. And remember something else. If you ever as much look at Anna Kohl again I'll come after you with a butcher knife. You got that, pig?" He kicked Willie in the ribs. "Got it?"

Willie got it. He moaned through the dirt and the slime and the blood.

"You better get it, pig. You goddamn better. I'll take that knife and trim your shaft down one inch at a time."

He walked away through the yard, past the anxious Marjorie, under the gas lamps where people still waltzed to wax cylinders. He kept walking, as the party faded behind him.

It would always seem somehow that his youth had faded with it, that the last vestiges of his childhood lay buried in the slime with Willie Brown III. Anna withdrew, and the magic went out of their brother-and-sister routine for good. Teresa and Sammy survived, and found a way to cope with tragedy. Tom grew away from home. In another year he met a young suffragette named Nell Clement. They walked under the box elders and talked. The world moved on. The age of the press agent came; scandals seeped out of City Hall, and a killer was loose on Market Street, strangling whores with a silk stocking and leaving them nude in dark alleys.

He learned his business. He learned to pick locks, and one summer he lifted a badge from a dead cop, to use in emergencies. Bonfils and Tammen grew richer. The war came and went. Abe went overseas, to fight in the mud of France. And Tom got asthma, was twice rejected for military service, and rode out the war as Harry Tammen's golden boy, pounding out police beats and sifting through clues to bizarre murders.

CHAPTER
THREE

1

When the Coolidge administration was two months old, he closed the house in Golden, put the furniture in storage, and moved into town. His hope for an early understanding with Nell had collapsed, and the weeks had passed, and fall had come with colors and then snow. He was marking time: his drinking had increased; his reputation was in danger. People talked of him in the past tense, as if he had already joined the ranks of the walking dead. Sometimes Tammen called him in for long talks after work, and some of the talks contained blunt warnings. "Pull yourself together, son," he said one afternoon. "I know it's tough losing your family, but goddammit, you're heading for disaster." Tammen had always been one of his favorite people, always his champion when Bonfils wanted to fire him outright. Tammen loved playing the father figure. He had no sons, and years ago he had taken Gene Fowler in tow. When Fowler left, Tammen transferred his interest to Tom.

He was a pudgy man of medium height, with an oval face and the disposition of a chameleon. He loved it when people called him a rogue; he promoted it by telling of men he had conned. His generosity was offset by Bonfils' stinginess, and they were seen by the community as direct opposites in almost every respect. Tammen liked to talk about shortchanging the register when he had tended bar at the Windsor Hotel. Bonfils, who really had conned people, never talked of such things to anyone. Bonfils was deep and moody; Tammen lighthearted and gay. Bonfils was trim, without an inch of fat; Tammen was squat and plump. Bonfils liked to dress up in tweeds and checks; Tammen wore baggy suits and rumpled shirts. Bonfils carried himself erect when he walked; Tammen slouched. Bonfils would cut a man's pay even as Tammen was walking through the newsroom passing out dollar bills from his own pocket. A glass of wine was an indulgence for Bonfils. Tammen enjoyed whiskey; often on Sunday mornings, when his presence wouldn't inhibit the reporters who went there during the week, he could be found at the Denver Press Club, slouched over a glass in the half-lighted room.

In his early days, Tom quaked at the sight of them. Sometimes Bonfils would come out of his office and stare across the room. His eyes always seemed to end up on Tom. Very early in his career, he got the feeling that Bonfils disliked him. There was some magnetism there, which had persisted through the years. He doubted that he'd spoken two hundred words to the man in all that time. There had been his drunken display on the street the night Harding died, and once at Christmastime he had met Bonfils on the stairs and had boldly wished him a happy holiday. Bonfils stared at him, eyes probing for a motive. Finally he nodded and went up the stairs, inviting Tom to beat a quick retreat through the front door into Champa Street.

Bonfils was known to fire people on a whim, and Tom kept out of his way. Later, when he had gained Tammen's friendship and the respect of reporters across town, he became bolder. But even then he seldom ventured up front for talks with Tammen unless he was summoned. The front office, by reputation and appearance, was intimidating. The partners each had a private office, Tammen's to the right, Bonfils' to the far left, and between them was a large reception room where countless advertisers, tipsters, socialites, power seekers, and political candidates had writhed in agony awaiting an audience. The room was painted deep red and was known across town as the Bucket of Blood.

Now at night he had taken to drifting around the building, wandering past the Bucket of Blood and peering inside. He was spending a lot of time here these days. It was like his learning years, with one critical difference. Then he'd been working; now he was drinking. Sometimes he would sit alone in Goodwin's darkroom and take it straight from the bottle, feeding the kitty with paper money instead of coins. Goodwin began finding him slumped on the floor when he came in for work. When there was time, Goodwin and Malloy would carry him down a fire escape and push him into a car, to be taken home later that morning and put to bed. Home for him now was a two-room apartment on Capitol Hill. Most of his things from the house in Golden were still in boxes stacked in a corner. In moments of sober reflection, he would sit in his room and stare at the boxes, and his resentment was great. His wife was stubborn; her stubbornness was appalling, but it bolstered his own.

There were two bright spots in his life. One was the weekly visit he had with Michael and Paul. The other was that, strangely, without any planning or understanding of why it had happened, he had begun to write again.

2

On days when his hangover wasn't too bad, he worked for an hour before going down to the *Post*. It had begun spontaneously, with the opening of a box. There he found his unfinished, unstarted novel, his notes on Preston Porter and Louise Frost. At first the work was limited to more note-taking. He would put Shaughnessy in, expand his role. Shaughnessy's importance as a balance against the madness of the town would be great.

At the end of the week he had nothing, so he shelved the project and started a short story, completely unrelated to what he had come to consider his "major work." It went fast and easy, and it sold first time out, to one of the New York pulps, for thirty dollars. He propped the check up on the mirror while he shaved. "By God," he said aloud, "the old man ain't dead yet." But his hand shook as he held the razor: too much bad whiskey the night before. That morning he finished another story and sent it off to New York. It came back and he sent it out again. He found the apartment ideal: There were no distractions from Nell or the kids, no scenery to watch while empty pages lay at his fingertips. There was just this room. His window looked out into an alley, a garage door, and a row of garbage cans. The house was run by a man named Harvey Settle, a balding, burly fellow in his mid-fifties. Settle was a Kleagle in the Ku Klux Klan. He had tried three times now to get Tom to join.

Settle had provided his tenants, all men, with some interesting maid service. Three times a week a lovely blond girl named Georgeann came in and moved things around, dusted, changed sheets. He thought Georgeann was Swedish; she was certainly Scandinavian. She talked in very broken English and braided her hair. She was still in her late teens. She had immigrated to America hoping for a husband and opportunity. Now she was a hooker in Harvey Settle's boardinghouse. He was tempted, as he continued to be tempted at work by Alice Wilder. Sometimes the thought of Georgeann filled his day. He would pass her in the hall and the memory of her perfume would linger through the morning. She would look up and meet his eyes. "Gut morning, Mr. Hastings." "Good morning, Georgeann." And he moved on, in anger and growing frustration.

The arrangement was simple. Men who used Georgeann's full services paid Harvey Settle an extra five dollars. It was a widespread practice in Denver, since George Creel and Sheriff Glen Duffield closed down the Market Street red-light district. Creel was a reporter-turned-cop. He had worked for the *Rocky Mountain News* in the early teens, crusading against Mayor Speer until the administration toppled. The new mayor, Henry J. Arnold, made Creel police commissioner, and by 1915 the whorehouse district had been closed for good. The maid system had come along to take its place. But to a writer like Tom, the maid system was a pale substitute. Market Street had color and lights. His first experience with sex had come with a whore on Market Street. Her name was Laurie, and she worked in a crib on the fringe of the district, well away from the more prosperous houses run by Mattie Silks and Jennie Rogers. He met her on Christmas eve, just before his seventeenth birthday.

It happened suddenly. A door opened and she was there. She had a shawl around her neck and she was enjoying the chill of the night air. Her hair was long and fair, not unlike Georgeann's, and she looked at him and her eyes stopped him cold. She might have been twenty, no more, and she saw him for what he was, a cherry-green kid with everything in the world to learn. What is it about virgin boys that excites whores like that? He would never know. Her eyes never left his face, and he began looking around for his lost poise.

She smiled. "Hello."

He swallowed and said something neither of them understood.

"You want to fuck, paperboy?"

He thought his heart would burst, right there on the street. He had never heard that word from a woman, and this one was so soft, her voice so mellow, her face so tiny and babylike. He dropped his papers in the snow and followed her into a fantasy world of yellow light. Somewhere a piano was playing, something with a ragtime beat. The floors were reddish; the walls were blue. Ungodly colors. Her hair was the color of bright sunshine. That was what he remembered now, the colors red and blue and yellow, and a dark, flat mole, somewhere under the nipple of her right breast. She took him to a room at street level, a small chamber that fronted Market Street, and the room was lighted by oil lamp and there were rugs and mirrors. She helped him and he lasted thirty seconds, ending with a shudder as a group of carolers walked past the window singing "O, Come all Ye Faithful."

Laurie was like a dope pusher. The first one is always on the house, maybe because it's the first, maybe because it's Christmas, or because business is slow and she's bored. After that you pay your way. But sometimes when he was short and the need was great, she let him in for a cut rate. He learned to pace himself. He learned not to go near Market Street on weekends because she'd be busy and he'd be rushed. He developed staying power. When he'd been with Laurie half a dozen times he could last five minutes and more, and he was starting to feel like a character out of *Moll Flanders*.

He thought he loved her. But that all ended one morning when the cops found her body in an alley near the viaduct. The whorehouse killer had found a new victim, and Laurie the whore became Tom's second experience with murder.

The trolley clanged to a stop at Sixteenth and Champa. Another day.

3

The Denver Press Club was having a party that Saturday night, a fund-raiser for its new building on Glenarm Street. Tom thought he might go and take Nell. He called the estate but she was still asleep. He talked to Paul, and asked him to be sure and have his mother return the call. He waited for two hours, then, impatient and bored, hopped the trolley downtown. It was his day off, but since his separation he had taken to drifting in on Saturdays, sitting around the photo lab, drinking and talking with friends. He knew that once he had that first one, the party and all his good intentions would be out the window, so he sat at his desk and tried calling her again. A servant told him *Miss* Clement (that drove him crazy, for a full hour after the call) wasn't in yet, and she was expected to be tied up all evening. Her father was giving her a birthday party that night, and they were having some old friends in.

So he'd blown it again; hadn't even remembered her goddamn

birthday, for Christ's sake, and he knew how much silly things like that meant to her. He called a florist and ordered a dozen roses, to be delivered to the Clement estate no later than six o'clock, but he had to cancel the order when he remembered that his paycheck was already gone, most of next week's was spoken for and he was living on the free lunch at Miller's speakeasy until he could pay off his bar tab. Miller didn't mind; that's why he brought back the free lunch idea in the first place. Sucker people in, build big tabs, get a piece of your goddamn soul in his ledger books.

He was back to drifting again, wandering aimlessly through the downtown streets. On days like this one, he thought he'd do anything she asked to get her back. He would say anything, give up anything, make any concession, if only this incredible loneliness could end. Weekends were miniature horror stories, complete and self-contained; he had enough loneliness on Sundays to supply the city room twice over. He would sit and watch the phone and think about writing, think about the old days in Golden, think, think and do nothing. She didn't call and neither did he, and by Monday morning his resistance was back at full peak. He slipped through the weeks that way, always dreading Saturday and the beginning of another long weekend.

He turned into Miller's and went up a long flight of stairs. It was a dark room, filled with people on any given Saturday night but half empty now in the hours just before the rush. There was a bar, and tables and a dance floor beyond. The Victrola was playing Whiteman's "Japanese Sandman," the flip side of "Whispering." He found Goodwin sitting at a table in a corner, drinking with Ollie Booker from the *Times* and Barney Gallagher of the *Express*. Gallagher had once worked at the *Post*, but in his last year he'd been used mostly as Tom's legman. He had tired of the role and quit, though everyone knew he was no writer and Tom had always insisted on equal by-lines on the stories they did. He never knew what Gallagher's problem was; he had come to believe that Gallagher just didn't like him. But he pushed in among them and signaled Miller for a bourbon on the cuff.

"Wonder boy arriveth," Gallagher said. "Sit down, wonder boy."

Booker and Gallagher were old Denver hacks, each in their forties, each quickly sinking into the walking death syndrome. Both had worked for every paper in Denver at one time or another, moving around as reporters always will, lured away, and back, and away again for a few extra dollars a week. They were talking shop: shop and women combined, the old reporter's stock conversation.

"I'll give her this much," Booker said. "She sure looks good."

"A looker and a helluva goddamn writer." Gallagher looked at Tom. "She's the best writer in Denver right now."

"Who?" Tom said.

"Marvel Millette," Booker said. "Barney's got his first hard-on since the war."

"Now what's an old fart like Gallagher doing sniffing around young stuff like that? Old married fart, I might add."

"What the hell do you know about it?" Gallagher said.

"Nothing, Barney, nothing. Hell, I never even met the lady."

"Boys, boys," Goodwin said. "Jesus Christ, can't we even have a quiet drink on a Saturday afternoon without screwing it up with a lot of two-bit bitching?"

"He's just too sensitive," Gallagher said. "There's just so much glory to go around in a town like this and now she's getting it all. Grow up, Hastings, you had your turn."

He tossed off his drink in one gulp. "I've always heard it was anatomically impossible for a man to get his head stuck up his ass, but Barney seems to have turned the trick. I'll drink with you guys later, when you find some better company."

And yet, when he had left them there, even Gallagher's needling seemed preferable to what lay ahead. The empty weekend stretched before him. He pushed out into the sunlight, staggering a bit, and blundered into a lady passing on the street. He stepped back to apologize. "Well, as I live and breathe, Miss Wilder."

She gave a half curtsy there on the street. "How gallant, Mr. Hastings."

"Fancy meeting you here. Where are you headed?"

"Home. I live this way."

"Could I walk with you? For a block or two?"

"That would be lovely."

They had coffee in a drug store on Sixteenth Street, at a table near a window that looked out at the thinning Saturday afternoon pedestrian traffic. She gazed at the crisscrossed trolley wires and at an old policeman with a handlebar moustache who stood in the street directing cars with a painted stop sign on a six-foot iron pole. "Cheer up, you could be doing that for a living."

"Is that why you're here, to cheer me up?"

She smiled. "I heard you're separated from your wife."

"Temporarily."

"And of course I didn't just happen to be passing when you came out of Miller's, I followed you from work, hoping we'd get a chance to talk. Like this."

She cleared his head in a hurry.

"And of course I wasn't walking home. My apartment's over three miles from here. In the other direction. My car's in the same parking lot, in the same block. I'm a terrible liar."

"Do you lie like that all the time?"

"Only when it gets me what I want."

"Which is exactly what?"

"Coffee with you."

They sat for a long time without talking. Finally she said, "My problem is that I have no ambition. I've never really loved anything the way you love your work. Or used to. Should I put that in the past tense?"

"Probably. How do you know so much?"

"By asking around."

"That'll get you in trouble. People will talk about you."

"They already do. Did you think I don't know that?"

"What about *your* work?"

"Somewhere back there I realized my limitations and quit trying. Somebody once told me no important work of art was ever done by a woman. I believed him."

He shook his head and clicked his tongue over his teeth. "Rule number one. Never, ever believe a man when he tells you something like that."

"This, ah, person, also told me you'd quit school after the seventh grade."

"He's a talkative devil, all right. Oh, well, my secret is out."

"Then it's true? That's amazing."

"And you're wondering how I manage to be so consistently brilliant on just the essentials of schooling. I read a lot."

"Yes. I was wondering how you do it." She touched his hand with the tip of her finger, drawing an imaginary doodle between his thumb and forefinger. He felt himself becoming aroused and withdrew his hand. He thought of Nell, surrounded by men, pampered by her father's money.

"Listen," he said.

She looked up, interested.

"You know about the Press Club bash tonight?"

She nodded.

"You want to go?"

"Sure I do."

"Same ground rules as before."

"Did we have ground rules before?"

He looked her in the eyes. "No complications. Remember?"

"Of course," she said. But there was a reddish tint to her cheeks that hadn't been there before, and he knew she was lying. Of course she was. Everything had its price.

98

4

He was impressed, in a sad kind of way, with her apartment. The first things he noticed were the paintings scattered around the living room. The sad part was how few of them were finished. Even the ones that looked finished had new paint marks, as if she'd had second thoughts and had gone back to the work. It gave him a strange feeling. He thought only writers did that.

She shared the place with a nurse, who was away visiting relatives and wouldn't be back for a week. She told him this as she showed him through, pausing at the open bedroom door long enough for the implication to hang there, suspended between them. Finally he moved on through.

He had gone home to shower, and returned to her place at eight. She was dressed provocatively, in a red silk dress that fairly rippled when she touched it and showed her slim figure to its best advantage. The hem came to the knee and the bottom had tassles that ran to mid-calf. Her stockings were silver and she wore a long strand of heavy beads. The dress was sleeveless, slightly out of season, but she wore a wrap. They went in his car, and parked in the lot near Champa Street.

The Press Club was small, and already it was packed. The ban against women had been lifted, for one night only, and unescorted females were bellied-up to the bar beside the men. Prohibition—what a goddamn laugh. Everyone pretended to be drinking soda, while the poison was mixed in below bar level, where no one could see. He had made up his mind to have no more drink tonight, but it made his mouth tingle to hear it: the laughter, the slurred talk, the clink of ice in a glass. A large group of politicians and lawyers stood talking near the door. Tom saw the mayor, Ben Stapleton, who had been elected this year by leaving unanswered the implication of aides that he would crusade against the Ku Klux Klan. Now he was standing in bad company: his circle included two Klan senators, two judges who were reportedly Klan members, and a pack of Klan lawyers. Tom's eyes moved around the circle, pausing at each face. He knew them all. To the mayor's left was his old friend, Willie Brown III. Their eyes met for the first time in more than a decade. Brown actually smiled. His face was warm and friendly, the face of a politician. When he smiled his upper lip quivered slightly and Tom saw the thin scar, extending from the lip almost to the nostril. Brown blinked, as if he couldn't quite remember something, and Tom moved on.

Standing next to Willie Brown were two judges, Clarence Morley and Thurman Hayes of the District Court. Both were building strong reputations as Klan judges. It was said that their jury lists were drawn up by John Galen Locke, in the Grand Dragon's secret chamber on Glenarm Place, and that Locke was preparing Morley for the governor's race next year. Morley was more a politician than Hayes, whose fear of reporters held him back. Sometimes Barney Gallagher sat in on Hayes' court, just for entertainment. In the press room, Gallagher had described a rape trial, when an east Denver contractor had reportedly raped his secretary. Hayes had learned of the incident and had persuaded the woman to file criminal charges against her boss. The trial was short, the jury swayed by the girl's emotional testimony. But then, with the jury retired for its verdict, word came from John Galen Locke that the defendant was a Cyclops in good standing, while the secretary had had questionable dealings with many men, including a Negro. The judge called the girl into chambers and tried to persuade her lawyer to drop the case. While they were talking, the bailiff knocked and said the jury was ready with its verdict. Again the judge pleaded with the girl, but she wouldn't budge. Everyone filed back into court to hear the jury's verdict. Judge Hayes paled as the foreman pronounced the Cyclops guilty. He leaned over his bench, seemed to be lost in thought for a long moment, then, in a soft monotone, he began to speak. Sometimes, he said, it became necessary for a judge, in the interests of justice, to intervene and override a jury's verdict. It was obvious to him that the secretary had lied, that a reasonable doubt existed as to the guilt of the accused. Thus he was appointing himself a thirteenth juror, and was casting his vote for acquittal. In the retrial Locke had packed the jury box with Klansmen and had produced six witnesses who told of the secretary's loose morals. The rapist walked out a free man.

For two weeks it had been a running gag in the press room: *Don't get raped in Denver*. People laughed, but Tom had started a file on the Ku Klux Klan. If he hadn't been so goddamn lazy lately, if he hadn't lost his wife and started drinking too much, he might have had it in print by now. Lay it out on the streets, exactly what these bastards were doing to this town, for everybody to read. Let Tammen use some of his red ink, and print their names in heavy black type beneath it, so they could be read across a crowded street. It wasn't the first time he'd considered crusading against the Klan, but it had always seemed like too much trouble. One of those endless mothers you get into and never get out of, something for a young fire-eater like Arthur McCantless. But Arthur's brain was between his legs; he was still chasing Alice like a pathetic pup, and besides, he just wasn't good enough. Not for something like this. Maybe, Tom thought vainly, nobody else in town is.

His eyes burned into the face of the rape judge, and Hayes shifted in discomfort. Standing beside the rape judge was Senator Philip Owens, who would write Locke's philosophy into law and try to push it past his senate subcommittee sometime next year. Beside Owens, laughing suddenly at some quiet joke, was more bad company: Saul Reismann and Rube Henry, a pair of shyster lawyers who worked for the Klan. Of the two, Reismann was infinitely more evil in Tom's mind, because he was also a Jew. The word was out in Denver: If any Jew wanted a chance at justice in the courtroom of Clarence Morley or Thurman Hayes, he first had to hire Reismann, who worked out the deal with Locke. Rube Henry was a lecher and a simple redneck from the South. He had come to Denver from Atlanta, where he was a member of the national Klan, reporting directly to the Imperial Wizard in matters of regional control. He had come to Denver to practice law, but it was a good bet that on any Friday night he could be found in west Denver, parading under a sheet through the Jewish neighborhood near Cheltenham School, shouting filth through the open windows just as the Sabbath was getting under way.

Beyond that initial wave he saw friendlier faces: Sidney Whipple and Ollie Booker and Carl Goodwin. Whipple was editor of the *Denver Express*, the only newspaper with an anti-Klan image. He had tried to hire Tom for years, but the *Express* was just too small, its impact too limited, for Tom's taste. Booker and Goodwin were already three sheets to the wind. O'Reilly was there, and Malloy, and with Malloy was a girl who would be the new wonder woman. Marvel Millette looked up from her drink. He was amazed at her youth. Her hair was jet black, long and fluffy, topped by the cloche hat and that infamous six-inch hatpin. It was the talk of the town. Booker said she could pick a lock with it. Tom doubted that, being no mean locksmith himself, but he didn't doubt the other half of the story, that it was a good weapon in a tight spot. She had already used it once, and the story had gone by word of mouth until now everyone in the room had heard it. One night after work she had been cornered by Rube Henry in the City Hall press room, and had finally resorted to punching him full of holes to drive him away.

Her eyes were quick and intelligent. She was sitting with a group of reporters and photographers, and Gallagher and Malloy seemed to be jockeying for her attention. She saw Alice and remembered her at once as an old schoolmate. "Alice," she said, offering a hand; "It's good to see you again."

"Hello, Marvel." Alice took her hand a bit timidly, then turned to Tom. "This is . . ."

"I know who he is. Mr. Tom Hastings, at last, in the flesh and blood." Her hand went from Alice to Tom. "At last I meet the idol of my youth."

He smiled, managing to look both flattered and doubtful.

"Don't laugh," she said. "It was because of your coverage of the Mary Wolfe case that I decided to go into journalism."

"To improve the art?" He said it as a joke, then realized that it must have sounded to others hanging over them as if he were fishing for a compliment.

She delivered the compliment without a pause. "Because it showed me, more than anything I'd ever seen, what could be done with words alone, without any fancy art or touched-up pictures." She looked at Alice, then at Goodwin, and she didn't apologize to either. "I know you must have felt that way when you were writing it."

Talk of past glories always made him squirm.

"What about now?" She looked him straight in the eye and it was all he could do to meet her. He smelled a setup. She was one of those castrating bitches, about to have him drawn and quartered for all to see. It was that old disease of ambitious reporters, to be on top of a world that no one else cares about or understands. He despised people who played it, as he once had, and women who played it were the worst of the lot.

But unless he misjudged her, there was no cruelty in her face. She only wanted to know, so perhaps he could forgive her a little if he let it drop at that. But others waited too, those who knew him, even more expectantly than Marvel Millette. Alice was tense at his elbow.

He fired the question back at her. "What about now?"

"What are you doing?"

Again, that look of honesty. Or was it an act? Was she in fact a calculating bitch, waiting to spring her trap? He smiled. "You don't really expect me to tell you that."

In the background, Gallagher cleared his throat.

"Oh, come now," she said. "We're just talking in general terms. I was wondering if they'd stuck you away on a beat somewhere. One of the great attractions of coming back to Denver was the prospect of crossing swords with you."

"I know, I know. You want to put the old man in his place." He laughed.

"I want to see how much I've learned."

"You've learned plenty, if what I see in the paper is any indication."

Abruptly, she drew in her horns and let him off the hook; the truth had come to her, and she looked as though someone had just dashed a cold drink in her face. So Marvel Millette was for real, and it had simply never occurred to her before this moment that he might have

102

lost his stuff. She asked Malloy to get her another drink, ginger ale straight, and suddenly there was a shift of attention toward the front door. Tammen came in alone. He moved past the circle of politicians without speaking. Only Bonfils would have created a bigger stir, and his appearance would have stopped the party dead. Tammen wore his standard three-piece suit, baggy around the ass and under the arms. A gold watch fob dangled from the vest. He moved through the crowd to the bar and got himself a drink, and a moment later his eyes came to rest on Tom and Marvel.

He came toward them, and the people parted the way the sea must have opened for Moses. He came straight to the fringes of their group and looked at Marvel. "So you're Marvel Millette."

"And you would be Mr. Harry Heye Tammen, Esquire."

Tammen grinned. "Goddamn sassy, just like I heard you were. Sassy and sharp. That's a goddamn good piece you got out for Sunday's paper."

She actually blushed. At her side, Malloy was in ecstasy. He eased closer, so people wouldn't miss knowing that she was with him.

"Sometime when you want to work for a real newspaper, drop by the *Post* and look me up," Tammen said. A burst of laughter from the political crowd up front caught his attention. Mayor Stapleton was laughing at something Rube Henry had said. "I guess they haven't seen it yet," Tammen said.

"Probably not," she said. "It must have just hit the streets."

Tammen nodded. "If Stapleton had seen it he sure as hell wouldn't be laughing. What do you say we tell him?"

He put his drink on the edge of the table and walked across the room, out the front door, and into the street. Gallagher leaned close. "Anybody know what he's talking about?"

"A story of mine for tomorrow's paper," Marvel said. "I guess he's gone to get one."

She was nervous, even Tom could see that: the uneasiness of the very young. He knew what it felt like, the prospect of facing on Monday the people you'd roasted in print on Sunday. Wondering how good your sources were, how many mistakes you'd made, how hard they'd come back at you. For her first real exposé, Marvel Millette was to be tested on the spot, in the presence of the man she had attacked. Tammen came back about five minutes later. He had two fat copies of the Sunday *News* under his arm. He paused near the door and spoke to the mayor; he gave Stapleton one copy and brought the other back to the reporters. Her story was on page one, just below the fold, under a headline that said MAYOR'S TIES TO KLAN REVEALED. The first two paragraphs said it all, everything reporters had known for months but no one had written. During his campaign last winter and spring,

Stapleton had begun a whispering campaign, let the word out that he would crusade against the Klan, while all along he had been in league with John Galen Locke, who was delivering the pro-Klan votes on the sly. Now Locke owned City Hall. Once Stapleton had even addressed two thousand Klansmen on Table Mountain above Golden. She had picked up some verbatim dialogue from that talk and had woven it through the jump, which took up most of page five. The only thing Tom didn't understand was how she had gotten it into the paper when the *News* managing editor was a Klansman and the paper was known to be soft on the Klan. Maybe it was something Locke wanted out, now that the elections were over and Stapleton was safely in. Maybe all newspapermen were crazy.

It was an interesting moment. The politicians and lawyers huddled over one table, the reporters were draped over another. Stapleton looked up briefly, trying to pick her face out of the crowd, missed her, missed her again, and went back to his reading. Tammen was enjoying himself immensely. "A goddamn good piece of work," he said again. "Naturally, if you come to work for us, you'd need to learn a few things about our style."

"I have. Just from reading you."

"Hit 'em where they live, hon, that's our motto. Nobody's sacred to us."

"That's not what I heard."

"You'll hear a lot; doesn't mean a thing. You get to be top dog, you'll always have a pack of pups snapping at your heels. Let me tell you something, then you go home and think about it. The *Denver Post* started with nothing. Just me and Fred Bonfils and a little money and a lot of guts. Today we sell more goddamn newspapers in Wyoming than any paper in that state. The circulation of the *Post* in Denver is three times all the other newspapers put together. You don't get that by printing what people don't want to read."

"I'm sure you don't."

"I'm sure too. I always was sure, even when people thought I was crazy. Maybe I am a little crazy. I never pretended to know much about business. Fred's the businessman. Bonfils. I'm just a guy from the sticks who got lucky. It took two of us to put it together, but Fred's the smart one."

"I heard you're a shrewd businessman."

"I told you, you'll hear a lot."

She didn't believe him, which was just what he intended.

"It takes guts to put out a good newspaper," Tammen said. "Guts start on the staff. If reporters've got no guts, the paper hasn't either. No guts, no teeth. No teeth, no bite. No bite, no readers. People want guts in their newspaper. If you see somebody get his head crushed under a car, I want to see it in the paper. If it makes you sick, I want that in there too. If you know some poor bastard who's getting screwed at City Hall, cut through the crap and say so. The hell with conventions. That's one thing that's wrong with your Stapleton piece, God damn it, you almost let the son of a bitch slide off the hook. You sure lost me when you started going through his side of it. Jesus, I thought it'd never end."

"That's called being fair, Mr. Tammen."

"I know what it's called, miss, it's called covering your ass. Let me tell you something about being fair. Being fair is just being right, and that's all it is. Why dignify the lie with equal play if you know it's a lie to start with?"

"It's too great a responsibility."

"What is?"

"To always be right."

He laughed and swished the ice around in his glass. "Sassy," he said. "Sassy and impudent. Jesus, I like that. You're not scared of me a bit, are you?"

"Why should I be?"

"People usually are." His eyes drifted across the room and for a while he just watched the politicians, huddled like partisan senators before a floor fight. "Sure," he said after a while, "sometimes we're wrong, but people know where we stand. We may be wrong but we're never in doubt, and if that gets us a reputation I say too goddamn bad. You bet we're yellow, but we're read, and we're true blue."

It was his favorite saying. She had heard it quoted from one end of town to the other. Now Stapleton had straightened up and folded the front section of the paper under his arm. He came toward them, still scanning the faces as though he couldn't quite remember what she looked like. He was flanked by Clarence Morley and the rape judge, leaving William Brown III and the lawyers near the door. Rube Henry was still nursing a hatpin wound in his hand, and he was staying away from Marvel Millette.

Tom enjoyed the fact that the seas didn't part for the mayor as they had for Tammen. Marvel held her head high and faced him evenly.

"Did you write that?"

"That's my name on it."

Tammen broke into a loud chuckle. "Sassy," he said, wheezing. "God damn."

The mayor glared at him. He looked back at Marvel and said, "I told you last week this was a pack of lies."

"And I quoted you to that effect."

"Yes, but the way you did it looks like *I'm* the liar."

"I'm sorry about that, Mr. Mayor. Are you?"

Now Tammen's laugh was belly-deep. He put his drink on the table and slapped his knee. Stapleton turned and left the party, taking his political entourage with him. Still breathing heavily, Tammen said, "Simply super, miss. Few words, straight to the point. Christ, I couldn't have handled it better myself. I'll raise your pay by ten a week."

She smiled and shook her head. "I'm flattered."

"Flattered, hell. Lady, I don't deal in flattery."

"Then thanks for an honest offer. I'll think about it."

"Make it fifteen."

"Not just yet. I want to get to know Denver better first."

"Twenty. Listen, Goddammit, I've got people on my staff who don't make twenty a week total."

Tom saw a streak of mischief cross her face. "I've heard about your raises, Mr. Tammen."

"What have you heard?"

"You offer a reporter more money, then, after the reporter quits and comes over to the *Post*, Mr. Bonfils calls her in and cuts her pay."

Tammen laughed out loud. That was what Tom liked best about Tammen: You couldn't offend him. "Hey," Tammen said, rising, "I didn't mean to break up the party. See you around, Marvel. You think about what I said."

5

He remembered another party, when the Denver Press Club was in a second-floor suite near Seventeenth and California. He had been riding high then, had just broken the Mary Wolfe case and Tammen was publicly calling him "the world's greatest detective." It was hard, watching that attention shift to Marvel Millette, but not as hard as he thought it would be. To be hurt by anything, you have to really care: his thought of wisdom for the day. Still there were times when he felt that old excitement, the tingle she must be feeling now, to have it all right there in front of you, to know that all you have to do is reach out and take it, because nobody else will. The quality of journalism could be appalling, and now he could lump himself in that bag, along with all the other hacks. She had taken his status, whatever that was, and now she was taking his story. The Klan piece. The one he'd been dumb enough to think only he could do. And the Stapleton article was only the beginning of what was now, in his mind, the Klan piece.

His willpower had deteriorated steadily through the evening, and he'd had more than a few drinks. He hadn't had a chance to talk to Marvel Millette again, and maybe that was just as well. Several times he caught her looking at him and once, when Alice had slipped away to the rest room, she made a move in his direction. But she was intercepted by Sidney Whipple of the *Express*. Another job offer, no doubt. Yes, Whipple would love her Klan piece as much as he hated the Klan. He saw her smile and shake her head, and then Alice was back, visibly tight, clutching his arm for support. "Hey," she said, "let's go home."

They walked along the street, and a midnight shower chased them into the *Post* building. They stood at the door watching the rain pound the street. "Looks like it's with us awhile," he said. "Might as well go up, have another drink." They staggered, laughing, up the long staircase and found themselves alone in the big, half-lighted newsroom. In the distance, AP machines clattered away, telling the world everything that happened while it slept. She disappeared into the rest room, using the men's because it was closer, and he sat at his desk and felt the first faint throb of tomorrow's hangover. When she returned she had sobered up; she sat at her own desk and dropped her heavy bag on the floor. A silver stocking hung carelessly over the edge of the bag. She had taken them off, had taken everything off but that red silk dress. Her breasts stood out against the silk, her legs parted slightly, and he felt a great surge of lust. It had been too long, far too long. His eyes saw the darkness there, warm and peaceful, liquid, deeper than infinity. Her hands went up and brushed her damp hair. Her bare underarms were as smooth as glass.

"Hey," she said again. "Let's go home. My place." She looked amused and patient. She was twenty-three, but looked ten years older now: a woman of the world. Her probing, relentless eyes made him feel silly and old-fashioned. It was the new era.

"She's gone, you know," Alice said.

It took him a full minute to realize that she was talking about his wife.

"I know it," she said. "I can tell. She doesn't appreciate you. Here, take my hand, let me show you something." She led him back to the photo studio, where everything was shut down and dark. They had to feel their way. She found the door to Goodwin's darkroom and slipped inside, drawing him in behind her. Her voice came at him out of the pitch darkness. "Once I dreamed of doing this. Watch." There were sounds as she moved things, pushing back everything from the waist-high table where Goodwin worked. Her fingers found a switch and purple light flooded over them. She hiked the dress up to her waist, rolling it in so it stayed up. "Watch," she said again. She got up on the table and spread her legs in a perfect split. "Ballet lessons, see? One, two, and split, gen-tle-men will drop their pants."

He did, and as he came closer she lifted her body off the table, bracing herself up on either side. She seemed to float out toward him, thrusting her groin up and out to receive him. They joined perfectly. She shuddered and gasped, and her finger hit the light button.

Darkness and liquid, deeper than infinity.

CHAPTER
FOUR

1

Rima was dying. Jessie sat at the window above the print shop and cried when David read about the fire. It was another Saturday, sometime in early winter, and the specter of Lieutenant Joe Moran and the Denver police seemed very far away. He had not had a midnight visit since Harding's death. No muggers had come out of dark corners with billyclubs and brass knuckles. No one had approached Jessie since that night, when Moran knocked softly on the door, waited a few moments, and drove away. She had been standing there, behind the curtains, a few feet away, and had had the good sense to be still.

At mid-morning he thought he might finish *Green Mansions* by noon, but Mrs. Wassermann brought in a manuscript to be printed. It was her son's book, a wretched thing titled *Armand LeFevre, or, Working for the Long Island Railroad: The Valiant Struggles of a*

Brave French Lad Establishing Himself in the New Land of His Choice. David knew the author well. Young Benny Wassermann had infiltrated his monthly round table meeting and had subjected them all to merciless readings. First he had tried experimental writing, but when no one understood it, he switched to teen fiction of an adventure-inspirational nature. The book was at least two years old. It had been turned down by a dozen publishers in New York and was still making the rounds. He explained to Mrs. Wassermann that it would be a waste of time, that to have a book privately printed would cost far more than they could ever regain in sales. "I'm not interested in sales," she said. "I just want one copy, leatherbound, with gold-leaf lettering. I want to give it to Benny at Chanukah."

They haggled and he agreed to do it for three-fifty. But there was no way he could have the book bound and ready by Chanukah: Even the New York publishers couldn't get a book out in less than four months. They compromised on February 12, Benny's birthday.

The Wassermanns were rich Jews for this part of town. They lived here by choice, preferring the sense of community to the discrimination and strife they had found downtown. Mrs. Wassermann's passion was talking about people. It was a trait she had passed along to her son, and to her daughter, Rosalie. David had done the printing for Rosalie's wedding last year. Usually he was impatient with Mrs. Wassermann's penchant for gossip, but sometimes he indulged her. Like today, when the two fifty-dollar bills she had given him as a deposit felt good in his pocket.

She lingered for perhaps ten minutes. She talked about the wandering eye of Mr. Jonas, the landlord who owned four houses on West Colfax between Hooker and Sheridan, including the one Sammy Kohl rented as a grocery. And speaking of the Kohls, the youngest son Gabriel was in trouble again at school. He had been expelled for fighting, and had fallen in with a gang of tough Jewish kids who roamed the downtown streets beating up the sons of Gentiles. They called themselves the Anti-Klan. Twelve years old or less, and already the boy was headed for a life of crime. "Do you know any of the Kohls, Mr. Waldo?" she asked. He nodded slowly. The crippled son Abe had begun coming to the round table. David had extended the invitation through Julia Howe and the deed was done. Julia and Abe had been sweethearts before the war. She had made a great show of sticking by her man when Abe came home shell-shocked, legless, and with sight in only one eye. Abe was a fine thinker and he loved books, but since the war his attention span was short. For no apparent reason his hands would begin to shake and Julia would cover them with her own until they calmed. Last month, about an hour into the session, Abe suddenly began to fidget, then, by

110

rapid degrees, grew very nervous. Julia excused herself and wheeled him home.

All the Kohls interested him, but his attention was still directed at the woman of the window, whose name he didn't know. Perhaps today he would find out from Julia, if she came by. Maybe even now, from gossipy old Mrs. Wassermann.

"Tell me about the Kohls," he said.

"Sammy is a lovely man. He understands everything, just like David Harum. Did you ever read that book, Mr. Waldo?"

He never had.

"And Benny tells me you're such a reader. If you read it, you'll know what I mean. Sammy Kohl has a clear vision. Not many people can you say that about. Teresa, ehhh . . ." She held out her hand, turning it over and over in the universal gesture of instability.

"What's wrong with her?"

"I said something was wrong? Sometimes she has her days is all."

"Don't we all?"

Mrs. Wassermann shrugged. "Let's see. I told you about the little one, and you know the one who lost his legs. There's an older boy of Sammy's who's gone somewhere. A bad apple, they say. And there's another who writes for one of the newspapers. He's *not* Sammy's son. Teresa's from an old marriage. I hear he's divorcing his wife."

"And there's a daughter, I heard."

Mrs. Wassermann made a face. "An ivory tower baby. She never comes out, never passes the time of day with anybody in the neighborhood, just sits up in her room day after day, brooding over some lost love affair. Some great tragedy, Mr. Waldo, that happened years ago. A spoiled child, Mr. Waldo, and I'm amazed that Sammy Kohl lets her get away with it. Once in a great while you can see her on the street, going from the house to Sammy's store. She walks past you like some princess, with never a word for anybody she meets along the way. She's got nothing to be high and mighty about, from what I hear . . ."

"What do you hear?"

"That affair of hers had its . . . elements, Mr. Waldo. I don't talk about things like that, but you know what I mean."

"What's her name?"

She looked at him curiously. "Save yourself the heartbreak, Mr. Waldo. Get interested in somebody nice and down-to-earth. I've still got one unmarried daughter at home."

Painfully he thought of Molly Wassermann. Mrs. Wassermann must be getting desperate to try palming off the hopelessly fat Molly on a Gentile.

"Do you know her name, Mrs. Wassermann?"

"I believe it's Anna."

"Ah."

Anna it was.

Anna.

Anna Kohl.

2

A telephone was ringing in the tiny office behind Sammy Kohl's grocery store. "Sam, it's Jacob Howe. I got to see you, right away. Now, Sam, as soon as you can get away from the store."

The call had come in the busiest part of his day, with the store full of shoppers. Sammy called Teresa at home and asked her to relieve him for an hour. The irritation he had felt had already turned to worry. Jacob Howe never used the telephone unless the need was great. Jacob never rode in cars or trolleys and had never been to a moving picture. His house had been wired for electricity only last year, and only then at his wife's insistence. Jacob Howe was of nineteenth-century America. He was a huge man, larger even than David Waldo, the printer. Jacob had arms bigger than most men's legs. He was a blacksmith by trade and lived with his wife Emily and their daughter Julia on the remains of an old farm a city block square. The land overlooked Sloan's Lake at its eastern end. Jacob worked out of a garage behind the house. He worked a long day, sunup to sunset, six days a week. Sometimes he drove a buckboard to neighboring farms and farm towns, and once a month he hitched a team and drove the ten miles south to Overland Park, where he spent two or three days shoeing racehorses.

The Howes had moved to west Denver in 1898, and had lived in the same house ever since. The Kohls had been there a year then, and Jacob and Sammy, being about the same age, had become warm friends. But it was a friendship marked by a certain distance. Both of them valued privacy. They saw each other once a week, usually on Sunday, and that was enough. They joked about being Civil War babies, though Sammy was six years older than Jacob and had been born four years before the war began.

They met each week over a mutual love of horseshoe pitching. Each Sunday they played their marathon games, pitching away the afternoon and quitting only when it grew too dark to see. Then they would sit under the canopy that Jacob had built outside his garage and drink the cider that Sammy had brought over from the store.

Often Teresa would walk over from Osceola Street and join them, and Emily would come out, and the four of them would sit under the lantern eating cheese and pie and talking world affairs. Jacob was a quiet man, but nervous, and politics wore him down quickly. He had lost a son in France. At least Sammy had gotten part of his son back from the war. Jacob Howe would have even settled for that.

Abel Kohl and Isaac Howe. Kids from Denver.

Kids going off to war, joking about taking the Kaiser's scalp. No earthly concept what they were doing, to themselves or their parents. He and Teresa had held up well. Emily Howe stood in the depot, dry-eyed and brave. In the end it was Jacob who had broken, collapsing in a sobbing heap into his wife's arms as the train window flashed past, the two grinning faces framed there for all time. One came home: more precisely, half of one, the shell of what had been Abel Kohl, reduced to a basket by a mine somewhere in Europe, near a town none of them could pronounce. Both legs gone, one ear dead and draining, one eye socket empty and covered by a black patch. Burns over most of his body, huge patches of hair burned off his head forever. Now he kept what was left cut short against his pink skull. His hands moved constantly and he shaved only once a week. Nerves attacked him without warning, and sometimes he would wheel his chair frantically across the room and crash into a wall. He screamed in his sleep. He dreamed that people were chasing him, and the memory of those dreams the day after reduced him to fits of nervous trembling.

Abel Kohl at twenty-seven.

You learn to live with anything, but sometimes Teresa found it hard. Once she hinted to Sammy that it might have been better if Abe hadn't come home. It was the only time he ever really lost his temper with her. He sat up and yelled across the room, "Better for who, for Abe or you?" She cowered before him, and for a month she was more attentive than ever. She jumped to Abe's every need. Then the despair washed over her again as she remembered the running, happy child he had been, and she left him more and more with Anna or Julia. She joined a woman's club; it bored her silly, but she never missed a meeting. She went to PTA meetings and got to know Gabriel's teachers. She began working odd shifts in the store. Sometimes she would turn up unexpectedly, saying simply, "I'll take over. You go home and rest awhile." Anything to get out of the house. Even when there was no business, she would show up suddenly, sitting beside him, keeping him company. "It's okay, Sam, Anna's with Abe; she's reading him a book," she would say, or perhaps, "Julia's with Abe. She came just before I left and said she'd stay the afternoon." Teresa thought Julia was a saint. The closest Julia had

113

ever come to doing wrong in Teresa's eyes was taking Abe to one of David Waldo's communist meetings. But the result of that—Abe's renewed interest in life—had vindicated Julia and had all but vindicated the mysterious Mr. Waldo as well. Maybe, Teresa was saying now, Mr. Waldo isn't even a communist after all.

None of them knew about Jessie Abbott. He watched her walk past and turn up the street toward the lake.

A strange pair. He should talk, what with his strange family. His daughter a recluse, his son a physical and emotional wreck, the youngest in trouble with street gangs, the stepson suddenly separated from his wife after eight years of what everybody thought was a happy marriage in spite of itself. And Ethan—God only knew where he was. The misfit firstborn, drifting away as he did twenty-three years ago now. Ethan had always been a blot on his conscience.

Was that why he'd sent the money? Two thousand dollars to buy off a conscience? A few coins to let an old man die in peace? Sammy had spent most of that afternoon staring at his bankbook. Four thousand total: the savings of twenty-five years in business. A lot of money, yes, but Teresa would need it to get through the years after he was gone. A time closer now than any of them knew. He touched the lump under his arm, as he'd done that afternoon, even as he wired Ethan half of his life savings. The money went to some anonymous Western Union office in Dallas, Texas, and the following month came a plea for another thousand from New Orleans. And Sammy Kohl, fool that he was, had almost sent that too, but that afternoon Abe had had a fit of screaming and that brought him back to his senses with a jolt. Instead he had sent a letter to the telegraph office in New Orleans. A letter Ethan still hadn't answered.

Mr. Jonas the landlord drove up outside, just as Teresa appeared far up Colfax. Jonas came inside and Sammy passed over a thin envelope containing the month's rent. "Weather is so unpredictable here," Jonas said. "I saw some black clouds coming down. Maybe tonight it rains, keeps the Klandals off the street." He laughed without mirth and went out. Teresa came and Sammy followed her with his eyes. She still wore those old prewar dresses, too long and out of date, as Anna did, as Julia did. At fifty-two, Teresa could wear the old style gracefully, but Anna and Julia should be more modern. He wondered what Julia would look like in jeans and sweatshirt, dressed up in Jessie Abbott's clothes for just a day. And he realized as Teresa reached for the door that he had been thinking of Julia as family, even though now, in all likelihood, she never would be. In 1915 she and Abe had had an understanding. A ring had been given and accepted, but they had decided to wait until Abe came home. People thought the war would be finished in three weeks. Incredible. It was all like something in a story, only the ending had not turned out happily ever after, and he wondered what would happen to Abe and Julia now. Would they just go on as they were, with Julia giving up her life, or would she tire of the part she was playing and decide sainthood wasn't for her? Sammy had seen people change profoundly, with much less provocation. The long dresses would go first, then the plain hairstyle. She had already stopped wearing her ring, so long ago that he had forgotten when he had first noticed it.

Julia in blue jeans.

Teresa took off her bonnet and went to work. Sammy took off his apron. "How's Abe?" he said. She didn't look up. "The same." Always the same; he was always that way to her. Now she did look up and she tried to smile. "He's fine," she said with good second effort. "He's home with Anna, waiting for Julia to come."

How fine would he be if Julia didn't come? Tonight he would go to the temple and pray for Abe and Julia. Give them both peace, let them find strength in themselves so neither would suffer because of the other. That was for tonight. Now he walked over to Jacob Howe's place. It was a short walk, two blocks up and one over. He came in through the backyard, and he could hear Jacob's hammer on the anvil as he unhooked the gate and let himself in. The yard was dry and dusty. A batch of chickens scattered, telegraphing his arrival to Jacob. Jacob stood in the garage, hammer suspended in midair. Sweat rolled off his brow. He dropped the hammer on the table and motioned Sammy inside. As always, it was hot and close in Jacob Howe's garage. The forge took up the center of the room, a brick hulk with a long metal stack. The hearth was coal-hot. Beside it was Jacob's anvil, beside that a storage bin for the scraps of iron and junk that Jacob picked up at roadside. The only floor was the well-packed earth. A pot-bellied stove stood in a far corner, for use in winter, when heat from the forge alone wouldn't do. Scattered around were projects in various stages of completion. A large can of water sat at the end of Jacob's workbench, a dipper draped over the side. Sammy drank out of courtesy and waited while Jacob downed two dippersful. Then they walked out across Jacob's land, down toward Newton Street, where a glade of trees was stirred by the wind that blew in from the lake.

For a long time neither spoke. Jacob rolled himself a cigarette and stood watching the silvery water. Whatever it was, it wasn't coming easy. After a while Jacob said, "Here, maybe it's best I show you." He led Sammy out of the glade, around the perimeter of the place, toward the house. Soon Sammy saw a large black spot, where the earth had been charred for a diameter of perhaps twenty feet. A pile of black ashes stood in the center, along with bits of lumber that had only partly burned. Sammy bent and touched the charred wood. "What's this?" He picked up a piece and it clung to another, as if the two had been joined by nails. He straightened up and looked at Jacob. "What is it?" he asked again.

"They burned a cross here last night." Jacob tried to roll another cigarette, but his hands trembled too much.

"*Here?*" Sammy's eyes opened wide, as if he couldn't understand what he was hearing. "Why?"

Jacob shrugged. It suddenly occurred to Sammy that he didn't know what religion the Howes were. They never seemed to go to church anywhere.

"Why this?"

Jacob shrugged. But Jacob wouldn't meet his eyes, and Sammy Kohl knew there was more, and that for Jacob the hardest part was still to come.

"Julia," Jacob said in a while.

A big piece of it fell into place. Julia. Of course.

"Julia and Abe," Sammy said.

Jacob nodded.

"Did you just guess that or did somebody tell you?"

"Told me." Jacob gave up on the smoke and threw the paper and tobacco on the ground.

"Who told you?"

"Coupla men. Came here last week." Jacob paused, then fumbled again for his tobacco pouch. "Said some bad things. Things I wouldn't tell you."

"About me?"

"You. Abe. All of you." Again Jacob began spilling tobacco. "These two guys just walked right in, unhitched the gate and came right up into my forge. Next thing I knew they were standing there in my light."

"Had you ever seen them before?"

He shook his head. "I asked them what their names were and what their business was. They said they were from Indiana, where they worked for an outfit called the Horse Thief Detective Association. But they didn't sound like Hoosiers. They both had southern accents."

"Did they tell you their names?"

"One called the other Nate. That's all I remember. Just Nate."

"Then what happened?"

"They said a new tide was sweeping the country, a backlash of decent folk, they called it. A white rebellion against lawlessness and injustice. They were out recruiting for the new campaign. Was I against lawlessness or was I not? I said sure I was. Was I for decency in schools? Sure I was. Was I for the high ideals of the white race?"

Sammy just looked at him.

116

"They said the Catholic and the Jew and the black man is the enemy of justice. They said the inferior races were out to make over the world into one yellow strain, a race of high yellas."

"And what did you say?"

"Me? Nothing. You know I don't argue. I just want to be left alone. That's all I ever want."

"Then what did they do?"

"They brought out a paper for me to sign. Said it'd cost me ten dollars to join."

"Did you sign it?"

"No, I said I wanted to think it over. I ain't got ten dollars to just throw away on anybody that walks through my door. The big one, this Nate, said I should think hard because the thing was picking up people all across the country, and people who weren't with them would have to be counted against."

"Ah, Jacob, Jacob, why didn't you throw them out?"

"That's not my way, Sam. You know that. I might not like what a man's saying to me, but I always hear him out."

Sammy nodded impatiently. "Then how did it get around to Abe and Julia? What did they say?"

"Just some things, Sam. I don't like to bother you."

"These people just walk in here, people you and I don't even know, and they start talking about me to you and now you say you don't want to bother me?"

"You know what I mean."

Sammy touched his friend's arm, feeling the fear there, along with the ash and sweat. "Hey, Jacob."

Jacob struggled with his cigarette and managed to get it rolled, then lit it with trembling hands.

"It's hard, Sam. A bad time for something like this. Business isn't that good anymore, I'm on the road more and more and Emily don't like that. More than half of what I do is in the country now. The auto is ruining me, Sam. A fire in my shop would put me under."

"These people threatened you?"

"Not in so many words. But I never thought of myself as a stupid man, Sam. I've got to think about things like that."

"What you've got to do is tell the police."

Jacob went on as if Sammy hadn't spoken. "I've got my wife and daughter. They come first. Before anybody else."

Sammy just watched him.

"Before any friendship," Jacob said. "I'm on the road a lot now. I can't be worried about Emily and Julia home alone."

"All right, Jacob. Get to the point."

Jacob tried, but his voice broke. It didn't matter; Sammy knew now what the point was. He could have walked away then and saved Jacob the trouble. But life wasn't that easy, and Sammy Kohl didn't just walk away from twenty-five years of friendship without seeing it all laid out before him.

"Don't you think it'd be better, Sam, if Julia and Abe kinda stand back and look at their situation for a little while?"

"Sure, except my boy can't stand," Sammy said bitterly. "Maybe Julia ought to stand back twice as far, for both of them."

"You know what I'm saying."

"I know what you're saying, all right. Listen, Jacob, you think my boy's not a good American?"

"Nobody ever said that."

"Somebody said it, only nobody had the courage to come right out with it. Maybe they think Abe lost his legs bombing Wall Street instead of fighting in the ditches in Europe. Now you tell me, Jacob, what in the name of God did my boy go to war for?"

Jacob's mouth hardened. "I had a boy too."

"Who Teresa thinks is better off than ours."

"That's a terrible thing to say, Sam."

"That's what I told her. But now I'm not so sure."

They stood quietly for a time, letting the heat of the argument pass. Then Sammy said, "Have you talked to Julia yet?"

"Yes."

"How does she feel about it?"

"What do you expect? She doesn't like it."

"Then it's all your doing," Sammy said evenly. "Whatever happens is all on your head." He turned and walked away toward the road. "Good-bye, Jacob."

"Sam."

He stopped and listened without turning.

"I didn't do this right," Jacob said. "I wanted you to understand my side of it. Your friendship means a lot to me."

Not nearly enough, he thought. He didn't want to talk anymore. He left Jacob there and walked out to the road. Jacob stood very still, watching him until he disappeared beyond the undergrowth.

Sammy needed his God now, to help him break the news to Abe. God help him with that. He didn't need a temple; he could ask for God's help right here, on a dusty road near his house. The temple of the world, his father had called it. He stepped off the road into a thicket, and he dropped to his knees and prayed, and after a while he felt better. The despair had gone, but no answers had come. He felt the cancer under his arm, saw a bank account suddenly cut in half, and a store going to ruin through his wife's poor business sense, a daughter alone, a legless son waiting for a girl who wasn't coming.

118

Prayer hadn't answered that question for him. He would have to do it himself.

Someone called his name. He turned and saw Julia coming along behind him. She walked slowly in the warmth of the Indian summer day, her long dress gathered cumbersomely over her ankles. She looked like Anna's blood sister. Her hair was knotted primly behind her head, her mouth set in grim defiance. They walked the last few yards up Osceola Street together.

"Abe's waiting for me."

He nodded.

"I'm twenty-eight years old," she said. "My father doesn't run my life anymore, Sam. But this thing is tearing him up. He needs us both to help him. Just try to understand him a little." She opened the gate and went in. Sammy stood and watched her until she disappeared into the house. Was this not proof of the power of prayer? In the synagogue or the temple of the world, it made no difference. God was always listening. But he hurried away, gripped by the sudden fear that God and Julia would change their minds.

At the corner, he turned toward the store. Far down the street he saw them, an army of men in white sheets and hoods, marching through the dust. The weekend ordeal was beginning early.

3

Every week there were more of them. Today the line seemed to stretch into infinity. They came along West Colfax in double columns, marching abreast on each side of the trolley track, chanting in that strange language. *Klakom klukom kokem klikom, panther anther hokum sibla.* Others walked along the sidewalk passing out leaflets. He brushed past the outstretched hand of the hooded man and found another coming along in his wake. This time he slapped the leaflet out of the man's hand and stared up into the tiny eye slits. "Who are you?" he said.

The man took another leaflet and held it out to him. He could see now that it had the word JEW headlined in red.

"I asked who you are. Are you afraid to give me your name? Why do you need a hood to cover your face?"

Still the man didn't answer. Sammy walked away. He found the store packed with people who had come in from the street when the Klan started marching. Teresa was working steadily, ringing up petty purchases as fast as she could add the figures. Sammy put on his apron and went around to help her. Slowly they worked through the line, and as they passed through, the people huddled near the plate window and watched the parade outside. Then the door opened and two of the hooded men came inside. Leaflets appeared, working their way through the crowd. Sammy rushed around the counter. "You! You get out of my store!"

The men continued moving among the people. "Teresa," Sammy said, "call the cops." She picked up the telephone and asked for the police station. "I want to report some trespassers," she said. There was a long pause, and while she waited one of the men crossed the room and faced her across the counter.

"Save your breath, Mrs. Kohl."

She watched him while she spoke into the mouthpiece. "We need some policemen over here right away," she said. "People in our store, causing trouble. That's right, disturbing the peace."

The hooded man waited until she had given her address and hung up. Then he leaned over the counter and said, "You called police, Mrs. Kohl? Well, here we are. *We* are the police."

"Get out of my store," Sammy said. "I don't care what you do outside, but you get out of my store right now."

"We *are* the police, Mrs. Kohl." The voice sounded intelligent and educated and dangerous. "All you people, think about that."

He moved to the door and went out. The customers milled around for another minute, chattering and laughing nervously. Abruptly the group broke up and the people hurried away to their homes.

Sammy and Teresa sank into their chairs, tense and exhausted. The police never did come.

Later they locked the front door and counted up the money. Sammy picked up the leaflets that had fallen to the floor and filled a paper bag with them. In the alley, as he was stuffing the bag into the garbage, he opened one of the leaflets and looked at it. The headline said DOING BUSINESS WITH JEWS IS BAD BUSINESS. Beneath that, a warning, also in red: WE KNOW WHO YOU ARE. OUR EYES ARE EVERYWHERE. Sammy crumpled it and went inside. Teresa was putting the store in order, taking off her apron, making ready to leave.

"Thomas is coming," she said. "He called this afternoon while you were away and I asked him to dinner."

He nodded.

"What did Jacob want?"

"Nothing," Sammy said, and his tone told her that there would be no more talk of Jacob Howe.

They walked home in the gathering dusk. Leaflets blew down the street, and Colfax Avenue looked like New York after a tickertape parade. The street was deserted; the Klan had gathered in the park near Sloan's Lake. They could hear someone making a fiery speech, punctuated by cheers. The voices drifted over the rooftops and were whipped along with the wind.

Julia and Anna had a dinner going and a fire on. Abe sat alone at the front window, fidgeting, watching the street nervously. Gabriel huddled by the fire, a schoolbook propped open while his eyes scanned the room. He seemed to be watching Anna, and Sammy saw hostility in his eyes. They had had another fight, he guessed. Tom hadn't yet arrived. Sammy went into the kitchen, where Anna was washing something over the sink. He kissed her behind the head; she turned and smiled. "Hello, Papa, how was your day?" He sighed, and his sigh said *you shouldn't ask*. He kissed her fingers, which smelled of Octagon soap. "I've asked Julia to stay for supper," Anna said. "She's cooking the vegetables, and helping Gabie with his homework."

Sammy nodded, happy to have her. He thought, at least tonight, that Teresa was right. If there were such things as saints, Julia might qualify. There was a thump at the front door and Tom arrived. Sammy went out to meet him. "Better put your car around behind the house," he said. "The Klandals are restless tonight." Sammy didn't have a car, so the driveway behind the house was always empty. Sammy got a large canvas from the basement and drew it over the car.

"They stoning cars now?" Tom said.

"There've been some incidents. Broken windshields. Smashed windows. Scratched paint. Things like that. Always on Saturday and Sunday you find it, the day after they've been here."

They went into the living room, which was dim and cozy. Tom went over and clapped Abe on the shoulder and sat on the floor beside the wheelchair. Anna came in, bent and kissed him lightly on the forehead. "How are things, brother?" she said. Tom made a face and bounced his head from side to side. "Getting along," he said. "Where's Gabriel?"

"He was here a minute ago; must be upstairs with Julia. She's staying for dinner."

Sammy went into the kitchen. Anna sat in a chair beside Tom. "Anything new in your life?" she said.

"With Nellie you mean? No, I guess we're just two stubborn people." There was a silence, then he said, "It'll work out, though."

"I'm sure of that."

"What about yourself? Decided to end your exile from the world yet?"

He was the only one who could talk to her like that, but even so, she blushed and shrugged him off. Teresa came in and hugged Tom. She fussed over Abe and chased them all across the hall to wash up. She had taken over the kitchen now, finishing what Anna and Julia had started. Tantalizing aromas drifted through the house, of beef and cabbage and baking bread. *Family*. It had been years since he had eaten dinner in this house, and now every smell and sound, the close, warm feeling of the air itself, seeped into his pores and drew him back in time. A time before Nell and Gabriel, when these same people had sat around this same table to celebrate Passover. Even Julia had been here then. Younger, brighter, she had sat across from Abe, wearing green instead of the gray she now wore. Her hair was rich and thick and loose, and Abe's eyes were full of incredible storybook love. But the things Tom remembered best about that year were the stories and the music and the matzos after the meal. Teresa playing the piano, Sammy with his violin, singing like a cantor in a temple, and later telling about the old religion and its customs. Moses leading the people out of Egypt. The people eating unleavened bread in the wilderness, and the bread was symbolized by the matzos, those hard little wafers that they ate for days afterward. He had not had one since.

Sammy took his place at the table and offered up thanks to the Creator, blessings to the table, to good friends and neighbors. Thanks for Julia and for Thomas, who have not broken bread with us for so long. Hope, he thought, for Ethan, wherever he is tonight. He finished with a few words in Yiddish, which none of them understood.

They ate. Sitting in the candlelight near the end of the table, Abe looked almost like the Abe of old. Gabriel's eyes went from face to face, finally resting darkly on the lovely face of Anna. Abe wanted to talk. Julia's friend in the print shop had opened new vistas for him and he was excited. He loved David Waldo. The group talked books and ideas, politics, even social mores. Nothing was taboo. "Nothing is embarrassing or in poor taste when people are honest with each other. That's the trouble with the world today; there's too much hypocrisy, too much covering up of real emotion. There are too many conventions. Don't you think so?"

Anna looked up, aware suddenly that he was looking at her. "Why ask me? I'm sure I don't know anything about the world or its conventions."

"Maybe that's the point."

"You know, Abe, this kind of discussion makes me very nervous."

"I know it does." But it was his hand, not hers, that had begun to tremble. "The point I'm getting at is that maybe it shouldn't."

Julia touched his arm and frowned, but he said, "No. Now, I'm going to say this, now, while I'm feeling good about it. While we're all here close and everything feels right. Anna, David Waldo admires you. He told me so."

"Where was I when he said that?" Julia said.

"You were . . . indisposed."

Everyone laughed but Anna, who had gone scarlet. "That's absurd," she said. "I don't even know the man; wouldn't know him if I passed him on the street."

"He's a big man," Sammy said. "Big muscular fellow with a black beard."

"He sounds awful," Anna said. "Let's talk about something else."

"I've invited him to come by sometime," Abe said.

"Come by? You mean here, to the house? Then you can entertain him yourself." She didn't often get angry at Abe, but just now she was furious. Gabriel's eyes never left her face. She searched for an ally in Tom, but found him cool, detached, amused. He smiled at her and said, "Maybe it's time you were getting out."

She folded her napkin and put her fork beside her cup. "Listen, everybody, I will be the judge of that. When I get out, who I go with or if I go at all."

Suddenly she was angry with everyone. It seemed like one giant conspiracy, but then Teresa came to her rescue. "You heard her," she said across the table. "I think that closes the discussion. Tom, pass the cabbage."

"Mom, you wouldn't have any matzos out there?"

"I might."

"It's been eight years since I tasted one. You know what I'd really like to do tonight? Have another celebration, like the last time. Remember, when Sammy sang and everyone got close to the fire and talked?"

Teresa looked at Sammy.

"Why not?" he said. He could still pray for Abe and Julia here, in his home. He stoked up the fire. Teresa brought out the matzos, warmed over the oven, and a jar of honey and a tub of butter. Sammy put a religious record on the Victrola and Teresa put out the lights as Julia came in with the candles. They all sat near the fire, Julia on the floor by Abe's wheelchair. But Sammy seemed reluctant to start, and at last Teresa turned to Tom and said, "Tell us about your life these days, son. What's been happening to you?"

Jesus, he thought, if you only knew. The mainstream of his life seemed remote and untouchable. His mother was asking, as tactfully as she could, how things were with himself and his wife, and he couldn't even answer that. They had seen each other just this afternoon. They had walked in Cheesman Park with Michael and Paul and now, looking back on it, he wondered if they had lost the ability to be honest. She was still playing games with him, and he realized with a shock that he had played the game too, giving it right back to her. Words calculated to hurt, as Michael and Paul lingered just out of earshot. As far as she was concerned, she was enjoying herself. She was enjoying her big house and her father's money after all the years of not having any. But there was an edge of desperation to her voice and he knew that she was as unhappy as he was.

For a time he had even considered telling her the one thing that would have ended the argument then and there. He had committed adultery, but no, it wasn't even that simple, she had driven him to it. She should know about Alice and Georgeann, that the blame rested on her shoulders and no others. But he didn't tell her, just as now he didn't tell Sammy and Teresa. How could any of them understand about Alice, and about Georgeann, who had followed Alice into his bed?

That Monday, opening his eyes and finding Alice in bed beside him, he knew his life had changed. He awoke thinking that murder must be like this; the second time there's nothing to it. Once you've killed, once you've been unfaithful to your wife, what difference does it make whether it's once or a hundred times, with one woman or a dozen? And as Alice began to pressure him, as it became so painfully obvious that there was a truly horrible price to pay, he looked elsewhere. That night when Georgeann came in, Tom met her in the hall. Quickly, before any of the others could get to her, he came close and pressed his last five dollars into her hand. A few moments later she let herself into his apartment. They sat and talked. Her English was even less competent than he had thought. But in this other thing, which to his amusement she called "affairs of the heart," her language was sharp and clear and universal. Her hair was yellow, like the hair of another whore he had known. It curled in thick tufts around her ears. Her lips were soft and moist, her eyes pretty. He had brought out some wine and together they drank the whole bottle. Georgeann had two children. She was twenty years old and was trying to make her way in America. She didn't like whoring, but it didn't shame her. And he liked her, something he hadn't intended doing. He didn't want to like or dislike her, only to use her.

She knew her business. Affairs of the heart. It made him laugh every time he thought of it. What she did with that hard, writhing body that night had nothing to do with the heart. Or had it? In the morning she was gone and his five dollars was there on the table. And she had never taken money from him, in all the nights that followed. He made it up to her by taking her to restaurants he couldn't afford, where they sat at window tables and drank illegal wine. By Monday of every week he was broke. Two weeks ago his tab at Miller's had been

124

cut off for nonpayment and he was waiting now for a check from a New York pulp that owed him, so he could get back on Miller's good side. Sometimes those goddamned magazines took forever.

And that's all there is, Mom—my lousy life in a nutshell. Nell, Alice, Georgeann, booze, and the ghost of this *Rocky Mountain News* bitch, Marvel Millette, whose three incisive pieces on the Ku Klux Klan had begun to stick in his craw.

He didn't tell them any of it, didn't even try to lie. He just shrugged his shoulders and waited for everyone's attention to go somewhere else. Sammy began to sing above the Victrola music. His voice drew people together, brought out family unity. Julia sat hunched toward the fire, belonging. Only Anna was unhappy. She slipped out in the middle of the song and went quietly upstairs. Tom saw her go. A few minutes later, he eased out of his chair and followed her up. When she opened her door she looked slightly embarrassed, like a child caught skipping classes. "I had a headache," she said. "You'll tell them for me?"

"I was hoping we could sit a while and talk."

"You're missing the celebration. They're doing it for you."

But she let him in and motioned him to a chair. He realized how seldom he had been in her room. He sat looking at her bed and soon his eyes drifted up to the signed picture of Aimee Semple McPherson.

"Are you a Christian now?"

"Yes."

Old Sam must love that, he thought. But he didn't say anything. Who was he to make judgments on her?

And anyway, he wanted her confidence again. The picture seemed to stand in the way of that, as if the miraculous Aimee had come in with him, and only she had Anna's trust. Tom had taken Anna, that day two years ago, to watch Aimee perform her wonders. They went to the auditorium, where Aimee was conducting a mass healing service. Aimee wore a white gown and seemed to glide before her audience. As the healing began, boys carried their feeble fathers to the platform, and Aimee clutched them and took their hands. She called them her children. She dipped her fingers in oil and made the sign of the cross on their heads. She shouted to Jesus to make them whole. An old man got up from his stretcher and began to walk. A crippled boy let out a whoop and threw his cane away. A woman blind from birth shouted that she could see. People grabbed at the skirts of the miracle woman and tried to touch her hand. She kneeled and blew softly into the ears of the deaf. When she glided off the stage to a soft piano tune, canes and crutches hung from the chandeliers.

Anna was trembling. She had Tom take her to Aimee's hotel room, where she was barred by a man in a derby hat. But then Aimee appeared, her face flushed with victory. Impulsively Anna dropped to her feet and clutched Aimee's hand. Aimee held her and stroked her hair. "My troubled child," she said. "Troubled by sins of the flesh. Don't ask how I know. Just pray and Jee-sus will make you whole again. Abandon thy selfishness and turn to Christ. Spend your days at the altar of the home, in Godly meditation, and you shall find peace."

It was as if Aimee Semple McPherson had personally turned that final key, locking her here in this room for all time: a prisoner in spirit if not in fact. He could see that she didn't want to talk, but he wouldn't be bullied by her eyes into leaving.

"How is Mr. Bonfils?" she asked. She never failed to ask for Bonfils, as if she knew the man. She looked out into the night, standing for a long moment as if frozen. "Here they come, brother," she said at last. "It's good you covered your car."

He joined her at the window. Far up Osceola Street a long column of hooded, sheeted men had turned in from Colfax. They marched in the yellow glare of torches. "They're coming here," she said, trembling. He took her shoulders in his hands and they watched together as the ranks grew and the chanting became louder. *Klakom klukom kokem klikom.* Then, as they approached the house, the words changed, becoming *Jews get out, Jews get out.* Downstairs the singing had stopped. The family would be huddled at the living-room window, watching. The torches strung out to Colfax Avenue and still they came, two abreast. The chanting never stopped. They came past the house and turned along the lake, circling the block and starting up Newton Street. They went up one block, down another, and from the oval window Tom and Anna could see the torches zigzagging through the streets like miniature, incandescent rocks carried in perfect step by countless worker ants. Softly she said, "The world's going crazy, brother." He squeezed her shoulders and she turned and looked at him. "I hate them, Tom," she said. "God, how I hate them. It goes even beyond hatred. People like that—if I could strike them dead this minute, I would. I swear it. Every black-hearted one of them." She looked away from the picture of Aimee Semple McPherson, as if the thought had made her suddenly unworthy. After a while he left her there. Downstairs the needle was rasping on the record and everyone had gathered at the window to watch the parading men outside. Tom turned off the Victrola and stood behind them. From here the view was quite different, but just as effective. The men rose up, two by two, the torches flickering over their heads, the chant unbroken, its single demand clear and penetrating. Once Tom saw Teresa cross herself, in the Catholic way, when she thought no one was looking. He had never known her to go to the Catholic Church.

126

Still they came. The chant *Jews get out* saturated the house and worked its way through the walls. He knew they would be hearing it long after the Klan had left. From his spot near the window, Abe said, "They could kill us all right now and nobody would ever find out who had done it." The words sobered everyone. Julia squeezed his arm, but he said, "They could. There are so many of them and look, they all wear masks. The police wouldn't help us. David Waldo says half of them *are* police. What could we do? They could march right in here and string us all to the rafters."

"Abe!" Teresa got up and threw another log on the fire.

"You're forgetting one little thing, brother," Tom said. "They're all cowards. That's why they wear masks. They haven't got the guts."

"They had the guts in Los Angeles," Abe said. "And in Louisiana. Or don't you read your own newspaper?"

"Those were *suspected* Klan murders. Nobody's proven anything."

"Who else would do something like that? Cut people up, cut their heads off, rip off their arms, then bury them in some big grave in the country. And saying that nobody's proven anything just goes back to my point. These people can do anything they want and get away with it."

"I want an end to this kind of talk," Teresa said. "Right now."

Tom reached over Julia's shoulder and drew the curtains tight. The room was bathed in opaque orange. "Hey," Tom said, "what happened to the party?" But no one felt like it now. "Wouldn't you think that many grown men could find something better to do on a Saturday night? They could be home, beating their wives and kids." Everyone laughed, but it was uneasy laughter, strained and forced. Suddenly Julia became concerned for her family and began looking for her wrap.

"Child, you can't go out there with those maniacs on the street," Teresa said. But Julia tossed the wrap around her neck and made for the door.

Abe began to cry. Teresa cuddled his head. Julia stopped at the door like a person being torn apart.

"Look, I'll walk her home," Tom said. "Those goons even look at us the wrong way and we'll spit in their eyes."

"I should go with you," Sammy said.

They moved toward the door. Tom said, "You need to stay here, Sam. Everybody's upset tonight. They need you here."

Tom held the door for Julia and they went out onto the front porch. The whole world seemed red, the marching men rising up like figures in some melodrama. Tom took Julia's arm and they walked down to the edge of the street. Behind them, Sammy had opened the curtain and the family stood watching. Anna had opened the curtains upstairs and watched from the oval window. They turned toward Sloan's Lake, walking beside the ditch, almost in step with the tides of Klansmen. "I think they're heading for my place," Julia said. She hurried ahead and he had to step up his own pace to keep up.

She was right. The Klan was gathering on the vacant land surrounding Jacob Howe's farmhouse, and a cross was going up. Around it, five hundred torches lit up the night. The chanting had stopped now and the lot was alive with talk, laughter, and soft murmurings. The cross was anchored and touched off to wild cheering. The wood, soaked with kerosene, burned quickly, becoming a shapeless inferno in the wind. The house stood out in the glow of fires. It was locked tight and boarded up, its shutters drawn and nailed as if no one had lived there for years. The men had made a full circle around it, and now someone started the chant again. Here the words were different: they were chanting *Jew lovers, get out*. Again Tom took Julia's arm and they began to move through the outer ranks toward the house. A path opened for them and the chanting became disjointed and fractured, then stopped completely. Everything was quiet as they crossed the clearing toward the front porch. Tom escorted her up the steps to her front door. The door was locked. He pounded it with his fist but no one came. Julia called out but still no one came. She put her mouth to the door and called again.

The door jerked open and Jacob Howe was there, hovering over them. "You idiot!" he shouted. "Have you lost your mind?" He pulled Julia inside and slammed the door. A wooden bolt slipped into place. Tom stepped down from the front porch and faced the mob alone, and for the first time he felt the fingers of fear. He had been Julia's protector, but in a real way she had been his. He walked toward them. Again the ranks parted, politely, almost respectfully. He squared his shoulders and walked among them, into the circle and across it. The only sound was the wind whipping the fire, the same sound a sheet makes whipping in the wind on a clothesline. He had reached the outer circle when something soft hit his head. A rotten tomato. Laughter began and spread out through the mob. Another tomato hit him, breaking open and oozing down his shirt. Jeers began, then whistles and catcalls. He passed under the cross and went straight toward them. Something hard hit his head, slicing through to the bone. Blood ran down his cheek.

"Hey Jewboy," someone yelled. "You gonna pertect the little lady all by yourself?"

Another stone nicked his cheek, then another.

"I bet he's got nigger blood," someone said.

Again the mob proved its color by parting and giving him a wide berth. Hands seemed to grope at him as he came out of the circle of light, but he didn't flinch and the hands didn't touch him. Soon he was clear of the Howe property, and moving at an even pace toward the street. The stones rained after him. Some hit him on the head and back, but he didn't run.

As he reached the street the chanting began again: *Jew lovers out of town.* The cross crumbled and a great cheer went up. He stopped once and looked back. Already the mob was moving out, leaving the embers on the Howes' backyard as a reminder of its coming. The Ku Klux Klan wouldn't stop, not ever. Abe was right. The murders in Louisiana and California were only the beginning. They wouldn't stop until they were stopped. "It's time," he said, watching the crumbling cross. "Time somebody put you pricks in your place."

And who else was there to do it but the great Hastings? Marvel Millette's articles had been nothing compared with what he would do. Marvel was clever, but far too cautious. She had to be careful just to make print at the *News.* He didn't know how Bonfils felt about the Ku Klux Klan, but he thought he could get almost anything past Tammen. His stories would shame hers. He would chase her back to Cleveland, where journalism was tamer and the people more civilized. Just the thought made him smile.

In his mind the pieces were already falling into place. He would take the bastards on with a frontal attack. Start by getting a full Klan roster, every son of a bitch that Locke had in his files. A list of the most prominent members would accompany his first piece. All the political bigshots who preached calm in public and stoked terror in private. He would reconstruct the rape story and drive Mr. Judge Thurman Hayes off the bench. He would take on Judge Clarence Morley, then go after Locke himself. And along the way he would expose Rube Henry and Saul Reismann, those insidious Klan lawyers, and see how deep was the involvement of his old enemy, Willie Brown III.

He jumped the gate at Sammy's house and stripped back the canvas covering his car. He wanted to begin tonight, now, while the feeling was hot. As if he could do it all in one night, after years of lethargy. As if, on this night alone, he could show them the truth of that old saw, that the pen is mightier than the sword.

4

It was Wednesday of the following week, and Abe sat alone in the living room near the window. Twenty minutes ago Anna had come in from the garden, flushed and hot. "Brother, I need a bath," she said,

heading upstairs. "I'll be back down to fix lunch in a few minutes."
Then David Waldo arrived. He was dressed formally, in a black jacket
and tie. His shoes were shined and his beard neatly trimmed. It was
the first time Abe had seen him in a tie. "I thought I'd take you up on
your invitation," David said. "I hope this isn't a bad time."

Abe pushed back from the door and let him in. "We live pretty
much as we choose here during the day. Anna and I do what we want
to, so one time's as good as any other."

David stood in the living room and looked deeper into the house.
His eyes and ears were alert for any noise or movement.

"She's upstairs, taking a bath," Abe said. As he spoke, they heard
her footsteps move from the bathroom down the hall. Then she
appeared below the second landing and he forgot about his nerves as
he watched her come. She didn't look up, didn't see him until she had
come fully into the room. She had dressed in an old dress, perhaps
figuring on working through the afternoon. Her forehead was still
damp from her bath and her hair had been let down. It was long and
thick.

"Anna, you have a visitor." Abe turned and wheeled himself out of
the room, and she was left alone with David Waldo.

Her cheeks went red; her dark eyes penetrated his. He thought she
was every bit as lovely as he'd imagined from a distance. "My name is
David," he said.

She was embarrassed; even from across the room he could see that.
She didn't move toward him; just stood for a long moment clutching
the dress under her throat, as though it revealed too much. At last she
said, very stiff and formal, "Sir, I wouldn't like to be rude in my
father's house. But surely my brother must have told you that I don't
receive visitors."

He nodded.

"And still you came?"

"I had to come."

Her eyes never left his. He had a strong face, what she could see of
it behind the beard, and she thought she saw kindness there. There
was honesty in his words, and that deepened her embarrassment.
Along with the honesty came an almost instant familiarity, establish-
ment of emotions that were never established between men and
women in the first moments after meeting. She looked at him coldly,
giving him nothing. "What would you do if you felt you had to jump
in a fire?" she said.

"I would probably jump."

"Then, sir, you must be very foolish."

"I would plead guilty to that."

He grinned widely, thinking how ridiculous, how formal and
Victorian and straight-laced they would seem to a stranger watching.

People out of time and place, caught up in the hypocrisy of a fading era. But he didn't push her. She watched him for a long moment, as though undecided as to what she should do with him.

"You've come at a terrible time. As you can see, I've been working in the garden, and expected to finish this afternoon. Clearing out the dead things for winter, you know. My mother depends on me. To look after the house. And Abe."

"If you have things to do I wouldn't stand in your way."

She lowered her eyes. "Well, then."

"Can I help you?"

"Oh, no." Then, after the slightest pause: "Thank you."

"I'm very good in gardens. And afterward I thought I'd wheel Abe around the lake. If you wouldn't mind."

"Why should I? It's a lovely day." She still hadn't moved. "It's nice of you to visit with my brother, Mr. Waldo. He gets out so seldom. The wheelchair is too heavy for me to push it that far."

"I enjoy his company."

"Do you?"

"Of course. Could I persuade you to come with us?"

"I couldn't."

"If I pitched in and helped you."

"No, really. The garden isn't half of it. There's the housework . . ."

"Miss Anna, I'll tell you the truth," he said. "The house looks great to me."

"You aren't my mother." She made a gesture of dismissal. But when he asked, she showed him the garden. They walked back among the tiny evergreens, past vines of dead and decaying flowers. "It's all but gone now," she said. "So much work for such a short season."

"I've admired it from the road. Did you do it all yourself?"

"Oh, no."

But she had, of course, and she wondered at once why she had lied. Would taking credit have seemed immodest? She realized with some surprise that she had been drawn into that old game between the sexes, that she was playing it for the first time in so many years. Wondering what he was thinking. Judging her own responses accordingly. Weighing each word before she spoke. They walked far back, to the fence, where she and Tom had shared their secrets as children.

They looked out toward the lake.

"I wish you'd change your mind."

She shook her head.

"Come on. Come along with us."

She didn't respond one way or the other, and he knew then that she was actually thinking it over.

"I'd have to dress and do my hair," she said in a while. "No, no, it would take much too long."

"We'll wait for you."

And they did.

A chilling breeze blew across the lake, but none of them seemed to notice. They went slowly, stopping often, and Abe was obviously enjoying his part in it. He felt useful and whole again, if only for an afternoon. They didn't talk much, just walked and enjoyed the roughness of the fall air. As they rounded the eastern tip of the lake, he told her something about his round table meetings. She responded with polite interest. He invited her to come to one. She said she couldn't possibly. Then, as they were walking up the north shore, he saw Jessie walking on the south. His first reaction was shock, then guilt; a loss of poise, like a man caught cheating on his wife. Jessie walked along the water's edge, meandering, stopping when they stopped, then moving along when they started again. She did not look their way.

He left Anna and Abe an hour later. Again, she was polite, but she gave him no assurance that she would receive him in the future. He waited in the shop for the next hour, but Jessie didn't come. As dusk approached, he pulled on his coat and walked east, toward the train yards. The breeze had become a wind, and snow flurries were blowing in from the west. The tarpaper shack loomed above the valley, and David crossed the meadow and pushed open the door. Jordan Abbott lay on his cot, wrapped in dirty blankets and whiskey vapors. He was shivering. David went to the ash heap and started a fire. When he had it going, he boiled a pot of water and sprinkled in grounds from a cloth sack of coffee on the table. He poured it through a strainer into two cups and pulled Abbott into a sitting position, propping him back against the wall.

"Has Jessie come by here?"

Abbott shook his head.

"We've got to talk," David said. "What I've got to tell you isn't going to be easy for either of us."

Abbott watched him, suddenly alert. His eyes were wary and dangerous.

"Jessie's been with me two years now," David said. "There's nothing more I can do with her."

The coward's way out. He took a deep breath and tried again. "Jordan, listen to me. She depends on me too much. It may actually be hurting her to stay with me."

More cowardice, deep and penetrating.

"I think it's time she came back to you."

Abbott just stared at him.

"Jordan?"

"You've found another woman for yourself," Abbott said.

"There's a woman, but . . ."

"Don't tell me about it. I don't want to hear it."

"It's not what you think."

"I don't care what it is."

"Well, I'm going to tell you, whether you want to hear it or not. What's happening between Jessie and me started a long time ago."

"Then why didn't you kick her out?" Abbott said. "A long time ago."

"Listen, old man, I love her as much as you do. Can't you forget yourself for a minute and try to understand what she's doing to me? She tears me apart the way she dominates my time. I read her the same books, we talk about the same things, if I try to get into anything deeper it's like talking calculus with a child. You think this is easy for me? It's like cutting off one of my arms. Or like giving up a daughter."

"Don't give me that. She's been more than a daughter to you."

"At your suggestion. Don't forget that."

"Well, at least you've taken care not to have children."

David grasped at anything Abbott would give him. "I didn't want to use her."

"Thank you very much for that." Abbott stared into the fire. "Well, what do you want me to do? You've had your fun but I'm two years older. Some days it's all I can do to stand up in the morning. My lungs are going and my kidneys are shot. How long do you think I can last? Six months? Three? And what happens to her then? Or don't you give a damn?"

"Jordan . . ."

"Now that you've got something else on the sly."

"Ah, Jordan, it's not like that. Would you just listen to me?"

Abbott, now fully awake and sober, said, "All right, then, leave her to me."

Abbott's words chilled him, and he knew now that it wouldn't be quite that simple.

"What are you going to do?" he said.

"Don't you worry yourself about that," Abbott said. "Abbotts have always taken care of their own."

"I need to know. You've got to have a plan."

"What my plans are are my own goddamn business and no one else's. You just bring her by and leave her off. Don't bother coming in with her."

"I can't do that."

A faint smile began around the edge of Abbott's mouth. "Then I guess that's your problem, isn't it?"

CHAPTER
FIVE

1

The heavy snows of early winter had covered the Clement estate, bringing an illusion of isolation. Ice formed in a thin crust over the pond behind the house; long fingers of it drooped down from the wooden lip that hung over the outside of the bow window. Nell Clement Hastings, alone in her thirtieth year, sat at the window as if frozen there by the winter storm. Only her eyelids moved, blinking periodically as she stared off at some point in space. She imagined people living in *her* house. They were strangers who didn't appreciate the skylight as they had. She saw breakfast scenes in the kitchen: four people without faces eating lumps of gray matter off plain white plates. They ate with their fingers. Later, naked, the mother and father made love on a bed in the sun under the skylight. Her hands touched her body and she tingled as they moved, inside the pockets of her dress, the right hand moving through the hole she hadn't bothered to mend, dropping, dropping into an eternity of darkness, probing, then finding the magic place that stood up under her finger like a child's pet responds to a caress. She shifted her hips and felt that old warmth. It was like turning back the clock to her youth. She hadn't done this in more than eight years.

Later she still sat there, savoring the fantasy over the reality. When she opened her eyes, her boys were there on the snow beneath her, playing. She felt a flash of shame, then drove it away. It was silly. Victorian. Michael was pelting Paul with snowballs, taking advantage of Paul's blindness again. She was about to tap on the window when she heard Tom's voice, as clearly as if he'd been standing behind her. *Goddammit, Nell, leave them alone. Don't protect him so much. It's a tough world and he needs to cope with it on his own.* So she watched a while longer and felt pain for her son. Paul was shouting to Michael now, yelling that he had had enough. Michael laughed and danced around him, peppering him with crusty pieces of snow. Paul had begun to cry. He had dropped his cane and was on his knees, groping. That's enough, she thought, but still she didn't move. Michael danced up behind Paul and pushed him hard, sending him face-first into the snowbank. Paul lay absolutely still. Nell shivered. *Surely he's playing,* she thought. *A little push like that. I'll wait a minute.* Paul didn't move. Michael eased closer. "Paul?" She just heard his tiny voice through the frosty window. Still Paul didn't move. "*Paul!*" Now there was fear in Michael's voice. He struggled through the snow and grabbed Paul's coat, rolling him over on his back. Suddenly Paul's fingers closed around Michael's leg. He jerked Michael's foot and sent him into the snow on his back. Paul gripped his neck with one hand and scooped up some snow with the other. He pushed the snow into Michael's face, packing his mouth and nose until Michael began screaming with terror. Nell sat back, laughing and clapping her hands. "Good for you, Paul, bravo!" That too had its price, and the price was nagging guilt. She would feel it in spurts all through the afternoon and evening, the price of cheering one son over the other. Michael was becoming a little monster, and how much of that was her fault? Hers and Tom's? Because of his blindness, they had loved the first son more, with predictable results. What to do about it now, that was the question. Now that she was left to raise them alone.

She had to be careful or the resentment would start again. Of course she hadn't been left, surely he would come back to her; all she had to do this moment was lift the telephone. He was such a silly, proud man at times. It was clear to her now, three months after she had left him, that there had been a mistake, and the mistake was hers. She had misjudged him. She had given him a week, two at the outside. By then he would be climbing the wall in loneliness.

Loneliness weighed on him like poverty weighed on her, so the last thing she expected was that he would give up the house and move alone into Capitol Hill. When he called and told her she was shocked. Now she knew that it had been her last good chance to say, "Don't do that, Thomas, I'm coming home." So simple. But instead she let precious seconds go by while he talked on, asking about new schedules for seeing the kids. It was her first real understanding that something had ended. There would be no more house with the skylight. She had hated that house, had been so determined not to return to it, and now that the option was gone she felt like crying. And they hung up, farther apart than ever.

Stubborn, stubborn.

Stubborn goddamn fool.

What was he doing for women? Ah, no, she wasn't going to ruin her day with thinking like that.

She had lost track of the hours she had spent at this window. She was ready to call a truce, but how to do it eluded her. One day a perfect plan would come to her, the next day she discarded it as too obvious and unworkable. The best, simplest way was to meet him somewhere and tell him she had been wrong. Give up pride, admit defeat. Unconditional surrender. Yes. She was ready to take him back under almost any circumstances. Yet day after day her hand had hovered near the telephone. It flitted through her mind constantly, but she didn't call.

Couldn't.

She simply couldn't pick up the telephone.

"Call me, damn you!" she had screamed at it one day. But the phone wouldn't be bullied, and the echoes of her own voice came back at her.

That, of course, was her main problem. This big empty house, steeped in luxury, was driving her crazy. She walked through it now and her footsteps echoed in the empty halls. She was a prisoner of her father's world, where women did nothing. Gregory Clement was away at his luggage plant in St. Louis. He had been gone for two weeks and was due back this afternoon, but until he came the house was empty of all but herself and the boys. An empty mansion, with sixteen rooms on two floors, and no one to live in them. In her mother's day every room had been filled. There had been no such thing as wasted space. Relatives too numerous to remember had come crowding in on them, but always from her side of the family. No one came to visit after her death. Servants had had their own wing upstairs, and they had had servants in great numbers. She remembered one Christmas when twenty-two people had been in attendance around the cedar tree in the front room. Only Gregory Clement, who didn't hold with such things, did not come down.

For his wife old Gregory had bent a lot. He would put up with her relatives, let her make merry; he would let people hang from the chandeliers if it pleased her. Alberta Clement was a Southern belle he had met in Savannah forty years ago. She became his proudest possession, a woman of great beauty even into her middle age. She was delicate and frail; she had had two miscarriages before Nell was born. With Nell the doctors had confined her to bed for almost the entire term. Gregory hired Woodrow, then Buffie, and every morning at exactly nine o'clock, Alberta Clement was served breakfast in her room on a silver tray. And when the baby was born, when it was a daughter instead of the son he wanted and doctors warned against having another, he pushed aside his disappointment and took the child into the fold, adding her name in the ledger of his mind.

The ledger marked *things owned.*

After eight years with Tom, she had almost forgotten how possessive the old man was. She had read the story of Elizabeth Barrett and Robert Browning. She thought of Elizabeth's tyrannical old Victorian father, and thought, my father is a lot like that. A stern old taskmaster, cracking a whip. In her childhood he had set her schedule. He decided who would see her, where she would go, what her activities would be, who her friends were. Once, at seventeen, she had defied him and he had taken her to an institution to live out her rebellion. Sixteen days locked up with crazies, the only consolation being that they were upper-class crazies. If her absence bothered Alberta, Nell never heard of it. In the end, Alberta was just another of old Gregory's possessions. He let her have her frills, but in the important matters, such as dealing with a troubled child, he would make the decisions.

Riding home that day, the old man had touched her hand and said, ever so gently, "Now you understand, don't you, my dear?"

"Yes, Papa."

"Everything I do for you, I do out of love."

"Yes, Papa."

"It's because I love you that we had to go through this."

She nodded.

"You had to be made to understand that the course you were on would only lead to disaster."

She didn't say anything.

"You understand that, don't you?"

"Yes, Papa."

"This, this young man you were seeing. He means nothing in the

137

long run of things. As a young lady, you haven't yet come to an understanding of your own desires. You'll see, it will pass, and you'll come to thank me for it."

"Yes, Papa."

And really, who could tell, maybe he had been right. The young man had passed from her life, giving her Tom and ultimately the boys. That the old man had also hated Tom, still hated him violently, she shrugged off with the attitude that you couldn't win them all. Even Gregory Clement couldn't be right all the time. At first the old man had maintained his distance, refusing to drive to Golden even to see his grandsons. Then, after the death of her mother, he began coming around. Gregory Clement was stunned by the loss of his wife. Now he came to Golden once or twice a week, to take the boys for drives in the mountains, to amusement parks, to the estate for overnight visits. He never came inside her house, with the exception of that one time, and he always came when Tom was working. If Tom came home unexpectedly, the old man would climb into the Packard and leave at once. And for all those years she had been true to the bargain she had made with herself. As long as her husband was unwelcome at the Clement house, she would stay away too.

Father and daughter. How quickly things change.

Father and daughter. Master and slave girl.

She was losing ground. She knew it now. It had started last month, when abruptly, without any warning or provocation, old Gregory had fired Buffie, the maid.

She had come into the kitchen to find Buffie in such distress that speech was impossible. She went looking for Woodrow and found him sitting near the door in the parlor. "What is it, what's happened?" He looked at her in disbelief. "The old master has fired Buffie." She shook her head. There had been a mistake. Gregory Clement didn't discharge servants who had worked for him thirty years. She went to his study and found him reading a report from the St. Louis plant.

"Father, Woodrow says you've fired Buffie."

He looked up and took off his glasses. "Fired is a terrible word."

"Well then, what did you do?"

"My dear, I've been running this house for more than thirty years. In that time I've had to do a great many things I dislike doing."

"What's the trouble, Papa? Was she rude?"

"She is simply not necessary anymore."

"I still don't understand."

"I'm closing down part of the house. It's far too big a place for just the four of us. We rattle around too much, and we don't have guests like we did when your mother was alive. We simply don't need all this room."

138

"But Papa, surely there must be something she can do. To just fire her after all these years . . ."

"I didn't just fire her, as you and Woodrow so charmingly put it. I've given her excellent references and will pay her a year's salary. I've also offered to pay her regular wages until she finds another situation. Now what could be fairer than that?"

Hans, the grounds man, was next. One by one the part-time servants began disappearing from the house. Three weeks after it began, the old man fired Woodrow, and the house was suddenly empty. Of all the original servants only Orrin remained, manning the guardhouse by day and living at night in the tiny cottage in a glade behind the big house.

That night the old man called her to him. "I've long felt that we should be more like a family. One close-knit family group, just you and the boys and me. So I'm moving you downstairs, next to my room."

"But my room's always been upstairs. I love it there."

His smile was thin, laced with bitterness. "Not always, as you'll remember. You were gone for many years. In the long run this will work out better."

She reminded him that her visit was only temporary.

"Yes, well, we'll see. But for now, let's try it my way."

He moved her into the room adjoining his. It had a bow window that looked out over the side lawn and there was much more space than she had ever had. "Just what I need," she muttered to herself. "More room."

The boys shared a room on the other side of the old man. There were adjoining doors both ways. And so, Gregory Clement began to arrange their lives. In the afternoon a woman came in to cook the evening meal. Whenever something more needed doing, Orrin did it, or found the manpower to have it done. Orrin seemed to know where he could find men to do almost everything. "Now," said Gregory Clement, "isn't this pleasant?" But Michael made a face and said, "I want to go back home." In anger, the old man sent them off to bed.

"They should get more sleep," he told her. "You're not raising them properly. They'll grow up temperamental and unruly. They should be in bed by seven-thirty."

"Really, Papa, they're beyond that now."

"Beyond what, a little old-fashioned discipline? That's just what they've lacked all these years and it's starting to show."

"They are beyond a seven-thirty curfew," she said firmly. "This year we've been letting them stay up till eight-thirty. Nine on weekends."

He waved his hand, dismissing her. "Never mind. Let's try it my way for a few months and see what happens."

"Papa, I won't be here for a few months. I told you . . ."

"We'll give them the discipline of a structured schedule. Let them know what's expected of them, give them responsibilities and duties and let them know we expect them to be carried out."

"As long as they have play time too. With other boys their own age."

"Boys need only one thing to get along in this life. They need to become self-sufficient, and the sooner the better. And they won't get that from playing at life with a bunch of sniveling neighborhood brats. Most children these days are rude, ignorant, and have no respect for their elders. The less Michael and Paul have to do with children like that, the better."

"They can learn from children of all kinds."

"Oh, really, now. Next you'll be wanting them to associate with coloreds as well."

"I wouldn't want them to be forbidden to."

"Colored people will not be satisfied until they're swimming in the country club pool. And another thing: Paul spends far too much time listening to wireless. Let's take it away from him for a while and see if his studies perk up."

"We can't do that. It means too much to him."

"Far more than it should, if you want my opinion. Besides, I don't believe in wireless."

"How on earth could you not believe in it?"

"It's absurd. Preposterous. The idea, sending sound through the air without wires."

"Have you ever tried listening to Paul's set?"

"I won't be a party to it. I think it's a trick, some illusion invented by the communists to brainwash our children."

"Honestly, Papa."

Thirty minutes later they retired. She changed into her nightgown and settled back with a book. Suddenly the lights went out.

She knocked on her father's door. "Father, the lights are out."

"I know they are. I turned them off."

"What for?"

"Because it's time for bed." He spoke patiently, the way a father speaks to a five year old. She crawled between her sheets, feeling a chill that went deeper than the season.

In the morning she decided to call Tom at work and arrange a meeting. She lifted the phone but the line was dead. She clicked the handle. For a few seconds nothing happened. Then a familiar voice said, "Yes?"

"Orrin? Is that you?"

"Yes, miss."

"What are you doing on the line?"

"I'm handling the switchboard, miss."

"Switchboard? What switchboard?"

"We've had one installed in the guardhouse."

"A switchboard for four people? Don't be ridiculous."

"It's to weed out nuisance calls, Miss Nell."

"Well, put me through to an outside line, right now."

"You'll have to give me the number, miss. I'll ring it from here."

She gave him the number of the *Post* newsroom.

There were clicks. A buzz. Then Orrin came on the line again. "There must be some trouble on that line, miss. I can't seem to get through."

She slammed down the telephone, knocking it off the table. Two minutes later she stormed into her father's study. Gregory Clement was on the phone as she came in. He hung up at once and faced her across his desk.

"Papa, Orrin tells me you've installed a switchboard in the guardhouse. Does that mean that I can't call out?"

"It means you have to go through the switchboard."

"Why?"

"I've been getting a lot of nuisance calls."

"Well, it makes me feel like a prisoner."

"There's certainly no reason for that. You're as free to come and go as I am. Has anyone ever stopped you from going anywhere you wanted to go?"

"Why must I always take *him* with me?"

"Orrin? He's there for your own protection, my dear. People aren't safe in the world today. If you read the newspapers, as I do . . ."

"Well, why can't I read them? I asked for the *Post* two weeks ago and I haven't seen it yet."

"I felt you'd be better off with some other newspaper. The *Post* is much too sordid for family reading. Doesn't the *Times* interest you?"

"That's not the point. The point is that you've taken it upon yourself to set my hours, to run my children, to set my reading standard, and now to monitor my telephone calls."

"Until I die, I am the master of this house."

"Then perhaps I'd better leave," she said quietly.

"I'm sorry you feel that way, my dear. I have enjoyed having you, and I've tried to influence you in what I think is the right direction after the, ah, misguidance of the past."

"I will leave," she said. "Today."

"If that's your wish. You see, my dear, you aren't a prisoner here at all. I fully recognize that you're a grown woman with a life of your own. Orrin will gather your things and drive you." He reached for the telephone. "Orrin, you will please have the car ready in thirty minutes, to deliver Miss Nell downtown. To, ah, where will you go, my dear?"

She looked at him defiantly. "He can take me to the *Denver Post* building."

"You'll be going downtown, Orrin, to the *Denver Post*." As he hung up, she whirled away and moved quickly toward the hall door. "Before you leave, I should tell you a few things."

She turned and met his eyes evenly.

"First," he said, "you and the boys will always be welcome in my house, at any hour of the day or night. If things outside don't suit you, you have only to call me. Secondly, if you do leave, you'll have to make it, as they say, entirely on your own. I think you know my feeling about rebellious children. And finally, there are a few things you may not know about your, ah, husband." He pried the word out of himself. He shuffled through some papers on his desk and found the one he sought. "I can now tell you with absolute certainty that he is not the man you think."

"I won't listen to this."

"It will be to your own good if you do, but again the choice is yours." When she didn't move, he put on a pair of spectacles and looked at the paper. "On the night of October 13, he went to a party at the Denver Press Club, in the company of a Miss Alice Wilder."

"I know her. I met her once. She's an artist at the *Post*. What of it?"

"Miss Wilder, as the name implies, seems to be of our cursed modern generation. You *know* what I mean. Two days later, Miss Wilder visited your Mr. Hastings at his apartment on Capitol Hill. She stayed the night."

"I don't believe it."

"Here's the report. You can read it for yourself."

She shook her head and sank weakly into a chair.

"There's more," the old man said. "This so-called apartment where your Mr. Hastings lives . . . you haven't seen it, have you?"

She shook her head.

"Of course not. Orrin has orders not to take you there. That's why, my dear, you always meet your Mr. Hastings in the park when he visits with the children. Once again, you see, I've protected you from things you didn't need to know. Now you must know, so you'll have the facts with which to make an intelligent decision. The right decision. Shall I go on?"

She didn't say anything.

"This apartment where he lives is notorious as a hangout for the worst kind of man. The owner has employed a series of maids who minister to their needs. I hesitate to elaborate. I'm sure, my dear, since you've been married these eight years, I don't have to. You know what I mean." He cleared his throat. "The newest of these maids is an immigrant woman named Georgeann Johanssen, who has two children born out of wedlock. This Georgeann woman seems to have taken a special interest in your Mr. Hastings. They have been seen together in public." Gregory Clement shook his head. "The audacity of the man is simply beyond belief, though nothing he does surprises me. I know this hurts you, and I'm sorry I had to do it. If there'd been any other possible way . . ."

"I'd like to leave now."

The old man looked hurt. "You're still going, then?"

"Yes."

His mouth set into a thin frown. "Very well. Orrin will be up for your things directly."

Orrin came exactly twenty minutes later. She had the children dressed and ready and her small bags packed. She didn't see her father as they left, and Orrin drove downtown without comment, watching her constantly in the mirror with those beady vampire eyes. She got out on Champa Street and stood there with her little boys, watching him drive away. She took Paul's hand and they went inside. She found a guard and asked him to call upstairs for her husband.

He wasn't in. The guard didn't know where he might be. "If he's a reporter, ma'am, he's liable to be most anywhere. I could call the newsroom back. Somebody on city desk might know."

"Please."

When the guard had finished his call, he said, "Nobody's seen him for at least two days, ma'am. He's away on some assignment. Maybe even out of state."

She faced the street and the coming night with meager resources. She had no money; Gregory Clement had never given the women in his house any money to spend. Instead he had always maintained charge accounts in Denver's best department stores, where they could buy what they wanted and he could screen the purchases as the bills came in. In the three months that she had been under his roof, he had taken complete control of her finances. Everything she wanted, she got. The boys were clothed in new outfits, which they still wore, but none of them had even a quarter of the old man's money. Now, looking through her pocketbook, she found only the dollar and change that she had left home with in August.

They walked southeast, into Court Place, where the Arapahoe County Courthouse was. They found a bench where she could sit and think.

The snow began.

At first it came as an elusive flutter. Then the wind began to drive it, blowing it horizontally, sleetlike, across the street. She gathered the boys under her arm and climbed the steps of the courthouse. For a long time they stood just inside the vestibule. Michael began to complain. She tried Tom's apartment and got no answer. She cursed him under her breath.

"Poor darlings." She hugged them close, wrapping them in her shawl until they were warm again. They waited some more. Darkness had come over the city.

All her life Nell had been taught to depend on men. First her father, then Tom. There had always been a man there to protect her. She was regal and aristocratic, and in a savage society she would be the first to perish without her men beside her. She had spunk but she wasn't tough. Her instinct for survival was dull from no use. She would not do whatever she had to do to get through the stormy night with her children. Instead she would run home to her father.

"The hell I will," she said aloud. "We'll see about that."

But a look outside made her shiver, and her confidence oozed away. The snow was drifting now, building up in six-inch banks on the sidewalk. The streetlights swirled in mist and all of Denver was cast in a cold gloom. The city was hostile and formidable and black.

The building closed. A guard locked the doors. She gathered the boys in the folds of her dress and they began to walk. Michael and Paul wore coats but she hadn't dressed for the sudden snow. She tried not to let them see her shivering. On Sixteenth Street they caught a trolley. It was rush hour. The cab was packed with red-faced people. A young man with a neat moustache stood and gave her his seat near the door. He looked at her kindly and with interest. She glanced at him periodically as the trolley lurched between stops. His hands were rough, the nails bitten off short. Beneath his coat were the coveralls of a warehouseman. He couldn't have been more than twenty-five. It was Friday, pay day in many places. He would have money in his pocket. She was beginning to think like a survivor.

But the jump between thought and voice was deep; between voice and movement deeper still. The man got off at the next corner.

She thought he might have spoken to her except for the children. The children had put him off.

They got off on Champa. Paul slipped on the ice and cut his hand. Michael started to cry. She held Paul's hand with her own to stop the bleeding, and they hurried along Champa Street to the *Post* front door. Workers were pouring out into the night. She waited, looking for a friendly face, someone she knew. She felt the red in her cheeks as her hat began to droop down over her ears.

She looked up the iron staircase and saw, coming down, the slim figure of Alice Wilder. Their eyes met, then Alice slipped quickly past

144

her and hurried along the street toward the lot where she had parked her car.

She should take survival lessons from Alice Wilder before she tried this again. A survival course, along with a bonus lesson on how to steal someone's man. Two lessons for the price of one: a bargain in these days of inflation and prosperity.

She felt like crying. She thought, I'm at the end of my rope. I can't do this anymore. I'm not tough at all.

She thought of friends. Who would help her? She had friends on Grant Street. But she hadn't seen them in two years, since Eli Eaker had won a seat in the State Senate. Tom didn't socialize with potential news sources.

Well, damn Tom. Damn his ethics. It would be so fitting if that was the next myth to crumble. The myth of his ethics. They had already lost the myth of their compatibility. Then the myth of his fidelity. What came next?

The myth of her pride.

She called her father. In a while Orrin came by in the green Packard and they were warm again. By eight o'clock the boys were packed off to bed and she was sitting by the fire with Gregory Clement, sipping a toddy as if nothing had happened.

Two weeks had passed. Now Gregory Clement was in St. Louis, it was snowing again, and she still hadn't heard from Tom.

In that time, her emotions had gone full circle. First came the fear that their separation might indeed become permanent. She would forget about Alice Wilder and that Georgeann woman. She would bear that cross in silence, pretend she had never heard their names. Then she settled into a time of calm and reason. They would talk it out between them and she would take her part of the blame. It was the modern way. Next came a wave of anger, uncontrollable, intense and obstinate. She would confront him with what she knew was true. She would slap his face, a thousand times harder than that night in Golden. By the end of the second week her anger had dissolved and the fear was back. Another fight might drive him away for good, and if that happened she thought she might kill herself.

And that was how Nell Clement Hastings happened to be here, sitting in the first-floor bow window, alone in a house of cold rooms. Now it seemed that she had never done anything but sit here and watch the snow pile up. Regret the past. Dream erotic, shameful thoughts. Masturbate like a silly adolescent, then feel guilty about it. Think how foolish and Victorian the guilt was. And always worry about herself and her sons, under the old man's thumb.

Remember a time when anything seemed possible. A picnic on the estate for all the Kohls. Her father, then as now, was in St. Louis. Tom had found an excuse not to come: he'd had to work that day. Anna wouldn't come, but Sammy and Teresa had been here, and Abe had brought Julia Howe and her brother, Isaac. It was a start, a break in the ice. She had had some of her friends in, the young people of her childhood, but they had separated themselves from the Kohls and talked drivel from the society pages. Later they had played croquet on the lawn. The snobs beat the bumpkins all hollow and everybody on the snob squad had a jolly good laugh. But Abe, who wasn't used to being defeated at anything, got out his football and the trouble started. Abe was the fastest runner any of them had ever seen. He bowled them over and a fight erupted. A table turned, spilling the punch and breaking the crystal service that had been in Alberta Clement's family for sixty years. Words were exchanged between Alberta and Teresa. Sammy apologized, gathering his fiery wife in tow before real trouble started. Inside the mansion, Alberta Clement collapsed in nervous exhaustion and refused to come out of her room, even to answer Nell's telephone calls, until old Gregory came home that Thursday.

Remember that, along with the hundred and one times the old man had told her about birds and butterflies. Birds and butterflies don't mix. Dogs don't mix with cats. Frogs don't mix with turtles. Things stay in their natural orders. It's the same with people. Races don't mix. Religions work best within their own. Catholics don't mix with Buddhists. In the six-thousand-year history of civilization, races have never lived side by side without warring.

Argue with him. Tell him the Jews aren't a race and get nowhere with that. Then think about Tom and how right this minute she would take him back under any circumstances he might want to name.

But he didn't call. It had been more than two weeks since he had seen his boys and that wasn't like him. The newspaper world might call that an angle. The boys had begun asking for their father; wasn't that a valid reason for parental concern? Damn it, someone in that building, if only Tammen himself, had to know where her husband was.

She picked up the telephone. "Orrin, have the car ready in ten minutes. We're going downtown."

"Sorry, miss. I can't do that."

"What do you mean you can't do it? I'm telling you to do it."

"Mr. Gregory told me to hold the fort as she is, miss."

Suddenly she was seized by unspeakable fury. She knocked the telephone off the table and kicked it against the wall. She jerked on a coat and stalked outside. It was a long march across the meadow to the guardhouse, hard going now that there was no one to scrape the walks. He saw her coming and he opened the door and came out. She saw him fumbling with the gate and realized with growing horror that he was locking it. He turned and faced her, a medieval figure in black. They stood watching each other across a thirty-foot stretch of snow. Her breath came in tiny white puffs. His was invisible.

"Now," she said when she could talk. "Would you mind telling me . . . exactly what the goddamned hell you think you're doing?"

"Just following orders, miss."

"Open that gate."

"Miss, I can't."

"Don't tell me you can't!" She screamed the words and came at him as though she might tear him apart with her hands. "Open that gate, damn you!"

"I'm sorry, miss."

"You bastard, you'll be a lot sorrier if you don't do what I tell you."

He didn't move. She came toward him faster, as fast as she could slog her way through the snow. But when she got close, he simply stepped back into the guardhouse and locked the door.

She beat on the window with her fists, but the glass was reinforced with wire. He just stood there, watching with those dark eyes.

She turned and walked slowly toward the house. Behind her she heard the guardhouse door open as he came out. She ripped off her gloves and in one motion scooped up a handful of snow, packed it, turned and threw it. It hit him above the left eye, knocking his hat off. She felt like laughing and crying at once, and suddenly she felt afraid. He started toward her, just one step, and she ran slipping and falling all the way to the house.

When Gregory Clement arrived that afternoon, she confronted him in the hall even before he had his coat off. She demanded that Orrin be fired. The old man nodded patiently and said that sometimes Orrin took his orders too seriously. He would speak to him.

As night fell she climbed through the empty house into the gable loft. From there she had a clear view of the entire front meadow, the guardhouse, and the street beyond. She saw the old man go out for his talk with Orrin. They sat together in the guardhouse for a long time, talking and smoking cigars.

CHAPTER
SIX

1

Tom had been on the road with Goodwin for more than a week. He knew he hadn't been good company, but Goodwin never complained as long as Tom had plenty of whiskey. And that was something he always had.

They made the grand tour of the state, starting on the plains east of Denver and making a great loop. They were on a graveled state road, somewhere south of Julesburg, feeling their way along on one of Tammen's so-called fact-finding missions. It was disguised to the city desk as a political journey, to feel the pulse of the state, since next year would bring elections for local office as well as for Congress and president. But Tom was interested in only one thing: gathering facts on the Ku Klux Klan.

The morning after the cross-burning at Jacob Howe's farm, he had put it to Tammen straight. He wanted to get the Klan, and to beat

148

Marvel Millette. And Tammen had grinned and said, "It's high time you got your ass motivated again. Don't talk to me about any goddamned Pulitzer Prize, I don't give a damn about that. Just go beat the *News*." And Tom had said, "I'll need some advance money. I want to survey the whole state. And I need to know what to tell the desk." Tammen peeled off some bills from his billfold, giving him enough, but barely. "You'll get what you need from me right now, and keep your mouth shut. If Fred finds out we're spending money for something like this I'll have to send him fishing for a week to get him over it. I'll tell the desk." Tammen sat back, implying dismissal, but Tom said, "One more thing. I don't want to do it for nothing." The implication was explicit. If either Bonfils or Tammen had friends in the Ku Klux Klan he didn't want to know it. He was simply serving rather bold notice on Tammen that he didn't want to work a month and then watch the story die of editorial strangulation. And Tammen had said, "It's just another story to me. It all depends on what you get, just like everything else. Now get the hell out of here and leave me alone. I got a terrible bellyache."

It wasn't much of a guarantee, but in this business there were no guarantees. Goodwin was assigned to him and the night before they left Tom got out his state map and drew a huge half-circle, hitting the prairie towns to the east where Klan strength would be most evident. The circle ended near Utah, in the butte town of Grand Junction, and there Tom wrote a date and circled it in red. He had learned through City Hall sources that a major national meeting of the Klan would be held there in three weeks, with delegates expected from both coasts; from Indiana, Texas, and Ohio. Hiram Wesley Evans, who some said was next in line to become Imperial Wizard, would be coming up from Texas by private train. John Galen Locke would play host, and Grand Junction had been selected because it was centrally located and far away from the attention of the national press. This would be no fiery session on the mountaintop. Its participants would be few and they would probably wear blue suits and ties. They would meet in the Grand Hotel downtown, mapping out strategy for taking over a state. One state, then another, then a region, then a country. Through his reading, he now knew enough to make an educated guess. Colorado and Indiana were almost certain to fall to Klan politicians in next year's elections. Ohio was possibe. The Klan was showing surprising strength in California and in scattered states throughout the Midwest. It had a solid lock on the South. The strategy was frightening because it used the political system so well. Grab the statehouses, then the city halls, pack the police departments and the state boards of licensing. Regulate the trades, starve out anybody who wasn't pure white American. Run candidates for every position of authority, especially positions in law enforcement. Intimidate voters; browbeat the stupid and naïve. Work up to Congressional and Senate races, and finally to the White House itself. That was why Grand Junction was important, and why he had to be there.

It was ironic and somehow fitting that their first stop was in Limon. Now, twenty-three years after Preston Porter had been burned at the stake, every face was a stranger's and the air no longer had that smell of insanity to it. He had no time for sentiment, so he didn't bother going to Shaughnessy's or to the old Frost ranch. He and Goodwin walked the streets, picking up what they could. They were dressed simply, in jeans and flannel shirts and western hats. Only the cumbersome box camera that Goodwin carried gave them away as something other than ranchers. They walked the length of the town, down the same street where he had once walked Louise Frost home from school, past the building, still standing, where Ethan had stood watching as they came past. He stopped people and asked questions. No one wanted to talk.

It was the same at the town hall, where he interviewed the mayor and the county sheriff. Maybe the Porter affair had purified Limon's spirit. Maybe the people still remembered and wanted no part of anything like the Ku Klux Klan. Or maybe it was here, right under his nose, and he'd just missed it. Later, in the car, Goodwin had said, "Assuming anybody gives you anything worth a damn, which they haven't so far, do you really think it'll see the light of day? I mean, you really don't expect to get this stuff published, right? It's all a put-on, just to get out of town for a few days."

"Depends on what we get. That's a direct quote from the little boss."

"Christ. The answers that fit with the questions you're asking'll never get in the *Denver Post*. You remember I said that."

Tom hadn't told him much of it. He hadn't wanted Goodwin along at all, but Tammen had insisted. Tammen and his goddamn pictures. So he told Goodwin what he had to tell him: that they were doing a statewide survey on the strength of the Ku Klux Klan, that what they got was for Tammen's information and might or might not be used in a story. He had told Goodwin to expect to be gone at least three weeks. Now he said, "Don't worry, it's out here. I can feel it. It'll probably run hot and cold all the way."

How right that was. He came looking for Klan nests and he found them. The plains were alive with bigots, ugly people full of hate who gathered at train stations and watched everyone who got off. Men who talked in soft tones of old-fashioned, southern-style lynchings. Old-timers who wistfully remembered slavery times, before the Jews owned everything and niggers got uppity, before communists were a

150

threat. The hostile towns wore their feelings everywhere, wrapped around telephone poles like armbands, posted on the doors of sagging, abandoned buildings, in the murderous looks of their people. In their tenth day on the road they came to a small town off the main drag. They were still on the plains, somewhere east of Pueblo. The sign at the town limit said:

BARKER, COLO.
Elevation 4,025 Feet
Population 87

And under it, someone had painted in:

And not a nigger, jewboy
or cat-licker amongst 'em

Goodwin took a picture of it. Farther along, down its one main street, they saw a hand-made poster that said NIGGER, DON'T SETTLE HERE. Goodwin pulled to the curb and got out to take another picture. Tom rolled down his window. "Look there," he said, pointing to a sign in a saloon window. The sign said KLAN MEETING THURSDAY NIGHT, 8 P.M.

"I bet the whole town's in the Klan."

"We gonna stick around, go to the meeting?" Goodwin said.

Tom shook his head. "I wish we could. We'll be a long way from here by Thursday."

2

But there were other meetings, other people to see. Now they were across the mountains. The weather had broken and Pueblo was behind them. The mountain towns were like those on the plains. Some were silent, some vocal, and a few of the smallest were locked up and owned outright by the Ku Klux Klan. Even in the quiet towns there were undercurrents. There was something in the air. Even Goodwin noticed it as dark faces watched them from open doorways.

Tom had filled four notebooks with impressions and quotes. This was the muscle that pieces like his were made of. Goodwin had at least two hundred shots and some of them, he had to admit, might come in handy later. But Goodwin's continued pessimism was like a weight on the car. He griped without letup about the worthlessness of the assignment, and about Tom's technique in interviewing. There had been a girl on the street in Pueblo, obviously a bigot, and Goodwin thought Tom's soapboxing questions had lost her.

"The minute she mentioned that lynching she saw in Mississippi you started turning her off," Goodwin said.

"Nobody's perfect, Carl, unless maybe it's you. I know you'da done it exactly right."

"Nobody said that. The only trouble with you is you're *too* goddamn biased. You want the Klan to always be wrong, and they're not. It's just not that simple."

"When they lynch people, it's that simple."

"Jesus Christ, that's why you lost that girl, just when you had her eating out of your goddamn hand. She'da probably told you lots more."

"That's where you're wrong, Carl. She told me everything there was."

Goodwin shrugged and sighed and Tom, suddenly angry, said, "Listen, *you* take the goddamn pictures, *I'll* write the goddamn story." They glared at each other the rest of the afternoon.

In a small town in a valley, they attended a Klan meeting in a fundamentalist church. There wasn't a hood or a sheet in sight. "Who needs a mask when everybody in town belongs?" he said as they drove out of town. The head man seemed to be the preacher, a man named Jensen, who inflamed the crowd with his wailing cries of danger. He told them how the nigger was simply the forerunner of the real menace, the chaos that was coming when America turned away from God. The Church of Rome, with its Pope of the foreign tongue and its virgin goddess, would prove the ultimate threat to the valley and its way of life. The Church of Rome would never be satisfied until it had regained the power of its bloody medieval history, the power to write law and punish true Christians with its sword. The people burned a cross in the yard and wailed passionately as other speakers took on the Jews and the communists. Goodwin and Tom didn't talk much the morning after. Once Tom asked if Goodwin still considered the assignment a farce. "Biggest goddamn crock I ever covered," Goodwin said. Tom looked at him for a while. "Then tell me one thing," he said. "What if there's an election tomorrow? Say these people had a clear-cut choice between some guy running on the Constitution and the Bill of Rights, or some goddamn madman trying to be a dictator. Who do you think they'd vote for?"

Goodwin just grunted.

Now they drifted with the wind, going far back to tiny hill towns that weren't on any map. The zigzag course took them northwest, toward Grand Junction and their date with the national Klan. They walked unpaved streets and talked their way across the western slope. In

Canon City they met a gas station manager, a Kleagle by night who bragged, even after they had identified themselves, that he had the town locked up, had signed up most of the white personnel at the state penitentiary. A minister in Salida preached the gospel on Sunday and on Monday helped burn a cross on a Catholic family's lawn. In one little town, Tom interviewed the mayor, who had a framed picture of John Galen Locke on a table behind his desk. When he saw Tom looking at the picture, he coughed and cleared his throat. "My brother-in-law," he said, turning the picture down.

They arrived in Grand Junction two days early. Tom checked them into the Timberline Hotel downtown and they had their first hot baths and uninterrupted sleep since Pueblo. That night Tom brought out the bottle and they drank through the dinner hour. The next morning he left Goodwin sleeping and set out walking across town. He took up a position in the lobby of the Grand Hotel, settling back with a newspaper over his face and waiting for something to happen.

Two hours later, John Galen Locke entered the lobby and checked in. Locke was carrying a heavy, tantalizing briefcase. He made his own way upstairs. Tom sat still, watching the floor indicator. When it stopped, he got up and moved toward the front desk. But he froze at once, dropped into another chair and held the paper up to eye level. Just coming in through the front door, looking uneasily from side to side, was Marvel Millette.

3

She stood in the shadows near a magazine rack and pretended to be interested in the new *Collier's*, hiding her face behind the huge book as Tom hid his behind the newspaper. Tom sat absolutely still, remembering to turn a page occasionally, but carefully, without closing the paper and leaving his face exposed. In a while Marvel put down the magazine, obviously satisfied that Locke had gone up, and made her way to the desk. She spoke briefly to the desk clerk, a sleepy man with a walrus moustache. She handed the man a bill and went up the stairs. Tom abandoned his plan to bribe the clerk and instead approached the desk as a potential customer. "I'd like a room on the third floor," he said.

"Third floor's mighty popular. This is the last room." He handed over a key and took Tom's money.

"Yeah, I know," Tom said. "That's my party. Anybody from there get around to renting a conference room yet?"

"Mr. Lowell from Omaha did that yesterday."

"Good. I hope it's a good room. You know, private."

"It's private, all right. It's the mezz room. You know—mezzanine. It's built right into the middle of the hotel, between the second and third floors. No windows, just one door, one set of stairs leading down to it from the end of the third-floor hall. That private enough?"

"It'll do. Can I look at your register, see who's here?"

"Be my guest, pal."

He flipped the register around and scanned the names on the third floor. The clerk got a call, and while he was away Tom made notes from the register. One man had put Cheyenne as his hometown, another Seattle, another Indianapolis. There was no one from Georgia, or from any state in the deep South.

The man from Omaha was actually from Texas: Hiram Wesley Evans, the Imperial Wizard designate himself. Tom sat in a café across the street and watched as Evans and Locke came out at noon and stalked off together, seeking a restaurant. He waited, but Marvel didn't show, and soon he decided to risk walking over and casing the hotel layout. He took the elevator to the third floor, checked into his room, then walked down the hall to the stairwell at the end. He started down, and came to a landing between floors, where a dark hall branched away, leading into the center of the building. The hall dead-ended at a locked door. He returned to his room for another look around. It was a plain chamber, once elegant but falling into disrepair. The ceiling was broken by a small trapdoor, which he guessed went up into the heating system. Just outside the window was an iron fire escape. There was nothing in the room high enough to enable him to reach the trapdoor, so he returned to the lobby, moving carefully. The lobby, a contrast to the morning rush, was almost deserted. When he saw that the lobby was deserted, he hurried across it, moved to the far end, and pushed through a door marked EMPLOYEES ONLY.

He was in a dark utility room. The walls were bare cement, covered with gray paint. At the end, a set of iron steps went down into a basement. He went down into another storeroom of sorts. Huge cartons of food and miscellaneous property were stacked about. He walked through it and entered the boiler room, where the antiquated furnace squatted, breathing steam. Beyond, but in the same room, was a work area for the maintenance man.

A long workbench dominated the area, its tools neatly stacked in their places. Just beyond that, an iron ladder led straight up to a trapdoor in the ceiling. In the top drawer of the workbench he found a flashlight. Slipping it in a back pocket, he began to climb.

He climbed in total darkness, feeling his way with his hands while the light created a hard lump against his backside. He came to a break and a maze of pipes, branching off in all directions. One of them leaked steam. Now he used the light. He was standing on the iron ladder, at third-floor level, he guessed. The crawlspace branched away, horizontally, in both directions, and he pulled himself off the ladder, crawling to the east, toward the mezzanine.

Soon he found that each room had its own door, each in the corner of the main room ceiling. He stopped at each room as he went, shining the light on the remains of numberless vigils by maintenance men through the years. Old candle wax, orange peelings, paper bags gave evidence that they had made a regular practice of sitting here, listening to people talk, laugh, drink, and screw in the rooms below. He squirmed ahead and came to another break. This one dipped down at a forty-five degree angle while the main passage continued ahead. He eased his body into the lower passage, squirming past the hot pipes that reached at him from all sides like monkeybars on a child's playground. Down he went as hot water soaked through his shirt and burned his back.

At the bottom he found the trapdoor and pulled it up. He was looking down into the Klan's conference room.

Now it was empty and dark. He played the light below him, and he could see a long conference table surrounded by chairs. He stuck the flashlight into his belt and lowered himself through the ceiling until he was hanging by his fingers. He let go and dropped onto a table about three feet below. He moved to the wall where the door was, where only a thin line of gray stood out against the black floor. He felt around until he found the light.

It was a plain room, with no closets or bathrooms. Near the far wall was a rack for hats and coats; near the head of the table, a blackboard. In front of each chair was a pad of paper and beside each pad a few sharpened pencils.

He took off his shoes and threw them up into the crawlspace. Then he brushed off the table and brushed his socks so they would leave no mark. He reached over from the table and turned out the light, stood, crouched, leaped up, and caught the rim with his fingers. Painfully, with great effort, he drew himself up into the hole.

4

When Tom returned to the Timberline, Goodwin had gone out. He retrieved his bag of burglar tools and hurried back to the Grand Hotel, slipping quietly into his room and preparing to go to work.

The small leather bag contained lockpicks, a jimmy, files, a vise, a screwdriver with interchangeable heads, a set of flat blades for prying without leaving marks, and a tube of graphite. In the bottom of the bag was a glass jar containing perhaps fifty key blanks, which would fit the commonest locks and needed only to be filed out.

He set up shop in the corner of his room, clamping the vise to the edge of a table and laying out his tools behind it. He waited until Locke and Evans came out for dinner, then he hurried inside, took a pair of identical key blanks from his bag and went down the hall to Locke's door. He sprayed the key with graphite and shoved it into the slot, turning it hard both ways until, when he removed it, he could see the faint teeth marks of the tumblers. He did the same thing at Evans' door. In his room he clamped the keys into the jaws of the vise and filed out the grooves with a sharp, triangular file. The key to Evans' room stuck, but Locke's opened at once. He finished off the Locke key, filing away the burrs, sanding it down and labeling it with a piece of tape. He cut deeper into Evans' key and tried again. It still didn't work.

He gave up for the moment and sat in the lobby, the newspaper covering his face. Locke and Evans didn't return, but thirty minutes later another man came in, flanked by two hard-looking bodyguards. The man signed himself in and went upstairs. Tom crossed the lobby and looked at the register. The signature said D.C. Stephenson of Indianapolis. Tom knew D.C. Stephenson as the Grand Dragon of Indiana. With all of Locke's plans about secrecy, Stephenson hadn't even bothered to change his name.

It fit with what he knew about the man. Ruthless and arrogant, Stephenson had an unquenchable thirst for power and for high political office. He was in a second-floor room at the far end of the hall. Tom thought the cast was now complete; Stephenson would be the last to arrive. He looked down his list, at Jones of Ohio and Smith from the coast, and wondered who they really were and where they had come from.

He didn't return to the Timberline that night. In the morning, two rough-looking men stationed themselves at the stairwell that led down to the mezzanine. Half an hour later they were joined by Stephenson's men, and the four of them stood talking. They all seemed to know each other. The laughter stopped as Hiram Wesley Evans arrived. The men split up, one from each group remaining at the head of the stairs while the others went down with Evans and posted themselves at the conference room door. At exactly two minutes past nine Locke appeared, walking briskly to the stairwell and disappearing down it. Other footsteps came quickly in Locke's wake. By nine-fifteen the hall was quiet again. Tom slipped out and took the iron stairs to the basement, and climbed the ladder into the

156

crawlspace. He had fashioned a head harness for the flashlight, and now he wore it, miner-style. He reached the split and wedged himself down through the pipes. He burned his hands and scalded his cheek, but he didn't hurry. His moves had to be slow and precise, and above all, quiet. He eased into position above the trapdoor and listened. Steam seeped into him as he reached into his coat and took out his notebook, placing it on the floor just below his eyes.

The room below was ominously quiet. He was beginning to worry when suddenly Locke said, "Gentlemen, shall we begin?" Tom wrote it down. Already his pad was soggy and steam rolled off his brow. Another voice, softer but more authoritative, said, "We wait for Steve." He wrote that down, guessing that the speaker had been Evans. A third voice said, "Well, where the hell is he? He's got a helluva nerve, keeping us waiting like this." And Evans said, "That's Steve for you." Then came the sound of a chair scraping as Evans got up and went to the door. "You there," he said to one of the guards, "where is Mr. Stephenson?" The guard muttered something and Evans came back to the table. Tom hugged his notebook against his shirt to protect it, but soon his shirt too was soaked through, and the little pocket where he crouched was filling with steam.

Stephenson arrived about ten minutes later. The loud man had been in the midst of a loud rebuke when suddenly the door opened and everything went quiet. Stephenson went to the far head of the table and said, "Gentlemen, I must apologize for my tardiness. The President of the United States kept me unduly long, talking matters of state by telephone." Tom wrote down the words exactly. Another hush had spread across the room. Stephenson's entrance had produced precisely the right effect, upstaging Evans and stealing his thunder. Tom wrote down his impression to that effect. The paper shredded and came apart as he turned the page.

He wished then that he could see as well as hear. He would probably see Evans going red under Stephenson's unrelenting eyes. From what he knew of Evans, he wasn't a man to be pushed. None of them were. Stephenson sat, taking the lead from Locke with identical words. "Gentlemen, shall we begin?"

Evans began with an assessment of Klan strength, giving first the national picture, then the situation by regions. He put Indiana last, a deliberate slap at Stephenson, letting everyone know that, after all, Indiana was just one state and not a very important one at that. Stephenson said nothing. Evans talked on, filling the room with figures and statistics. Tom copied as much as he could, but Evans spoke quickly when he knew his material, and some of it got past him. Evans was talking regionally again, but narrowing even that scope down, getting into states and asking for elaboration from the Dragons who lived there. Tom copied their names and got what he could of what they said. By then his notebook was in tatters and his back was blistering from the steam. He came up for air.

He stayed up longer than he wanted to, and when he finally crawled back into his hole, Evans and Stephenson were arguing. Evans was emphasizing the need for calm. If there must be violence, the Klan mustn't be connected to it except, perhaps, by rumor. There must be no more lynchings like California and Louisiana until after the national elections. Terrorist tactics had their place, but not now. Locke agreed. Why bomb Catholic churches if it made their priests martyrs? Why create any sentiment that worked to the advantage of the Jews, Catholics, or niggers? Their job now was to stoke the public distrust that already existed toward minorities, to isolate the majority and draw strength from it. Evans said the only time violence might work was if it could be laid to the communists and not on the Klan's head. And he was having trouble in the South, keeping people in line.

"We're not having any trouble in Indiana," Stephenson said.

"There've been national reports of night-riding in Indiana," Evans said. "Here—here's a *New York Times* article that ran just last week." Evans shuffled through some papers and read the clipping aloud. It told of public floggings and tar-and-feather parties on the plains, near a tree that had been used in frontier days for hangings.

Stephenson laughed. "Well, what of it? You think I care what some idiot in New York writes?"

"That's just the point, Steve. You'd better care, if this movement is to go anywhere nationally."

"You're getting old," Stephenson said.

"That may be," Evans said, his temper flaring. "But when I'm running this organization, the Indiana branch will goddamn well do as I say."

Again Locke played statesman. "What do you say, gentlemen, to a break and some liquid refreshment? In my room?"

Chairs creaked and the room emptied into the stairwell. Tom crawled out into the upper shaft. He was drenched with sweat and the skin along his spine was raw from his assbone to his shoulder blades.

The argument resumed about twenty minutes later and ran through the morning. Evans remained passive, Stephenson militant, with Locke skillfully walking a tightrope between them. Frequently Evans' voice grew heavy with warning. "I will put you on notice, then," he said at one point. "If I see any more reports in the national press regarding overt violence in Indiana, I'll take the appropriate steps to have you removed from the Klan." Stephenson, brash and sure of himself, said, "What steps? And what's your definition of violence?" Evans, still bristling, said, "You know damn well what steps, and if you don't know what violence is, look it up in the dictionary."

"Gentlemen, gentlemen, this isn't getting us anywhere," Locke said. "Steve, I think we all know what Hiram is talking about. Some of the troops get a little too enthusiastic sometimes, that's all. What we're talking about here is overt lawbreaking, and the need to keep them reined in tighter until next year. There's a big risk; a lot is at stake."

"In Indiana there's no risk. In Indiana *I'm* the law."

"All right," Locke said slowly. "I know how you mean that."

"I mean it just the way I say it."

"All right. And I feel the same about Colorado, but at the same time I know what Hiram's saying. There's a bigger objective here than any single state can handle."

"But one rebellious state can derail the whole train," Evans said.

"It doesn't mean we can't harass and agitate and scare the hell out of them," Locke said. "I'm all for that. I think we do that as well here as anywhere."

"You need to come down south," Evans said, and everyone laughed.

"Listen, let me tell you about Colorado," Locke said. His voice became laced with excitement as the emphasis of the meeting shifted. "Right now I have Denver locked up. The mayor is in my hands; so are several key members of city council. Next spring, after the mayor's been in a year, I'll dictate selection of a new police chief. But Denver alone isn't enough. Now we're going after the whole state. Next fall we'll run candidates for every state office. I expect to win without a warm-up. We'll run Judge Clarence Morley for governor, and we'll have candidates for lieutenant governor, the supreme court, state auditor, secretary of state, and attorney general. We'll get control of the state House of Representatives and we'll make some good inroads into the Senate. A candidate from the Klan Auxiliary will run for superintendent of instruction. We will place people on the university board of regents. I expect to win most, if not all, of these races. Control of the state house will enable us to pass laws barring ethnic outsiders from entering the state. If we're successful in this, the national implications are enormous. If we can do it, other states can, and we can quite literally run the goddamn niggers back to Africa."

A cheer went up. Locke said, "The chief of police will play an important part in our Denver plan. We will make Denver an unpleasant place for unpleasant people, gentlemen, I assure you of that. Laws on vagrancy and loitering will be tightened, and the state militia will be placed at our command. The governor will dissolve all state licensing boards and get each of these licensed trades under control of one person. One of our people, gentlemen. Then we can decide who may and may not practice his trade in our state. With control of the regents, we can squeeze undesirables out of the university. If that doesn't work, we can go through the state house and cut off the university's flow of money. We are truly on the verge of becoming a major power in this nation. This afternoon I'll show you my membership list for Colorado. You'll be amazed at the powerful heads of government who have joined us, and the thing I'm stressing to you, Steve, is that we've accomplished most of it in just over a year. We've locked up Denver and are about to grab the whole pie, and all without any atrocities that can be laid on our doorstep. The people here look on us as benevolent big brothers, protectors of their homes and lives and their women."

"Which is exactly right," Evans said.

There was a murmur of agreement around the room. After a moment, Stephenson said, "I don't quarrel with that. I think we've done at least as well in Indiana as you've done here. Or any of you anywhere. What I'm telling you is that I will not be dictated to on the affairs of my own state. We'll continue to handle our own problems in our own way, and if you, Hiram, are telling me to disband the Horse Thief Detectives, I'd advise you to forget it and let me handle my own problems."

Evans shouted something and pounded the table with his fist. Again Locke stepped between them, suggesting that the talks resume after lunch. He had made reservations for all at the city's best restaurant. Chairs scraped and people shuffled out. Tom pulled himself out of his sweatbox, feeling lightheaded and faint. He needed a salt tablet, but there was no time. He had ninety minutes, perhaps two hours at the outside, and the real work was just beginning.

5

In the lobby he grabbed a telephone and had an operator connect him with Goodwin's room at the Timberline. "Jesus Christ!" Goodwin shouted. "Where the hell have you been?"

"Never mind that now; just get over to the Grand Hotel on the double. Bring your best cameras for closeup work. Documents and stuff, and plenty of film. You'll probably need a tripod. Come up to the third floor and meet me in Room 312. The door'll be unlocked and I'll be waiting there for you."

He went quickly to Locke's room and let himself in. It was a plain room, exactly like his. He crossed the room to the closet and in five minutes picked that lock open. Pushed into a corner of the closet was the fat briefcase.

He took out the briefcase and put it face-up on the bed. It too was locked, but the lock was flimsy and he picked it open in a minute. Inside were sheaths of papers, hundreds of letters and files and reports. All were original copies, sealed and stamped with the red insignia of the Ku Klux Klan. He began leafing through them with his fingers, and suddenly he knew he had found it all.

With Locke's files as a resource, a reporter could write stories for five years and still not hit bottom. One paper outlined the internal structure of the Colorado Klan; below it, a thick file contained the state membership lists. The most powerful business and political leaders in the state were Klansmen. It was what the press had always known in general terms. Now he began to see who they were.

Cops he had known for years.

A cyclops in the Chamber of Commerce.

Kleagles at City Hall.

And money. Christ, money beyond belief. That came next, the money report. At ten dollars for each new member, the Klan was hauling in the money with a rake. Three dollars of the ten went to the recruiting Kleagle. A King Kleagle, who ran the recruiting effort for the entire state, got one dollar for every member in his realm. A Grand Goblin, in charge of one of the Klan's nine national regions, got fifty cents for every member in the domain. The rest of the money was split between state and national headquarters.

The business angle. It would make an entire series by itself. The big business world of the Ku Klux Klan.

He wondered how much tax they were paying, and that was another angle. If he couldn't get the bastards with a frontal attack, maybe they were vulnerable on tax evasion.

He heard footsteps in the hall, and a moment later Goodwin came in. Tom closed and locked the door, then motioned toward the open briefcase. "Set up to shoot those papers, on the double."

Goodwin's eyes opened wide. "All of them?"

"As many as we can shoot in an hour, just as fast as you can pull the trigger."

Goodwin set up his tripod near the window. He opened the shade all the way and turned on the overhead light. Tom froze as footsteps approached in the hall. They stopped just outside the door. He heard a thump and a faint rustle of paper. Goodwin's eyes were wide. Tom held his fingers to his lips and crossed the room to the door. A moment later another set of footsteps came along the hall. Even before they reached the door, an angry exchange of words filled the hallway.

"Well, where the hell have you been?"

"Now, Nate, don't start on me. I told you, I'm sick of being ordered around."

"You were supposed to *be* here. Goddammit, if I can't trust you to do something right . . ."

"I just slipped away for a sandwich. And a piss poor one at that. We sit here in a dark hallway eating tunafish while they're across town having prime rib."

"All right, never mind. You just keep an eye on that door, like Mr. Locke says. I'll be back later."

Tom waited until the footsteps had died away, then he crossed to the window where Goodwin, pale and shaky, stood watching. Tom held his fingers to his lips. "One of them's still outside," he whispered.

Goodwin swallowed. "How do we get out, then?"

"Leave that to me." He passed over the roster of Klan members. "Start shooting," he said. "This first."

They moved with the speed and precision of assembly-line workers in an auto plant. Tom rifled the files, picked out what he wanted, took off the clips that bound them, and passed the individual sheets to Goodwin. The camera clicked incessantly, pausing only when Goodwin reloaded the film. They went through the file in a hopscotch fashion, passing over good material to get to better, because there was no way they could get it all. While they worked, Tom watched the clock.

Thirty minutes had passed since Locke and his friends had gone to lunch. They were into the financial statements now, a report that detailed everything the Colorado Klan had taken in since 1920. It ran more than fifty pages, showing the individual names of large contributors. Goodwin's camera clicked monotonously, and the shutter sounded like shots on a rifle range. Tom's nerves wound tighter with the ticking of the clock, but the lure of pages not yet uncovered drew him on. He was cutting it thin and he knew it. "Just a few more pages, then we go," he said. But then he came to a file on Colorado's relations with the national Klan in Atlanta. It was fifty pages of small type, with handwritten notes by Locke in the margin, and a look inside showed strife, differences in philosophy, and deep-rooted bitterness. He knew he had to have it. By the end of two hours, his

162

instinct was almost screaming at him. "That's it, Carl," he said in a whisper. "Pack in your gear, we're folding up shop."

Goodwin began dismantling his tripod. Tom replaced the papers neatly in Locke's briefcase, snapped the latch and returned it exactly as it had been in the closet. In the hall he heard a faint, familiar click, the sound of the elevator door. He motioned to the trapdoor in the ceiling and made a cup of his hands. Goodwin stepped up close, just as the sound of many men came toward them in the hall. Tom boosted him up and Goodwin pushed open the trapdoor, reaching inside the lip and putting his camera inside first. With Tom pushing from the rear, he writhed up into the black hole.

Voices drifted in to them. The men had stopped and someone outside was talking. A voice telling a nigger-with-a-big-cock joke sent everyone into hysterics. The laughter died and there were more shuffling footsteps. A key scraped against the lock.

Tom had remade the bed, pulled the shade and turned off the overhead light, and above him Goodwin had struggled into a kneeling position over the trapdoor. He reached his arm down and Tom leaped up from the floor, catching Goodwin by the wrist. The key turned and the door opened, and there stood John Galen Locke, not twenty feet away, just turning to speak with someone in the hall while Tom twisted in the air behind him. Tom strained at Goodwin's arm, gripping his shirt, tearing it, struggling upward. His pencil dropped to the floor as his head came into the hole, then his shoulders. He got his elbows under him and braced against both sides. Kicking his feet like a swimmer, he squirted up into the dark.

Total darkness closed in around them.

They heard Locke come into the room.

"This pencil wasn't here when I left. Who's been in here, Nate?"

"Nobody, Mr. Locke. Honest to God, sir, nobody's come in or out the whole time."

"Somebody was watching that door all the time?"

"Yes sir, Mr. Locke. Just like you said."

"Then where'd this pencil come from?" There was a long pause. Locke said, "Nate, do you know where that trapdoor goes?"

"Probably up in the heating system."

"Go down and ask the manager. Tell him to call me on the phone and let me know."

Tom tugged at Goodwin's shirt. Carefully he climbed up the inclined crawlspace, counting the doors as he went. When he had found the one he wanted, he lifted the door, hung from the lip, and dropped onto his bed. Goodwin handed down the camera, then the tripod, then the bag—that precious leather pouch containing the exposed film. With a sigh, Goodwin struggled through the hole and dropped into the room. They waited near the door, breathing hard and not talking until they heard the man Nate come past with the manager and the house dick.

"Let's get out of here."

They walked to the stairs and down. Twenty minutes later they were back at the Timberline, still breathing hard. Goodwin, with hands that were just beginning to shake, broke out the bottle for their first drink of the long night.

6

At dusk Goodwin turned their bathroom into a crude darkroom and developed one roll of film. Tom came in and held the negative up to the light. "Beautiful, Carl, just lovely," he said. He said a silent prayer of thanks that Tammen had made him bring a photog. "Man, look at that. I can even read the names on the negatives." He took out one of Tammen's twenties. "Tonight we eat and drink on the *Post*, my friend. And tomorrow we head for Denver."

They locked the film in Goodwin's suitcase, stashed it in a closet, and covered the suitcase with a blanket. Driving across town, Tom said, "The thing that really makes this sweet is how we've put the screws to this dame from the *News*. Did I tell you she's here?"

"Nobody tells me anything," Goodwin said. "I'm just the hired help around here."

"I saw her that first day in the lobby, haven't seen her since. I wonder if she went home." He settled back and closed his eyes, sipping gin from his flask and feeling self-satisfied. "God Jesus, Carl, I'd give ten bucks to be in the *News* city room when our first piece breaks. It'll be incredible, the look on her face. She'll never be the same again."

"I'll still believe it when I see it," Goodwin said. "Christ, I don't even know what this goddamn story *is* yet. I still don't know what the hell I was shooting today."

"The most important stuff you'll ever shoot."

"That's what they all say. Tommy, you sound like some punk kid right out of J-school."

"That's just how I feel."

He took a long slug on his flask, draining it. "Carl, those documents you shot are gonna run the Ku Kluxers right out of our town."

Goodwin just grunted.

Hours later, stuffed with good food and more than a little drink, they parted company in one of the town's hotter nightspots. Goodwin spotted a photog he knew from Wichita days, and they huddled in a corner, talking shop. Tom drifted across the street to a restaurant and went upstairs, where a speakeasy occupied most of the second floor. He sat alone and drank, savoring the day, wanting to keep the feeling it gave him. He had taken control of his life again, and no sad thought must cross his mind. Nell. The boys. Her old man. Alice. Georgeann. Abe and Julia. Anna. Ethan. Everything pushed back for his burst of positive energy. Tonight, he thought, I could solve the problems of a nation.

Unwritten passages leaped through his mind, whole and powerful. He let them go, positive that he'd be able to recall them at will. The stories were already there and alive, in some journalistic vat— complete, whole beings, waiting to be drained onto his paper. It would flow like rich red wine: flow and flow and never stop. Written with the power it deserved, done as well as he could write it, it might well win the Pulitzer Prize.

Glory and power. It had been so long that he'd almost forgotten the feeling. Images of red ink, of 72-point type spread over an eight-column page. His by-line the only thing people would see. The people who counted with him. Tammen, Marvel, and that wiseass, Barney Gallagher. Reporters. His goddamn peers.

And under it, a sample page from the Locke files, the most telling of the membership pages, blown up and reproduced in detail, Klan insignia and all. He would have to talk with Alice about the possibility of having the Klan insignia reproduced for page one, in that off-red ink that Locke used. As Tammen would say, it would make one hell of a page.

He picked up a hooker in the speakeasy, and it seemed like the easiest thing he had ever done. Dawn hadn't yet broken the eastern sky when he picked his way across town to the Timberline. He came up the elevator and stopped outside his door, groping through his pocket for the key. He pushed open the door, closed it behind him, and leaned back on it, feeling the first wave of hangover chills and headache. Something moved in the pitch darkness, just beyond his vision, and he stood up against the door. "Carl? That you?" He felt along the wall for a light, found it, flipped the switch, and nothing happened. He was alert now, peering ahead, listening. The sound came closer, took shape before him and moved out of Goodwin's room toward the window. Then, so fast that he hardly knew what had happened, she threw up the window and stepped out onto the fire escape.

Marvel.

He saw her for just a second in the moonlight, and the heavy cloth bag she held made his terror run deep. The bitch had their pictures.

By the time he got out on the fire escape landing, she was a full level below him, banging down the iron steps with tiny, precise movements. He took half the landing at once, twisting his ankle on a missed step, falling and hitting the bottom on his elbows. The ladder rolled down under her weight, landing her gently on the ground. It jerked up with a clatter as she stepped off, and he hobbled down the steps and gripped the rungs and started down. She had cleared the alley and he had one brief glimpse of her, far across the street. She had ducked into a park, heavily overgrown with trees and bushes. She had disappeared when he came limping out of the alley, but he hurried across the street, his eyes scanning the entire length of the park. Pain had all but immobilized him, but panic drove him on. At this point she would think only of hiding, not running. She had no way of knowing how badly he had sprained his ankle, and would never try to outrun him if he had two good legs under him. So he moved carefully, peeling back the layers of branches and trying like a good bird dog not to flush her out until he was close enough to pick her off.

He saw her. Her round white face was there before him, peering out of a grove about twenty yards ahead. She disappeared into the underbrush as he plunged in after her. He circled the grove and picked her up as she broke out on the other side. From there it was a straight dash to the street. She beat him to it by thirty yards, burst out of the garden path, and ran into the arms of a patroling cop.

What happened then would always be somewhat hazy in his later attempts to recall it. She seemed to swoon in the cop's arms. He heard the words *masher* and *rape*, and the cop came at him, dropping her there on the grass. He remembered the cop's beefy pug face, the gravel sound of the voice as the cop said, "That's as far as you go, mister," and his own weak voice saying, "Sure, officer . . . whatever you say." He must have swung from the hip. The cop's head snapped back and he dropped without a whimper, sprawled flat on the sidewalk. Tom stepped over the body and faced Marvel Millette across the street.

"Now you know," he said, trying not to let his ankle show as he stepped into the street toward her. "I'm not playing games with you. I'll have that bag if I've got to take it off your dead body."

"Sure," she said. "I've had enough."

She started across toward him, waited for a milk truck to pass, and when the truck had passed she was gone with it. He ran full-tilt behind it, yelling for the driver to stop while Marvel hung on the running board, screaming for him to open the throttle. The truck lagged for a moment, as if the driver couldn't decide, and Tom closed on it with each jump. His fingers touched the back door handles and he twisted one and got it open. "I said open it up!" Marvel shouted. "Move it or I'll crawl in there and scratch your eyes out!" The truck surged ahead as Tom made a last desperate try, leaping at the flapping rear door. He went on his face in the dirt. His breakfast was a mix of truck fumes and dust. For dessert he had the sour bile of defeat.

Back at the Timberline, he began going through the town's hotels, calling each one in the chance that she had used her own name. He found her on the fifth try, in a small place he knew about six blocks away. She was just checking out and came on at once. "Mr. Hastings, I presume?"

"I'll kill you with my bare hands."

"It's good to see you haven't lost your spirit, Mr. Hastings. Even though you are slowing down in your old age. I expected your call five minutes ago."

"Oh, you bloody little bitch."

"Actually, I do sympathize with you. I know how it feels, but what can I do now? We do what we have to in this business, isn't that right? You should know that better than anybody, Mr. Hastings. Honestly, if I could share it with you, I would. Of course that's out of the question."

"Of course."

"Well, then, was there something else?"

He slammed down the telephone and ran the whole six blocks to her hotel. He pulled up lame as he came into the lobby. The clerk told him he had missed her by no more than two minutes.

She had left alone, in a taxi, and that told him something too. He called the depot and learned that the next train for Denver would leave at nine-thirty. Then he got a change of clothes, showered, and set off across town to see if he might spot her by chance. He was limping badly.

By eight forty-five he had given up the aimless search and had settled in a corner of the depot to wait. She came in thirty minutes later, looking crisp and fresh and carrying only a small overnight bag. She had, of course, mailed the film to herself in Denver. She went to the ticket booth and bought passage to Denver, then moved out onto the platform to wait. He bought a ticket, then called the Timberline to leave word for Goodwin, who still hadn't returned from the long night.

The train came in from Salt Lake City. Tom followed her into a compartment near the end of the train and sat in a corner, watching her. Her eyes were fixed on the gliding white expanse outside the frosty window. When the train stopped, a young man in a business suit tried to sit beside her, but she told him the seat was taken.

In a while Tom swallowed his pride and hobbled up the aisle. She heard him coming and she gathered up her bag and put it under her feet, making room for him. He sank down and stared at the back of the next seat.

"That's better, love," she said. Her smile was brilliant.

7

"All right," he said. "We've got it established now, how incredibly clever you are. We've got a definitive ruling on that. Now, where's my film?"

She sighed. "Come on, Mr. Hastings, I did hope you'd be an improvement over this dreary landscape."

"Miss, I'm through playing games. I want that film."

"I'm sure you do. There must be some goodies on it."

He stared at the seat, wondering what on earth would move her.

"What have I got to do to get that film away from you?"

"How can I answer that until I've had it developed and see what's on it? It might not be of any use to me at all. In which case I'll return it at once, with my apologies for your trouble."

"You don't believe that."

"What, that it'll be no good? Ah . . . no." She smiled again, cool and without mercy.

He turned it over in his mind and came up blank.

"So," she said suddenly, "let's change the subject, okay? I've been meaning to call you ever since that Press Club thing."

"What for?"

"Thought I'd invite you to lunch sometime. I wanted to apologize for some of the things I said, the way I acted in general. I know you thought I was being bitchy and superior, but I really wasn't."

"It just never occurred to you that I might have lost my stuff."

"I wouldn't put it that way. Naturally, since then I've heard a few things."

"I'm sure you have."

168

"Talk doesn't mean anything. The only thing that matters is what comes out on the street. Nothing people say can change that. So I went back and looked up your clips."

"And found what?" He was sorry at once. He knew full well what she had found.

Her eyes, which he now noticed were a light shade of brown, burned into his with a relentlessness he had seldom encountered in a woman. "In this business we're surrounded by whole waves of mediocrity, in our peers, in the editors who work around us, all the way to the top. It's hard to stay out of that."

"You missed your calling. You should have been a social worker."

"It doesn't necessarily mean you've lost your stuff. I don't think real talent ever dies, Mr. Hastings. It gets dull from lack of use, but it comes to a fine point again with very little honing. No sir, the man who wrote the Mary Wolfe piece doesn't just lose that touch. I bet you don't have any idea how good that was. I bet you never go back and reread your own clips."

He just looked at her. After a long while, he said, "I know how good it was."

"But there comes a time when you wonder why you try so hard, isn't that right? You can grind out third-rate stuff like all the other hacks around you, work a third as hard and they'll all be just as happy and resent you a hell of a lot less. They'll like you so much better if you play the game with them. The fact that it destroys you, makes you a non-entity like the rest of them, actually works to your advantage after a while. Because it takes a lot of effort to be good at something, doesn't it? I'm just twenty-six, but I've felt it."

"You're really sure of yourself, aren't you?"

"What, that I'm good? You're damned right I am. It's important to me."

"Why let it be, if nobody cares?"

"I care. It's what keeps me alive. That's why, after just a few months at the *News*, people call me a prima donna. That's when they're feeling nice. Some of the things they call me I couldn't put in a family newspaper. The thing nobody understands is that I'm not out to do anyone in. Even you, Mr. Hastings. You're just my competition for this one story, that's all. I really wish I knew a way we could both get it. You probably think I'm lying, but I really do feel a debt to you."

"Give me my film and consider the debt paid in full."

"You'll have to be more ingenious than that, my friend. What good would it do either of us if I just handed it back to you on a silver platter?"

"Wait a minute, are you telling me you're doing this for *my* sake?"

"No, but it might work out that way."

"Oh, brother."

"Look at it as part of the honing process we talked about earlier. You've had things your own way in this town for so long that you don't know what competition is. You underestimated me, played me for a pushover. Next time I'll expect a better fight. This time you lose, Mr. Hastings. But I predict bigger and better things for both of us ahead."

They ate lunch together in the train's diner. It was a sullen, quiet meal. He glared at her and after a while she gave up trying to talk. After lunch they took their seats, and he stretched out beside her, closed his eyes, and pretended to sleep. But his mind was alert and in turmoil. It was so easy for her to talk about the honing process; she had no earthly concept what this story meant to him. A dozen plans passed through his mind and he discarded them all.

Each stop brought him closer to professional disaster. By next week it would be all over town, how Marvel Millette had screwed Tom Hastings out of the story of the decade. People like Barney Gallagher would never, ever let him live that down. Gallagher would be laughing for months. Years. He looked within himself, at yet another possibility: the chance of writing something from his notes, from the Evans-Stephenson confrontation, from memory, from the one roll of film that Goodwin had developed. It would buy him some time until he could find a way of getting to her. Just now he couldn't imagine what that might be.

They were pulling into Golden. It was after ten. The train had been delayed on the passes, and now the distant lights of Denver shimmered in the snow. The train circled a ridge above his old house, and he saw that someone new was living there. It filled him with sadness and self-pity. Light shone up through their skylight like a beacon, and for a moment he felt like a man who had lost everything. Wife, children, job, friends. All gone. What was left were tinsel things. Booze, whores, and dead time without end.

He shook it off as the outskirts loomed outside his window. He could start over on everything tomorrow. He would call Nell, and he would begin to write. Maybe he'd call Fowler in New York, to talk over the chances of getting to this Marvel bitch. She was a cool one. She wouldn't be an easy mark, even for Fowler. The train clanged into Union Station and they got up without another word to each other. He watched from the door as she walked through the snow, under the electric WELCOME arch, and disappeared into the night.

The sign taunted him.

WELCOME, sucker. Welcome.

Welcome to Denver.

CHAPTER
SEVEN

1

David had hardly believed his good fortune when she answered his knock. No one was home and she couldn't let him in, but she would accompany him for a turn around the lake. Gabriel had gone to school and Teresa had taken Abe to a doctor in Denver. Abe had been doing poorly of late. His back was bothering him, and the ends of his legs were hurting where the saw had cut through bone. But when they were walking Anna was clearly enjoying herself, and the problems of everyone else seemed distant and trivial. Even his trouble with Jessie and her father seemed insignificant beside the pure joy he felt at being here and having her with him. He thought that this was a woman he would marry, if the obstacles could be cleared. They didn't talk much but their eyes met frequently, hers peering intently into his huge, dark face, then darting away to some carriage sloshing through the snow, to kids having a snowball fight, to other people walking past. It was the first time he had heard her laugh, and he laughed too, at the simple pleasure he felt in her pleasure. Near the west end of the lake he touched her shoulder, then withdrew his hand as if he had touched fire.

"I was wondering. Could I call you Anna?"

"If you wish."

"Would you call me David?"

She shook her head. "Mr. Waldo seems more proper."

"Not to me."

"Say it's more comfortable, then. I'm comfortable with that."

"Then let's leave it that way for now."

They walked up past St. Anthony's Hospital. Nearing Osceola Street, he took her arm again, determined not to lose her just yet. He propelled her past Osceola and into the next block. "Let me buy you something out of your father's store." The money from the second payment on Benny Wassermann's book lay heavy in his pocket. She laughed and refused to take him seriously until suddenly they were there. The store was doing a brisk business and the whole family was manning the counter. Sammy and Teresa were filling orders from grocery lists, while Abe, back from the doctor, sat at the cash box in his wheelchair, taking money. Even Gabriel, home from school, was running deliveries and helping the ladies with their larger bundles.

Inside, Anna seemed embarrassed and uneasy. Several of the ladies waiting near the counter looked at her and Teresa came up from the rear of the store. Anna introduced them. "Mr. Waldo came by to see Abe, but he wasn't there, so I took a turn around the lake with him. It's such a lovely, cold day."

Teresa nodded. "Well, Mr. Waldo, we meet at last. I've heard a lot about you."

"In a neighborhood like this, it would surprise me if you hadn't."

"Meaning that you've heard about me too," she said. "People gossip too much around here. Is that what you're trying to say, Mr. Waldo?"

"That's pretty close. Sometimes it's hard not to get drawn into that yourself, and to remember that you can't believe everything you hear."

"Exactly." Teresa offered her hand and David took it, holding it gently for a moment. She looked at Abe, who was busy and couldn't hear them. "You've added something to his life and I thank you for that."

"He's added something to mine, too."

"How nice of you to say that. Someday I'll have to get over to one of those meetings, see exactly what it is that you discuss so heatedly."

"I hope you will."

172

"After all," she said, trying to smile and not quite making it, "both Anna and Abe are pretty impressionable still."

"Honestly, Mother!" Anna pouted, and a flash of schoolgirl beauty came over her. He could almost see the virgin creature she had been, ten years ago and more. He wondered if she could still be virgin, and his eyes shifted abruptly to her face. Her icy composure was returning by degrees, but quickly, giving her only a moment's vulnerability. But he thought then that, yes, she might well be a virgin, even at thirty, even in this day and age. He hoped not.

David and Teresa exchanged good-byes and he moved down the counter toward the door. "I wanted to buy you something, remember?" Abe pointed to the johnnycake jar. "I couldn't possibly," Anna said, shaking her head. But David bought two and she nibbled hers as they moved toward the door. He held the door and she moved out into the street, just as Sammy's voice called out to him from the rear of the store. "Would you wait for me?" he said. "Your father's calling me."

He went back between the shelves. Sammy looked down at him from the sliding ladder. "You're taking Anna home now?"

"Yes, sir."

"That's good. I think the time has come for us to talk about this. Don't you, Mr. Waldo?"

"Any time you say, sir."

"Could you stop over tonight, after I close up? Say nine o'clock."

"I'll be here."

Sammy turned and went back to his work. As David came out into the street, Anna said, "Well, can you tell me about it, or is it some male secret?"

"He wants to talk to me."

"I guess that's not surprising. Just don't let him bully you, Mr. Waldo."

Her words surprised and excited him. They seemed to imply an intimacy that hadn't been there before. "Is there something for him to bully me about?"

"He may think so," she said in that flat, cool way.

She allowed him to escort her across, and they had just reached Osceola Street when the police car came. David saw it first, easing past them, and the sight of Moran in the front seat frightened him now as it never had before. There was a driver and at least one other cop in back. The car moved slowly ahead and stopped on the street just outside the Kohls' front gate.

"Police," Anna said. She had never had any contact with police. "Do you know them, Mr. Waldo?"

"Yes, I know them."

"What on earth could they want at our house?"

He didn't answer her, not immediately. For perhaps thirty seconds his mind went totally blank, even while his feet carried him up the street toward the parked car. The door opened and Moran got out. He came around to the front gate and stood there, flanked by others.

David knew then what was to happen, and that he had only a few minutes to prepare her for it. "Anna, please listen to me and believe what I say. These men are trouble, Anna. The one in the middle is a very, very bad man. Whatever happens here, I need you to remember that. Forget about his uniform, and forget that he's supposed to represent law and order. He and I have been enemies for a long time."

They drew near now, within earshot, and he risked a final look at her, to see what effect his words had had. Her face had gone pale and her eyes were wide with fright. He touched her arm. "Don't worry, they won't hurt you. Just remember what I said, and let me tell you about it later. Would you do that? Anna?"

She didn't answer; didn't even nod. She followed him to the gate like a sleepwalker. He hoped she would go inside, but she waited with him while Moran came toward them. One of the cops had pushed back his coat, revealing a gun and a club. Her eyes were fixed on the gun.

"Put your hands against the car, Waldo," Moran said.

He knew an argument would only make matters worse. He turned and spread his hands against the car, suffering the humiliation of the search while she watched. He heard her ask what he had done, but no one bothered to tell her. "I haven't done anything," he said over his shoulder. One of the cops gripped him roughly by his coat and spun him around, frisking him down the front. He wished she would look at him. When she didn't, he said, "Anna, just remember what I told you. This is an old story between Mr. Moran and myself, and that's all there is to it."

Moran stepped up and brought out a set of brass handcuffs. "We'll see about that."

"Come on, Moran, you don't need those. I told you I'd go with you."

But Moran jerked his arms behind him and snapped the lock over one wrist. And suddenly, for a brief moment, David Waldo fought back. He was not a man of temper, but in that moment rage blotted out the last trace of reason. He pulled his hands free and the loose, swinging handcuffs struck Moran across the face. Moran stepped back, stunned. He slipped on the ice and went down to his knees. He was up at once, charging like a maddened bull. He swung at David with his fist, slipped and went down again, this time flat on his back. By then the other two had their billies drawn. David threw up his arms in a gesture of surrender, but one of the clubs cracked down on

174

his head and he fell to his knees. Moran, struggling to his feet, came at him again. He had the face of a madman. "Let me have the son of a bitch," he said. The two cops held David's arms behind him while Moran took one of the clubs and beat it back and forth across his face. Blood dripped into the snow. The sight of it brought Anna out of her shell. "Stop it!" she screamed. "You, stop that!" He saw her vaguely, clutching at Moran's neck. Her voice was the last thing he heard.

He saw bars. He was in a small holding cell, about eight feet square, that looked into a courtyard behind the jail. His head throbbed and his nose had crusted over. Dried blood was everywhere: in his hair, down the front of his coat. His face was black with it. His eye was swollen and his left ear was draining. He touched the stuff draining out of his ear and it looked pink, like pus mixed with blood. All he could hear on that side was a loud whistle.

Moran came in. Even in the dim half-light, David could see the red mark across Moran's face where the handcuffs had struck him. He hoped it hurt like hell. But Moran smiled as he came close. "I've been waiting a long time for you to do something stupid like that, Waldo. And now you have."

David sat up and held his head.

"They say misery loves company, Waldo. If that's true, you'll be happy to know you're just the first of many."

"What's that supposed to mean?"

"It means we're going to run you goddamn communists out of town, Waldo."

"I've told you befor I'm not a communist."

"Communist, anarchist, Marxist, red pig. You bastards have a dozen ways of disguising what you really are, don't you?" Moran came around to the cell door, where a beam of red sunlight hit him from the window. "I thought you'd be interested in knowing what's going to happen to you, so I stuck around to fill you in."

"You're too kind, Moran."

"Tomorrow you'll be taken before Judge Thurman Hayes. Do you know the judge?"

David just looked at him.

"He's a friend of mine. You might say a fraternal brother. He has the same interest in good government that I have. The same concerns too. He's especially interested in stemming the Red influence."

"I need a doctor. One of you broke my ear."

"Maybe you'll think twice before you go at a policeman again, Waldo. I'm going to enjoy seeing what Hayes does to you." He stood there watching for a moment, then said, "How's that little pussy of yours? The dumb one."

David sank onto a hard cot set into the wall. Still Moran didn't leave. He walked along the bars and stood just outside the finger of light. "The charges are resisting arrest, assaulting an officer, and assault with a deadly weapon. Do you know your law, Waldo?"

He didn't say anything.

"In case you're interested, the last one's a serious felony. With luck you'll be out in two years. You got a lawyer, Waldo?"

David threw his feet up onto the cot and turned over, facing the wall. Moran didn't speak again, and a moment later David heard him leave. The jail was quiet for a while. Then a key scraped and the inner door swung open. Someone had come into his cell.

"Mr. Waldo?"

He sat up. Facing him was a lean, gaunt man, wearing a colorful tie and a beard, neatly trimmed.

"My name is Saul Reismann. I'm an attorney. Judge Hayes asked me to interview you and see if you qualify for my representation in court."

2

There was no longer any question about it: David Waldo had disrupted her life. Since his first visit, things had been different. She was different and she liked the difference. Liking it frightened her more than the experience itself. She didn't know what to make of this gentle, bearded giant with his intensity and his soft voice and his quiet sophistication.

And this afternoon—she didn't know what to think of that either. She understood about brutal police. She knew from Sammy and Abe that some policemen were even in the Ku Klux Klan, which persecuted them. So David's story about a sadistic cop might be true, and she didn't know what to do about *that* either. Now, sitting alone in her room, she was tense and nervous and afraid for his safety. She had spent the afternoon looking for help, but it had been so long since she had needed help of any kind that she had no idea where to go. She called police headquarters and they told her nothing. When she asked how he was, the man on the other end just grunted and hung up.

Finally she thought of brother Tom, but he was out of touch. She called the *Denver Post*. Someone on city desk told her that he had been out of town and had returned just this morning. He had been in the office briefly and had gone home to write. She tried calling him in

176

Golden, and only after her third try did she remember that he didn't live in Golden any more.

It took her nearly thirty minutes to get his home number from the *Post* operator. On the fifth ring a woman answered. Her voice was young and foreign. She said she was the maid. Mr. Hastings was not home. Reluctantly she tried calling Nell at her father's estate, but that didn't work either. Someone intercepted the call and refused to put her through.

And now she sat, feeling cowardly and inadequate. At dusk Teresa and Gabriel and Abe came home. She realized then that she hadn't even begun dinner. Teresa came up and Anna faked sickness. She lay on her bed after her mother had left and cried into her pillow.

The phone rang. She rushed downstairs, but it was only Sammy, wondering why Gabriel hadn't yet brought his dinner over.

She went into the kitchen, told Teresa she was better, offered to help. Anything was better than doing nothing.

"What happened?" Teresa said. "You and your Mr. Waldo have a fight already?"

She blushed and turned away. She set the table while Teresa cooked. Gabriel took Sammy's dinner over ninety minutes late and when he came back the four of them ate in stony silence. After dinner Julia arrived, pushing Abe into the front room where they could talk. As they were clearing the table, Teresa said, "He's a nice man, Mr. Waldo. Don't you agree?"

"Yes. Very nice."

"You like him?"

"He's interesting enough, I guess."

"Would you go with him again if he asked you?"

"I suppose I might. If he asks me. Why, would it bother you?"

"Your father thinks he's a communist."

"Really?" She looked surprised, and was.

"And naturally he'd like it better if he were Jewish."

He'd like it better if I were Jewish, she thought. But she said, "Where did he pick that up, about Mr. Waldo being a communist?"

"Things people say. You know how people are in this neighborhood."

Yes, she knew how people were.

"Like I told Sam, we'll have to give him the benefit of the doubt till we know more about him," Teresa said. "Later tonight he'll be talking to your father, after the store closes, when they can be alone."

"Oh, yes. I'd forgotten." She stared off into space, thinking that now there wouldn't be any talk because David was in jail and only she knew it. Sammy would close the store and wait, but David wouldn't come and she didn't know what she could do about that either. Somehow she was afraid to tell anyone, especially her family, what had happened. She apologized for not doing her chores and Teresa kissed her on the cheek. She was sleeping an hour later when Teresa came to her room and knocked. "Anna, Mr. Waldo is here. He thinks it's important that he talk to you, but he won't come inside."

"He's . . . *here?*" She couldn't believe it. "Where?"

"On the front porch. He won't come in. I told him you could have all the privacy you want in the back drawing room, but he wouldn't hear of it. So if you see him, it'll have to be on the front porch. And take your wrap."

She could see at once why he wouldn't come in. By standing back in the shadows and keeping his head cocked to one side, he had managed to keep his face partly hidden from Teresa. The entire left side was puffed and lumpy, giving his head an out-of-balance, grotesque look. The left eye was shut tight, as if it had been stitched that way. He dabbed constantly at his ear.

"Oh!" Her hand went up. Cool and trembling, her fingers touched the side of his face. "Oh, you poor thing."

He grasped her hand and held it against his lips. All her icy aloofness had vanished and she was that lovely young schoolgirl again, touching his beard with her free hand. For a frozen moment she cradled his head, as a girl might hold a wounded brother. "You poor, poor dear." He took her left hand and kissed that too, and she didn't pull away. They stood together in the dark, just touching.

He told her he had seen a lawyer and had arranged bail.

"Never mind that now. Something's got to be done about your hurts."

"This is nothing," he said. "Nothing." He had taken her hands down from her lips, but still held them tightly in his own. "Everything's fine now that I'm here. I just had to get back here tonight, and for a while that looked so impossible. None of this hurt half as much as having you see that happen. That's all that ran through my head the whole time, just the cold bloody fear of what you must be thinking."

"I didn't know what to think."

"It was my own fault. I should have taken more care."

"How? Aren't you free to walk the streets like everyone else? Why should this one man persecute you like that?"

"Believe me, there's nothing more than what you saw with your own eyes. Moran is just a very bad man who's been on my back for a long time. It's become a feud between us."

"What I can't understand is why. It doesn't make any sense."

178

"Probably not, in your life. I guess you've never known a man like Moran, and I've known too many."

"How could they let such a man be a policeman?"

"What else would you expect him to do? Being a bloody cop, that's an ideal job for somebody like Moran. They terrorize anybody who doesn't think exactly like they do. They've got force on their side and the law to back it up."

"My brother has told me about brutal police. My half-brother, Tom. He's a newspaper reporter. But I never understood it then, either. Why would the city hire sick people like that to be policemen?"

"Anna, Anna, I could write a book about that, if I could just be the writer I once thought I was, just for a year. What's between me and the police goes back a lifetime. Might as well ask why cats are enemies with dogs. After so long it's like instinct."

"Aren't you ever afraid?"

"Sometimes. Like I told you, none of that matters. My biggest fear is what you think."

"Never mind me. Aren't you afraid for your life?"

"Sometimes that too."

"Do you goad him on?"

"Sometimes, I guess. I can't help it. There's simply no way for Moran and me to hold a conversation without goading on both sides."

She looked suddenly weary and frustrated, and beneath it all, slightly angry. It had all been more than she wanted to handle. All she wanted was pleasant company and a walk around the lake. "Well, what do you want from me?" she said. "What can I do about it?"

"For God's sake, just believe me. Promise you won't worry about it."

She didn't say anything.

"Anna?" His voice was anxious, strained.

"It's a bit late to say don't worry, isn't it, Mr. Waldo? If a doctor told you that you had some emotional illness but you shouldn't worry, wouldn't you worry anyway?"

"Is that how you feel?"

"Sometimes."

"Would it help if I just left you alone?"

"No."

He took up her hands again. "Talk to your brother, the newspaperman. If he knows anything about police in this town he's bound to know Virgil Moran. Ask him what kind of guy Moran is, if you don't believe me."

"I do believe you, Mr. Waldo."

He let out a long sigh of relief.

"But I'll talk to Thomas anyway. Maybe he'll know something you can do about it, some higher-up who might help you. Not to change the subject, Mr. Waldo, but had you forgotten your appointment with my father?"

"Oh, God, yes, I had forgotten."

"I'll call him for you, tell him you've suddenly taken ill." She drew him into the light, where she could see his face. "He's heard you're a communist. Is that true?"

"I don't believe in any government, communist or capitalist."

She shivered visibly. "That sounds awfully radical to me."

"The Reds have more government than anybody. Look, if you've got to have labels, call me an anarchist. A peaceful anarchist."

She shook her head. "You know, every instinct I have tells me to run away from you just as fast as I can. Nice people aren't supposed to talk like you talk. There's something subversive and threatening about it."

"I don't give a damn about Lenin or Trotsky, but I don't care much for Coolidge either. I just don't participate in government."

"Not even to vote?"

"Not since my misguided youth."

"You really are the strangest man I've ever known, Mr. Waldo. Do you have any religion?"

He shook his head.

"You don't believe in God?" She said this in half-shocked breathlessness, her hand to her lips. She had never known an atheist.

He didn't answer; didn't have to. At last she said, "Will you come in and let me wash your face?"

"I couldn't. It would be too humiliating."

"Then be sure and do it yourself. You run along now, and see a doctor about that ear. Take care of yourself, Mr. Waldo, and come see me tomorrow, if you can."

She stepped back into the hall and closed the door.

3

At the same moment, Jacob Howe opened his front door, two blocks away, and came out onto his porch. He lit a store-bought cigarette, drew it down to his knuckles in a few long drags and ground it under his heel as he crossed the yard to his shop. In the garage he turned on a light and sat on a keg by the door. He lit another smoke and watched the lights of a steamer on Sloan's Lake. His hand shook as he held the cigarette, and he got up and went to the forge, still warm from the day's work.

He was waiting for Julia to come home from Abe's, and there was no telling how long the wait might be or how inclined she might be to talk when she came. He dreaded talking to her. The truth was that Jacob Howe had always been a timid man, afraid of embarrassment, of confrontation and mostly of physical pain. It was a phobia, blown up beyond all reason in his mind, as vivid as the fears others had of heights or of bugs. Even the threat of pain reduced Jacob to a quivering bag of nerves. It had always caused him trouble. As a child, he had been bullied by kids who loved to make the giant crawl before them in the school playground. He left school in the fifth grade and ran away from home. Truant officers caught him and his father whipped him with more cruelty than anything he had known at school. In the eighth grade he ran away again, riding the rods to Denver, where he would make his life for the next forty-six years. He had not communicated with his family since 1877.

He hadn't seen Sammy Kohl since that day, sometime last month, when they had had their discussion about Abe and Julia. Sammy had stopped coming by on Sundays, and it had never occurred to Jacob to walk the other way. Something long-standing and fine had ended, and it distressed Jacob as nothing had since the death of his son. He had known Sammy Kohl almost as long as he had known his wife— more than twenty-five years. How could such friendships dissolve in a few moments of misunderstanding? Maybe it was inevitable, this breach between the Howes and the Kohls, and had been since the day their sons had gone off to war. Fate. The gods. Whatever you call it. The moment they lifted Abe out of that troop train, legless, shattered, his skin blistered raw from mustard gas, Jacob Howe knew there would be trouble someday over Abe and Julia. People thought of Jacob as a primitive man, but in his primitive way he understood the human spirit. He knew both Abe and Julia, and understood everything that was happening between them. Everything but this Klan menace. Nobody could have foreseen that five years ago.

He knew the pain that was with her, but he had no answers. Somehow she would have to find the courage to walk away from Abe and begin living her own life again. People could only give so much, then they began dying inside. And he knew something else, that Julia's loyalty wasn't as deep as her capacity for guilt. Beneath that quiet, lovely face was a woman in turmoil, slipping past her best years, chained to a cripple.

He lit another smoke and looked down the road. She was taking a long time tonight. Things must be going badly for Abe.

He was lost in some dream when the car approached, and he didn't notice that it had stopped in front of him until the doors slammed and the two men stood watching him from the road.

He stood up, turning over the nail keg, and his shakes began again. He dropped the cigarette and stepped on it, and for a long moment they just stood staring, just watching each other from a distance of fifty feet. Then the men moved to the gate, unhitched it, and came in. One of them was much larger than the other, and he led the way across the yard. Jacob flinched. His hand moved inside the door and flicked off the light. He stepped out into the moonlight and closed the door behind him.

"I'm just closing up," Jacob said. He was glad he had turned off the light, so they wouldn't see his trembling hands.

"Me and Pike been out of town." It was the one called Nate who spoke. "We just got back yesterday. We're wondering about people we seen before we left."

"People like you," Pike said.

"We're wondering if they been thinking about the things we talked about. The country being in the shape it's in, we wouldn't like to let the grass grow under our feet, now would we?"

Jacob turned up his palms. "Gentlemen, I told you before, I'm not a political man."

"It ain't a question of politics, pilgrim. There just comes a time when a man's got to take a stand. Wouldn't you agree with that?"

"I don't know."

"When two opposing forces meet, and it's a death fight, and only one of them's going to survive, and the future of the nation depends on which one, wouldn't you say that calls for some commitment one way or another?" Nate grinned, obviously proud of the speech.

But Jacob only shrugged his shoulders.

"You don't seem too anxious to help out, friend."

"All I want is to be left alone."

"If you're not with us, then you must be against us. I hate to put it that way, but that's how it looks to me."

"Well, then," Jacob said. "What do you want me to do?"

"We already told you that."

"Well, if I do that—if I give you ten dollars and sign my name—will you leave me alone? Will you stop burning crosses on my land?"

"The ten dollars don't buy off your obligation," Nate said. "I need to tell you that. Your application's still got to be approved, and the man can still boot you out anytime you don't pass muster. We keep the ten either way."

"I don't know. I don't know." Jacob was trembling all over. "Why can't you just leave me alone?"

Nate seemed suddenly weary and out of patience. He stepped

toward Jacob and Jacob cringed back against his garage. A short cry escaped his throat.

Nate grinned. "Hey, Pike, look what we got here. A genuine, giant white-liver. You scared of us, pilgrim?"

Jacob didn't say anything. Nate moved toward him and he cringed back toward the door. The two men looked at each other and snickered, then burst out laughing.

"All right," Jacob said. "What do you want?"

"Gimme the paper, Pike." Nate opened the garage and turned on the light. Jacob crouched above his work table and tried to read the paper, but he saw only the red insignia and the words "Ku Klux Klan." At the bottom there was a place for his signature.

He signed, and became a member of the Klan.

"Now the ten dollars," Nate said.

The money disappeared into Nate's hands. "Being a member of the Knights of the Ku Klux Klan is a privilege and a responsibility," Nate said. "You are responsible for the daily conduct of your family and friends. In many ways you are your brother's keeper. You are expected to report flagrant breaches of Christian faith and acceptable moral standards which you may observe, and to help stamp out the growing threat of anarchy and lawlessness. Brother, do not take this lightly." He said his speech in solemn tones, a speech he had learned from John Galen Locke. It was the longest speech he knew. Their eyes met and Nate smiled, not unkindly.

And when they had gone, Jacob Howe felt suddenly weary and sick of heart. He cried like a child over his forge, weeping into his folded arms for a long time. It was very late when he made his way through the dark yard toward his home and the comfort of his wife. A light snow was beginning. He had forgotten about Julia. From the shadows of the great elm tree, she watched him pass. The voice of Nate Newton hung over the yard, as if the man hadn't gone away at all.

4

If they had been watching more carefully, Nate Newton and Elvin Pike would have seen the lonely figure of David Waldo as their car moved along Colfax Avenue toward Denver. In the hour since he had left Anna Kohl, David had walked the streets, full of dread at what must come next. And it had to happen now, it had to be tonight, any more procrastination was unthinkable. He stepped under the tiny awning over the door of his print shop, and the snow swirled around him. For a long time he listened for some movement inside, but nothing happened. He pictured Jessie lying in the dark upstairs, waiting. She knew something was happening: In her simple way, she had to know it. He had been moody and withdrawn, and they had not been really together since that afternoon when she had seen him with Anna and Abe. She would lie beside him each night, sweet-smelling from her bath, and they never touched and nothing ever happened. He had identified Jessie Abbott's one inhibition. She could ask him to read, but not to love her.

So the time had come. He started up the winding staircase. He had always believed that a thing was over when it was over, and he hated drawn-out scenes and long speeches. But she wasn't just another girl to him. He opened the door and came into the dim room. She was sitting on the side of the bed, fully dressed, her heavy coat over her lap. Her eyes were fixed on his, as clear and yellow as he had ever seen them. She showed no surprise, no emotion at all, at the condition of his face. He looked down and saw that her boots were on, and her heavy jeans, and the bed was made up exactly as she had left it that morning. At her feet was a small canvas bag, the same one she'd had when she moved in, two winters before. It was packed and pinned across the top with safety pins. He saw her front-door key, placed deliberately on the table beside the bed. His eyes moved across and found her face again—her smooth nose; the yellow eyes; the taffy hair, washed and brushed out for its full length down her back. She is so incredibly pretty, he thought. He wanted her. He saw and thought all these things in the few seconds before he understood what it meant.

"Well, then." It was idiotic, but that was all he could think of.

She didn't say anything.

Two years, and at the end of it they were both speechless. He leaned over to touch her but she drew away. It was the first time she had ever done that. He didn't try again.

They looked at each other. It was ridiculous. Of course they had some things to say, and the things were important. He forced himself. "Where are you going?"

She shrugged and he saw that her tears were very near, that she couldn't speak if she tried.

"Back to Jordan?"

She nodded and made a valiant effort. Abbott had taken her walking tonight. He had told her that David didn't want her anymore. They were going south for the winter, to Miami, where the weather was warmer.

"Things just . . . didn't work out . . . like I'd hoped they would," he said. "Do you understand that?"

She shook her head. For her, life was a page in a book, or their bare arms touching before a fireplace, where the only sound for an hour was the popping of a coal brick.

"Maybe your father can explain it to you."

The coward's way out.

She got up and picked up her bag. She had sniffed back her tears and was making a great effort to smile.

"Maybe we'll see each other," he said.

She just looked at him. It was like saying good-bye to a childhood friend.

"Later, when you get back from Miami."

He went to a window. Outside the snow was heavy, and a wind rattled the panes. When he turned, she was gone.

He hurried down behind her and caught her at the door. He held her against him, feeling her heartbeat.

He squeezed her hand and buttoned her coat. "In case you ever need me, I want us to stay in touch." He pressed her key into her hand, and tucked the old copy of *Green Mansions* into her bag. Something for Abbott to read her, for those long winter nights around the campfire.

She walked away without looking back. He watched until the storm closed in around her.

CHAPTER
EIGHT

1

Friday night had come, and Tom Hastings had settled down at his desk for what was to be the hardest writing of his life. He was writing from memory, trying to work into his lead piece all the political figures, judges, cops, and officials whose names he could remember from the Locke files. He knew her story would also go on Sunday, and the difference between them would be strong and immediately clear, to anyone who had ever been inside a newsroom. At that moment he could have strangled her. By seven o'clock he realized that he had lost this round, and would have to think it through from another angle to have even a hope of making a decent showing against her.

Marvel Millette was simply too tough, too world-wise, to fall for something now. He had tried throughout the week, with laughable results. He had sent a man to the *News* posing as a deputy sheriff from Grand Junction, with a warrant for her arrest and a subpoena for the film. The man was an actor appearing in a play at the Auditorium.

He had cost a week's pay. The warrants and forms Tom had bought from an engraver downtown. They cost another week's pay, and he still owed the guy for that. He hadn't eaten much since Tuesday, and his welcome for Miller's free lunch was wearing thin. That was the least of his problems. Two weeks' pay had dissolved in five minutes of futility. The actor had played his part and had reported to Tom an hour later. After a moment of indecision, Marvel Millette had laughed him out of the newsroom.

It had been a day of phone calls: a last-minute call to New York, where Gene Fowler was employed at the *American*. A roar of delight at the sound of his voice, and then total silence on Fowler's end as Tom told him about Grand Junction. When he had finished, Fowler said, "The problem is, Tommy, you've got her worked up now and just one day left to get your film back. She's bound to be on edge, expecting something." He paused for a long time, then said, "Have you tried her with *méthode d'amour?*"

"You're kidding." But he knew with horrible certainty that Fowler was not kidding, that what he was getting was his last possible chance.

"Women are funny creatures, Tommy. Sometimes they respond to a little loving when nothing else will turn the trick. Even the tough ones. Sometimes especially the tough ones. This goddamn Marvel sounds like a dame after my own heart. Is she a looker?"

"Some guys might think so. Tell you the truth, Gene, I hadn't noticed."

"Oh, Tommy, you're slipping. Christ on crutches, I wish I was back there."

More telephoning. At mid-afternoon, after a barrage of calls to the people who would be mentioned in his story, Nell reached him at his desk. She sounded overjoyed to hear his voice.

"Tom! I've been trying to reach you for a week!"

"I've been out of town. Can I call you back?"

Her voice chilled at once. "No, you can't call me back. My God, I haven't talked to you in almost a month and the first thing you say is can I call you back?"

"I'm sorry. It's just one hell of a bad time."

"Aren't they all? Don't you have time for your children anymore?"

"I'm sorry. I really am. Would you apologize for me? Tell them I'll see them soon."

"To-om! What does that mean? Next month? Next year? Are you planning to see them for Christmas?"

"Sure I am. Look, I'm sorry, but I'll have to call you back."

"Well you can't. I'm not home anyway. I'm downtown shopping. In fact I've got to go now myself. Orrin's coming for me."

"I'll call you later at home."

"No," she said. "No, don't do that."

"What's the old man doing, tapping your phone?"

The silence stretched between them. She said, "Don't you think it's time we got together and talked things out?"

"If that's what you want."

"Well don't do me any favors." She caught her breath and said, "Wait a minute, let's stop right there. Everything's going wrong. Damn it, Tom, I didn't call to pick a fight. I didn't want to snap at you, but I do think we need to talk."

"Fine. How about Sunday?"

"What's wrong with tomorrow? Oh, don't tell me." She sighed. "You've got to work tomorrow."

"Listen, Sunday would be perfect." Perfect, he thought, in many ways. By Sunday it would be over. Both their stories would be out for the eyes of the world, and he might well want nothing more than a walk in the park with his boys.

"Sunday, then," she said calmly. "We'll meet in City Park at noon."

She rang off and he went back to work. It went badly. The story wasn't, as they say in the business, writing itself. He struggled with each paragraph, substituting arrogance for fact, invective for documentation. He shuffled through the pictures on the one roll of film she hadn't gotten, the one Goodwin had developed in their bathroom at the Timberline. The entire roll contained the middle of a long report. Few names, no local dynamite. Given the explosive potential of her first-day piece, he might not use this at all.

At last he turned to his notes, the paper matted together from the steam pipes, and he knew at once that he held in his hands the one chance to knock her wind out. Here was the hidden angle, the one set of facts that she couldn't have. He rolled the paper into his machine and began to write.

GRAND JUNCTION—A Ku Klux Klan plot to take over the United States, by states and regions, was hatched here last week, in a secret hotel room far from press scrutiny.

The plot calls for manipulation of the American political system, though delegates were split in their opinions on Klan violence and open terrorism. Current plans call for at least six states outside the solid South—including Colorado—to become Klan controlled after next fall's elections. The Colorado Klan will run a solid slate of candidates for state Senate, House, judgeships, education boards, and numerous other posts of public trust.

Representatives to the Grand Junction meeting

came from as far away as Ohio and Texas, though their names and home states were disguised. Dr. John Galen Locke, Grand Dragon of the Colorado Klan, was host for the group, which met at the Grand Hotel and held all-day sessions in a semi-secret room with one door and no windows.

Among the notables attending were D.C. Stephenson and Hiram Wesley Evans, prominent Klansmen from Indiana and Texas. With trouble and scandal brewing in the national Klan hierarchy, Evans is thought to be next in line as Imperial Wizard, the ruling monarch of the group that has become known as "the invisible empire."

The Klan plans to work through conservative civic and political groups, including the most powerful and influential men in each city and state. In Denver the Klan has infiltrated virtually every level of commerce and politics. Its members include officers of the Chamber of Commerce, banks, established brokerage houses, and downtown department stores.

He ripped it out, studied the rough draft, and began listing the names beneath it. When he had written down all he could remember, he began calling them for reaction. First on his list was Joel Cregar, owner of a Denver emporium. He knew Cregar as a cigar-chewing fat man, bald and loud.

"Mr. Cregar, this is Tom Hastings, *Denver Post*. I'm doing a story on prominent people who are members of the Ku Klux Klan. Your name's come up."

"So?"

"So, what have you got to say about it?"

"What I've got to say is it's none of your goddamned business."

"All right." He wrote down the quote exactly, wondering if he could get the profanity past the copyeditors.

"Listen," Cregar said. "That information's supposed to be secret."

Tom wrote that down. "Naturally, I'm not bound by any agreement you may have made with Mr. Locke," he said.

"Then maybe you'll be bound by this," Cregar said. "You print that and I'll sue your ass off." He slammed down the phone.

Most of them went like that. Three admitted humbly that they were members, but swore that their interest was strictly passive. They had no truck with terrorism or violence. Tom took down the quotes. One man, a vice-president at Merchant's State bank, begged Tom not to reveal his membership. Tom struck out the quotes but left the name in.

Some threatened him. They threatened to have him fired, to cut off their ads in the *Post*. He took down those quotes too. At the end of three hours he had reached them all, and suddenly it had begun looking like a story.

He asked Alice about the possibility of having the Klan insignia reproduced for the top of the page, but she brushed him off and left early with Arthur McCantless. He forgot about the art. By evening he had settled in for the real writing, the rewrite, the polish. He finished off the main piece and started work on the sidebar before he could begin doubting it. The Sunday deadline was sixteen hours away.

The telephone rang.

"Mr. Tom Hastings? This is John Galen Locke. What do you mean, calling people and asking about Klan membership? These are powerful people you're bothering, and you and your superiors should be aware of that."

"That's what makes it news."

"Makes *what* news?"

"Their membership in the Klan. Would you have any comment on that?"

"I will not acknowledge the membership of anyone."

"That's your comment?"

"I have no comment. May I ask where you got your so-called information?"

"May I ask you, sir, how your dispute in Grand Junction turned out? Do you take over the country by intimidation and violence or by working through the system?"

Locke seemed stunned, unable to reply for a full minute. After a while the phone simply went dead, the earpiece placed gently on its hook. He had a vision of Locke sitting in some dark office, staring at the phone in horror and disbelief. He remembered the taunts at Julia's house, and he smiled.

The midnight hour approached, and he pulled the last pages out of his typewriter and read them over. The doubts persisted. She would mop up the street with him. He knew his lead was good: it was an element she probably didn't have, though with this bitch you could never be sure. Once past the lead, it thinned out fast. He thought about Fowler and his *méthode d'amour*. Fowler was such a crazy bastard, he'd probably do it. It was what separated fine reporters like Tom Hastings from great ones like Gene Fowler.

He had fifteen hours left. He put through the call.

He expected her to be at her desk, and she was. She answered the phone with the same cool efficiency she always had.

"Marvel Millette."

"Hello."

190

"Who is this? Mr. Hastings?"

"Right the first time."

"I've been expecting you."

"You have?" He managed to sound surprised, though of course he wasn't.

"Of course. I didn't think you'd go down without one last try."

"I just called to say congratulations. I'm throwing in the towel."

"Now is that a fact?" Her sarcasm, as it was intended, conveyed disbelief. "Well, I really appreciate it. And listen, Mr. Hastings, I'm not putting you on. I still think you're a hell of a reporter. I'm looking forward to learning a lot from you."

"Thanks."

"Oh, don't take it so hard. This time you just got careless. I'm really hoping we'll get to be friends."

"All right. Let's start now. Sure. I'm really washed out. Let's have a drink together and just unwind. And why don't you call me Tom?"

"All right, *Tom.* But listen, *Tom,* before you spend any money on me, I should be honest with you. This is just about as dumb as that deputy sheriff bit. I mean, this is the love bit, right, *Tom?* Take her out, tell her how gorgeous she is, fill her up with booze and hope she'll get drunk enough or giddy enough to hand over the stuff. Isn't that how it works? *Tom?*"

He was glad she couldn't see him. His face had gone red and his hand had come up to cover his eyes. He leaned in toward the mouthpiece.

"Miss Millette?"

"Yes, Tom?"

"What I'm about to say is a little out of character. I wouldn't normally speak this way to a lady. You do understand that?"

She laughed. "Am I about to get shocked by gutter language? For shame, sir! Your restraint this far has been admirable, I was so hoping it wouldn't sink to that. Tom? You still there?"

"Yes."

"Tell me, Tom, do you think I'm gorgeous?"

He hung up, deprived of even that final barb by her laughter.

He looked around the empty newsroom.

All right. So what? In the end it was just another story.

He marked his copy, dumped it in the basket on city desk and prepared to go home. He wondered if Georgeann would be there tonight.

His telephone rang. It was Tammen. He had just gotten a call of protest from John Galen Locke. He had told Locke to go to hell and Locke was on the phone this minute to Bonfils. Tammen laughed.

191

"Sounds like you got the bastards on the run. You better plan on coming in tomorrow. We might need to talk."

"I was planning on it anyway, boss. See you then."

2

The first thing he saw as he came into the newsroom was an important-looking delegation of businessmen, sitting outside the Bucket of Blood. He saw Joel Cregar's bald head, and through the cigar smoke recognized other voices and faces of the enemy. Roy Garrison, member of civic clubs, president of a railroad. Arnold Wilson, owner of a dry goods store. Lowell Branch of The Golden Eagle. Faces of men he hadn't even called, men who hadn't been on his list. But they had been on Locke's list. Now that he saw them, it all came back. And they were smart. There wasn't a politician or utility man among them. They knew better than to throw any political weight at Bonfils and Tammen. The *Denver Post* never bowed to political pressure. Bonfils and Tammen had cut their teeth on politicians, and now even John Galen Locke was nowhere to be seen. His heated calls to Bonfils and Tammen had not been wise, and now he had backed off and let bigger fish fight his battle for him.

There was Walter Foley, a longtime friend of the *Post*, whose three stores advertised exclusively with Bonfils and Tammen and brought in tens of thousands yearly. Adam Hook was another heavy advertiser. Here they were, the pullers of strings, the holders of the company purse. His real bosses. The people who indirectly paid his salary.

It had been a gnawing fear all along; from his first meeting with Tammen he had worried about it. Now it bloomed into near paranoia. But Bonfils was an arrogant bastard. Friends or not, he kept them waiting almost fifteen minutes while he and Tammen conferred in private. When at last a receptionist stood and said, "Mr. Bonfils and Mr. Tammen will see you, gentlemen," the men stood up with much clearing of throats and scraping of chairs. Fifteen strong they marched into the Bucket of Blood, while across the newsroom the reporters, desk men, and artists shuffled papers and exchanged glances.

Everyone in the house knew that something was up, that Tom was at the hub of it and was drawing fire. He fought down the urge to hit Goodwin's darkroom for a quick one, and instead went to a coffeepot perking on a table near the copy desk. Soon he would be called in, and

192

it wouldn't do to face them with alcohol on his breath. Coffee was a penny a cup and he had to write an IOU for that.

Behind his chair, Alice Wilder, who hadn't given him the time of day yesterday, was suddenly in love with the goddamn image again. All her ice had melted, all the hurt was gone, and what was left was pure lust. He looked away from her and dropped into his chair. He had never been good at waiting. But it wasn't a long wait, not nearly as long as he had expected. The fifteen important men, after a conference of less than an hour, filed out the way they had come. None of them looked at him, and none smiled or spoke to anyone.

His telephone rang. It was Bonfils' secretary. "Mr. Hastings, please come to Mr. Bonfils' office."

He straightened his tie and stood up. Alice leaned over and whispered luck in his ear.

Bonfils and Tammen were alone in the room. They were seated on opposite sides of the desk, facing him as they must have faced the others, as equals. Tammen's face was soft and friendly; Bonfils looked dark and menacing. Bonfils motioned him to the front of the desk and didn't offer him a chair. On the desk between them, he saw, was his story.

Bonfils picked up the story and thumbed through it. He looked at Tom and said, "A lot of this goes without any attribution whatsoever. Where'd you get it?"

He told them how he had eavesdropped on the Klan meeting. Tammen grinned.

"I've got my notes on what was said," he told them.

"What about this other stuff?" Bonfils said. "These names, this unholy alliance business?"

He told them how he had gotten into Locke's room, picked open the briefcase and instructed Goodwin to shoot the papers. By then Tammen was openly laughing, his hand dropping in pain to his side.

"You've got these pictures?" Bonfils said.

"We lost some of them." His cheeks burned as he said it, but he looked Bonfils in the face. "*I* lost them. I got careless. There's no excuse for what happened. The names you see in the story are the ones I could remember from Locke's file."

Bonfils clasped his hands and leaned over the desk. "Tell me, Mr. Hastings, exactly how did you lose the pictures?"

"Marvel Millette got into my room and got them away from me."

Tammen had stopped laughing now. Bonfils never blinked an eye.

"Then the *News* has this too," Bonfils said.

Tom nodded. "I expect her story tomorrow too. She'll have most of what I put down in the body of my piece as her lead. I don't think she'll have the conspiracy angle."

There was a long moment of silence. Bonfils looked at Tammen and said, "Did you have anything else?" Tammen shook his head.

"What about the story?" Tom said.

Bonfils fixed those steel eyes on his and said, "That's all, Mr. Hastings."

At his desk he waited some more. The Saturday paper, thin and without much substance, came up from the press room. By noon he was so edgy that he dug out some obits and began writing them up. It had been so long since he'd written one that he had forgotten the style.

Alice asked him to buy her lunch. He smiled sadly. "Can't. I spent my last dime bribing people." She laughed and said, "Then let me take you to lunch." He shook his head. "Thanks anyway. I've got to hang tight here." She left with the kid, Arthur McCantless. By one o'clock the bulk of the Saturday crew had disappeared and the newsroom was quiet and still. He went back to Goodwin's darkroom and had a drink. It tasted so good he had another, feeding the kitty with IOU papers from his notebook.

Just before three o'clock the Sunday city edition came up from the pressroom. O'Reilly came over and dropped it on Tom's desk. "You didn't make it, Hastings," he said. "Too bad. Somebody should get those pricks." But it went without saying, that somebody wouldn't be Hastings the great or the *Denver Post*. Tom sat there, staring at it. There was no use looking inside. With this story, it was front page or nothing.

He went back to the darkroom and had himself a double.

There was still a chance, he thought. They might still be haggling over it, might still run it in the home edition. Maybe they were just waiting to see what the *News* had, making sure the comparison wouldn't shame them. He downed his drink and poured another, and suddenly he felt cheated and mean. The combination of the drink, the long days on the road, the hours of hard work, the money out of his own pocket, and the final humiliation of Marvel Millette weighed on him until, in a fury, he gripped the tiny shot glass like a baseball and hurled it through a window.

He staggered out into the newsroom. People had returned from lunch and now it seemed that everyone was staring again, watching him with that same apprehension he had felt all morning. He walked to his desk, grabbed up the Sunday *Post* and threw it across the newsroom. The pages fluttered and fell like giant snowflakes.

"Fuck this place," he said. His voice carried across the room, and every typewriter stopped. "This place and this job."

Bonfils and Tammen had come to the door of the Bucket of Blood. He grabbed up his coat, stared at them for a moment and walked out.

His first stop was at Miller's, where he persuaded the barkeep to reinstate his tab, for one night only. When the limit ran out, he went over to the Black Cat Saloon on Welton Street, across from the *Rocky Mountain News,* and sat at a table where he and Fowler had once downed two bottles of bourbon in just under three hours. *News* and *Times* reporters drifted in. He let Booker buy him a drink. When the freebies ran out, he went back to Miller's for the *Post* crowd. By then everyone had heard about his stormy exit, and many drifted over to offer condolences and the tip of an elbow. O'Reilly and Malloy came in; each was good for two drinks. O'Reilly said that Tammen had left word for Tom to call him and Tom said, quite loudly, that Tammen should screw himself. Soon he found himself standing at the bar with his foot on the brass rail, listening to Miller and Gallagher argue about the Coolidge administration. He was sure he was dreaming when he looked into the far corner and saw some middle-aged dame with beads, red hair, and rolled-down stockings trying to do the Charleston.

He felt a stirring at his elbow, and when he turned, Marvel Millette was standing beside him. He wanted to hit her, but he had never hit a woman and didn't know how. He tried to sneer, but in his drunkenness even that came off badly. He had hit bottom and his executioner was standing before him. He held up his hands as if to push her away, and dropped them limply at his side. "Get out of here," he said finally. "Just get away from me and leave me alone."

"Here." She threw a heavy brown box on the bar. "I brought your pictures back."

"Well thanks a goddamn lot, Miss Marvel Millette, you are still no lady in my book." He beckoned to Miller, who was serving people at the far end of the bar. "Miller, tell this . . . *lady* . . . the rule about unescorted females. She's bothering your customers."

Miller came over and said, "It's a house rule, miss."

She looked him in the eye and told him, in pure reporter's lingo, what he could do with the house rule. Miller made a face and retreated.

"Okay, so you've got the biggest balls in the house," Tom said. "That's a helluva accomplishment."

"Mr. Hastings, you are drunk."

"An acute observation."

"You are an offensive, sloppy drunk."

"Your powers of observation are"—he belched loudly—"simply amazing."

"The pictures are all there, both the negatives and the finished prints."

"Fine. Great. So what the hell are you waiting around for? What do you want, a goddamn receipt?"

But she stood for another moment, watching him sadly. "Isn't this a sight? The great Tom Hastings, standing alone in a bar crying in his beer. Feeling soooo sorry for himself."

He grabbed her shoulder. "Listen, you, if you know what's good for you you'll move your little ass out of here. I'm about five seconds away from putting you in a hospital."

"Oh, you big strong man! You disgust me with your he-man threats." She knocked his hand away. "And get your hand off my shoulder, buster, I don't like being manhandled. I've had enough of you and this town with its suck-up journalism. You sulk and cry like you're the only one who's ever been scooped or had a story killed. Jesus, I'll tell you about killing stories, I've had more stuff killed both here and in Cleveland than you ever heard of. So don't come whining or sniveling to me about your problems at the *Post* because I've got problems too. And while I'm thinking about it, let me tell you one more thing. If you ever again hint that I'm some kind of male freak just because I went head-to-head with you and won, you *will* have to put me in the hospital because I'll come after you and tear your goddamn eyes out."

She turned and walked out. Tom just stood there, speechless and very sober. From the end of the bar, Miller grinned and said, "I guess you can consider yourself told off, Hastings."

It was raining when he left Miller's. He left the box of pictures in Miller's safe and walked along Sixteenth Street, getting wet to the skin. In an all-night diner he started to buy a *News* from a blind man sitting near the door, then he remembered that he didn't have the two cents. He did get close enough to see the page before the shepherd dog on the blind man's leash began to growl and prick its ears.

Her story wasn't there.

He didn't know if that cheered him up or made him sadder. He walked on, letting the cold rain soak away his drunk, and suddenly he was on Welton Street, standing under the electric sign that thrust the single word NEWS out over the sidewalk. He began to climb the narrow, creaky staircase, pushed through the swinging doors at the top, and looked out across the newsroom. His first sight of the copy desk with its ring of living corpses almost turned him back into the street. Three stand-up telephones stood against a far wall. No one was using them. Someone on the desk made a feeble joke and no one laughed. No one seemed to give a damn. They shuffled papers and did all the routine stuff and none of them cared that the best story of the year would never see print.

The walls were covered with telephone numbers: politicians, friends, lovers, sources. He followed the numbers around to her desk, where she sat looking out into the night. She was staring at some people in the Orient Hotel next door. It took a long time for her to see his reflection in the glass and turn around. Her eyes were red, giving him a mild shock. He would never have believed that Marvel Millette had any tears inside her.

"I wanted to say I'm sorry," he said. "Sorry for what I said and sorry about your story."

"Thank you, Mr. Hastings."

He walked home in the rain. When he stumbled into his apartment on Capitol Hill, he found a note from Georgeann, written in her blundering style. A Mr. Tammen had called. She didn't understand it but it sounded like he said not to be stupid. Come in Monday and talk but stay away from Mr. Bon-fees. And he had a ten-dollar raise, beginning next week.

He went to the cabinet and broke out a bottle. Later, when his drunkenness had settled in again, he saw that Georgeann had also brought in his mail. There was a desperate-sounding, almost incoherent note from Nell, written a week ago, long before she had reached him by phone. Under it was a slim envelope from New York, a thirty-dollar check from *Red Mask* magazine.

3

Even before Tom had gone to bed, Nell was up and planning her escape. The day had a storybook excitement to it, a feeling she hadn't had since her youth. Her father's ability to crush her flares of rebellion had given him a visible lift. He was every inch the old master again. His rules were arbitrary and stern, and he was especially hard on the boys. There would be no more horseplay, no going out after dark, no giggling after he pulled the master switch. There would be no intercourse with the ruffians in the neighborhood. Paul had always gone to a special school, but now the old man took Michael out of the public school and put him in private classes as well. He made them report to him every afternoon on their progress that day. And Nell fared little better. Without ever telling her so, he confined her to the grounds for a week, punishment for another flare of defiance. He simply made certain that Orrin wasn't available to drive her.

In desperation she had slipped out through a crack in the fence, catching a tram into town. She answered ads for governess and elementary school teacher and was told that she didn't qualify. She had no experience at anything. The only thing she had ever done, other than being a wife and mother, was work for the vote. The only political work in town, on the few fledgling campaigns gearing up for 1924, was strictly voluntary. By the end of the day, she had been offered one job, as a maid in an old downtown hotel, but the only apartment she could afford on that salary was grimy and cold, and it had bugs. Even then she might have taken it, just to spite the old man, had it not been for her sons. Now she wondered which was worse for them, physical hardship or this slow bleeding of the soul.

She had gone wearily home, to endure his lecture in silence. She winced when he told her again that she must never venture alone into the world of communists and radicals, and that everything he did for them, he did in love.

All that week she had tried to get Tom, and now that she had him, now that he would meet her in the park, she intended to make the most of it. She bathed in cold water, in a dark part of the house that they didn't use anymore. She had no truck with makeup, and she hoped the chill would bring a rosiness to her skin that would last through the day. She stood before the full-length mirror and pinched her cheeks, bringing out their color. Her dress was important, and she selected a pale red thing that might entice Tom without arousing the old man's suspicion. At breakfast she played her hand.

"Father, isn't this a lovely day?"

He looked vaguely at the window. "It is nice."

"I was thinking about taking the boys to City Park. After the rain last night, everything will be fresh and pretty. Michael's been looking so pale lately."

"Don't they have the run of the place here?"

"Yes, but it's too easy for them to stay inside if they're home."

"They should have set hours to play outside, and it should be mandatory that they do."

She smiled sweetly and said in her best singsong voice, "You're right, Papa, and we'll work on it. But just for today . . . please."

He nodded and touched his mouth with a napkin. "I have some reports from our St. Louis plant to read, so I can use the quiet time. Orrin will drive you. When will you go?"

"Noonish, if that's okay."

"If that means twelve o'clock, fine. I do wish you'd speak proper English, and stay away from those abominable modern slang expressions."

And so, just before noon, the green Packard pulled up the horseshoe drive and the three of them got in the back seat. She kept the window between them and Orrin until they approached the park. Then she opened it and directed him around the lake toward the pavilion on the west side. They arrived at a quarter past twelve, just late enough and not too late. *Fashionably* late. It was a term Tom despised. She felt like giggling. He was always right on time for everything.

He wasn't there.

She walked through the empty pavilion. Orrin watched the boys. She drifted away from them and softly called his name. Nothing happened. She couldn't believe it. Her eyes began to burn: the beginnings of what would be, if he didn't show up damned soon, unspeakable rage. At one o'clock, she sank wearily on a bench. She was heartsick. At two o'clock Orrin came across the small stretch of sand in front of the bandstand and looked in at her. "It's getting late," he said. "We'd better leave now."

"Not just yet."

"Mr. Clement will be expecting us back, miss."

"It won't kill him to wait another hour."

Then, to her disbelief and horror, he reached out and took her arm. "Please, miss, Mr. Clement was very specific about timing." He drew her out of the pavilion toward the car. She jerked her hand away and twisted an ankle, dropping in pain to the ground.

"Now see what you've done! Oh, this time you've gone too bloody far."

Orrin picked her up and whisked her to the car while Michael watched from lakeside. She tried to kick him as he lowered her gently into the back seat and closed the door. She lunged at the other door, but he came around and gripped her wrist with those strong little fingers. "Come now, miss," he said. "You've had your fun now. Let's be going home without all this fuss." For Orrin it was a long speech, and she never got to hear the rest of it because suddenly Michael screamed. It was a shout of joy. Across the brown, snow-spotted grass, Tom was coming.

Michael ran to him, shrieking at the top of his lungs. Tom scooped up his tiny son and held him against his chest. Paul, now aware that his father had arrived, was groping around trying to find him. Still clutching Michael against him, Tom walked to Paul and swept him up with his free arm.

"Now, Orrin," she said. "Will you let me out, or will you explain to Mr. Hastings why you are fighting with his wife?"

Orrin hung there in confusion. "Miss Nell," he said. His voice had a pleading strain to it, a pathetic quality she had never heard, but now in triumph she was ruthless and impatient. "I said get out of my way!" She pushed him and he fell back through the door, landing on his back in the gravel.

She walked toward Tom, composing her thoughts. She was furious with him, but that must not show. Not here, not now. His face was full of apology, and in his eyes she saw the unmistakable, red evidence of another old enemy. He had been drinking and had overslept. He admitted that much. And his car wouldn't start.

She forced herself to smile. "It's all right, it's fine." But she had to turn away, facing Orrin. She clenched her teeth, took a deep breath, and looked again at her husband. "I'm glad you came when you did, though. We were just about to leave."

"I was afraid you had."

"Well," she said lightly, "the boys wanted to see their father." She forced herself to say, "And so did I," and she smiled.

He said, "You're looking good."

"Do you think so?"

"Great."

"I've lost weight, you know."

"I didn't notice."

She looked at the ground and her teeth closed over her tongue, just enough to hurt. He never did notice. He only noticed when presidents die, and then it was always too late.

"You look a little ragged, to tell the truth," she said. "Haven't you been taking care of yourself?"

"It's been a rough month."

But he didn't tell her about it, and that was fine. She didn't want to hear about his rough month anyway. She could well imagine. She let him lead her down to lakeside, and felt neglected while he wrestled and talked with the boys. After half an hour of this, she felt ready to scream. "I know you don't get to see them much, Thomas, but I really must be getting them in. It is getting late. They have studying to do."

"Sure," he said. "It's my fault we haven't seen each other much. We'll make that up, I promise. We'll get back on our Saturday schedule and stay on it. How does that sound?"

Michael said it sounded great.

"Paul?"

"I don't want to see you on Saturdays. I want us to live together like we used to do."

Nell looked at Tom, her face full of hope. But he was looking at Paul.

"Hey, kiddo, don't you like your grandpa's place?"

"I hate him," Paul said.

"Paul!" Nell grabbed his shoulders.

"Leave him alone," Tom said. There was a dangerous look in his eyes and she backed away. He took Paul's head in his hands and said, "What's wrong, son? You look fine."

"Grandpa's too mean to us," Michael said.

"Mean how? How's your grandpa been mean to you?"

"He makes me go to this crummy school," Michael said.

"Then he makes us sit for hours and tell him what we've learned," Paul said.

"He won't let us off the grounds," Michael said.

"We can't play with anybody."

"And he makes us go to our room right after supper every night."

"And put the lights out at seven o'clock."

"Now he won't even let Mom go out."

"Michael!" She stamped her foot. "I said that's enough!"

"It's true," Paul said. "She can't even make a phone call without him spying on her. Last week he told me . . ."

"Yes? Told you what?"

"He said you didn't care about us anymore."

Horrified, Nell sank to the grass and stared at her son.

"Did you know that?" Tom said to her.

She shook her head.

"It's true," Paul said. "I swear it."

"You don't have to swear to me, kiddo. Your grandpa and I go back a long way." Tom took the boys under each arm. He mussed Paul's hair. Looking straight at Nell, he said, "I've got to get them away from him."

She nodded, waiting.

After a while Paul asked him again. Tom clasped his son around the shoulder. "I'd have you come live with me, but that wouldn't work out. The place where I live now is . . . too crowded. There isn't room."

Nell turned away and looked out toward the street.

"Christmas is coming," Paul said.

"I want a bike," said Michael.

"Well, Mike, I don't know," Tom said. "Bikes are pretty expensive."

"Oh, Michael, shut up!" Paul said. "All I want this year is for us to move back together and have it like it was before."

Nell laughed nervously. "Well," she said, still looking away. "How about that?"

"Nothing's ever as simple as it sounds, is it?" Tom said. To Paul: "Your mom and I still have to talk."

"About that?"

"About a lot of things." To Nell: "Are you staying down? To talk?"

"If you want me to."

They had reached the sandy area where Orrin stood waiting.

"If I can't get the car started, you'll have to catch a trolley back," Tom said.

She shrugged.

"Mr. Clement is expecting them home for dinner," Orrin said.

Nell gave him a bitter smile. "I think he'll survive, Orrin. You can take the boys home, tell him I'll be along later."

"We all came out together; we should all go back." Orrin came around the car and pulled open the door, shooing the boys over in the seat.

"I'm not going."

"That's it, then." Tom reached over and took her arm.

Orrin hurried after them. "Miss Nell, please, I can't let you do this." He tagged along about ten yards behind them, like a child undecided about what to do next. Tom stopped and turned. Orrin stopped. "You wait here," Tom said. He met Orrin over a mound of snow. She couldn't hear what was said, but Tom's voice had a nasty, cutting edge to it. He jabbed Orrin once with his right hand, and Orrin stepped back. They circled the mound of snow like two kids preparing for battle. And then Tom said something that made Orrin back away. They looked at each other for a moment, then Orrin turned and walked to the car.

When Tom came back to her, he didn't take her arm. There was a coldness in his eyes that frightened her. They walked out to Seventeenth and stood under a tree at a trolley stop. "I hope you've got sixteen cents for our trolley fares," he said. She didn't, and they began to walk.

4

He couldn't take her to his room; that much was understood. They walked downtown, and he put her in a restaurant booth, in a place near the *Post*, while he went to Miller's and cashed his check. Miller kept ten on account and gave him twenty.

They went to the Savoy, a hotel a few blocks away. The room cost five-fifty, and had a window that looked across Broadway and up Seventeenth Street. He threw his coat on the bed and sat in one of the chairs facing her. She looked flushed, whether from the long walk or the embarrassment of being suddenly alone with him he couldn't tell. In fact, she was embarrassed. She had planned his seduction so many times that now, faced with the time and place, she was afraid to try. In the bathroom she reassured herself, looking at her pretty face in the glass, staring for a long time at her eyes. When she came out, she moved past all three chairs and sat on the edge of the bed. She untied her bonnet and took down the pins that tied her hair, just as she might have done in preparing for bed. Her hair had grown since he had seen it. Gregory Clement couldn't abide the popular haircuts, so she had let it grow. She wet her lips with her tongue and unbuttoned her dress. "All right," she said. "I'm here now, if you want me."

Her own words terrified her. She was so afraid of rejection that it almost paralyzed her. But she saw at once that he wanted her. He stood and began to undress, like a man robbed of voice, ears, and eyes, with only one form of communication left to him. She didn't care. Her dress dropped to the floor, her underthings with it, and the instant they came together on the bed she knew she had won. He was hers again.

Then he did a strange thing, and it shattered her confidence and troubled her for the rest of the day. Tom, who had always despised birth control, asked if she had brought her diaphragm.

She blushed and tried to laugh. "Really, dearest, I didn't come here with this in mind."

They both knew the lie of that. He reached for his wallet. Her arms wrapped around him and she tried to draw him away. But he found what he was looking for and put it on. "Is that . . . thing . . . standard equipment for your wallet these days?" she said. He didn't answer. She played with it, teasing, and at the same time not teasing, trying to work it off. He wrestled her arms back. She giggled and told him how silly he was, how she was giving up on birth control, how she wanted to feel him inside her. But he never did let her have it and after a while she gave up and let him put it inside her. Even with the sheath of rubber separating them it was over in a few moments. The second time, a while later, was longer and better for her. She rolled on top and spread her legs. They stayed locked together for a long time, while she stared dreamily into his eyes and smiled.

Still naked, she lay beside him, in the hollow of his arm, and for most of the next hour she told him how bankrupt her life had been without him and how everything she had believed had failed. He didn't respond. She wondered if he had been comparing her with those others, the Georgeanns, the Alice Wilders, heaven only knew how many others. Using rubbers on her as if she were one of his one-night whores. She pushed away from him, got up, dressed, went into the bathroom, and shut the door hard. She cried, then splashed her face with cold water. When she came out, he was sitting on the edge of the bed, putting on his shoes. He didn't ask why she had been crying. He seemed to know.

For the first time, she saw pain in his face, but she was too angry to respond to it. When she spoke again, her words were meant to cut. "Now that you've gotten that out of your system, now what?"

He shrugged. "I wish I knew."

Midnight was near, and she felt farther from him than ever. It had snowed again. They walked through it to Capitol Hill, neither saying a word. At an all-night gas station he called a friend who owed him. The man, a mechanic, came out on this snowy Sunday night, got his Model T started, and squared the debt. That was the world he lived in. A world where people owed people. A world of tips and sources, seedy people, debts, booze, and whores. The world she hated.

He had had a heater installed, but now it wasn't working. He kept a thin wood chisel on the seat beside him, to scrape away the frost that collected on the inside of the windshield. On Colorado Boulevard he found a place, a small diner where they could eat something and talk.

The talk came hard. They had been sitting for almost fifteen minutes when she said, "The way I see it, it's fairly simple. You have a nice family. Do you love us or not?"

He nodded, too slowly for her liking.

"Maybe it's just the boys you love," she said. "Could that be it, Thomas? Could you still love the boys but be out of love with their mother?"

He didn't answer for a long time. She said his name again, imploring him in that tiny voice, reaching out but not quite touching his hand.

"That's not it either."

When he looked at her, now and always, he felt that old familiar mix of feelings. Respect, interest, affection. Joy. Pain. That must be what love was.

"Well, then, what's to stop us from moving back together right this minute? I've told you I'm ready. I can't do any more than that, can I? No more nonsense about your work, I promise you that." She did touch his hand then, but after a moment he drew it away and rubbed his eyes.

"Tom, the boys do need their father."

"You think I don't know that? The old man's not doing them any favors, is he?"

"He's doing what he thinks is right. That's all we can do, any of us."

"Oh, listen, don't defend him to me, and for Christ's sake let's not fight about that. At least not till we get this other stuff out."

"All right."

"I quit my job yesterday."

That took her by surprise. She couldn't quite keep a small sigh of pleasure from him, or a slight smile from the corners of her mouth.

"Don't get too excited yet. Tammen wants me to stay. And even if I do quit, do you have the faintest idea what I'd do for a living? You know anything that'd pay me sixty-five a week?"

"I don't care."

"Nell, you're dreaming."

"I don't *care!* I don't! We won't starve."

"How easy for you to say that. *I'm* the one who's got to make it come true. And it wouldn't even be as good as what we had. Not for a long time. I owe money."

"I don't care about any of that. I'll go to work. Thomas, what have I got to do to convince you?"

"I know exactly what you're thinking. It's your old man's money again. No matter how hard he lays down the law, he'll never let Michael and Paul suffer. Isn't that it, now? Old Gregory will always come through, if things really got tough? Well, I can tell you, you might as well forget it. If you come back to me I'll never take another dime from that old son of a bitch, and neither will you."

She fought back the urge to remind him that her father was feeding his sons, even now, while he sat penniless and without work, running the old man down in a cheap café. Why was she like that? Why did he always bring out her need to destroy herself? "Sometimes I think you're trying to punish me. I'd lay down my life for you, and all you can say are spiteful things like that. Didn't I give myself to you today without any shame at all? I've told you some things that have made me very vulnerable, and you're still punishing me for leaving you. How long am I going to have to pay for that?"

"Wait a minute, you're getting off the point. The whole crux of this thing is what we do to each other. You and me. It's got nothing to do with the kids or Tammen or the goddamn old man. It's got nothing to do with anybody but us. I didn't tell you, but I've started to write again. That check I cashed today was from a piece I sold to a New York magazine. Why couldn't I do that when we were living together? Why didn't I ever start that novel I wanted to write?"

"I see. Now you're blaming me for that too."

"I'm not blaming anybody. I'm looking for answers." He shook his head. "We go around and around in crazy circles. 'Do you love me, Tom?' 'Well, of course I do.' 'Then why can't we get back together, tonight, this very minute?' 'Because.' 'Because why?' Goddammit, I don't know why. All I do know is nothing's so simple anymore. I feel like a man who's been asleep for eight years. Now I'm awake and you want me to go back to sleep again. The longer it goes on, the more I realize how right you are and always have been. The job stinks. It's every bit as frivolous and inconsequential as you've always said it was. And so am I."

"I *never* said that."

"You said it every time I looked at you, every time I had to leave you on a Saturday night. My trouble is, I'm just too slow on the uptake. See, Nell, I can't read minds all that well. Now I can look back and see where things started coming apart, but just once, in plain English, I wish you'd said, 'Tom, that goddamn job of yours is ruining our marriage.'"

"I'm sorry. I really thought I had."

"Look, all I'm telling you is don't expect any easy answers out of me tonight. A lot has happened in the past forty-eight hours and I'm just not up to it. I'm due at my desk in just over seven hours and right this minute I couldn't tell you if I'm going to show up or not. If I don't, I haven't got a hint what I will do. Now you're here, wanting to move in and set up housekeeping again, and I don't know what to do about that either. The whole world's unhappy, and I got the feeling you want me to work it all out here and now."

She knew then that he had sentenced her to another confrontation with her father. She looked him in the face and said, "All right, then, if that's how it has to be. When?"

"I don't know."

"Well, can you call me this week? No, I'll call you later this week. That'll work out better. Is that okay with you?"

"You can call me any time you want."

It was after one o'clock when he let her off outside the estate. A faint light burned outside the guardhouse, and beyond the wireglass she could see the shadowy figure of Orrin propped against a wall, waiting. The lights were also on in the big house. At the gate, she leaned over and kissed the corner of his mouth, hoping to put off for another few minutes what she knew must be faced alone.

"Remember," he said, "I want to see the kids next Saturday."

"I'll try to arrange it."

"Do arrange it. I'll be coming for them right at noon. And tell the old man he'd better back off, because if he tries to stop me I'll kick his house down."

They parted that way, on a threat. She watched him drive away, took a deep breath, and walked slowly toward the house. Orrin came out and unlocked the gate. She walked past him without looking at him or saying a word.

Gregory Clement waited for her at the front door. Silhouetted against the hall chandelier, he looked thin and tall and terrifying. He stepped aside and she came past, into the ring of light where she could see him better. His face shocked her. He was livid, pale, and angrier than she had ever seen him. The tiny vial containing his heart pills stood open on the hall table. She didn't comment on that, so certain was she that he had left them there for her benefit alone. He had spoken for years of a mild heart condition, had had two attacks since her mother's death, and now the implication hung between them as she faced him.

"Young lady, what you have done today is totally without honor or principle. Lying, sneaking away like some spiteful child. Lacking even the decency or courage to tell me what you were doing."

"Would you have let me go?"

"That's not the point."

"That's exactly the point. Would you?"

"I can see now there'll have to be some changes made around here."

"What does that mean, Father?"

"The remedy must fit the case." He looked at her for a long moment, then said, "We will discuss it further in the morning."

He turned off the lights in the hall. She closed her door and, suddenly weary, began to undress. Her light went out and she finished undressing in the dark. She went to the window to draw the drapes and saw Orrin standing on the lawn, watching her room from the edge of the trees. The clouds had blown over and a half moon was out, casting the yard in silver and black. He just stood and watched, as unmoving as the statues. She closed the drapes and lay on her bed, too tired to be bothered even by that.

She opened her eyes and looked at her clock. The room was still dark, though outside, she knew, the morning had come. At last she braved the cold room and the cold floor, throwing on her clothes and hurrying out into the front hall. Her father's heart pills remained where he had left them. No one was about. She called his name but no one answered. The fireplace remained unlit, cold. She heard the sounds of his feet outside; he was knocking the snow off his boots. He opened the door and she heard the quiet hum of the Packard's motor as Orrin pulled the car into the drive.

"Father, where are the boys?"

"I've sent them to school. Orrin's just getting back now."

"Are you still angry?"

"Did you expect I wouldn't be?"

"I'm sorry," she said.

"No, you're not sorry, so let's not start off the day lying to each other. What happened yesterday was calculated and premeditated on your part, and we must take steps to see that it doesn't happen again. You know, my dear, I've never been able to abide liars or cheats. The only times that you and I have ever had any serious disagreement were over the larger issues of lying. Isn't that true?"

"I don't know, Papa. If you're talking about old times, that's all such a long time ago."

"Not so long that you've forgotten. Did you know your Mr. Hastings threatened to have me arrested?"

"What?"

"Isn't that extraordinary? Orrin swears it's true. Apparently he told Orrin he'd have me put in jail if I held you here against your will. Now I ask you one more time, is anyone holding you against your will?"

"Papa . . ."

"Answer the question, my dear. Didn't we have a long talk about just this subject not so long ago?"

"Yes, Papa."

"And didn't you agree then that you would stay here and abide by the rules of my house as long as you did?"

"Yes, Papa."

"But you didn't do that, did you?"

She just looked at him.

"No." His lips pressed together. "Get your coat. We're going for a ride."

They drove southwest, away from the city. The roads had been plowed by farmers with horses, and the early-morning traffic was sparse. For a while there was no talk, and then, abruptly, the old man began talking about the boys. He said that Paul especially was becoming sullen and uncooperative, that corrective measures would have to be taken soon. Nell reached over and banged the glass shut, angry that Orrin should hear them discussing her children. Gregory Clement smiled at this bit of temper, then resumed his droning monologue. "What we have is a case of old-fashioned discipline. When a child misbehaves, it's up to the parent to correct that behavior with whatever means he has available to him. Disobedience and rebellion are simply not to be tolerated." She only half listened as he went on and on, but suddenly something he had said brought her mind into sharp focus. Somewhere on the snowy plains he had stopped talking about Paul and had started talking about her. She was a child again, being punished for slipping away to meet her lover. Punished with whatever means the parent had available to him. Even then she didn't make the connection, not until she saw the wire fence and the guard ahead, and the huge wire gate sliding back. It had been a long time, but she would never forget the rolling grounds and the squat gray buildings of the asylum. He was trying to frighten her.

She sat still and composed, refusing to be lured into that trap. Let him think he was scaring her with his crude attempt to punish. She was a woman now, not a child to be scolded and bullied and locked away. They pulled up before a large building. Orrin, looking unusually tense, leaped out and held the door. She stepped out into the warm sunshine. The snow was melting off the walk under her feet. The old man smiled kindly and took her hand. She played the role: "Do you have business here?" she said. So wide-eyed, so innocent. He smiled and led her up the snowswept walk.

Only when they were inside and the doctor came in did she become openly hostile and impatient. "Really, Father, don't you think this nonsense has gone far enough?" The doctor looked at her, but didn't speak. When he did speak, his words were directed to her father. They talked as if she weren't there. The doctor looked at an old chart. She saw her name, *Nell Clement*, written in elaborate scroll on the outside of the folder under the date, March 3, 1908. Just sticking above the folder's edge was a paper headlined REPORT FROM THE LUNACY BOARD.

Gregory Clement was telling the doctor that she had suffered a relapse. After all these years, she had reverted to the strange behavior patterns that had characterized her adolescence. Possibly a bad marriage, now over, was at the root of it. Gregory Clement said she had exhibited certain self-destructive tendencies, especially in the past twenty-four hours, and he was afraid she might harm herself.

The old man and the doctor retired to another room, to talk in private. When he came out, she saw that the doctor carried a series of new-looking forms. Only then did she realize that it was no game, that he had signed her away in the name of love. Her first reaction was anger; her instinct was to fight. But she had been here before, and knew that got her nowhere. Gregory Clement put on his hat. She clutched at his arm and cried, "Father!" But he wouldn't look at her. He left her there, staring after him in disbelief as he and Orrin walked down the corridor and disappeared into the front walk.

She felt the doctor's hand on her shoulder. She spun away and lashed out, pushing him off balance. But the doctor, who was an old hand at dealing with lunatics, simply skipped once and never lost his footing. He came toward her slowly, his palms turned up. "Let's be calm and talk it over," he said. "You've got nothing to fear from me."

"There's nothing to talk over. There's nothing wrong with me and I demand to be released at once."

She got nowhere with that, so she let the doctor seat her and they talked. She answered his questions. Then she told him that she was a married woman, outside her father's legal authority, and they had no right to hold her. The doctor didn't react to that at all.

An orderly took her back to the ward, where she was given a bed in a far corner. The windows were covered by heavy wire, inside and out. Directly across from her was an old woman who never stopped staring.

All right, she could cope with it. At any moment now he would walk through the door and the punishment would be over. But the hours passed, the shadows lengthened across the room, and he didn't come.

She heard shrieking somewhere, far back in another room. Some poor lost fool who didn't know better, didn't understand how to cope. Shrieking was simply playing into their hands. It was what they expected. Calm, cool reason was the only way to deal with these people. How well she knew that.

It wasn't until her third day that her nerves shattered and her reason took flight. She made a break for the door and it took three strong men to hold her back. She bit and scratched and cursed them, until they wrestled her into a strait jacket and carried her to a padded cell.

When she didn't call by Thursday, he tried calling her at the estate. The telephone rang twenty times, but no one answered.

At noon on Saturday he drove over to pick up his boys. He found the gate locked and the guardhouse boarded up. He took a hammer from the toolbox he kept under the rumbleseat and smashed open the lock. He drove up the horseshoe drive and parked in front of the mansion. The windows were boarded up and all the doors were locked. He pulled off one of the boards and looked inside. It was as deserted as a mountain ghost town.

5

The press room at City Hall had once been the county morgue. On a slow day, police-beat reporters from all four Denver dailies could be found slouched over wooden desks, some only half awake. Even the tiny *Denver Express* had a police reporter. It was an important run, though still just a run, where a man was tied to a specific desk within four specific walls, and unless something big was happening, the hours were pretty well established and there was little danger of overtime. It was the first concession he had made for her. He had taken Tammen's raise, asked for and got immediate transfer to the police beat and had even started paying off his bills. His tab at Miller's had been cut in half, and he had knocked down the debt to the engraver downtown. His drinking had increased but so had his eating. He had gotten thinner and older-looking since his weeks on the road with Goodwin.

He lost himself in the daily routine. With three other papers scratching for police news, there were endless rounds to make, bases to touch, tips and leads to cover, and a hell of a lot of writing to do. He wrote his own stuff, dictating polished copy to rewrite men while others phoned in notes. When there wasn't time to write, he dictated on his feet, organizing a smooth, professional story in his mind. He dictated periods, commas and paragraphs, and was always two graphs ahead in his mental composition. His writing became leaner and sharper, and by the end of his first week he had his first front-pager of the new run, a brewing scandal involving one of Mayor Stapleton's aides.

On Tuesday of his second week he tried Nell again. Still no answer. It angered him that she had left like that, but maybe even that would work out for the best. It would give him more time to pull his life together. At noon that day, Marvel came by and invited him to lunch. He turned her down, saying he had too much work to do. He was cool and distant. These were the hours when he cleared his desk, doing all the crummy little assignments that nobody else wanted, writing up everything that everyone said, pounding the Underwood until his fingers cracked open. At four o'clock each day he would have his first drink, sitting at the *Post* desk one floor beneath the police station, openly breaking the law. Occasionally a cop drifted in, and when that happened Tom just gestured toward the open bottle and offered a shot. Sometimes they refused. Just as often they took the shot, tossing it off quickly before hitting the streets.

On balance it wasn't a bad life; it was something he thought he could live with, and he was anxious to tell his wife about his progress. How like her to start playing games again, right at the worst possible time. He decided to wait it out and work harder. There were a few small problems. Gallagher managed to make him feel inferior every time they met. A problem came up with the kid, Arthur McCantless, but he had handled that one quickly and decisively. The kid had begun sitting on the desk as a part-time editor. Was anything as clumsy as an arrogant youth on the way up? Twice he had received abrupt calls from McCantless, demanding elaboration on minor points in his police stuff. Twice he'd gone chasing after the source in an honest effort to oblige. When McCantless called the third time, he shouted into the phone, "Jesus, Hastings, this won't do." Tom guessed the shouting was for Alice Wilder's benefit. Calmly, he said, "Hold it, Arthur. Just calm down. I'm eating my lunch. When I get done I'll come back to the office and we can talk it over there. If you still want to shout, you can do it from the alley. That's where you'll be after I throw your ass through that second-story window. See you in a while, kid." And that problem had ended.

At night he went home alone and pounded out stories for exotic magazines back east. Sometimes he worked straight through until ten o'clock, when Georgeann came. Georgeann was another problem, though he knew she didn't have to be. When it was over, he would simply tell her and she would disappear. No ties, no strings attached, except that she had been with him many weeks now, he had come to love the feeling of her warm body near his, and he knew it would hurt him to say the words. Nothing was ever simple. He wondered where she went when she left him at midnight. He tried to imagine her life, complete with children, and couldn't.

She had never taken his money. He knew that she did take money from others, and there were many, but she always came to him fresh from a bath. He guessed he loved her, but it was a strange love that bred no jealousy or possessiveness. Away from home, he never thought of her, and he never fretted over how she made her money. It was only late at night, as he sat beating away on his old typewriter, that his eyes would drift up to the clock and the old excitement would begin.

At ten o'clock he washed up, turned off the light and got into bed. A few minutes later the key scraped in the lock. She moved through the dark room and eased in beside him.

In his third week on cops, he dashed off an angry letter to Nell. He rewrote it, took out most of the harshest barbs and put it in the morning mail.

Most of the press had cleared out, heading for Miller's and the free lunch. He was shuffling through his notes when a soft female voice from the hallway brought him to his feet. "Pardon me, sir, could you please tell me where I might find Mr. Tom Hastings?"

Anna came to the door.

"I don't believe it," he said. "What on earth brings you down here? Is something wrong at home?"

"No, no. You always said I should start seeing the world, so I'm starting."

"You'll excuse the expression, but this is a hell of a place to start."

He found her a chair and sat her beside his desk. She sat primly, her hands in her lap, like a transplant from another time. Her ears were alert to passing noises in the hall, and her eyes rolled back often, in response to something she had heard. She took in everything. "So this is a press room." There was a sense of wonder in her voice. "Why the tiled floor? And what are the drains for?"

"You shouldn't ask. Have you had lunch yet?"

He took her to a fine restaurant on Seventeenth Street, a place where brokers ate. At every table people talked stocks and bonds, profit and loss, and margin. His first unspoken-for paycheck and another forty dollars from New York had brought some of the glow back to the world, and even a five-dollar lunch tab wasn't beyond him. Anna was amazed at the hustle of the downtown. She couldn't take her eyes off the brokers and lawyers in their three-piece suits, but the thing that really amazed her was how few horses there were on the streets. "In the blinking of an eye they're all gone." He didn't remind her that the blinking of her eye had been more than ten years long. She rushed on, a bit out of breath. "This morning I walked along Curtis Street. I couldn't believe the cinema houses. It's just incredible! The whole street is full of cinema and vaudeville, and a few other places that look pretty wicked."

"It's called the Broadway of the West."

"I want to see a movie sometime. Can ladies go without escorts?"

"In the daytime. At night it's not too smart, but that's when the lights are all on. But I'll be your escort. I'll be proud to take you."

"That scandal over Mabel Normand was so monstrous, what with that horrid murder, but it hasn't seemed to hurt her any. They're showing two of her pictures downtown. I guess people have to satisfy their lusts for blood, don't they? Have you seen her?"

212

"Oh, sure."

She rambled on, talking about ladies' fashions and how far hems had come up, how reading didn't quite prepare you for the experience. He thought she'd look good in one of Alice Wilder's things. She seemed made for silk. Get her out of that ten-year-old dress and into something modern and she'd set Denver on its ear. He was trying to think of a tactful way of saying that when suddenly she told him why she had really come.

"Someone I know is going to court today. I've been meaning to call and ask your opinion, but I've been putting it off. Now it's here and I can't put it off any longer."

"Is this a lady friend?"

He thought her embarrassment was incredibly charming.

"I didn't say it was a friend at all. It's a man, a friend of Abe's. I just happened to have met him."

"What did he do?"

"He hit a policeman. Do you know a policeman named Moran?"

"Is he the cop your friend hit?"

"Yes. I saw it happen. He really was provoked."

"I can believe that. Moran's a bad actor. That's just my opinion. Some of the guys down here get along fine with him."

She looked relieved, as if she'd chosen sides in a fight and had only now learned that she had picked the right side. "David said you'd say that."

"David, uh . . . Waldo?"

"Yes. Do you know him?"

"I remember the name. Isn't he the guy Abe was setting you up for?"

"Please, Thomas, don't tease me now. This is too serious."

"Who's the judge?"

"I don't know his name."

"Does your friend have a lawyer?"

"Yes, they got him one right away."

"Who are they?"

"The people at the jail. Isn't that how it works?"

"Uh, no, not exactly. Has your friend got any money?"

"How would I know? I told you . . ."

"I know, he's Abe's friend. Well, do you think he's indigent?"

"I doubt that. I think he owns the building his store's in, for what that's worth."

"It's worth something. His lawyer wouldn't happen to be named Henry, would it? Or Reismann?"

"I really couldn't say. Does that matter?"

"It might. Do you know what they're charging him with?"

She shook her head. He sat, quiet for a moment, drumming his fingers on the table. He was thinking of all the reasons why he shouldn't get involved in this, and heading the list was his restricted job. He couldn't just go charging off anymore without reporting to someone on city desk. It was a court reporter's story, plain and simple.

"Look," he said. "Let's get back to the office. You wait for me while I clear up a few things and I'll walk over to the courthouse with you. Are you being called to testify?"

"Goodness, no. Will I be?"

"You should be, if you saw what happened."

"Dear God, you mean I'll have to get up in front of all those people . . ."

"Don't get excited yet. It may not come to that at all. Got your wrap?"

6

David Waldo's hearing was at two-thirty, in the courtroom of District Judge Thurman Hayes. The rape judge.

Tom and Anna sat in a pew at the rear of the courtroom. They were the only spectators. About five minutes after they arrived, a slim balding man from the district attorney's office came in, flanked by Virgil Joseph Moran. They took seats at a table before the bench, and almost immediately Saul Reismann came in and sat at the opposite table. Moran turned and saw Tom and Anna, then leaned over and said something to the prosecutor.

David Waldo arrived. He came down the aisle without seeing Anna, and settled into a chair at the defense table to wait. Soon the bailiff entered, and Judge Hayes came in to the bang of a gavel. "All rise." Tom and Anna rose. The judge sat, and looked at them. His eyes met Tom's, and for perhaps thirty seconds there was a staredown between them. Hayes loved publicity when it was good, but he had a fear of bad press that had made him a laughingstock in the press room. At last he looked away. He put on a pair of glasses and read from a paper before him. "People versus David Waldo. The defendant will stand."

David stood and faced the bench.

"You are charged with resisting arrest." The judge looked suddenly troubled. He took off his glasses and rubbed his eyes. When he looked up again, his eyes found Tom. "Mr. Hastings," he said softly.

Tom stood. Everyone turned and looked at them. Anna went red and avoided David Waldo's eyes.

"Mr. Hastings," the judge said again. "May I ask what interest the press has in my humble court?"

"The interest of justice, your honor."

"Surely the interest of justice is better served elsewhere. I can assure you that these proceedings are most mundane. Usually the people want something more exciting issues in their newspaper reading."

"Respectfully, judge, the press reserves the right to decide that question for itself."

The judge nodded shortly and the hearing began. It was apparent at once that a deal was in the works. The three charges, resisting arrest, assaulting an officer, and assault with a deadly weapon, had been amended, reduced to the single least serious among them.

"How do you wish to plead?"

David looked at Moran, whose face was a gray mask. "Not guilty," he said. His voice was so soft it barely carried to the back of the room. Immediately Saul Reismann stood and drew David off to one side. He gestured fiercely and spoke in a raspy whisper. The judge looked over his glasses at the DA.

"He's pleading not guilty. Are there any witnesses?"

"There were two officers with Lieutenant Moran at the time, your honor."

"Oh, well, then." The judge looked at David. "Any other witnesses?"

"No, your honor," the prosecutor said.

Anna stiffened. Tom placed a hand on her leg.

Saul Reismann approached the bench. "Your honor, I think my client wants to change his plea."

Again David faced the rape judge.

"What is your plea, sir?"

"Guilty."

"You'll have to speak up."

"*Guilty!*"

"Very well. The defendant pleads guilty to a charge of resisting arrest." The judge looked first at Tom, then at David. "Now I ask you, Mr. Waldo, did anyone coerce you into making this plea?"

"No."

"Did anyone promise you anything, or otherwise indicate that this court might be more lenient to a plea of guilty?"

"No."

"Then you make this plea of your own free will and choice, knowing that the penalty for this crime may be a fine and a term of imprisonment?"

"Yes."

"All right, the court accepts the plea of guilty and is prepared to pass sentence now." There was a long pause while the judge continued reading through the complaint. He took off his glasses and faced David Waldo and Saul Reismann. "This court's feelings about crimes of violence are well-known in this city. The current wave of anarchy and lawlessness must be stopped. The defendant may consider himself fortunate that the more serious charges in this case were dropped. In the coming months he may reflect upon his situation, and on the court's practice to be lenient on first offenders. Let me assure you, Mr. Waldo, that any recurrence of violence on your part will bring about a far different sentence. The court sentences you to ninety days in the county jail and a two-hundred-dollar fine."

The gavel banged. The judge glided off the bench.

Anna was near tears. Tom patted her knee and said, "You and Mr. Waldo wait for me here." He went back behind the bench, through the open door to the judge's office. He gave the clerk his name and in a moment he was admitted to the plush chamber, filled with the mementos of a legal lifetime. Behind the mahogany desk were shelves of law books and a picture of Judge Hayes shaking hands with Warren Harding. The judge had taken off his robe and was seated in shirtsleeves and suspenders behind his desk. He looked friendly but wary, motioning Tom to a chair with a wave of his hand.

"All right, Hastings, what's it about? Usually you newshounds shun this ordinary stuff like the plague."

"My sister was a witness. She saw what happened between Waldo and the cops. It wasn't quite like it came out in court."

"If she saw it, why didn't she come forward?"

"She wasn't called. It was all done pretty fast, your honor."

"The man pleaded guilty. You heard that yourself."

"On the advice of counsel. Listen, judge, let's quit playing around. You know Saul Reismann as well as I do."

"That sounds like contempt of court, Hastings. Talk like that could get you in a lot of trouble."

"Is that your comment, your honor?"

Hayes watched him for a long time. "My relations with the press have always been cordial, haven't they?"

"You always manage to do all right in print, sir."

"Just what is it you want?"

"I told you that in court."

"Ah, yes, justice. The grand elusive ideal. But subject to interpretation, wouldn't you say?"

"Not in this case."

Hayes just stared at him. He didn't call Anna in, didn't ask what had really happened that day on Osceola Street. He just watched Tom's eyes, and when he spoke again his voice was a friendly growl, almost conspiratorial.

"All right, God damn you." He laughed, then the laugh melted away and he had gone serious again. His face was full of judicial dignity. "We can suspend the jail sentence, subject to the defendant's good behavior for the next six months. He'll have to pay the fine. You see, Hastings, this court is always anxious to hear additional facts, even after judgment has been passed. Does that satisfy the *Post's* interpretation of justice?"

"It'll do, your honor." He moved out into the courtroom, where Anna stood waiting with David Waldo.

7

David Waldo climbed the winding staircase to his apartment above the print shop. It was late and he had been walking alone through west Denver. Three times he had gone past her house. He had stood in the trees, watching her window as in that delicious beginning, when nothing had happened between them, and anything was possible. Twice he had seen her dark head pass the window, cocked slightly toward the street as if she sensed his presence. The last time she had come into full view she smiled down into the street; for a full hour David had walked around the lake, happy beyond belief.

That afternoon after his appearance in court he had taken her to Curtis Street, to see the new Mabel Normand film. He would remember the day as their first real date, done on the spur of the moment after a quick cup of coffee with her brother in a restaurant near the courthouse. Tom had suggested it. She had been enchanted with the film, and she seemed almost drunk with excitement that he would not be going to jail after all. She thought Mabel Normand was very lovely. Afterward, as they had arranged, they met Tom and the three of them had dinner. David thought her brother was first-rate. Their talk across dinner was free and easy, and suddenly Tom was gone, back to the police station to finish his day's work. David and Anna stood on a corner and watched him until he disappeared into Larimer Street. "He's very sad these days," she said. "He's having trouble with his wife."

They sat alone in the trolley and watched the electric lights float past the window, and in time he deposited her by the door. He kissed her hand. Not satisfied with that, he watched her house from the trees across the road. It was late when she finally turned out the light. He walked and lost track of time. When finally he turned toward his store, he saw two police cars circling the block. He waited in the shadows until they were gone, then he ran like a fugitive to his door, where he finally got inside after two fumbling attempts to get the key in its slot.

That brought him to the top of the stairs. The upper room was in total darkness, but he knew it so well that he crossed it without a pause. There was no sound, but he could feel a presence just ahead. A familiar scent came riding on a cold mist that seemed to come from the bathroom. "Jessie?" He leaned over and turned on a light.

The place was empty. If she had been there, and he was sure she had, she was either gone now or in hiding. He searched thoroughly and found nothing. In the bathroom, he bent over and felt the tub. It was damp. So was the heavy towel that hung over the gas heater, which was still warm. And the bed, though it seemed made up as he'd left it that morning, was slightly warmer on one side, as if someone had been there and had only recently left.

It wasn't the first time she had done it. Last week he had almost caught her here, coming home early one night to hear scurrying mouselike sounds. She ran out through the shop's back door. He chased her across a field, down a gulch, and along a drainage ditch, where he lost her in the bushes. He walked along both sides of the ditch for an hour, begging her to come out and talk, but the only answer he got was from a neighborhood alley cat.

Now he tried to sleep, but sleep wouldn't come. He thought that perhaps he would marry Anna and move to Alaska, where he could get a fresh start. He thought of Canada, where perhaps there were no brutal cops or bigoted judges, where land was still free for the taking. He wondered if she would leave her family. And inevitably, involuntarily, his thoughts always came back to Jessie.

He got up, dressed, and went out. He walked east, to the railroad yards. He covered the distance quickly, coming up toward the tarpaper shack under a heavy cloud cover. The shack was empty, but inside were unmistakable signs of recent habitation: brown bottles without labels, the unstirred ashes of a fire not quite cold, a pair of beans cans, still moist inside. So they hadn't gone to Miami; hadn't gone anywhere. He rummaged through the old man's cot and found a library copy of *War and Peace*. It was two years overdue. Near the pile of rags where she slept was a sheet of paper and a pencil. On the paper, in shaky stick letters, she had printed the name RIMA. He tore the paper in half, took up the pencil, and wrote a note.

> Jordan,
>> Please come see me. This has got to stop.
>>> David

But Abbott didn't come and it didn't stop. She came again the following week and twice the week after that. She was still coming in January, when David Waldo and Anna Kohl were married.

End of Book One

BOOK TWO

BOOK
OF
DAVID

CHAPTER ONE

1

Tides of change were on the land. In Denver and across America, acts of brutality and oppression that had long been practiced, but always condemned, became marks of respect. In private suburban clubs and in homes from North Denver to Capitol Hill, men met to drink, laugh, and slap backs, then don the hoods and sheets of the oppressors and 'stalk the night. The victims were the poor, the weak, those with no power. In west Denver they watched from windows as the fiery parades came every Friday, returned on Saturday, and the rows of the hooded marchers grew with each passing week. Each Friday morning, in the yards near Cheltenham School, the Jewish fathers nailed heavy sheets of plywood over their lower floor windows, and the houses remained boarded until Sunday, when the Sabbath had ended.

The fear ran across racial and religious neighborhoods, trickling from west Denver into the downtown. The oppressors marched everywhere. Huge turnouts could be summoned at any hour of the day, at any day of the week, in any part of town. They came up Sixteenth Street, walking three abreast in a show of solidarity and strength, while along the sidewalks their leaders went store to store, loudly demanding that all blacks, Jews, and Catholics be fired.

The undercurrent of the city that spring was like that of a town beseiged, though no guns could be seen, no trenches lined the perimeter, no shells burst across the night sky. The seige came down in a state of mind and in an economic boycott. Stores that hired Negroes found their windows smashed at night. Mysterious fires broke out, and acts of vandalism went unreported. In an alley near Cheltenham School, a pair of newsboys watched from the bushes as four men ransacked Sammy Kohl's store. In the morning, when police reporters from the *Post* and *News* combed through the blotter, they would find no mention of it, no report made, no complaint filed. Sammy Kohl simply didn't report it. Even when Mr. Silverman, who lived behind the store, told Sammy that he had seen the men, and that one had been a policeman, Sammy didn't report it. Instead, twice a week, and always on different nights, he slept on a cot in the store, a shotgun within easy reach.

Across town, in a paint store on Welton Street, John Wentworth was forced to fire Richard Watson, whose father had worked for his father and who, himself, had worked in the Wentworth store for thirty years. Richard Watson was a paint mixer who had never been to school. From experience, Richard Watson could mix exactly the right reds with flat whites to produce the perfect shade of pink. He did this by instinct, the way an old housewife cooks, without any chart or recipe book. It was said of Richard Watson, first of all, that he knew his job. He had worked himself up to sixty cents an hour, and now brought home thirty dollars for a fifty-hour week. But the Klan took offense when John Wentworth hired a Kleagle's son, at thirty-five cents an hour, to deliver the paint that Richard Watson mixed. The night of his first paycheck, the boy complained to his father. "Pa, they got a nigger in that store that makes twice as much as I do." And the father, red-faced and arrogant with the intoxication of his sudden power, stalked out to see what could be done. That night, John Wentworth had visitors.

It was a story told a thousand times that year, but seldom for any public record. Why appeal to police, when the police are the enemy? Historians, looking back at those sparse records, tell us that Denver and Colorado were free of night riding, that Klan terror tactics were confined to California, Indiana, and the deep South. What really happened is bound in folklore. We know that by early 1924, John

Galen Locke was running Denver and had begun to grasp at the state machinery as well. When Republicans assembled at the Auditorium for their state convention, Locke arrived in a red Pierce Arrow and supervised from a private box high above the floor. Like a feudal emperor he directed the convention's progress. The delegates bowed and did his bidding. Judge Clarence Morley became Locke's hand-picked candidate for governor. Locke was running at least four benches of the district court. He rigged trials and drew up jury lists. Klan lawyers gave the high sign and cases were arbitrarily dismissed, thrown out of court, or twisted to Locke's will.

In March, Locke plucked off the police department, forcing Mayor Ben Stapleton to appoint William Candlish as chief. Candlish was an assayer with no police experience, and when rumors filtered through the press corps that his appointment was imminent, reporters scattered across town to find the mayor. If true, it was a big story. Stapleton faced the press with patient denials. He was not appointing Candlish to anything. But when the mayor arrived at City Hall, he found the forms already filled out, lacking only his signature. Clipped to the form was a note from Locke, directing Stapleton to sign it.

A feeling began to mount that Stapleton had betrayed Denver, and recall petitions were circulated. District Attorney Philip Van Cise and Judge Ben Lindsey of the Denver Juvenile Court were harsh critics of Locke and of Stapleton, and other anti-Klan forces began to muster. An Irish-American group, the Ancient Order of Hibernians, waged an unofficial street war against Klansmen, slashing tires and upholstery and ripping wires out of cars parked at Klan rallies. For a brief spark the *Denver Post* came to life, running brutal front-page attacks against the Klan without ever mentioning the civic leaders who were its members. The *Post* took up the chant for Stapleton's recall, openly branding the mayor a Klan lackey, and when 26,000 signatures were obtained, Bonfils picked up the call. He supported the candidacy of Stapleton's foe, Dewey C. Bailey, and blistered the mayor in daily front-page articles and with cruel editorial cartoons. One cartoon had Stapleton in a cloak and hood, sitting behind the mayor's desk with a bullwhip in his hand, his foot resting on a book of Constitutional law. Another showed the mayor bowing at the feet of the Klan chief. On election day, the *Post* ran a cartoon titled "The Hooded Boss," showing a ghostlike apparition hovering over the city skyline. The caption read, *You will vote the way I tell you, and I will run this city as I please, and it pleases me to run it according to the secret laws and rules of the KKK.*

By mid-evening it was apparent that the editorial barrage had backfired. Stapleton won by 31,000 votes, better than two-to-one, and the people handed their city over to John Galen Locke. That night two crosses were burned on Table Mountain above Golden, one red and one white. Klansmen whooping with the taste of victory replaced their bumper stickers reading "Stapleton Stays" with new ones that said "Morley For Governor." In the morning, Bonfils drew in his horns, wrote a tame editorial congratulating Locke on the "perfect machine" he had assembled, and dropped the Klan issue from the pages of his newspaper. Locke was interviewed in his Glenarm Street office and claimed total credit for Stapleton's stunning victory. After long months of secrecy, the ghost was finally out of the closet.

It had been a long winter, a longer summer. Far back in January, the night the recall petitions were just getting moving, Sammy Kohl slept in his store. Richard Watson, unable to find work, moved out of his Marion Street apartment, packed his family into an old Hudson, and struck out for Chicago, where he hoped things would be better. The press didn't cover his departure, nor did it take note, two days later, when Isaac Jefferson and his wife Bess fled in terror after getting a Klan threat in their mailbox. Only the tiny *Denver Express,* with its trivial circulation and its featherweight punch, kept up a consistent, unending attack against Locke's Klan. For that its advertisers were boycotted and its windows were smashed by bullets, fired from speeding cars at midnight.

2

For David Waldo, the first few months of 1924 were the most exciting times of his life. His trouble with police seemed part of a distant past, his business picked up and, most important, his friendship with Anna Kohl had become what even in his fantasies he had not really hoped for. In late November she began calling him *David;* in December he became *Davie,* and by January even old Sammy was resolving himself to the fact that they would marry. He had never had his talk with David Waldo, but events had gone beyond that now. Anna and David were married in the mountains at the end of January, with an unorthodox rabbi doing the ceremony. Sammy, dressed in orthodox Jewish garb for the unusual wedding, gave the bride away. His face was blank. Behind him, Teresa looked satisfied and happy. Abe sat in his wheelchair, watching the billowing grass. Tom was David's best man. During the winter an intense friendship had formed between them. At least once a week, without any prearrangement, one would show up at the other's domain. They would sit and talk for long stretches at a time. Tom had begun coming to David's round table meetings, and by Christmas Anna was coming too. They added spice and heat to the dialogue, so much so that Benny Wassermann dropped out. David was amazed at the quickness of Anna's mind. She could go through a book in an afternoon, absorbing the finest details with total recall. "The genius is out of the bag now, Dave," Tom said one afternoon. "She used to do stuff like that in school too. Never study, always straight A's anyway, embarrass the hell out of the rest of us dummies." Anna, sitting in a corner, looked up from her book, stuck out her tongue, and blushed.

In addition to the monthly sessions, Tom would suddenly appear at David's doorstep. "Hey, Dave, got some time?" he would say, and David would make some time. They would sit at the big table with the curtains drawn, David's OUT TO LUNCH sign discouraging potential customers. Their talks were varied and full, though David always felt afterward that Tom had skirted around the personal problems that were really on his mind. He did tell David that he had received a letter from his wife, who had taken the two children and moved to St. Louis. She had decided to divorce him. He said this with regret, but without bitterness, then he moved on to something else and never brought it up again. What they talked about most of the time was the state of the world, politics, Coolidge prosperity, stocks, the Ku Klux Klan, and journalism. David surprised Tom with his keen interest in the press, and with the revelation that he too had been a reporter, with the *Oakland Trib* more than twenty years ago. They talked writing and literature. Tom told him about the book he had always wanted to write, but now never would, and David described his strange friendship years ago with Jack London. They passed the days, sitting, talking, exploring each other's mind. David didn't drink, and it kept Tom out of bars.

Sometimes David turned up unannounced at his Capitol Hill rooming house, or at the City Hall press room. He met Georgeann Johannsen and liked her very much. The three of them had dinner one night, and David held a long talk with her in broken Swedish while Tom just watched. Georgeann laughed, enjoying immensely the novelty of talking her own tongue again while someone else struggled with the words. There were few bad moments between them. Once or twice, going down the steps to the press room, David met Lieutenant Moran coming up, but those times were exceptional. He learned what Tom's deadlines were, and he seldom arrived before twelve-thirty. On good days they bought their lunch at a take-out sandwich shop on Lawrence Street, then walked down the tree-lined path that followed Cherry Creek southeast from City Hall. After a while Tom would find a place to sit, and the talk would start.

At the end of their first month, David confessed that he was hopelessly in love with Tom's sister and would marry her if he could. Tom told him about Anna's long affair with Willie Brown III, and what had come of it. "I'm telling you this because she won't, and if it makes any difference to you then you ought to know now, before this goes any further. Things like this have a way of cropping up sometime and causing a hell of a lot of pain, so I'm going to take it on myself and tell you, even if it's none of my business, to do it. Gabriel isn't our brother, he's Anna's son. Maybe you've already guessed that. He's Anna's and Willie Brown's. He was born in the Florence Crittendon Home way out on Colfax, just a few miles from our house. It was a great big tragedy, and nobody ever mentions it around our house, ever. That's why Anna's been living the way she has, isolating herself from the rest of the world, living up in that room, going on religious kicks with this silly Aimee Semple McPherson person. It's a form of penitence, if you can believe that in this day and age. Maybe if social mores before the war had been what they are today, none of this would be happening. You and I wouldn't be sitting here talking like this, probably wouldn't know each other at all. For ten years I've been hoping somebody would come along and do what you're doing— walk into that house and take her out, get her out of that goddamn room and away from those dusty scrapbooks and that dumb, stifling religion. I think she's worth it."

"I know she is."

"I'll tell you anything you want to know. First there was this big shock wave at home. Sammy looked sick for days on end. Mom just sank into a gloomy depression. Big sin, big fall from grace. And Anna began sitting upstairs alone. She'd eat in her room, never came down for anything. Finally one night Sammy and Teresa had it out. They decided to keep the child. Old Sam decided that. No matter what, the kid had Kohl blood and would be raised in the family. The only question was how. Anna was starting to show, so they had to make a decision soon. Neither Sammy nor Mom had any family, nobody they could trust to send her to. None of us had any money. In the end it was decided that she should go to the home and have the kid there. Gabriel became Teresa's menopause baby. He was born when she was forty-two years old. It's still incredible to me that nobody in that neighborhood of busybodies questioned it; as far as I know, nobody does to this day. Gabriel himself doesn't know, and that's another reason why you can't ever say anything. I've always thought that was a mistake. Jesus, can you imagine the shock now if the kid learned that his sister is his mother? But Mom, God bless her, she's like a bulldog when she decides how something should be done, and I guess it's too late to change it now. I'll give her this. She sure fooled everybody."

3

On their wedding night, David and Anna Waldo seemed reluctant to break away from the small crowd that had gathered in the living room of the Kohl home to wish them well. David was drunk with joy, laughing and at ease with everyone. Anna was shy. She tried to withdraw from all the attention, but people milled around, talking and joking, occasionally peppering their talk with sly double entendres. These were her father's friends; she had always thought of them as adults and of herself as a child. Now, with their sly winks and racy talk, they seemed to be welcoming her out of her long childhood and into the real world.

Anna, partly out of habit and partly from a last-minute attack of nerves, tried to help her mother clear away the dishes, but Teresa shooed her away. They were pushed bodily out onto the porch, and immediately the lights went out. They stood trying to see each other, unable to in the sudden dark. In a moment David took his wife's arm and led her down the steps into the yard. Their first walk home was peaceful and lovely. Even the broken glass from last night's Klan march didn't break the spell of the day. She leaned her head against him and they crossed Colfax, and she thought surely, *surely*, he must hear my silly heart beating. How could she tell anyone what she was feeling then? As a child she had thought herself in love with Bonfils, and later there was this Willie Brown thing, and in all her life there had been nothing else. Now here beside her was this gentle giant who called himself David Waldo, whose existence six months ago was unknown to her, and they were married. Everything paled beside that fact: her family, her years of self-torture, Bonfils, Gabriel. Even, God save us, Willie Brown III. Tomorrow, she thought, I will go home and fetch my scrapbooks, and I will burn them.

Somehow the print shop looked different and felt different tonight. Coloring was different, dark images magnified. She would call this home now. Her eyes adjusted and took it in: the round table, the worn curtains, his work area out back, incredibly cluttered. "I meant to straighten it up," he said. "Somehow there just wasn't time." She squeezed his hand. "Never mind, I'll do it for you." He led her around the table and sat, facing her. "Would you like some coffee? Or tea? I'll fix us some." But no, she didn't want anything. The faint light from the street outlined her pale face against her black hair. He touched her cheek. She closed her eyes and quickly, nervously, he moved away.

"I did straighten up, upstairs," he said. His voice was suddenly loud. "Come up and see."

They went upstairs. Her body was tingly, like a mass of raw nerves. She wondered if he felt the same. He led her into a huge room that took up most of the upper floor and served as a combination living room and eating area. There was a small partitioned kitchen and a fireplace. Beyond, a smaller room contained the bed; beyond that, the bathroom. He lit a kerosene lamp, and in the dim light he looked at her with unmistakable hunger and passion.

"It's not much."

"It's fine."

He looked at her. "I am so lucky. All my life I've thought of myself as an ill-fated man. But this . . . God, this erases it all." He waited a moment, then said, "I'm forty years old and I don't know what to do. I don't want to rush you."

She sat on the bed and clutched his hand against her breast. "Dear Davie. Sweet, sweet man."

He let her undress in private. In the bathroom, he splashed his eyes with cold water, took off his shirt, and looked at himself in the mirror. Suddenly his back stiffened and his fists drew tight. His nostrils had caught that old soap scent, faint but unmistakable, bringing back thoughts of a thousand other nights. He went to the bathtub and held the lamp over his head. In the bottom of the tub was a trace of cold water, and beside it were three short, curly hairs. Brown, not black like his. He washed them down the drain, then carried the lamp into the bedroom. She was in bed; only her wide eyes and the dark, tangled mass of her hair showed above the covers.

"I'll be back," he said. "Just going down to make sure we're locked in tight."

In the shop, he rummaged among the presses and stacks of papers, checking into each corner. He climbed down the creaky stairs to the basement, but no one was there. The back door was still locked with the bolt. He braced a chair against the front door and again climbed the stairs to the bedroom.

Trembling, he slipped in beside her. They touched: fingers, then hands. Her fear was great. She wondered if he would expect a virgin. Could he possibly at her age? Then they joined and she gave a little sigh and ran a fingernail along his cheek. Her fears vanished. It was not like that last time, that only time. There was no pain; no frantic, fumbling hands clutching at her. There was just this warm, flowing sensation, and she began to move with him. "Ah, Davie, sweet love."

227

When, five minutes later, she suddenly jerked upright in bed, he clutched her hard against him, thinking she had reached orgasm. But already her excitement had died, replaced by another emotion as strong and primitive. She was afraid again. What had made her jump was not orgasm at all, but the stark, irrational certainty that someone had been standing over his left shoulder, watching them. Of course no one was there and she never told him about it. He would think he had married a mad woman.

4

Throughout the first week of her marriage, the uneasiness persisted. Noises came to her in the night, when he was sleeping, and during the long stretches when he was out making a delivery on some job. Sometimes on gray winter afternoons she would lie awake on her back, staring up at the ceiling and listening to the house. What bothered her were the things that happened not when she was listening, but when she was busy. When they were talking over a warm fire, when she was rattling around in the kitchen preparing their dinner, suddenly something would happen. She would stop, uncertain of what she had just heard. Sometimes it was just a feeling that brought her up short. By the middle of the second week, she was beginning to wonder if the house was haunted. She checked out three books on ghosts from the library, including one long scholarly work, and read them all in a single day. Finally she settled on the most likely theory: the newness of everything. She was a new bride, living in a house that was new to her. Everything had happened so fast, and she'd had precious little time to adjust. She had never lived outside her father's house, hadn't spent a night outside Osceola Street since her long ago childhood with Gail Jaffe. She had been a prisoner of her room, where she knew every rattle and squeak by heart, for more than three thousand days and nights. Was it any wonder, then, that a new place startled her? The thought made her feel better, but the illusions persisted.

Their lovemaking improved throughout the month. They became easier with each other; she was less tense. Still, time after time, she was tempted to sit up in bed and stare into the face of . . . *what*? She knew there would be no one, and she would feel silly again. So she lay there with her eyes closed, trying not to let *it* ruin things. She tried to come with him and sometimes she did. The times became more frequent, and her sexual frustrations began to dissolve and drain away.

One day in the third week she suffered a horrible attack of nerves, which lasted through the afternoon. It was Monday. There had been a tray of sliced beef in the icebox from yesterday's dinner, and she had planned to have it for lunch. She opened the icebox door, but the tray wasn't there. The butcher knife that had been on the tray was gone too. She found the tray, washed and stored, in the cabinet above the sink, but she couldn't find the knife anywhere. She climbed down the stairs to the shop, where David was wrapping some handbills for delivery downtown. "Say, Davie, did you eat up that bit of beef that was left over from yesterday?" He shook his head and went on with his work. He was excited about something; he wouldn't tell her what. Promptly at one o'clock he dashed out into the snow, packing four thousand circulars on his back, and headed for Denver. Alone in the house, the mystery of the missing beef became larger, more annoying than before. She decided to search the house. "If there's a ghost here," she said aloud, "then I'm going to find it."

She felt very foolish, but she started with the attic. It was a large unfinished space above the apartment. There was one trapdoor, which opened from the bedroom. She stood on a box on top of a table and pushed it up, sticking her head through the small hole. It was dusty and close; there was no light. Her eyes adjusted and she saw a pile of papers and rags in a corner, two more stacks of newspapers against a far wall, and several large cardboard boxes. "Hello, anybody here?" She laughed at her silliness and peered deeper into the gloom. It was a firetrap. She made a mental note to ask him about it, and perhaps this weekend they'd get up here and clear it out.

She tried to tackle the basement next. It opened down a set of rickety stairs at the very back of the shop. Its floor was rough concrete and the walls were simply two-by-eights nailed together and braced by two-by-fours. There were gaps between the boards, and the earth beyond pushed in relentlessly. It brought up an old childhood phobia, the fear of being buried, but she pushed ahead anyway. Paper was everywhere, in huge piles around the foot of the stairs, scattered across the floor, in opened, half-used boxes. She put down the lantern and tried to straighten it up, but the sound of a scurrying rat frightened her off. When David returned from town, she forgot to tell him about the attic. He was too excited to let her talk. He had bought her a new dress, something conservatively stylish, still far too bold for her. But he made her try it on. He took her hand and held her at arm's length. "Simply beautiful," he said. She gave a half curtsy and laughed. Then he told her that she could wear the dress in San

Francisco, give it a good breaking-in where there was no danger of running into anyone they might know. He had bought two tickets on the Union Pacific, leaving a week from Friday. They hadn't had their honeymoon yet.

5

A huge winter storm had rolled down from the mountains, catching Denver in the middle of its work week. It began Wednesday morning, and by nightfall traffic was clogged on all four major roads out of town. Trolley service ran late and was finally discontinued as snow drifted across the tracks and obliterated them.

For Sammy Kohl, it was to be a night of uneasiness and trouble. He had planned to stay over in the store, but a last-minute need to be with his family made him change his mind. The store was empty and quiet. Sammy had eaten the supper that Teresa had sent, and now he sat at the counter near the door, watching the snow swirl outside. He was thinking of Anna. His suppers hadn't been the same since she'd married David Waldo. Teresa was a good cook, but Sammy had always thought that Anna was a little better. David Waldo was a lucky man. Sammy tried to keep the bitterness out of his heart as he thought that, but it was hard not to feel that David had reached into his house and snatched away its most precious jewel. This courtship and marriage had overwhelmed him; it had all happened so fast. David Waldo made him feel uncomfortable. He didn't want to dislike Anna's husband, and really, there was much about David that was likable and even admirable. He seemed to work hard, and he did love her. David had brought her out of her shell so remarkably that they all had to be grateful. The fact that he had lived openly with this other woman, this Jessie Abbott, and until fairly recently, bothered Sammy a lot. He wondered if Anna knew that, and if she knew that Jessie was still out there, watching. Once last week Anna had come to the store, and Sammy had felt a strong urge to tell her. *Watch out, daughter. Be careful.* But he couldn't do that. The time for watching out was past.

He had been surprised and a little shocked the night before, when Jessie came past his window. He had slept in the store, and the clatter of a passing trolley had stirred him out of a dream. He took a book from his office and propped himself up near the counter to read. He had been there only a few minutes when Jessie walked past. An old man walked with her. They came past his storefront and stopped at the corner. The old man spat. For a moment they stood there, outlined against the streetlamp, then they crossed and continued on up Colfax. Three hours later they came back. Sammy hadn't moved. He sat and watched them come, like ghost figures in the night. Just as they reached the storefront, Jessie looked in and saw him. Her eyes found his face, and she smiled.

His troubled family. Anna, happy on the surface, had trouble brewing that none of them understood. And what could a father do about a son like Abe, or about Tom and Nell? Another old man's heartache. He had always liked Nell, even if the others in his family didn't share the feeling. And Ethan, God bless him, wherever he was. Always requesting money. The latest had come just last week, from New York. Ethan had sounded so desperate, so unhappy, that again Sammy Kohl had split his bank account in half, sending one thousand dollars to a hotel address in New York City. He sent a note, emphasizing that it was a loan, which would have to be repaid as soon as Ethan could send it. And he knew that this note, like all the others, was futile. He comforted himself with the thought that perhaps he was wrong, perhaps he would live a long time yet and build the account up again. But now he knew the futility of that too. Two days ago the pain had started, and this morning after his bath he had found another lump, this time in his groin.

He had come to resent people, and that was no way to leave this earth. He resented Ethan for demanding too much, and David Waldo for taking his little girl. He resented Jacob Howe for trying to deprive Abe of the last remaining pleasure in his life. He resented himself for not being a better man, and most of all he resented the Ku Klux Klan for keeping him in his store, away from his family. He wondered how many more nights they would have together. So tonight he would go home, and the Ku Kluxers would do what they would. He broke open the shotgun's barrel and slipped the shells into a side pocket, turned out the lights, and walked home with the open gun cradled across his arm.

He was passing David's shop when he saw, or thought he saw, a light in the upper window. It was just a flicker, so faint and so brief that it might have been his imagination. Both upper windows remained black and empty.

Sammy had never been a man of mirages or spirits. He walked home and, as Teresa came to the door, he said, "Did Anna give you a key to their house before she went away? Get it for me, will you please?" Sammy took the key and trudged back to the shop, the gun still cradled in his arm. At the door he slipped two shells into the barrels, then he went inside. He had never been in David's place, and his eyes weren't what they once were, but he used no lights. He found the shop sloppy and the upper rooms tidy and neat. Only the bed was mussed, and that puzzled him. The spread was rumpled as if someone had just jumped up from making love. The thought of Anna and David together on this bed embarrassed him. He left quickly and walked home.

When he came in, Teresa had just hung up the telephone. "It's Julia," she said. "They've got trouble at the Howes'."

"What trouble?"

"Some trouble out in Jacob's shop. Julia was too excited. I couldn't get much out of her. She said Jacob won't let her or Emily come out with him, and there are some more men just outside the door."

"All right." Sammy nodded. "You call Julia back. Tell her I'll be there in a second."

"You going by yourself?"

"You see anybody else to go with me?"

"Call Thomas."

"Takes too long. In this snow, he'd never get here."

"Then I'll call him."

"You call, then. I'm going."

He approached the Howe place from the east, circling the block and coming up from the blind side. A large car was parked at the side. Sammy paused at the gate. His fingers felt stiff and unresponsive on the trigger. He went into the yard and circled the house. Suddenly they were standing before him, not twenty yards away. They were standing near the back porch, smoking. He cocked the hammers on the gun and moved noiselessly through the snow. At the edge of the house, he leveled the gun and said, "Okay, stick 'em up." For a moment the men stared at him, like comedy figures in a cinema short. Then they saw the gun. Slowly their hands went over their heads. Sammy motioned with the gun and they stepped away from the house. He moved toward the shop. As they came close to the open door, he heard voices, one gruff and hard, the other high-pitched, whining. He had reached the door when he realized with a shock that the whining voice was Jacob's. He pushed open the door and saw a pale yellow light: a lantern, hanging from a nail over the forge. Jacob had backed into a corner and two more men stood before him laughing.

"I told you men . . . ," Jacob said. "I told you before, I don't want no trouble."

"He don't want no trouble. You hear that, Pike? The big man don't want no trouble. Is that what you said, big man?"

"I told you. I did what you said, now why don't you leave me alone?"

"Your membership's been refused, big man. It looks like you're not a good enough citizen to be in the Klan."

232

"What must I do then?"

"The big man wants to know what he must do, Pike."

"What must I do for you to leave me alone? All I want is to live in peace."

Both men burst out laughing.

"Listen, big man, if you want peace, we'll give you some peace. It's simple. Won't we give him some peace, Pike? Here, come closer, big man, I'll tell you how."

Jacob took a step out of his corner, his eyes full of suspicion and fear.

"Here, big man. Here's some peace." A fist lashed out and Jacob went down. He flopped on the floor, crawling into his corner as if somehow he could claw his way through the wall and away.

"Here's some more peace." Nate kicked him in the ribs.

Jacob buried his face in his hands. "Please stop it. Please! I'll do anything you say, only Jesus God stop this."

Sammy pushed open the door wide. He stood still, in the open doorway, where he could see all four men. Nate saw the gun first. He backed away from Jacob, a smile crossing his face.

"Well, Pike, it's the jewboy."

"Get out of here," Sammy said.

"Jewboy, come down to help his friend. Fine friend you got here, jewboy."

"I mean right now." Sammy's thumb touched the hammer over the right barrel. "Get off this land."

Worry began spreading across Pike's face.

"I will kill you, mister," Sammy said.

"You ever kill a man before, jewboy?"

"No, but don't press your luck. I don't consider you much of a man."

Nate looked at him. "Okay, we'll leave. Pleasant dreams, big man. We'll be seeing you around."

Jacob didn't move. Long after the car had gone he lay on the floor, hiding his face in his arms. Sammy stood over him until his fingers froze to the gun barrel. He watched the cowering man who had been his friend and neither of them spoke. His finger jerked and one barrel fired into a snowbank. Emily and Julia rushed out onto the porch. Sammy passed them on his way out.

"Sam?" Emily looked down anxiously from the steps. "Sam, what happened?"

"Ask him."

Emily rushed across the yard to the shop. Sammy and Julia stared at each other for a moment, then Julia turned and went back into the house.

A week later Teresa and Emily crossed paths in a neighborhood meat market. Emily said they had sold the farm and would move to Durango, a mountain town in the southwest corner of the state. Jacob had been there as a young man and had liked the wild country. He hadn't been back since 1885. He hoped the rural life-style would be better for his business. Teresa said she was sorry. The women talked for less than five minutes.

There was no send-off. The night before they left, Emily called Teresa and they talked for a few minutes. Julia came to see Abe one last time. Sammy saw the relief in her face. This was her release at last. She looked almost radiant as she left. Abe sat, staring out at the warm winter rain like a dead man.

The morning dawned cold and foggy. Sammy stood on the porch, and across the field he could hear the old truck that Jacob Howe had bought, idling in the yard by the shop. The Howes had sold everything: furniture, some clothing, even some of Jacob's work tools. They carried only what could be packed in the truck. Sammy Kohl stood on the edge of his porch and listened to them leave. He stood there for a long time after the clatter of Jacob's truck had faded.

By the time David and Anna had returned from San Francisco, new tenants had moved into the Howe place. They were quiet people and no one ever saw them. But the abrupt change stirred David's curiosity, and one afternoon he went to the courthouse to check the deed. The property had been bought by Saul Reismann, acting for an unincorporated group of businessmen whose directors were not named.

6

For Anna the days whirled like horses on a carousel. She was removed from her old life by an immense gulf, yet still joined by geography and emotion. She had the best of both worlds. During the day, when David was busy in his shop, she could wander over to Osceola Street and visit with Teresa or keep Abe company. Now, at any hour of the day, she could be seen wheeling her brother along Colfax between the family home and David's shop. She did the shopping for both families, and became known in stores and produce shops all along the avenue. The proprietors smiled and called her "Mrs. Waldo." She loved the sound of it. Sometimes she went alone, and sometimes with Abe, who didn't seem to care. Abe had sunk into a gloomy, unending despair. He spent as much time these days at David's as he did at home, and at last David installed a lift so Abe could be pulled up to the apartment. It worked by sheer muscle power, a simple wooden platform attached to ropes and pulleys. Only David could move it.

Anna loved housework. She liked to talk while she worked, so Abe was pleasant to have around. But at least once a week she took a day for herself, to venture out and explore the world.

She heard soapbox speeches, shouted by madman as people went past. The specter of someone shouting in public was new to her. In the old order, anyone who shouted had to be someone of authority. But the shoppers brushed by, some looking openly annoyed, and after a while she did too. She sought escape in books and cinema. She had come to love film, and now she spent long afternoons in the dark, watching the silver flicker. She saw Colleen Moore and Norma Talmadge. She saw *Passion* with Pola Negri three times. The slapstick was annoying, but she was attracted to racy, suggestive titles. She saw *Mad Love* and *Sinners in Silk*, *Flaming Youth* and *Married Flirts*. She was awed by *The Sheik*, though she didn't particularly like Valentino. At night she returned to west Denver; David would drop his work, and they would eat together in a tiny café three blocks from the store. Then, except on weekend nights when the Klan was marching, they would walk around the lake like courting lovers, returning home to a warm fire and bed.

Now there was little to distinguish her from the thousands of smartly-dressed shoppers who flocked into Sixteenth Street. Her outdated dresses were folded in mothballs and stashed in a trunk. When she held them up at a mirror, they looked like pieces in a museum. So fast had the world changed. David had bought her another new outfit in San Francisco and a third when they returned. She was becoming chic and smart, and her confidence grew with each day. When in the spring she read that a legislator in Utah had drafted a bill limiting skirt lengths in public places to three inches above the ankle, she laughed with delight. *My God*, she thought, *if they passed that here, even I would go to jail.*

She had her hair cut, but not bobbed. She settled on a medium cut, just below the shoulder, and it made her hair look darker and thicker. Catching a sudden glimpse of herself in a mirror, she stopped short and thought how provocative she looked. She looked almost . . . sexy.

There it is. The new me.

She decided she liked it. Yes, she would keep the new her. And so the days passed, and Anna Kohl Waldo, like some statue modified by the chisel of a fickle artist, joined the new society.

7

Her transformation was so rapid that David had trouble keeping up with her. In their long nightly talks before the fire, she displayed a keen, quick mind that never stopped surprising him. She read everything. By mid-April she was reading five books a week, two of them fiction, and was going through three newspapers a day. At night she pounced upon him eagerly, always with some new idea or some thought about world affairs. Often they were still talking at ten o'clock when he turned out the lights and doused the fire. He loved her so much that the thought of her mortality terrified him. For the first time in his life, David Waldo began thinking about a child.

He thought about a son of his own, and about her natural son, Gabriel, who still lived only a block away. A pleasant enough kid, with sandy-colored hair and freckles across the bridge of his nose. He wondered if Gabriel resembled his father. More than once he wanted to tell her what he knew, that it didn't matter, and try to find some way of getting at the truth for all of them. But Gabriel didn't talk much and Anna still grew moody and quiet in the boy's presence. It was easier to think about sons of his own. He had no doubt that she would conceive sooner or later. Her age didn't worry him. The fact that she had had a child early in life would help her when the time came, and he had no reason to worry about his fertility. It was early in the game. David began planning for the event. He thought about it and decided to save some money for the child each month. He didn't trust banks. Coolidge prosperity was all on paper, and someday the economy would tumble like a house of cards. Banks would close and nobody would find work. So he saved his money in a heavy canvas bag, strapped across the front and locked with a tiny padlock. He stored it in the basement, in a small hole behind the wallboards, scooping out the earth with his hands and burying it deep. Each week he worked longer hours so there would be more to put in. He worked ever harder until she complained. Then, wisely, he slacked off and gave her more of his time.

They were in fine health, but he worried about death. He worried especially about his own death, and what might become of her when he died. America did not treat its widows well. In May he said, "How would you like to go back to school?"

Her eyes opened wide. "Me?"

"Just in case."

"In case of what?"

236

"In case something happens to me."

"Please, love, don't talk nonsense."

"Just listen a minute. I'm eleven years older than you. Women usually outlive their husbands even when they're the same age. So if we assume that neither of us will live forever, we also have to assume that I'll go before you. Okay?"

She just looked at him.

"Okay, then, if that happens, I'd like you to be able to take care of yourself. That's all I'm saying. It might never come up. Or it might be twenty or thirty years from now."

"At least."

"All right, but take a look at that future time for yourself. I may be gone. Sammy and Teresa will almost surely be gone. God only knows where Tom will be. You may be saddled with Abe, and if we don't have children, who'll take care of you?"

"I'll take care of myself."

"Exactly. But you have to know how. Anna, it's a man's world. Men run everything. They make all the important decisions and pass all the laws. A man in his sixties will never want for food on his plate or a roof over his head, unless we get into the depression I think is coming. A man can mop floors . . ."

"I can mop floors."

"A man can mop floors or dig ditches. There's always been lots of day work for men. But a woman is at the mercy of the system. All right, forget the sermon. All I'm asking is if you'd like to go back and pick up some skills. Something that'll pull you out in a tight spot."

For a long time she just looked at him. Then she clapped her hands and gave a squeal of joy. "Could I really?"

"Give it some thought. Think about what you'd like to do."

"Maybe later I could even get a job somewhere. Does that shock you?"

He took her tiny oval face in his hands and laughed.

She went to St. Anthony's Hospital, on the south bank of Sloan's Lake, and volunteered for work with patients. By June, downtown Denver had lost its special magic and had become part of her routine. She had enrolled in a business school and was taking courses in typing and shorthand. On her own she studied bookkeeping. She straightened out David's messy books and overhauled his system. For the first half of 1924 they were as happy as two people can be. Only two things troubled them. Anna was still nervous about noises in the apartment, and David, after his respite from police harassment, had become a target of Klan pranksters.

8

On the morning of June 14, 1924, David came down from the apartment and found his windows soaped. Written in huge letters, backward so he could read it inside the shop, were the words DAVID WALDO, COMMUNIST. WE ARE WATCHING YOU. Quickly, before she could come down and see it, he drew a pail of hot water and washed it off. It was Saturday; there had been a huge Klan turnout the night before. He walked around the building looking for more vandalism, but the hooded marchers had moved on to other targets in the neighborhood. That night they returned. Their chants saturated the walls, and he stood in the upper-floor window, watching the procession and the flickering torchlight until Anna drew him away. On Sunday morning the window was marked again. This time the message was in red paint, and the words said DAVID WALDO, JEW FUCKER. He hurried back to the shop, rummaging through his desk for a scraper. By the time he had found one, Anna had come down. He scraped it off, starting with the most offensive word and working up. Like a man covered with leeches, he couldn't get the letters off fast enough. Anna sat at the round table and watched. After a while she realized that her presence only made matters worse, so she moved back through the shop and went out back to wait. But behind the shop, painted into the wood with that same red paint, were the words BOLSHEVIK JEW FUCKER, RED IS THE COLOR OF YOUR ROTTEN COMMUNIST HEART. WE ARE WATCHING YOU. WE WILL NOT GO AWAY. When David came back and saw it, he shook his head and sat on the ground with a sigh.

"That's so ugly," she said in her tiniest voice. "God, who would *do* something like that?"

He sighed and said, "People, Anna."

That night they came again, and now there was an ominous new element. For the first time they came on Sunday, using darkness instead of torchlight, quiet instead of noise. On Monday morning he found his entire storefront drenched in red. Someone had splashed a full can of red paint across the glass, the door, and even on the boardwalk out front. Small crooked fingers of it reached up toward the apartment, and tacked to the door was a note, stick-printed in red on stiff cardboard. The words at the top, larger than the rest, said, HOW DOES IT FEEL TO SCREW A JEW? He burned it and crushed the ashes. All that day the words stuck in his mind. Vile words, horrible and sick, once seen never forgotten. Gross sexual references to Anna's black hair, her mouth, and "hungry" eyes. Someone had been doing a lot of fantasying about Anna. He was sure he knew who.

It had the distinct Moran style.

At midnight, Tuesday, the phone began ringing. Anna got up, put on her robe, and hurried down the staircase.

"Hello?"

She clicked the cradle arm once and listened. "Somebody there?" She hung up and went back to bed. She had just drawn the covers up under her chin when it started again. "Let me," David said. He went down and lifted the earpiece. A thick, raspy voice said, "Look out the back window," and the caller hung up.

In the field behind the house, someone had erected a giant wooden cross, painted with a yellow paint that stood out against the dark. Four hooded men stood around it, one holding a torch. The torch was passed from hand to hand until one of the men stepped close and touched it to the base of the cross. Flames leaped up, forty feet into the black sky. The men paraded around the cross, then trickled away into the trees lining the field.

They talked about it over breakfast. "You know," he said, "this kind of thing will get nothing but worse. They'll get bolder and bolder. First thing you know they'll be doing stuff in broad daylight."

She shook her head. "Not their style."

"Well, it's got to be stopped."

"How?"

"I don't know how. All I know is we'll never have any peace until something's done." He paused for a long moment, as if lost in thought. "How would you like to move?"

"Do you really think that'll stop it? From what I've heard, these people are all over town."

"I wasn't talking about moving across town."

She blinked. "You mean . . . *move*? Out of state?"

"I've been reading about Alaska."

"Alaska! It's a frozen wasteland!"

"Oh, that's just what you hear. Some of it's really nice."

"But what about my family? What about my schooling and my job? How do you know you could even sell the house?"

"Let's just say I've got a hunch."

"Dear God, Davie, *Alaska?*"

"Like I said, it's just something to think about."

She shivered.

"All right," he said. "You think of something."

She thought a moment, then said, "Let's go see Thomas."

David went alone. He found Tom at his desk in the press room at City Hall. They had not seen each other in several weeks, and Tom looked haggard and tired. He looked much older, and his eyes were red. There was an air of defeat about him that David had never seen. They walked down to Cherry Creek and sat talking over the lunch hour. Tom looked hung over and his pants hadn't been pressed in a long time. He refused David's offer of a sandwich, and they just sat and talked. When David had finished, Tom said, "Well, what can I do about it? I tried once and didn't even make print with it. Now I'm stuck away over here, rewriting press releases and covering ax murders. They've clipped my balls good, and for the first time in my goddamn life I don't even feel like fighting back. Seems like every year there's less to fight for." He let a minute pass, then said, "Man, if I were you I'd get the hell out of here. I'd move so goddamn far away they'd never sniff me out. You've got a trade, you can always set up your own business somewhere else. Anywhere, as long as there are no bigots and no newspapers."

David shook his head. "Anna won't hold still for it."

"She doesn't know a good thing when she hears it. God damn the United States. Who was it that said that?"

"Philip Nolan. *The Man Without a Country.*"

"That's how I feel, like a man without a country. Old Philip Nolan had it right. The United States is a land of pigs. Just let them put me on that ship, I wouldn't care if I never touched land again. Just give me a few books and a lot of booze and the hell with everybody."

David touched his shoulder. "I'm sorry, old friend. I'd never have bothered you with this if I'd known you were feeling this bad already."

"I know you wouldn't. It just pisses me off so goddamn bad, Dave, to have stuff like this going on and not be able to touch it."

They walked back toward City Hall. Tom didn't say anything until they had reached Larimer Street. He stood for a long time, watching the City Hall building, and after a while some of the fight came back to his face. "These things that have been happening. You're sure it's Moran?"

"As sure as I can be without seeing him do it."

Tom nodded. "You want to try something?"

"Anything."

"No guarantee it'll work, but you won't be any worse off than you are now. You still got that note? The note, Dave, the one you found tacked to the front door."

"I burned it."

"Well, Goddammit, how the hell do you expect anybody to help you if you do dumb stuff like that? Jesus!" He mopped his brow with his shirtsleeve. "All right, forget it, it's done now. Maybe we won't need it

240

anyway. This is all one big bluff, so we might as well bluff his ass all the way down the line. You just sit back and let me do the talking, okay?"

They crossed the street and went into the police station. At the desk Tom asked for Moran, and the sergeant waved him back to a dark hallway and a row of anonymous offices. Moran sat at a desk at the end of the hall. He looked up and smiled. The smile vanished when he saw David.

"You know David Waldo?" Tom said.

Moran nodded.

"David's wife is my sister."

Moran gave a half snicker. "You can't blame me for that."

"Some things have come up at David's place. Maybe a police matter."

"There are plenty of cops up front. Tell it to them."

"I'd rather tell it to you, Moran." He rubbed his eyes. "Could I have a drink of water?"

Moran pulled a paper cup out of the dispenser and passed the water across his desk. Tom took it by the rim and drained it with one toss of his head.

"It'll take more than water to put out that fire, Hastings."

Suddenly Tom's eyes got hard. "All right, Moran, let's stop playing games. You were at David Waldo's store last night. You went out there with a bunch of goons from this department. All of you dressed up like monkeys and you burned a cross on the lot behind his store."

"Is that a fact?"

"Then you left a filthy note tacked to the door, full of slime right out of that rotten brain of yours. Only this time you made a mistake, cop. You left a fingerprint on the cardboard."

Moran didn't move. His eyes were hard on Tom's face.

"You cops work with so many ignorant people, you think every-body's dumb," Tom said. "So you get careless and leave a fingerprint." He held up the paper water cup. "It'll be interesting to see how the print on that cardboard matches this."

"Like you said, Hastings, let's quit playing around. Give me the cup."

"Not a chance. You can read about it in the *Post*."

"I seem to remember that you tried that once before."

"You know a lot for a two-bit flatfoot. Maybe you also know who killed it. Not politicians, not cops. Businessmen, Moran, all with a helluva personal stake. You think people like that give a good goddamn what happens to you? You think they'll take on Bonfils on your account? Man, you haven't been reading your paper lately. Have you seen what Bonfils has been doing to your boss in this recall flap?"

Moran didn't say anything.

"How's this sound, Moran? 'Tacked to the door was a message, its contents so vile they cannot be reported in this newspaper. Fingerprints taken from the cardboard matched those of Lieutenant Moran of the Denver Police. According to Waldo's wife, Anna, Moran has been conducting a campaign of harassment against Waldo for several years. Moran, contacted in his office at City Hall, had no comment.' That right, Moran? You got any comment for the *Post*?"

Moran just looked at him.

"If I write this one, you can bet your ass it'll go," Tom said. "You can kiss your ass good-bye while you're at it." He motioned to David and they went out. On the street, he said, "That's how you deal with punks like Moran. It's the only language they know. Now all you can do is wait and see if it does any good."

9

That night the street was quiet. In the morning there were no notes, no splashes of red paint. David walked around his store and breathed in the cool air of early summer. He walked far back into the field behind the house, kicking the ashes of the burnt cross. After a while Anna threw up a window and called him to breakfast.

When he came to the table, she was dressed for downtown. She had a typing session, which ran from nine to eleven, and a shorthand class that went from one till three. Over the long lunch hour, she walked the downtown streets and thought about who she was and how much her life had changed. David's comment about moving to Alaska showed her that anything was possible. Anything at all.

She found herself on Arapahoe Street, looking up at the apartment where Tom had lived long ago. A family lived there now. The sundeck door was open and diapers were flapping in the breeze. She remembered the day she'd almost jumped from that rooftop, and she thought of the things that had happened in that bedroom. She remembered the scrapbooks, which she hadn't burned after all, and soon she made her way across Sixteenth Street, into a huge, ornate office building that housed the Mountain States Coal Company. In the lobby was a directory. She found his name there, heading the list of officers under the name MOUNTAIN STATES COAL. Brown, William III. He had kept the "III" through all the years, in spite of the abuse he had taken from tough kids in school. He had once told her it sounded regal to him. William Brown III. Regal, yet common. A good political name.

Willie Brown.

The sun had dipped below the buildings as she made her way across the street. She would be late getting home. But now she did another strange thing. With her husband waiting for her, she sat in Herbert's and ate a double-scoop soda. She hadn't had one in years. She crossed the street and went into the building, for one more look at the directory before going home. She lingered there, and a few moments later the elevator door opened and Willie Brown stepped out. He came straight toward her and she froze. She knew his eyes were on her as he hurried past. He pushed the revolving door and went into the street. She looked up and he was gone. Her heart was beating wildly. She walked to the door, and out into a street crowded with shoppers. For a long moment she didn't see him. Then the throng parted and she had a clear look. He was standing about half a block away. He had stopped and turned, as though he had left something. Something he still couldn't quite remember.

Their eyes met. He started forward but she didn't wait. She hurried away, disappeared into the crowd at the Golden Eagle, and caught the next tram home.

CHAPTER TWO

1

On July 19, Sammy Kohl came down with an acute stomach pain, which doubled him over in the office behind the store. He lay on his cot and writhed in agony. When Teresa came in late that afternoon, she found the CLOSED sign up, though the front door remained unlocked. She found her husband feverish and shivering, and she called an ambulance and rode with it as it took him to Denver General.

When Sammy came home from the hospital, his pain was eased by drugs and Teresa knew the worst. No one else would know, for Sammy wanted it that way. He had never believed in worrying people about things that couldn't be helped.

Teresa faced it calmly, methodically, without ever talking with anyone. Now in her mind she made the hundred weekly decisions that Sammy had always made, deciding what should be ordered and how much, how much paid, how much charged, what her margin of profit should be. She bought conservatively, keeping a thin inventory in the store until she had a more firm control of the business. Sammy gave up sleeping in the store. Klan or no Klan, the activity was too tiring.

Teresa had begun making decisions that she couldn't yet implement. Sammy still worked his shift in the store, and she knew that she mustn't push too hard or he might feel buried before his death. But she couldn't quite conceal the fear, especially when they were alone at night. No words were necessary between them; he knew well enough what she was thinking. The great dread of her life had arrived quite suddenly and without warning. She was in her middle age. She had always had a fear of middle-aged poverty. She knew there was a bank account, probably enough to carry them over while she made the first mistakes in running a business alone. Sammy had never told her how much was there, but she had a fair idea. It would be enough at least to pull her through the trial-and-error time. She planned to press everyone into service with a single-minded ruthlessness. Abe would sit at his perch near the door, taking money. She would persuade Anna to drop her hospital work and help out part-time in the store. Even Tom could help, if she could get him here on Saturdays. Finally there was Gabriel. She would take him out of school and use him for deliveries in that first critical year, when she would either make it on her own or lose it all.

She never told Sammy any of these things. It simply wasn't his problem anymore, and she had to be free to deal with it her own way. Sammy would object most violently to her decision on Gabriel's schooling. She rationalized it. Dropping out for a year would do him good. It would get him out of that tough gang he had fallen in with, he would learn about the real world and he could go back in a year with a broader perspective. Still she knew that Sammy would fight her. He might even extract some deathbed promise. Far better to say nothing. In the end it didn't matter much. The day Sammy died, she lost the ability to decide anything. Teresa Hastings Kohl discovered that the Ku Klux Klan had truly come of age.

2

Across town, in the mahogany-lined mansion at 1061 Humboldt Street, Harry Tammen lay dying. Tom knew it, as surely as he knew that he was losing his last real friend at the *Denver Post*.

On the morning of July 20, the *Post* gave over its front page to the death story. Tammen had died hard, of stomach cancer, and Tom was surprised at the depths of his own grief. Alone and broke, he suffered the pain of another long hangover. He read the stories and went home sick.

A week later he was still sick. On the scarred, bottle-ringed table beside his bed, the telephone was ringing. Tom stared at it as he might stare at a hated enemy. Beside him, Georgeann sat up, the thin sheet falling down from her breasts.

"Tomas?"

He shook his head. It was the third time that morning that he had lain through the insistent ringing. The last time had caught them, as Georgeann put it, "in der middle of someting," and she had hardly noticed as it rang and rang forever. Now the insistence of the caller made her nervous. "Tomas?" she said again. "Da telefon."

Again he shook his head. It was Monday. He had called in sick, as he had at least twice a month for the past six months. His work record was a mess. He had no idea how much time he had missed, only that the total for 1924 must be greater than the entire eight years before. He really didn't care; there were days when he simply couldn't face that dingy press room and that desk and the cops. They were usually Mondays, when Georgeann came early and stayed late. Sometimes, like today, if she came early enough, she could take care of the rooms quickly and they could spend the morning in bed. That miserable job. How fast news of earth-shaking importance became a dusty conversation piece, then simplistic nostalgia. It was all grand theater. In the news business, nostalgia was yesterday. A scoop was a two-hour high between the three-month lows.

That goddamn telephone. Whoever it was wasn't about to give up. He reached across her, plucking the phone off its table.

"Hello."

It was Bonfils' secretary. "Mr. Hastings? Mr. Bonfils would like to see you this afternoon at three o'clock."

"Does he know I'm sick?"

"I didn't ask him that. Shall I check with him and call you back?"

"No. No thanks, I'll be there." He hung up and lay on his back, staring at the ceiling.

Georgeann leaned over him. "Trouple?"

"I don't know. I'm being called in on the carpet about something."

"Dat's bat?"

"Not too bat." He smiled at her. "At least they've given me the rest of the morning." He touched her breast, which hardened under his hand. She pushed him back gently. "Let me," she said. She rolled over, covering him with all that golden skin.

246

. . .

Later, in the tiny bathroom that looked down into an alley of cats and garbage cans, shaving with cold water because there was no hot, Tom Hastings drew his first truly sober breath in a week and stared at his own reflection. In another time it might have shocked him, but these days he was all but unshockable. His hair was going gray at the temples. The lines above his eyes had the definitive stamp of permanence. The lines had also attacked his mouth, drawing it tight, giving him a bitter look. Behind him, the door was open and the apartment was empty. Georgeann had gone on to other things. *Udder tings.* Affairs of the heart were finished for this July Monday, and just outside his bathroom door the coffeepot on his hotplate was perking for the second time. All the world in a gush of black liquid. His hands shook as he shaved. He cut himself and blotted it with an old handkerchief. Like it or not, he was meeting Bonfils in an hour, and if he really cared as little for the job as he pretended, why did his hand shake and why was his heart suddenly beating faster?

Once in the shower, it was Nell who haunted his thoughts. Harding was in the news again, with scandal beginning to engulf his top people, and Tom would never think of Harding without remembering that night, one year ago next week. He had an anniversary coming up and he had not seen his wife or children in almost eight months. Allegedly she wanted a divorce, but she was taking her sweet time about getting one. He was ready, as much as he would ever be. Let it be finished and done with.

Twice in recent months he had driven to the Clement estate, but the gate still hung open, the smashed lock rusting as he had left it. The windows were dark behind peeling plywood. He had received two letters, handwritten and postmarked St. Louis, advising him that she would be returning "at some future date" to discuss the terms of the divorce. He had fired off a brief note, demanding to know when, but she had never answered. She had always been reasonable, and he hoped now that there wouldn't be any ugliness over the boys. He was prepared to compromise, but not too much, and her old man couldn't be involved in the compromise in any way.

But he knew the way of the world and it frightened him. Any custody fight, backed by her father's money, could have only one logical conclusion, so he couldn't ask for too much. Reasonable visitation rights. It was enough. It was a soft position for old Hastings the fire-eater, but this was not the old Hastings and his options were few. In periodic sparks the old Hastings burst to the surface. Last week, when his restlessness had increased so sharply after Tammen's death, he had written her a nasty letter, demanding that she return and get it settled between them, but so far there had been no answer.

She had left him to stew, no doubt about it. He wondered if he should go to St. Louis. The old Hastings would have done it without thinking twice. Maybe it was exactly what she wanted, some commitment from him, evidence that he cared enough to chase her seven hundred miles across the plains. She might even change her mind about the divorce. Anything was possible.

But he had no idea what she was thinking or if she was thinking at all. She might well be guided here and there by the old man, moved around in his spidery grip without any idea what he was doing to her. It all had a strange, unreal ring to it. The last time he had seen her, she had been all but begging him to take her back. How could you figure a woman like that? Tender and loving one minute, cold and hard the next. She was giving him a good taste of life without her, without his boys, letting him see how bleak it could be. And bleak it was.

He thought she might be gone a month, six weeks at the outside. But Christmas came and went, and when the estate remained dark throughout Christmas week, he quickly bought presents for the boys, using all his eating money for the week, and shipped them to her St. Louis address. He got prompt, polite replies from both Michael and Paul. Both thanked him, said they were enjoying St. Louis, and were finding lots to do. And he waited, and winter became spring, and still she didn't write and still she didn't come. Summer came, and the impact of that first divorce letter began to wash over him. Still there was no indication when they were coming or if they were coming. Was she serious, or was she testing him after all? Was that what this was, some crazy goddamn test?

He couldn't imagine.

Denver glided past his open window and the harsh sunlight of mid-afternoon hurt his eyes. He felt tired and very old.

At exactly three o'clock *to the minute* he walked past the clattering typewriters, through the swinging door, to the Bucket of Blood. Bonfils' secretary asked him to wait. When he was finally admitted to Bonfils' inner chamber, he found the air heavy with smoke. Bonfils didn't smoke but he loved the smell. He was flanked by two bodyguards. One was smoking and blowing the smoke into Bonfils' face. In a corner stood a loaded shotgun. Bonfils had kept it handy since 1900, when a madman, outraged over a story, had come to the Bucket of Blood and shot both partners, Bonfils seriously. Now he looked up from his desk, where a red-bannered edition of today's *Post* lay open and marked. Abruptly, Bonfils said, "Mr. Hastings. Your resignation is accepted."

"Resignation?"

"I believe you resigned from this paper quite loudly some time ago. A little matter of dissatisfaction with one of your stories. I think that's all we have to discuss."

In the Bucket of Blood, he collected his last week's pay. He walked over to Welton Street and went up the wooden staircase to the *News*. The shock of getting fired had already worn off. People were always quitting and getting fired in this town. They always turned up on another paper, quit, or got fired there, and usually ended up back on the paper where they'd started. He walked in boldly and stalked up to city desk. The editor was a small, fiery man named Day. Day had once worked for the *Post;* he knew what Tom could do. Tom told him he wanted any reporting job they had open. Day jumped up and pumped his hand. He said he would be happy to have a reporter like Tom aboard. Tom's knowledge of the city and its politics would give the *News* added punch where it counted most. "You wait for me here," Day said. "I'll talk to them up front and see if I can't get you started tonight."

There it was. Suddenly he was a reporter for the *Rocky Mountain News.* He looked out across the half-empty newsroom and wondered which of these desks would be his. Near the window, Marvel Millette's desk was empty, but her chair was pushed back and a pocketbook perched on the edge. Day seemed to be taking a long time. Again that headache had started; deep, far back behind his eyes. He decided then that he wouldn't ask too much of himself in this new job. He wouldn't try too hard too fast to show Bonfils the mistake he'd made. He'd be here every day, show up sober and on time. Just do the work. Be a pro. Climbing back to the heights could come later.

Day came out of the front office and walked slowly to his desk. He looked grim. "I'm not having much luck with you, Hastings. They tell me nothing's open right now. Why not give me a call in a month?"

Tom stared at him. "Come on, Eddie, what the hell's going on? You know what I can do. Where's the snag?"

"It's the times, Hastings. You know how times are. Call me in a month."

"You think things'll be any different then?"

Day shrugged. "These are funny times. Who knows what a month will bring?"

He bought a bottle on the way home. Georgeann didn't come that night and he drank himself to sleep, alone. He awoke with a headache, with less than fifty dollars in his pocket. He had no checks coming from New York. He hadn't written anything in a very long time.

He thought he might call Nell. Suddenly he needed to hear her voice.

But he didn't do that. Instead he drank some more. That afternoon, just before dark, he drifted down to the lowers, where gaunt, displaced men lived in alleys and back lots. He knew a man there who would sell him all the whiskey he wanted, at a price too good to turn down.

3

Suddenly, and without warning, the terror began again. One morning red paint was splashed around David Waldo's shop, front and back. Almost every night after that something happened. Notes were slipped under the door: vile and putrid messages, coming, as David said, from the bottom of some black soul. Telephone calls, whispered obscenities. He tried to isolate her from the worst of it, but he couldn't know what she went through during the day when he wasn't around. That animal with the raspy voice had begun calling every day between eleven and one. If David answered, the voice just whispered some threat and the line went dead. David never told her what the caller had said, but she knew it had something to do with her. For hours afterward he would fume around the shop, muttering and throwing things.

But if Anna took the call, the talk dragged on, sometimes for as long as two minutes. There were drooling sex offers, perversions of sex, twisted suggestions involving Jews and animals. Words she had only heard in whispers, or by mistake from a nearby sandlot, when roughhousing boys didn't know she was close enough to have heard. At first she hung up the moment that vile mouth opened. Then one night David said, "I think the thing for us to do is not react, one way or another, to anything they do. If they don't get a reaction from us, maybe they'll go away." The next day she held the phone, sitting through the entire two-minute verbal attack. At the first pause, she said, "Is that all you have for us today? Good-bye, then." She pushed the phone away from her as if it had suddenly covered itself with slime.

She braced herself for these daily assaults, and thanked God silently whenever David was in and could take the calls. When the caller caught her alone, she screwed up her courage and answered it, trying to think of something else while he went on. She always hung up at the first break. Usually she said, "That's nice, sir. Have a nice day," and burst out sobbing as she pushed the phone away. But one afternoon, feeling especially tense and angry, she said, "Really, sir, you are sick. You are truly the sickest person I have ever encountered. Could I help you a find a psychiatrist?" This time it was the caller who hung up first. She threw up her arms and cried for joy. In the long war of nerves, she had won a tiny battle.

From this beachhead she fought back. "Really, sir, I was hoping our talk yesterday had ended all this," she said. "Haven't you found help yet?" There was a long pause while they listened to each other breathing. Then the caller screamed into the mouthpiece, "*I am not sick!*" and slammed down his telephone. She was actually smiling as she put her phone gently on its table. She fondled the cradle and patted it affectionately.

Words alone were losing their power. No longer was she shocked so easily. She thought she had heard all the words by now, and in every possible combination. Then suddenly the tactic changed, and she spent one of the most harrowing days of her life. They had been invited to the family home·for dinner. She had done her marketing early that morning, and had planned to spend her afternoon making her father's two favorite dishes. Almost from the beginning things had gone wrong. First she couldn't get the right kind of meat. The gas went out. The pipes and valves were in the breaker box, which David always kept locked. Now the door was wide open and the lock was missing. She found the gas valve, saw that it had been turned off, turned it back on and went upstairs to her cooking. Fifteen minutes later it went off again. She turned it on and sat at the back window, watching the alley and the field beyond. No one came. She sat for an hour, until the smells from the oven drifted through the apartment.

Then the noises began again. The apartment had been quiet for almost a month, as if their ghost had taken a holiday. Now those creaks and groans filtered down from above, as if someone had moved across the attic. She climbed onto the table and pushed up the trapdoor. No one was there, unless they were hiding back behind the boxes. But the noise had stopped, and she climbed down, took her dishes out of the oven and wrapped them, then put them into the icebox.

Outside it had begun to rain. The street was sloppy and deserted. She stood at the front window and saw not a soul. The stores along Colfax looked deserted and dark. A mist had covered the lake and was moving east toward Denver. She thought David was taking a long time. He had left just after lunch, backpacking brochures to customers downtown. She went into the bedroom and laid out some dry clothes. And she listened. The apartment was so quiet she could almost feel the presences around her.

If David didn't come soon, she thought she might scream. At least she might get out, walk over to the house or to the store, where all the family would be working through the busy day. She tried calling Tom. Someone at the *Post* told her he no longer worked there. She tried his apartment on Capitol Hill. No one answered. Immediately, as she hung up, her phone rang. There was no one on the line.

She sat by the back window and watched the rainfall in the field. The mist had closed around the trees, and they stood out as formless shapes, black against gray. Something moved against the black and she saw two tiny black holes. Eye slits. The sheet and hood of the Ku Klux Klan.

He was standing perhaps two hundred yards away, at the very edge of the field. She knew he must see her too, framed in the large back window, but in all the time they were there, he didn't move. She jerked the curtains shut and paced the apartment in anger. Most of her anger was directed at herself, as she remembered that her telephone victories had been won by indifference, not anger. She went to the window and opened the curtains, but she didn't see him again.

There was a knock at the door, insistent, almost frantic pounding. She hurried down and found no one there. The telephone rang. She closed and bolted the door, smiled grimly, and tried for a note of singsong cheer as she lifted the phone from its table.

"Hel-lo."

"Mrs. Waldo?" The male voice sounded tired and official.

"Yes, who is it?"

"My name is Burrows, ma'am. I'm with the Denver coroner's office."

"Coroner's office. Did you say coroner's office? What on earth do you want with me?"

He paused for a moment, the way a man does when he's facing a difficult job. 'This is going to be hard, ma'am. Maybe you'd better sit down and get a grip on yourself."

Her eyes went wide. She sank into a chair and clutched her breast.

"Mrs. Waldo, your husband was killed today."

"Wh . . . what?"

"I'm sorry, ma'am. This part of the job never gets any easier."

"What? Oh, Mr. . . .. Mr. . . ."

"Burrows, ma'am."

"Mr. Burrows, yes, there must be some mistake. Has to be." Her mouth had gone dry. "Sir, my husband just left here. . . not three hours ago."

"He was hit by a truck at Speer and Colfax, Mrs. Waldo. It was one of those crazy accidents, ma'am, nobody's fault really. Kid chased a cat into the street, made the driver swerve out of his lane. Your husband was trying to cross." There was another pause. Waves of shock washed over her. "Ma'am," he said, "if it's any consolation, he died immediately. Hit his head and felt no pain. The coroner wanted me to be sure and tell you that. It was quick and painless."

"Oh, Mr. Burrows, that can't be. It just can't."

"I'm sorry, Mrs. Waldo."

"No, you see, you've made a mistake. It has to be a mistake."

"I'm really sorry, ma'am." Another pause, then: "Ma'am?"

"Yes?"

"You'll have to come down. You know, make identification. Tomorrow will be fine on that. Mrs. Waldo?"

"Yes. . . yes."

"I am sorry."

"Yes . . yes."

"I am sorry."

"Yes."

She hung up, numb with shock and grief. Less than five minutes later she heard the door open downstairs and David's voice drifted up from the shop. "Anna! I'm back!"

She swallowed and gasped back a sob.

"Anna!"

"Yes, dear." She dabbed at her eyes. "I'm up here."

She heard his feet on the stairs. She hurried into the bathroom and drew the water for her bath. She stayed in the water for almost an hour, until all the grief, shock, relief, and joy had left her. All that was left as she went down to meet him was cold rage.

Later, while he bathed, she called the coroner's office and asked for Mr. Burrows. She wasn't surprised to learn that there was no Mr. Burrows on the coroner's staff. She hung up without giving her name.

At dusk they walked over to Osceola Street. David held the umbrella over her while she carried her two casseroles in a heavy cloth sack. At the corner he looked at her and asked how her day had been. She smiled and said everything had been quiet.

Teresa met them at the door. Abe sat in a wheelchair, staring into the fire. Gabriel sat in a corner reading a schoolbook. He didn't look up when Anna came in. A moment later he got up and left the room. Sammy was in the big chair near the window. In the few days since she had seen him, his cheeks had hollowed and his hair looked whiter. They sat around the fire while Teresa put Anna's dishes in the oven. Sammy asked politely how the printing business was. "I'll tell you something, children," he said a few minutes later. "The world is just beginning to open up. You know what I would do if I were young? I think I'd invest in the future. My money and my sweat. Look at the people who started the automobile now. Millionaires. They invested in the future twenty, thirty years ago."

David leaned forward and warmed his hands. "What would you invest in?"

"Radio. Air travel. Women's fashions. Cosmetics."

Anna laughed. "Cosmetics!"

"You laugh, young woman, but the day will come when you won't think of going out without your lipstick and your rouge. It will become a fantastic industry and the people in it will be rich."

David said, "Sam, the trouble is I'm too much like you. I don't really care about being rich. All I want is to lead a quiet life and be left alone."

"Tell me what you think is going to happen," Sammy said to David.

David thought for a moment. "I think a depression is coming. A depression like the world's never seen. That's the reason why I don't jump headlong into these jobs of the future, Sam. In another five or ten years it may all be plowed under again."

"Interesting," Sammy said.

"Take a look at it. Coolidge prosperity is all on paper. Someday somebody will get wise to that. He'll cash in his paper and there won't be enough money to cover it. Stocks will drop and banks will close. People will lose their life savings, then their jobs, then their homes. I think entire industries will fail, and the first to go might well be the newest. The first depression of the industrial era."

"And if that happens?"

"Then whatever crawls out of the muck and sets itself up as law may well become law. Our political system will get its greatest test. Most likely it'll be one man who makes the difference, not the millions who carry his brochures and lick his stamps. To me that's a terrifying thought."

"To me it sounds like H.G. Wells."

"All right." David leaned forward and gestured with his finger. "Here's what I see. The stocks fall. People panic. The banks close. Layoffs begin. Fighting breaks out. No one has the money to buy the goods, so the factories close. The President calls out the militia to keep order in the streets. This may drag on for years. Then suddenly somebody rises from nowhere and promises to deal with it, and the people, because they're so miserable, accept anything he tells them. The middle class is hardest hit. Middle class values will disappear. You know what shame poverty brings to the middle class, Sam. That's the voting class, and they'll vote for anyone who promises to end it. Once he's in, the new President can go two ways. If he's mad for power and glory, he could become the first dictator of the United States."

"Is this what you talk about in those meetings of yours?"

"Sometimes."

"Maybe . . . do you think I might come to one?"

"Sure," David said. "We haven't had one in a while . . ."

"Not since we got married," Anna said, blushing suddenly.

Sammy was quiet for a moment. Then he said, "That thought of yours, about the presidential dictator. What do you think would happen if the depression came now?"

"Well," David said, "Outside the two parties themselves, what's the strongest political organization in America today?"

"The Klan."

"Exactly." David looked at Anna. "And that's the day you and I go to Alaska, no questions asked."

"Maybe we should all go to Alaska," Sammy said, and everyone laughed.

Teresa called them from the dining room. Gabriel refused to come, saying he had a headache. Anna, already surprised at Sammy's thin appearance, was shocked when her mother had to come in and help him to the table. Teresa had set an extra plate, "just in case Thomas comes." But no one had seen or heard from Tom in more than a week. "I tried phoning him all day yesterday," Teresa said as they settled into the table. "He doesn't answer his phone."

"I called him today at the *Post*," Anna said. "Somebody told me he doesn't work there anymore."

"Really?" David was surprised. "I saw him last week. He didn't tell me he was quitting."

"How'd he look?" Teresa said.

"Tired mostly. Maybe a little worried."

They ate in silence, and afterward Teresa brought out the matzos and honey, and again she thought of Tom and how he enjoyed them. "Gabriel should have some of these, even if he doesn't eat anything else," she said. "Would you mind, Sam?"

"He should eat good food first."

"I'll just take him one on a little tray."

David said, "Would you let me take it to him?"

They all looked at him.

"I'd like to get to know him better. Would that be okay?"

Teresa beamed. "That would be fine."

Gabriel was sitting at the window, looking out across the moonlit backyard. David closed the door. "Your mother sent you this." He put the tray on the bed and sat on a wooden chair. Finally Gabriel, with a touch of hostility in his voice, said, "You going to sit there and watch me eat?"

"I thought maybe we could have a talk."

"What have we got to talk about?"

"Well, for one thing, I hear you're a pretty good delivery boy."

Gabriel just stared.

"Is that true or not?"

"There's no such thing as a good delivery boy. That doesn't take any skill. A trained monkey could do what I do around here."

"Not true."

"How do you know?"

Measuring his words carefully, David said, "I'm a delivery boy too. I run my own business, but I'm also the janitor *and* the delivery boy. Doesn't matter how good your work is if the merchandise doesn't get where it's going, on time and in decent shape. Take this morning. I got caught in a rainstorm halfway to town. I had a load of very perishable brochures with me. I was on a stretch of Colfax where there wasn't any shelter. My backpack's heavy canvas, but once it soaks through, it leaks. So what do I do?"

Gabriel reached over and took the wafer from the tray, biting an edge off without honey. "I always carry a sheet of plastic wrapping in my wagon. I also built a lid so the top can be sealed off. It's waterproof."

David just nodded. "How would you like to work for me?" he said.

"Doing what?"

"What do you think? Doing what you do for your dad."

"He's not . . ." Gabriel broke off and looked away. Then he said, "He's not paying me for that. It's just part of my chores."

David stared at the boy. Slowly, defensively, his eyes came up.

"Is that all you were going to say?" David said.

"What else?"

"I don't know. I just had the feeling you were going to say something else." He continued looking at Gabriel until the boy looked away. *He knows,* David thought. *This kid knows.* Somehow, he was sure of it, Gabriel had found out that Sammy Kohl wasn't his father. It would explain a lot of things: his sudden resentment of Anna, the moody spells, the bad temper that both Anna and Teresa had observed in recent months. He had to go slowly on this, and feel his way by instinct.

"Well, naturally it wouldn't be chores, what you do for me. I'd expect to pay you whatever the going rate is. And this is all providing you have any spare time. I wouldn't want to take you away from school or the store."

256

"The only spare time I've got is Saturday mornings, before the store gets busy."

"I've always got more deliveries than I can make on Saturday. What do you say?"

Gabriel shrugged.

David leaned forward. "Look, I'm offering you a straight business proposal, no frills or favors attached to it. The least you can do is give me a straight answer."

Gabriel looked him in the eye. "I'll do it."

What a fine, honest little guy he is, David thought. He didn't know Willie Brown, wouldn't know him if they passed on the street, but any man would be proud of a fine son like this. "All right," he said. "What's fair?"

"Albert Beser gets sixty cents."

"Sixty cents what?"

"An hour." Gabriel smiled. "He works for his sister's boyfriend. The guy is trying to make time."

"Well, nobody's trying to make time here. This is just between you and me. So what if I paid you fifty cents? You show up at eight o'clock every Saturday morning, work through till noon, and make yourself a couple of bucks."

Gabriel nodded.

"I'll count on you, then, unless either Sammy or Teresa objects. It'll get you some spending money and give me more time with your sister."

He said this deliberately, watching Gabriel's face. The boy's mouth turned down at the word "sister," and all his hostility and anger seemed to return. David touched his shoulder and left him there. He went to the table, certain that Gabriel knew it all. Gabriel knew. David knew. The only person who didn't know was Anna.

CHAPTER
THREE

1

The following Saturday Gabriel made three runs with his pushcart and earned two dollars. At noon he went to the store, but found it locked and dark. He knew that Sammy was having another bad day. This morning at opening time he had been unable to get out of bed, and Teresa had come down to open the store alone. Gabriel drifted back to David's, looking for more work. But David looked at the darkening sky and said, "No more today, son. Let's you and me take a walk instead."

They went around the northern edge of Sloan's Lake. Gabriel seemed tense and uncomfortable. They walked to the northwest edge and sat in the grass. Cars rattled along Sheridan Boulevard, but the street was hard-packed and there was little dust. David took a deep breath. There was simply no easy way. He said, "How long have you known about yourself and Anna?"

Gabriel looked out over the lake. When he spoke, his voice was strong. "I just found out for sure not long ago."

"How?"

"Abe told me."

"Now why would he do something like that?"

Gabriel shrugged. "Frustration maybe. He gets that way sometimes. You can't really blame him for anything he does. He's in pain all the time. He hurts inside too. Then it builds up until he's got nothing left but to let it out on somebody. I just happened to be around that day. The day Julia left."

"Is that why you're angry with Anna?"

"I hate her."

David waited a moment, while the emotion drained out of Gabriel's face. "All right," he said. "Maybe you do feel that way now."

"All my life I thought she was my sister."

"And all your life she's known you're her *son*. Think about that for a minute. Imagine living with your child and not being able to mother him."

"She doesn't care about me. She just doesn't give a damn."

"That's not true."

"I make her ashamed. That's why she hid away in her room all those years."

"That may be partly true. But listen, your mother is a highly strung, complicated woman. There are always lots of reasons for everything she does. Locking herself away may have been just what you say, an act of shame, but there was love in it too. I think she wanted to be near you."

"You're making that up."

"I honestly believe it. She herself might not know it, but I'm convinced it's true. And whatever shame she felt had nothing to do with you. It was all hers, and even at that it was a phony shame concocted by the society. She's starting to see that now. She's really starting to come around. Don't tell me you haven't seen the change in her."

"I've seen it."

David plucked at a blade of grass. A slight rain blew out of the west, but neither of them moved. "Listen, I think you're an exceptional kid. Just in the few times I've seen you, I think that. I don't know what'll happen between us, whether we'll ever be any more to each other than we are right now. There's no blood, so there'll have to be something else. Friendship, I hope, and trust. Your mother is my wife and I love her very much. I promise you this," David said. "I won't ever kid you, now or ever. You ask me a straight question and I'll give you as straight an answer as I know. What else can I offer you?"

Gabriel shrugged.

"Your father . . . Sammy . . . your *grand*father, Gabie . . ." David cleared his throat. "Honesty sometimes takes practice, doesn't it?"

The boy smiled.

"Your grandfather is dying."

"I know that."

"Teresa may or may not be able to keep the store. The next year will be full of changes. Childhood will disappear; you'll have to become a man before your time. It's not always going to be easy. I'd like to help you through some of it if you'll let me."

"I don't need any help."

"Maybe you still don't understand," David said. "I'd like you to come live with us."

"That's the craziest thing I ever heard," Gabriel said. "You just finished telling me you wouldn't kid me and now here you are."

"I'm not kidding."

"Then tell me how. How is that supposed to happen? Nobody but you even knows that I know anything."

"And we may not be able to tell them, at least not now. It'll take some time and care, patience, waiting for the right moment. I'm hoping I'll know it when it comes. We can't just spring it on everybody after dinner some night. Just try to imagine the shock it'll be to Anna. That's my problem, and I sure don't want to make any mistakes. And I don't want you to think I'm talking about tomorrow or next week. It might take several months to work it around till it's right. In the meantime, I want you to know that I'm here, and I'm thinking about it all the time." David touched the boy's shoulder.

"You're kidding us both. She doesn't want me. Why should I care about her?"

"You're doing just what she's doing, hiding from the truth. The truth is you need each other, but you're both afraid to face that. Afraid to put yourself on the line. But I know her, and I know it won't happen like that. Maybe to you she seems weak, but she isn't. She's got a streak of strength in her that none of us knew about. Grit and bone, Gabie. When the time comes, she'll do just fine."

"She wishes I'd never been born."

"Not true, son, not true. She wishes it had been different maybe, but never that. In the long run, Teresa may be a bigger problem than Anna. How do you tell a woman to stop mothering a child she's always known as hers? That's where your patience and understanding comes in. Whatever it takes, we've got to get past it and start living with the truth. That's what I'm shooting for. Family, Gabe, a feeling of belonging at last."

Gabriel stared away at the hospital across the lake. Again David touched his shoulder. "Trust me for a while," he said. "I'll try not to botch it."

They walked along Osceola Street in the mud. The house was locked and quiet. No one answered David's persistent knocking and Gabriel didn't have a key. They walked to the store. It was still locked and the CLOSED sign hung in the front-door window. They huddled under the flapping canopy, and an uneasy shiver began in David's neck. "Where the devil do you suppose everybody is?"

They looked up the rainswept street and waited, but no one came.

2

Teresa was less than five blocks away, sitting in the front seat of the Studebaker owned by Mr. Jonas, the landlord. He had turned up suddenly at noon, surprising her. The rent wasn't due for another week. Jonas told her he hadn't come for the rent. In the back office he told her he had sold the building. The new owner had plans for it and they would have to get out.

Now they sat in Jonas' car on the hill that overlooked the eastern edge of Sloan's Lake. She had asked twice if anything could be done, but Jonas just shrugged and looked sad. "I'm sorry, Mrs. Kohl," he said after a while. "What else can I say?"

"You might have let me know ahead of time. Maybe we could have worked something out."

"You couldn't, Mrs. Kohl. I know pretty well what kind of business you do. There was just no way for you to raise this kind of money on short notice. Somebody offered a good price, so Jonas took it. I just couldn't refuse, Mrs. Kohl."

"Did you tell them how long we've been here?"

"I told him everything. You been fine tenants. Always pay rent on time, been there many years, no trouble. I told him all that, but he wants the building for himself."

"Maybe I could talk to him. Would you tell me his name?"

Jonas shook his head.

"It's very important, Mr. Jonas. I can't tell you how important it is."

"Maybe not so much. Things always work out, Mrs. Kohl. There are lots of buildings."

"Around here?"

"Around here, around someplace else. Other neighborhoods, other towns. Other countries, Mrs. Kohl. Listen, I tell you something. After that I got to go. I am leaving here soon. One week, maybe ten days. I been smart, maybe a little lucky, I got enough money to last through my old age. I got a son in Oregon. He says there are plenty of trees and rivers there. Mountains and seashore. So I say to myself, why not? Sounds like a nice place to settle down, watch my grandson grow up. This place is no good for people like us, Mrs. Kohl."

"What do you mean, people like us?"

"Jews like you, foreigners like me. People are getting upset about foreigners. I think maybe I'll settle near Portland. I'll settle down and take some English, learn to speak real good, without an accent. Maybe change my name from Jonas. Not too much, just one letter. Maybe I'll call myself Jones. That sounds real American, don't you think so?"

"Mr. Jonas, if I told you what I think, you'd probably put me out here and make me walk home in the rain."

Jonas laughed. "Ah, you know Jonas better than that. I know you talk from disappointment. I understand that."

"Please tell me the name, Mr. Jonas. Please."

"It's not one man, but a group of men. I do business with just one, but he says he's just acting for somebody else. A lawyer named Reismann. He signs the paper, with what he calls power of attorney. And they pay cash, Mrs. Kohl. So you see why I have to sell, why it all comes so fast."

"I guess there's nothing more to discuss, is there, Mr. Jonas?"

"I'm sorry. You been good, fine people. There are other places."

"How long have we got?"

"New owners take over tomorrow. I told them your rent is paid through the first of the month."

"That's less than a week, Mr. Jonas."

"Discuss it with Mr. Reismann. He seems like a good man. I'm sure if you need more time, he'll work out something."

He dropped her on Osceola Street. By then the rain was blowing hard. She went up the steps without looking back, and heard him drive away as she opened the door. Inside, the house was stuffy and dark. She called Sammy and got no answer. She called Abe. Still nothing.

She didn't become alarmed until she called up the staircase and still got no answer. She came to the downstairs bedroom, far back in the corner of the house. It was a spare room that they used for guests. She looked in and saw Sammy, stretched out on the bed. Abe sat beside him in the wheelchair.

"Abe? Why didn't you answer me? You scared me half to death."

Abe made a great effort to meet her eyes. Teresa looked at Sammy, and noticed for the first time how pale his face was.

"He's dead, Mom," Abe said.

They sat together, and when Abe finally did meet her eyes, she saw his tears. Teresa did not cry. When she spoke, her voice was husky and soft.

"Did you call anyone?"

"What for? What can anybody do for him now?"

Teresa sniffed. She straightened up and pulled the blanket over Sammy's face. It was like closing her old life. She wheeled Abe out of the room, gliding him through the hall to the front room.

"When did it happen?"

"An hour, maybe two. I don't know. He said he didn't feel good. That's the last thing he said to me. 'I don't feel too good, I think I'll lie down again.' He came in and lay down and died. He's gone."

"Yes." Teresa blew her nose, sat beside her son, and thought. "I have to prepare him," she said. "We have to tell Thomas and Anna, then call the undertaker and the rabbi. So you see, there are things to do. Do you want to help me?"

He shook his head.

"No." She sighed. "Then you sit here and think about your papa. Remember him with love. And don't worry about it, son. I'll see to everything."

She went into the bathroom and began drawing a tub of hot water.

3

Afterward it seemed like she had sunk into a sea of detail. The rabbi came, and the undertaker, then Anna came with David and Gabriel in tow. The body was taken. No one could reach Tom, and David set out for Denver, to see if he might be found in any of his old newspaper haunts.

Anna stayed through the day, to help watch over Abe and prepare their dinner. None of them felt like eating. As soon as the body was gone, Teresa slipped upstairs and began looking through her husband's papers. Sammy would understand. There were things to do. Money things.

That was her third shock. She got out Sammy's savings book and found less than five hundred dollars on deposit. Huge withdrawals had been made in August of last year, and again in March, and again in June. She went deeper. It was a mistake. Perhaps Sammy had just transferred the money to another account. Maybe, like David, he had begun to worry about the coming depression and the possibility of bank closings. No doubt he had taken the money and put it into something more secure. She would find it. She folded the bankbook and put it aside. Under it she found the first letter from Ethan. Dated last July, it was a beggar's note, asking for money. Under it was another letter, asking for more, and under that another. She felt a growing sense of horror. The dates on the three letters roughly matched the withdrawal dates in the bankbook. She began clawing frantically through the papers, looking for some other answer.

There was none.

David had gone to the *Post,* and later to Tom's apartment on Capitol Hill. At Capitol Hill he met Georgeann coming down the stairs. She hadn't seen Tom in a week. He had just disappeared, leaving all his things behind. His rent was overdue and, in another few days, the manager would put his things out for the garbageman to collect. "Tell him I'll save what I can," she said. "Tell him come home."

David asked her if he might look through Tom's room. In a closet, Tom's clothes still hung loosely from hangers. Piled on the floor of the closet were several heavy cardboard boxes, containing notes, film, and huge piles of developed pictures. In a wastebasket near the desk he found two brown bottles, unlabeled, both empty, smelling faintly of alcohol.

Too tired to walk home, he caught a streetcar and sank back against the seat. He closed his eyes. He thought that Tom had gone off to St. Louis after his wife and children. That would be their best bet now, work through Tom's wife. The bell clanged and the streetcar jerked. His head rolled and he stared into the dark beyond the houses of East Colfax. He would be getting close to his stop. Another weary man going home to his wife. Anna would still be at Teresa's. He would go there first, pick up his wife, and put this horrible day in the past.

Far ahead an orange glow lit up the night sky. The conductor stopped and crouched beside his seat, peering out through the front window. "Wow, would you look at that! Big night for the Klan, it looks like." The conductor looked at David. "Saturday night, you know. They're always out here on Saturday nights, bothering the kikes." He stared at the glow as if hypnotized. "I make this run every weekend. Fridays and Saturdays really get wild, but man, I never seen anything like that." He took a gold watch out of his pocket and looked at it. "Quarter to two. Jesus Christ, look at that. Must be one helluva bonfire's all I can say. Looks like it's right out on the street."

They had reached the end of the pavement, where Hooker crossed Colfax. About seven blocks ahead, a tongue of flame leaped across the street.

The conductor pulled on a rope. "That's as far as we go," he said.

"Jesus, if the fire department don't get here pretty quick the whole block'll go up."

"Move," David said. "I'm getting off."

Outside, people ran past the stopped trolley toward the fire. He began to walk toward the fire, slowly at first, then faster. He broke into a trot, then a run.

It was his place.

By the time he reached Sammy Kohl's store, two blocks from his print shop, he could see that the whole lower floor was engulfed in flames. Some of the neighboring men, bare to the waist, had run out into the street and were trying to fight the fire with buckets of sand and water. David pushed his way behind the store and got at the head of a bucket brigade. The strong smell of kerosene was everywhere. Tiny pockets of flame kept erupting as the fire ate into the old wood. The papers in the basement ignited and fire shot up through the floor, blowing out the lower windows. A current of air sucked through the upper floor, knocking out the upper windows and pouring burning cinders down into the street. The flame sucked higher, into the attic, leaping through the papers and boxes, poking through the thin roof and joining at the rafters. David worked like a madman. He kept the water coming long after the others had given up. The building began to sag, then crumble, and finally a neighbor came and wrapped his arms around David and said, "Come, man, come now. There's nothing more to be done." The roof settled. More cinders and hot ash fell into the alley and scattered the men back into the field.

Bells clanged and the fire department arrived: two engines from downtown, roaring up through the smoke, blocking off Colfax, spewing hose from the underbellies of the trucks. David went looking for his wife. He found her on Colfax, watching from across the street. They had all come down from the house, Teresa and Gabriel, even Abe in his wheelchair. David and Anna stood arm in arm and watched it burn. It stopped before dawn, when there was nothing left.

David tried to smile. "Nothing more you can do here," he said. "Why don't you people go on home? I'll stay around for a while, just in case."

Anna squeezed his hand. "We'll take my old room, love. Straight down the hall on the second floor."

"I know."

Cars arrived. More firemen poured out, mixing with cops on both sides of the street. The fire investigator came. He was a huge, balding man in boots and a helmet. He stalked to the back of the building, flanked by a small knot of men. He walked under the cordon and pushed his way through the steaming back door. All around him firemen worked with axes and hoses, and the smell of charred wood hung heavy in the air. David told the cop at the cordon that he owned the building and they let him pass. Inside was an unreal world of crumbling walls and broken glass. Even the furniture was burned to the floor. In the center of the rear room, his printing press stood defiantly, too hot to touch. The fire investigator moved to the basement door, pulled what remained off its hinge, and played a light around the walls. He asked one of the cops what he thought. "Looks like a fire waiting to happen," the cop said. "Spontaneous combustion."

"That's what I was thinking." The fire investigator called for a ladder, and one of the firemen brought one from outside. David came closer, standing at the edge of the basement while the fire investigator lowered himself into the smoke-filled hole. They heard him pulling at some boards, and a few minutes later he came up. "Pretty bad wiring down there. That could have caused it."

"This fire was set."

The fire investigator looked up. "Who the hell are you?"

"This is my building."

"And how do you know it was set?"

"I could smell it. When I got here the smell of kerosene was so strong it could have knocked you over."

"We have ways of telling when a fire's been set. There are no indications on this one."

"By the time the fire department got here, there was no more house."

The man's mouth turned down. "Anybody else smell this kerosene?"

"There were ten men back there with me. They had to have smelled it."

"You know their names?"

"Some of them." David spelled out the names and the fire investigator took them down. He gave the paper to another man, told him to question the witnesses and report back as soon as he could. By then other firemen had crawled into the basement and were poking among the ashes. The fire investigator continued following the trail of wiring until it petered out in a maze of fused and burned circuits.

"Ask me, this is where it started. Bad circuits, right over the basement. What'd you have down there, papers?"

"Well, this was a print shop. There were papers everywhere."

"Uh-huh."

"That still doesn't explain the smell of kerosene."

"What about you? You ever use kerosene?"

"For what?"

266

"Wash with. Printing can be a messy job."

"I've got a gas can. I keep it downstairs. It was sealed with an airtight top."

"We'll see about that. You ever have any open around here, in cans or bottles?"

"No, never."

"Still, a man can make a mistake. I've got to tell you, mister, it don't look to me like you're the most careful sort."

"Is that what your report's going to say?"

"It'll be noted, along with anything else I find."

A fireman came through the back door. "I talked to three of those guys, Max. None of them smelled any kerosene."

"Talk to the others. We want to be sure."

Another voice called from the basement. The fire investigator picked his way through the timbers and came to the edge of the basement. Two men had found something in a far corner. One looked up, a sick frown spreading across his face. "Looks like we got us a body down here, Max."

4

They brought her up. He couldn't look and yet he couldn't look away. The men hoisted her up on an uncovered stretcher. One black arm dangled limply over the edge. The face was burned beyond recognition, all but the lush, tawny hair on one side of her head. David went out into the field, far back where the trees grew, and there wasn't a trace of burned wood or burned flesh in the air. He dropped to his knees and threw up.

He called himself a pacifist, but perhaps that was just a way of hiding a naturally violent temper. He could kill, tonight, now, if the enemy suddenly showed himself. If he only knew.

He didn't come back until they had taken her away. Now there were more questions, this time asked by a policeman. They wanted to know who she was, what she was doing there. He lied. He said he didn't know. Her body had no identifying marks. Only the sex could be told without an autopsy, and David knew that the autopsy wouldn't give them any more. Her teeth would show no sign of a dentist's work. There would be no public records on her, here or anywhere. The fire investigator thought she had been caught in the upper house and had run to the basement to escape. She had been overcome by smoke and finally the weight of the burning floor had settled down over her. It looked like she had been trying to crawl into the earth behind the basement wall. One hand had been burrowing into the earth, and even in death the fingers had held a small book so tightly that they had had to pry it loose. A fading copy of *Green Mansions*. Like her heroine Rima, dead in the fire.

Outside, the tiny groups of people broke up. Finally the police left, unsatisfied, promising more questions. Sunday dawned cold and misty. David moved among the final stragglers, seeking out the one face he knew must be there. He found the old man, overcome with grief, sitting in a gutter a block away.

"Jordan."

Abbott couldn't speak. He tried but managed only a slight cry.

"Jordan, what was she doing there? I need to know that."

The old man looked up at him, then slowly drew himself to his feet. He looked mean and dangerous. "What do you mean what was she doing there? She belonged there."

"Not anymore. I thought we had this out."

"We had nothing out!" Abbott spat on the ground at his feet. "I wish we'd never set eyes on you."

"Jordan, I'm married now."

"You think I care about that? You were married to her, in every way, till you got tired of her and threw her out. You had a responsibility, Waldo. You took it on yourself and then didn't live up to it."

Jordan sobbed into his hands, David touched his shoulder but he jerked away. "You keep your goddamn hands off me! This is all your fault. You with your royal Jewish wife. Somebody should walk in off the street and kill her, then you'd know something about how I feel today."

"My God, Jordan, don't even say that."

"Somebody should do it. Me. I should do it." Abbott looked at him and his eyes narrowed. "I told you once what I'd do. A hand for a hand."

"Jordan, listen to me . . ."

"An eye for an eye, Waldo. I told you what would happen. Rotten bitch with her royal ways. She don't deserve to live. I shoulda done it months ago, when I first thought of it. Stuck her lily-white neck with her own butcher knife. I shoulda done it then."

David grabbed the old man's shoulder. "Don't you say that, old man, don't even think it. Kill me if you've got to kill somebody, but don't you go near her. Jordan, I'm warning you . . ."

"Shoulda done it. Coulda, too, any one of a dozen times. Shoulda done it that day she stuck her head up through the trapdoor. Sitting right behind her with the butcher knife in my hand. She'da turned, she'da seen me. Shoulda put the knife in her neck and had it done then and there. Then you and Jessie can be like you were before. I can still do it. Maybe that'll make it right."

The old man turned and walked away toward the railroad yards. David stood there, too stunned and too frightened to move. After a while he went after Abbott, but the old man was gone. He looked through the shack, found no one there, and slowly came back along Colfax toward Osceola Street.

He felt eyes on him as he walked past the burned-out shell of his print shop. Faces watched him from dark windows, and he knew the talk would be going from house to house and from block to block.The Klan had gotten to David and Anna Waldo, and by midday the fear would be everywhere.

He slept through the morning in Anna's room, got up at ten, and pulled on yesterday's clothes. They still reeked of smoke, and he didn't even have a fresh shirt. They would both need clothes, and for that they needed money. He thought of the canvas bag, buried behind the walls of the burned-out basement. Anna's survival fund.

He found Anna and Teresa sitting over coffee in the kitchen. Abe sat in his wheelchair, staring into the yard. The *Rocky Mountain News* lay face-up on the table. Nobody seemed to be reading it. David picked it up and sat at the table beside his wife.

"There's nothing about the fire," Anna said, nodding toward the *News*.

"There wouldn't be. Happened too late at night, after they'd already gone to press. There'll probably be something tomorrow."

"Anything happen after we left? They got any idea how it started yet?"

"We know how it started," Teresa said. "I could smell it clear across the street."

"They don't believe that," David said. "They think I was careless with papers."

Anna just looked at him and sipped her coffee.

"There's something else," David said. "They found a body in the rubble down in the basement."

"Dear God!" Anna touched her lips with her fingers. "Do they know who it is?"

He shook his head. "They've taken her to the morgue for an autopsy."

"It was a woman?"

"Yes."

"Isn't that strange?"

"Klan auxiliary probably. I bet she was helping them torch the place, and got stuck in her own trap," Teresa said.

"Anything's possible, I guess. We should probably all be a little careful till we know for sure."

"Careful how?" Teresa said.

"Don't open the door for strangers, for one thing. There may be a lot we don't know about this yet."

"I won't be a prisoner in my own house."

"Nobody's suggesting that. Just be careful." He looked at Anna. "You especially."

He went into the living room and began looking through the want ads. No one had said it and no one would while Teresa was around, but he had become, in one day, the man of the house. The Kohls were now his responsibility. Five people to feed and now no income: It was a sobering thought. Even with that, he found it hard to concentrate on the narrow columns of fine print. The specter of Jordan Abbott loomed out of every shadow in the house, and David Waldo found his fear growing by the hour. Soon, he knew, he would be afraid to leave the house.

So he did leave. At the door he drew Anna aside and repeated his warning about strangers. The front door was to remain locked, whether Teresa liked it or not. He walked over to the shop, to look at the damage by daylight, and the sight of it depressed him as nothing had in years. Nothing could be salvaged, unless perhaps his printing press . . . He was kidding himself. He had lost it all, and with no insurance he was out of the printing business, for a good long while. He walked around the building and tried to get in through the back, but two policemen were still guarding it and wouldn't let him pass. He didn't argue. Let them probe around, finish their investigation, and have it over and done with. Time, then, for digging the canvas bags out of the soft earth.

He thought of Abbott again, and the thought sent him hurrying back to Osceola Street. That afternoon he had a nap and Anna washed his clothes. The evening meal was silent and depressing. They all retired early. Monday morning Teresa left for the funeral home, to see to arrangements for Sammy's funeral. Someone would have to try again to reach Tom. David said he would. Anna would stay home with Abe. Again he took the *News* to the living room and read the ads. The fire had made page five, with a spectacular picture and a small story about the "mystery woman's" death. He looked quickly through the rest of the paper. Hidden away behind the entertainment section was a small item that caught his interest.

MAN KILLED BY TRAIN

A man said to be in his late fifties or early sixties was killed last night when a freight train hit his prone body in the railroad yards west of Santa Fe Drive.

The man, who wasn't immediately identified, was sleeping or lying across the tracks when the train came through at a moderate speed.

The engineer, O.W. Benson, said he saw the man lying across the width of the tracks, but too late to stop. Benson said he blew his whistle and the man seemed to look up, then settle back again. Police are investigating the possibility of suicide.

He walked the twenty blocks to the train yards and again looked through the shack where Abbott and his daughter had lived. He found the coat that Abbott had been wearing, and inside the pocket, a picture of Jessie. On the table was a butcher knife that he recognized as his own. He waited for a long time, but Abbott didn't come. David knew he wouldn't.

He had liked Abbott, and now that the old man was gone, he felt only relief. It hurt him to burn the picture in the fireplace in the corner. He couldn't take his eyes off the flames as they licked across that lovely face, burning everything. He pulled some newspaper out of a crack and touched it to the flame, then dropped it on the floor near the wall. He piled on more papers until the wood caught.

Even before he had reached the road near the trees, the flames were licking through the cracks. The tar paper ignited and the shack went up in a puff. David didn't look back. He walked toward Osceola Street, to tell Anna that he'd overreacted, and she didn't have to watch her shadow after all.

CHAPTER
FOUR

1

The men came the following Monday, five days after Sammy Kohl's funeral. All that week Teresa had tried without success to get Mr. Saul Reismann on the telephone. He had not been in and had not returned her calls. Now the truck had pulled up outside the store and the two men stood beside it, watching the store and talking. Both smoked cigars and wore coveralls. There was menace about them and the way they came. The larger one walked as if he owned the earth, the other trailed a few steps behind. Just outside the door they paused. Teresa lifted the telephone and called home. Anna told her that David had already left. He had three job interviews in Denver today. The door swung open and the big man stepped inside. No one spoke. Teresa sat on her perch near the counter and watched as they walked along the aisles looking at the shelves of groceries. The big man drew the curtain and looked into the back room.

272

"Nobody's allowed back there," Teresa said. "You men want something, give me your list. I'll fetch it for you."

They ignored her. The big man pushed the curtain all the way back and stepped into the back room. The other one moved along the aisles, like a new owner taking inventory.

"What do you think, Pike?" the big man said. "Three, four hours?"

"That's about right."

"Let's get started."

He walked to the front door and propped it open with a wooden box.

"Hey, Nate," the small man called across the store. "Where do we put the stuff?"

"Just stack it on the street. It ain't our responsibility."

Teresa came around the counter. "Just what do you think you're doing?"

They moved around her as though she didn't exist. The one called Nate began taking cans down from the shelves. He threw them into a cardboard box, carried it outside, and dumped it in a pile near the door. At the door, Teresa stood in his way, but he eased her aside with his arm and went back for more cans. Teresa hurried along behind him, tugging at his shirt. "Stop that. Stop it!" He moved down the aisle, dragging her along with him.

"Hey, Nate," the smaller man said, laughing. "Looks like you picked yourself up an anchor."

Nate shook his head. It was as though they had worked out a plan, and part of the plan was to ignore her completely. She bent over and picked up a heavy can of beans, throwing it hard and hitting him on the left ear. It knocked him against the shelf and it tipped over, scattering cans across the floor.

"There, you son of a bitch, ignore that!"

"Why you . . . God . . . damn . . . bitch." He got to his feet and came at her. She ran into the street, screaming with terror. She didn't stop running until she had reached the house. She burst through the front door screaming. "Call the police! My God, call the police, they're wrecking the store!"

Twenty minutes later a police car arrived. Two uniformed cops came to the front door and talked with Teresa. "I'm going with you," Anna said. By the time they reached the store a small crowd had gathered, and the pile of merchandise on the street had grown into a six-foot heap. Nate Newton and Elvin Pike were still hauling it out, dumping everything together: cardboard boxes, paper packages, cans, even a chair. Some of the boxes had ripped open, spilling their contents into the street.

"All right you two, hold it right there." The cops, the men, and the two women converged on the street, and everyone started to talk at once. Nate Newton produced an eviction notice, signed by Judge Thurman Hayes of the District Court. "This woman was told to get out. I know she was told at least a week ago that the place had been sold and she'd have to get out."

The cop looked at the paper. "It's a legal paper, all right," he said to Teresa. "Did you know about this?"

"I've been trying for a week to reach the new owners."

"What difference does that make?" Newton said. "She was told to get out, so what more is there to talk about?"

The cop shook his head. But the second cop said, "Who appointed you to serve this notice, mister?"

Pike reached into his pocket and took out a wallet. Pinned to the leather was a deputy sheriff's badge.

"Well, that's it then," the first cop said. "It's a legal eviction notice, signed by a judge, and he's a deputy sheriff."

"Sworn in last Friday," Pike said.

Newton glared at him.

Anna said, "Sir, he may have a paper, but does that make it right?"

"It makes it legal. Look here, it's the judge's signature."

"Isn't there any due process in something like this? How can you just stand there and watch them put us out on a moment's notice? Do you know how long we've done business on this corner? Doesn't that mean anything?"

"It means you've got to move," the cop said.

"Unless you want to go to court yourself," the second cop said. "Maybe you could get a restraining order till it's worked out."

"We'll be out in the street by then. Can't you stop them until we've had a chance to talk?"

The cops looked at each other. No one spoke for almost a minute. At last Teresa sat on the walk and said, "Forget it, honey. I think Thomas would call this a stacked deck."

"That's it, then," the first cop said again.

"Just you men remember who that merchandise belongs to," his partner said. "I'm staying here to see that you do."

"Collins, for Christ's sake."

"You go back if you want to. I'm staying."

They stood on the corner, Teresa and Anna and the policeman, watching in silence while Newton and Pike unloaded the store. Now the work went slowly, carefully. Boxes and cans were stacked neatly against the outer wall. The sun got warmer and Collins, the policeman, took off his hat and sat against the building in the shade.

Soon another police car came. Collins' partner was driving and a gruff-looking man wearing a handlebar moustache and three stripes on his arm was sitting on the rider's side. The car stopped at the edge of the road and the sergeant said something to Collins. Collins got to his feet, looked at Teresa, and climbed into the back seat.

"I'm obliged to tell you, this stuff's got to be taken off the street," the sergeant said. "Otherwise I'll have to get the garbage trucks out after it."

"We'll move it," Teresa said.

"It's creating a public hazard the way it is. I'll give you till this afternoon to haul it away."

"There's just the two of us," Anna said. "My husband will be back this evening."

"Four o'clock, miss. If the collectors have to come after it, it's got to be done before they knock off for the day. What's not gone by four goes to the dump."

Newton came out with an armload of cans. He waited until the police car was out of sight, then dropped them on the street. He kicked the pile, so carefully stacked throughout the hour, and the cans clattered down off the walk and rolled into the gutter.

"Now look what I done, Pike. After all that work."

He stepped on a can of tomatoes. The top burst open and the red fluid oozed out, like the blood of a dying man.

2

They struggled with the merchandise all afternoon. Anna changed into her gardening clothes and by two o'clock her face and arms were streaked with dirt and sweat. She and Teresa filled burlap sacks with cans and packages, then hauled them over to Osceola Street. When the sacks were full, it took both of them to pull one. After a while they learned that it was faster and easier to carry half-sacks.

Gabriel came home from school. Between the three of them, they got the heavy cash register perched on top of his pushcart. It took them almost an hour to get it home.

Newton and Pike had finished by the time they got back to the store. The men had stripped it bare and were installing new locks on both doors. In the front window they had placed a sign, which said PRIVATE PROPERTY ABSOLUTELY NO TRESPASSING. The inside of the store looked desolate and somehow smaller, as if no one had used it in many months. It seemed impossible now that so much of their lives had been tied to this dusty, bare room that now resembled a warehouse more than a store, that now belonged to the Ku Klux Klan, that was and would be, from this day on, a grim reminder of happier times.

Newton and Pike were in no hurry to leave. They lingered near the door, watching as Gabriel loaded loose cans into his pushcart. The deadline had come and gone. It was well past four, and still at least half the store's stock littered the street. There were huge barrels of rice and flour, sugar and coffee beans. The shelving had been ripped out of the wall and piled on top of everything else, so that to get to the cans they first had to move the heavy boards. The counter too had been broken apart, so that it might pass through the front door. It sat in three huge pieces, immovable even by the three of them. They struggled with the smaller foodstuff and left the heavy items alone. Gabriel slipped and dumped his cart into the street. Newton and Pike laughed.

Anna shouted at them. "Shame on you, laughing at a child like that!" Newton just grinned at her. "Shame on us, Pike," Anna came toward them. "There'll be a price to pay for this. You'll both pay it in hell. Damn both your black souls."

They left as the garbage truck came. It was manned by a white driver and two black workers. They loaded the shelving and counter first, then the blacks bucked up the barrels of flour and rice. "Be careful with that, boy," the driver said. "Don't spill any." Suddenly Teresa felt the tears come. She dabbed at her eyes and choked them back. "Those barrels'll never make it to the dump," she said, avoiding Anna's eyes. Anna said, "Maybe he'd drop them at our place. It wouldn't hurt anything to ask." But Teresa put a hand on her arm. "We've done enough asking for one day, honey. This family don't ask favors from jackals like that."

By five-thirty the street was cleared, and the three of them walked slowly home. In a back room of the house they took a quick inventory and were amazed at how little there was. "That's it," Teresa said, sinking into a chair. "Twenty years of hard work and that's what we've got to show. A few cans of groceries, a few sacks of beans." David came in about thirty minutes later. He sat without reacting to Anna's weary description of their day, then he told them about his own day. He had found a job, stacking shelves at a market downtown. It was boys' work, paying a boy's wage. Ten dollars for fifty-five hours, ten hours a day, five on Saturday. But it was a start, a way back. They should all be happy for that. No one was. "In the morning I'll go out and see what I can find," Teresa said.

"So will I, of course," Anna said.

"Somebody needs to stay with Abe."

"Then you stay," Anna said.

After dinner David walked over to his shop. The cordon had been down for three days now, and the investigation was over. He hadn't told Teresa or Anna, but this afternoon he had stopped at City Hall to look up the fire investigator's report. There was no mention of arson.

The report made him look like a careless idiot. On the way home he had made another stop, in the Potter's Field section of Riverview Cemetery, where they were burying Jessie's body. The coroner had held it eight days and no one had claimed it, and now he had ordered it buried. The hole was dug by two winos from the lowers—thin, hard men with four-day beards and red eyes. The coffin was six pieces of wood, nailed together carelessly, with the points of the nails occasionally breaking through the wood. A minister in plain clothing came down and said a few words over the open grave, then departed, leaving David to watch the burying alone. There was no mound, no marker, nothing to indicate that the fresh-turned earth was a grave.

How different it was from Sammy Kohl's funeral a few days earlier. Sammy had been buried in a family plot bought by the Kohls years ago, and half of west Denver had come. The stranger, watching through the graveyard gates, would know that it was the funeral of a much-loved man.

It had cost them some money, and David had dug his canvas bags out of the soft earth of the shop basement. He sat on a keg near his rusting printing press and counted it. Two hundred dollars, no great fortune, but still twenty weeks' work in his new job. Eleven hundred hours.

There were other things: clothes for himself and for Anna. He didn't tell them where the money had come from. He was becoming tight-lipped, almost secretive in these new days of terror and threats. That night he'd taken a strange telephone call, and he didn't tell them about that either. For perhaps fifteen seconds there was only the sound of someone breathing on the other end. Then—and he still wasn't sure about this part of it—a voice whispered something. It sounded like his name. *Dave*. Dave. He clutched the mouthpiece close and said, "Tom? Is that you?" He heard a click and the line went dead.

Anna came into the room. "Who was it, love?"

"No one. Wrong connection."

She looked at him and shook her head. "Those people. Won't they ever be satisfied?"

3

On the morning of his fourth workday, David Waldo met the enemy. He was working in the storeroom, marking and stacking canned goods, when he saw two men through the tiny glass window. They went upstairs to the manager's office, and twenty minutes later a delivery boy came for David. The office was at the rear of the market, built into a mezzanine floor, with a plate glass window so the man could look over his kingdom without ever leaving his chair. The man's name was Sanders. He had inherited the market from his father, and was at least eight years younger than David.

He came to the point at once. "I'm afraid I can't use you, Waldo." He reached for a pink slip.

"What's the problem?"

"I don't hire radicals."

"What's that got to do with me?"

Again Sanders turned to his desk. He fished through a pile of papers until he found the one he wanted. "Your record goes back far, Waldo."

"Where'd you get that?"

"Were you arrested in Oakland, California, for interfering with police?"

"That was more than twenty years ago. I don't believe this."

"Those things are hard to live down, especially these days. What about this arrest in Chicago a few years later—swept in with a bunch of radicals who were armed with explosives."

"I was a kid then. And I didn't know about the explosives."

"Arrests, arrests, arrests. Were you still a kid in 1920, Waldo? Arrested in Boston in January, 1920. Held without bail for two weeks."

"And then released without charge. Does your record show that?"

"Nor has your record been exactly spotless since coming to Denver. Constant trouble with the police here. Arrested just this summer, pleaded guilty to resisting arrest. Fined, sentenced to jail, jail term suspended. If you ask me, the judge in that case showed remarkable leniency, considering your past record. Good God, man, where's your judgment? Waldo, if we associate with anarchists and communists, we're bound to get burned when the firing starts. That goes for the company as well as the individual." Now he did pick up the pink slip. "Here—I'll give you a voucher and the cashier up front will give you your money. Four days, eighteen and one-half cents an hour. I figure I owe you six-sixty. That sound about right?"

David didn't say anything.

Sanders tore off the slip and passed it across the desk. "We'll make it an even seven."

David walked away. He collected his seven dollars and went out into the autumn air. From the sidewalk he saw the two men, watching him from a truck parked across the street. The driver started the motor and drove away. Later, walking home, he saw the truck again. It was about two blocks behind, following him across the valley.

Anna came in about thirty minutes behind him. She was ecstatic. She had been hired by a broker on Seventeenth Street, to type and run errands. Her pay was twenty-five dollars a week. A fortune.

His news would wait. That night they celebrated. They had the last of the side meat and canned corn from the store.

4

The month of September was hard. Anna lost her job mysteriously and David found work in another market. But on his second day Newton and Pike showed up, confronted the manager, and had him fired. In the middle of the month, thieves broke into the storage room behind the house and made off with most of their canned goods, smashed the rest, and scattered the cans through the garden. "It looks like they've shifted tactics," David told her that night in bed. "It's an economic squeeze now, and we all need to understand that. I think they intend to starve us out."

He found work as an iceman. Every morning at three o'clock he got up and slipped out through the backyard. He doubled back up the hill over Sloan's Lake, cut through the trees and walked due east until he reached the railroad yards. He crisscrossed through the blocks, making certain he wasn't being followed before going to the icehouse. He arrived there at five, loaded the ice blocks onto the truck with tongs, got away by six and made his first run through the neighborhood near Park Hill, just east of downtown. It wasn't until his second run, through Capitol Hill at mid-morning, that he began to relax. He often stopped by to see Georgeann, hoping for some word from Tom, but there was never anything. Someone named Nelson had taken Tom's apartment.

Everything in those weeks had a feeling of impermanence about it. When he drew his first paycheck, he was elated to have lasted so long. It gave him a feeling of security, of his own cleverness. He told himself that he could outsmart them forever, an illusion that dissolved near the end of his second week, when Moran picked him up on suspicion of burglary.

He was held in city jail for two days on someone's word that he resembled a robber, seen running from the area at four o'clock in the morning. He never met his accuser. They paraded him into a police lineup, turned white lights in his face, made him turn one way and then another, and led him back to jail. When they finally released him, he hurried to the icehouse, to try to salvage his job. He was careless. Newton and Pike followed him.

That night he felt that rage stirring again. He wanted to smash things with his fist. Anna met him at the door, sat him in a chair, and rubbed his shoulders. "There, love," she said. "Things'll get better."

He shook his head. "Anna, I'm very much afraid that this is just the start."

She didn't say anything for a long time. They just sat in the darkening room, her fingers working the muscles of his neck. "All that means to me is we've got to think before we act," she said. "I did that today."

"Did what?"

"I thought about what you'd said. And I thought, what's the best way of fighting this nonsense? At least one of us has to have a job. Something untouchable, that the Klan for all its power won't trifle with."

"Tell me where it is and I'll go there tomorrow."

"I've already done that." She came around and looked at him. She was fairly ready to burst. "This afternoon I went downtown and talked to Mr. Bonfils at the *Denver Post.*"

5

She had been nervous, but not nearly the emotional disaster she'd feared. Sitting in the plum-colored waiting room that people called the Bucket of Blood, fidgeting in her lap, she thought that Mrs. Reynolds must have waited in a room like this one, perhaps in this same chair, for her first interview with Bonfils twenty-five years ago. Anna had walked in unannounced, not quite certain that Bonfils would see her. But a secretary in the Bucket of Blood had asked her to wait and here she was, staring at the closed inner door. She had given her married name. Let him ponder it. Let it intrigue him, prompt him to know why someone named Anna Waldo, whom he had never known, would want to talk to him. He wouldn't have to know who she really was; he'd never recognize her in a thousand years. She had changed a dozen times over from the little girl he'd known across the hedge, changed so much for the better. She was sharp and trim and some said pretty. She was thinking that when the door opened, startling her. A burly man came out, not Bonfils, but just beyond she caught a glimpse of that dark head in a swirl of smoke. Eccentric, unpredictable and, God help her, sensual. She chased that thought from her mind and denied she'd ever had it.

He had seen her too; she was certain of that. The minutes dragged and her confidence grew, in herself and in what she was doing. It all evaporated when the door opened again and he stood before her. He stood absolutely erect. He wore flashy tweeds. His black eyes riveted her where she sat and she held his gaze. *I must not waver. I must not look away.* But she did look away, and only then did he speak to her. His voice had reached her, clear and loud, and yet she had no idea what he'd said or what she was to do now. She stood and dropped her handbag, spilling its contents across the floor. Bonfils did not move. His bodyguard appeared, as if from the woodwork, kneeling at her feet and scooping up her things. She was ushered into his office, given a chair facing his desk and made to wait some more, while he dictated an order to someone in the outer room. If there had been an easy escape route, she'd have taken it. She heard him come in behind her, closing the door. He came around the desk. They were alone.

He wasn't as tall as she remembered. His eyes never left her face. His manner was brisk, his voice businesslike, and yet laced with good manners and distant charm. "Madam, I am at your service. What can I do for you?"

She was first embarrassed, then mortified. She had lost her voice. Her mouth moved like the mouth of a gaffed fish, but nothing came. She knew she must look grotesque, and without warning, the tears came. Bonfils passed her a linen and brought her some cool water. He waited, looking down into Champa Street while she composed herself. She thought he must be used to this. How many women must come to him weeping, pleading the cause of a brother, a husband, a boyfriend. He had to be used to it, and yet there was about him an air of discomfort. He looked almost like the crushed lover of two decades ago, pouring out his grief to a little girl on a park bench.

"Madam?"

She stood and for just an instant their eyes met again. "Do I know you?"

"No." She said it too quickly, almost defensively. Again Bonfils gestured toward the chair. She sat and faced him, noticing for the first time that he was getting gray. How distinguished he will be in old age, she thought.

"Miss?" When she still didn't speak, Bonfils said, "Am I so terrible and fearsome that I reduce a lady to speechlessness and tears just by walking into a room? Are you quite certain, Mrs. Waldo, that we haven't met?"

She shook her head, feeling more like a fool than ever.

"I don't know your name," Bonfils said, "but that face. I don't forget faces . . ."

"It's been too long ago to mention."

"Then we have met."

"So long ago, sir, that it's not worth mentioning."

"Mention it, please, just to satisfy my curiosity. I won't sleep tonight unless you tell me. Do tell me."

"I was a child."

He frowned and puzzled it, a man peeling back the years.

"I last saw you in August, 1907."

"The little girl of the park."

She smiled. "I was thirteen years old."

"The little girl in Cheesman Park. That was you?"

She nodded. Her confidence had come surging back.

His dark eyes panned her face. "Yes," he said. "Yes. I told you about . . . myself. Naturally that was all made up. Just stories for a little girl. I know you didn't believe a word."

"I believed every word, and still do."

"See how vulnerable a little girl is? That's why the *Post* crusades so hard for the rights of working children. Children are ready to believe everything you tell them."

"I also saved the clippings."

"What clippings?"

"About Mrs. Reynolds."

He sat and regarded her across the vast expanse of his desk. "But it was just a story. Now that you've grown up you can see that."

She sensed her advantage and grew bolder. "Now that I'm grown-up, I know that anything is possible."

"The clippings—I've never read them. What did they say?"

"Just straight factual reports of her life and death. How kind she was."

"Nothing about me."

"No, sir."

"Then see? It was all a story, made up by a man with time on his hands, for a child with an alert imagination."

"I think not, sir."

There was a long moment of silence, while Bonfils stared with relentless intensity. Suddenly his eyes grew dark again, and the hardness reappeared around his mouth. "Well, what can I do for you? I hope you didn't come here to hold the past over my head."

"Mr. Bonfils, that's a horrible thing to say."

"What then? I'm a busy man."

"I need a job."

He just stared, giving her the jitters and finally bringing back her panic. She tried to lay her case before him all at once. "My family is being persecuted by the Ku Klux Klan. They took our business and now they have people following us everywhere, both my husband and me. They threaten employers and cause us to lose work. I need a job where the employer fears no one. All we want is to live in peace and be left alone. My husband could work for you too. He was a reporter once."

"I have more reporters now than I need. Where did he work?"

"In Oakland. On a paper called the *Oakland Tribune*. Around the turn of the century. He knew Jack London."

"Just what I need, a reporter who hasn't worked in twenty-five years, who thinks he's Jack London. What about you? What do you do?"

"I type and run errands. I take excellent shorthand. I answer the telephone well, and I get things straight. I have a good voice, don't you think?"

"Where did you learn to type?"

"I've always done some, but they polished me off at business school. That's where I got the shorthand too."

"If I had something for you here, would you continue your classes?"

"As you'd like, sir."

"You'd have to go at night. Your husband might not like that."

"He'd like it fine, Mr. Bonfils. He's very open-minded about things like that. He's a remarkable man in many ways."

"He sounds like a fool."

She bristled. "Do you always form opinions about people you don't know?"

"Are you serious? Young lady, that's my business. Anyway, I stand by my judgment. Any man who lets his wife stay out after dark is a fool. He bores me already. Here—take a pencil and pad. Let me give you a letter. When I'm done, go outside and find yourself a typewriter, type it up on *Post* bond, exactly the way I gave it to you, and bring it back to me."

He dictated a long, abusive letter to the Tramway Company, which she suspected was fiction designed solely to test her. When she brought it to him ten minutes later, he read it and reread it. When he spoke, his voice had lost that hard edge. "You were staying with people next door," he said. "A family of Jews lived there."

"Gail Jaffe was my friend."

"She still lives there," Bonfils said. "I was passing once not long ago and I saw her. Did you know her father hated me?"

"Yes."

"One morning he died on the lawn outside their house. I saw him collapse. He'd had a heart attack. Harry Tammen and I were coming down to work together. Jaffe came out on his lawn to get his newspaper and we saw him fall over backward and clutch at his chest. Like this, here. I ran up on the lawn and ripped open his collar. He looked at me with the eyes of a shot deer. I will never forget what he said to me then. Do you know what that was?"

"No, sir."

"He called me a pig. A dying man. He looked up into my face and called me a pig. This man—I was trying to save his life, and he formed his mouth to spit at me. He died before he could. We'd never spoken to each other, and I've always wondered why a man I barely knew would hate me as much as that man did. Do you know why, little girl?"

"He hated your newspaper."

"All right, that I can understand. But because of that he hated me too, enough that he didn't want my help even in death. You see what hate does?"

"I know what hate does, sir."

"You said you were being persecuted. Do you know why the Klan hates you?"

"I guess because we're Jews. And perhaps because we've tried to defy them."

"Yes. Well, it doesn't matter to me what you are. I don't think I can use your husband, but I might have a job for you. Report to Mr. Roberts on the fourth floor, starting tomorrow." He put her letter in an envelope and sealed it. "And mail this on your way out."

"How can I thank you?"

"By being worth what I pay you."

She nodded her head and smiled, gathered her bag and moved to the door.

"Little girl?"

"I hope you aren't going to keep calling me that."

"I'll call you Mrs. Waldo."

"That would be fine. Anna if you like."

"Remember the time I invited you through the hedge?"

"Of course I do."

"I told you I had something for you. And you said . . ."

"I said I wasn't allowed."

"I had some candy for you. Peppermints, shipped from New England. Did you ever wonder about that?"

"Many times."

"It took you a long time to cross the hedge and find out."

6

She couldn't resist wandering through the old neighborhood. Late that afternoon she came upon Bonfils' old house. It had been many years since she'd seen it. The hedge was gone now, replaced by a haphazard row of tiny trees. Bonfils had moved years ago into another house, and the new owners were letting the place run down. Next door, the Jaffe home looked as trim and well-kept as ever. Nothing about it had changed in the least. She stopped for a moment outside the gate, then went up the walk almost reluctantly. At the door she was met by a dumpy little woman in a maid's uniform. "Is Miss Jaffe, pardon me, Mrs. Owens, in?" The maid stared suspiciously and she said, "Please tell her Anna Kohl is here."

She was shown into the living room. It was exactly as she remembered it. In a moment she heard a shriek from the upper floor, and Gail came floating down the staircase with her arms outstretched. They hugged and Anna blushed in happy embarrassment. "My God, look at me. Would you believe this?" Gail was obviously drowning in the flapper craze. "Wasn't I always the shy one, quiet and mousy? I always wanted to be like you. Now look at us. I wear loud clothes, go to parties, do the Charleston on tabletops, and, what the hell, I still wish I could be like you. You look like you're leading a nice quiet happy life."

"With all this," Anna said, "I'd imagine that you could live just about any way you want to."

"All this, if you'll pardon the expression, can be an incredible pain in the ass. Come on, let's sit and talk. Trudy is fixing us some tea."

They sat at a table covered with the latest New York magazines. The table was immense. On the far end, someone had become bored with a Mah-jongg game and had scattered the tiles across the board. A pile of books turned spines-out revealed all the superficial titles that made intellectuals sound intellectual at parties. On top was *Pocket University*, the publishing sensation she'd been reading about. It filled a person with instant facts, made him an authority on anything and had been ripped to shreds by real intellectuals like Mencken as a piece of tripe. Gail herself looked strangely distant and shallow. She looked older than Anna, though as Anna recalled it, she was actually somewhat younger. Her eyes were tired-looking. The flapper thing had run through her like consumption, leaving her too weak to shake it off. She wore makeup, far too much and in the wrong places. Her dress was silky and loose, designed especially to hide her large breasts. No woman in 1924 wanted to be compared with a cow, and

Gail kept crossing and uncrossing her arms as though she could somehow hide the truth. Her hair was bobbed. Anna thought it was the most charming thing she had done to herself. It emphasized the natural roundness of her face, which Anna had always liked and wanted for herself.

Gail's husband, Philip, was a state senator. They were currently separated, though that situation seemed to change with the wind. They had two boys who were away at military school. Anna asked how her being Jewish had affected her husband's career, and Gail said, "I stopped going to Temple when I met Philip and I never saw any reason to go back. Eventually I joined his church. That's a bore too, but we have to go anyway. That's the kind of crap you do when you're in politics." Their marriage was a classic conflict of liberal and conservative philosophies. Senator Philip Owens was chairman of a powerful senate committee that would be screening the bills offered by the administration next year. Everyone expected the administration to be Klan-dominated. "I don't see how they can lose after that recall fiasco, do you?" Gail said. "Anyway, I think Phil will play along with anything Mr. Locke wants, and his own political star will rise like a balloon if he does. The whole goddamn thing bores me to tears. All our friends were suck-ups with axes to grind. Once the sex thing cooled off, all we had left were all the things we couldn't stand about each other. Even the sex stopped after a while, what with Phil out lifting the skirts of anything he could lay his hands on. It got so I was afraid to let him touch me. I never knew what he might bring in off the street."

Anna was shocked. She had never heard anyone talk so frankly about sex. She had read about the liberation that had come with the Vote, but had never expected to meet one of its products. But Gail Jaffe Owens looked the part. She chain-smoked and her talk was liberally peppered with "Christs" and "hells" and "goddamns." Trudy brought tea, the afternoon waned, and shadows lengthened across the room. "Listen to me gabbing away," Gail said. "I haven't heard a thing about you. You must be married now." Anna told her that she had married a wonderful man who was, she thought, hopefully out of jail and on his way home by now. She had just gone to work for Mr. Bonfils at the *Denver Post*. "Dear old Mr. Bonfils," Gail said. "Remember how Daddy hated him? I'm surprised your husband will let you work."

"He encourages me. He wants me to be self-reliant and skilled."

"Sensible man. Phil wouldn't let me step out of the house without him. And work—Christ, you'd think I wanted to burn the American flag on the statehouse steps. Your husband sounds just about perfect."

She smiled.

"If you're still trying to take classes, won't that run you late getting home?"

"Maybe, sometimes."

"In winter too. If you ever get stuck, you know where I live. It'll be a ball. We can stay up late like we did when we were kids. You could even have your old room. Same room, same bed. Nothing ever changes around here."

"It gives me a good feeling to see that," Anna said. "You need to know that there are some things that don't change. Of course, I'll want to make it home if I can." She stood. "Speaking of which, I'd better get going now if I want to make it before dark."

Gail took her hand. "Thanks *so* much for coming to see me. Please come back. And bring that lovely husband of yours."

Gail escorted her to the door. "Remember what I said. Anytime!" Anna hurried up the walk. She turned and waved as a cold wind blew against her. Gail was standing in the vestibule, smoking another cigarette and looking very lonely.

7

On Sundays the family went to visit Sammy's grave. David hired a carriage and drove the team along the back streets. Teresa put flowers on the headstone and afterward they had a picnic lunch at Sloan's Lake park. Anna was so happy that laughter was always at her lips. She had worked for the *Post* for two weeks without disaster, and again Bonfils had become her hero. That first morning she had come boldly out through the front door, smiled at Newton and Pike, and caught the trolley downtown. She saw their truck following, and at her stop she had actually waited for them to catch up. Then she walked a block up and disappeared into the *Post* building. After her third day they had stopped coming.

David too had found work. None of them knew where. He kept his secret even from his wife, saying only that she would have less to worry about if she didn't know. He brought home fifteen dollars a week, little more than half her salary, and worked half again as long. Even Gabriel was working, selling the *Rocky Mountain News* before school and making his collections in the afternoon.

He awoke each morning at three, crept downstairs, and found David at the kitchen table, eating a breakfast of shredded wheat and cream. Gabriel would sit with David and drink a glass of milk. They talked about the problems of the day, about school and staying alive. At quarter to four, with still no trace of light in the east, they slipped out the back way, making sure the door was locked, and crept off through the garden, going through a hole in the back fence. Each day they took a new route, usually ending up at Colfax, far from home, in time to get the four-thirty tram downtown. David would walk Gabriel through the streets toward Welton Street, cutting away on Sixteenth and leaving the boy to walk the last block to the *News* building himself.

David felt the bond between them grow. He felt it now, watching Anna gather up the basket after their picnic and wheel Abe down toward the eastern shore. Teresa went with them. David and Gabriel sat alone on the grass. For perhaps a week now he had known that Gabriel had something on his mind, but he had decided to let the boy find his own way to let it out. When it did come, now, it was natural and smooth. Gabriel watched the water for a while and said, "I've been wanting to tell you something. I don't hate her anymore."

"That's good. For a boy to hate his mother is a bad thing."

"I still get impatient. I want it to be out in the open. When can it can it be? Why can't we just tell her?"

"Put yourself in her place. How did you feel when Abe just told you?"

"Mad. Just so damned mad you couldn't believe it. It was like I'd been deceived all my life."

"You had been. You had every right to feel that way. But in a way, we're doing the same thing to her, now. We're still playing that game."

"It's their game. They started it, not us."

"It doesn't matter who started it. It's going to surprise her, shock her maybe, and that calls for a little care."

"Don't you think the longer you put it off the worse it'll be?"

"Maybe, maybe. It's so hard to know what's right."

Gabriel was quiet for a moment. "I never really hated her," he said. "Not really."

"I know. How could anybody hate her?"

"It's going to feel funny, calling her Mother."

"You'll get used to it in no time. Just be patient." He rolled over and got to his feet. "I'm going to catch up with them. You want to come?"

Gabriel shook his head. David hurried off toward the shore. He began to trot. His heart was light. He thought he had seen something very dear in Gabriel's face. He had seen trust. More important, perhaps, the beginnings of love.

8

On Election Day she went to Gail's for dinner. The invitation had included David, but he thought he might have to work late that night, and did. The occasion, Gail said, was her temporary reconciliation with Senator Philip Owens, something she emphasized was not to be taken too seriously. It was the fourth time they had reconciled this year. Owens had invited some of his political friends and their wives, and the men would probably spend the evening listening to election returns on the radio. "We can watch them fight over the earphones," Gail said. "When that gets boring, we can get out in the patio and talk."

She put on her best dress and waited on the porch for the car that Gail had promised to send. All afternoon Teresa had been nagging her over the impropriety of going out nights alone, and her own argument, that Gail was a very old friend and David *wanted* her to go, had done nothing to stop it. The chauffeur arrived, and the car whisked her across town. The Jaffe mansion lit up the block. There were lights on every floor. Gas globes burned atop brick gateposts. Gail had said a small dinner party, but to Anna, who had never cooked for more than eight people, it looked immense. Cars lined the block on both sides of the street and people came in a steady stream. She began having second thoughts about her dress, her hair and most of all her shoes, which were a year old. The chauffeur turned into the drive and pulled up behind a line of cars.

It was like stepping out on another planet. All the chandeliers were lit, and the candlelit patio at the side of the house hummed with conversation and laughter. Waiters were everywhere. She wondered where they had come from, when two weeks ago there had been just the maid. Gail greeted her at the door with a cry and a hug. She tried to blend into a crowd. "No no no, you don't!" Gail said, laughing. "Here's some people for you to meet. Eli and Pat Eaker, this is my oldest living friend on the face of this earth, Anna Kohl. It's Anna Waldo now, isn't it? Where's that husband of yours?"

"He had to work."

"Eli's a senator, on the rules committee with Phil. Speaking of whom, did anybody see where that handsome old devil went?"

Senator Eaker looked at her with interest. Still looking, but talking to Gail, he said, "I think he's outside."

"Eli and Phil form the backbone of the conservative coalition in the Senate," Gail said. "They're somewhere to the right of Louie the Fourteenth."

Everyone laughed but Mrs. Eaker. Anna thought she had a superior air. Her hand was cold and her eyes moved beyond people in a tired, bored way. More people pushed in behind her, and at last she escaped the hated limelight, moving back into the room while Gail greeted the new arrivals. Waiters moved past her with brimming trays of silver and glass, luscious-looking tidbits, drinks, hors d'oeuvres. The house drink was a fruity punch, heavily spiked. Anna had never tasted alcohol. Across the room, she saw that a man had brought out a hip flask and was putting more spike in the fruit drink. She sipped it, then put it down and looked to see if anyone was watching. Senator Eaker stared at her, his lips curled back in a soft laugh. He came toward her.

"Drink not to your liking?"

"I'm just surprised. I didn't expect it."

"What, demon rum? Have they spiked the punch? I'll run the law in on them." He roared with laughter and Anna tried to smile. She tried to continue his joke, but coming from her the words sounded prim and prudish.

"Isn't it strange how in this room full of lawmakers you find so many lawbreakers?"

"What's strange about it? It's a bad law, lady, and not our doing. I don't have to remind you, this is something the Feds imposed upon us. Now let them figure out what to do with their law."

"I'm surprised to find a conservative who feels that way."

"Prohibition's got nothing to do with conservative or liberal. It's just a matter of what's right for the country."

He sounded like a man on the campaign trail. Vaguely, he offended her.

"Still," she said. "Shouldn't legislators at least try to follow the law till it's changed? I'd think you'd be morally bound to set us sinners an example."

"Young lady, are you presuming to lecture me?"

Again she tried to laugh. "I guess I was. I'm sorry."

"In that case, you're forgiven. That's the trouble with women, you have no political sense at all. No concept of what's possible and what isn't. God only knows what'll happen to the country now that you've got the vote. I guess you voted Democrat."

"No." She felt ashamed, anticipating his next question. She hadn't voted at all.

But he said, "At least you've shown some sense. But you seem to think laws like Prohibition are made and repealed overnight. You need a lesson in politics."

"Maybe so."

"Now what does that mean? Why do I get the feeling you're a Democrat in disguise?"

"Maybe because I'm Gail's friend and we think alike. But I promise you, sir, I'm not in any disguise."

"Then what did that last crack mean?"

"Just that politics, if I understand it . . ."

"Which you don't. But go on, I'm fascinated." He put on his most bored look.

"Politics is simply trying to decide what people will vote for."

"Greatly simplistic, miss."

"Like most truths."

She felt sassy and angry now, her temper flaring at the man's bullying. "And if it's true, which I believe, then my judgment is as good as yours. Maybe better, since I'm one of the people and closer in hear to the voter than you are."

"I don't do too badly. I've been elected to the Senate twice now, both times by big margins. Maybe I know a little of what the people want."

"Then why don't you tell me? What do they want?"

"Law and order. A repression of this radical surge. They want us to pass some laws that'll give the police some teeth. They'd like to see some people deported, sent back to Italy or wherever they came from. The people of this country are getting sick and goddamn tired of all this lawlessness."

"And that, sir, sounds exactly like the Ku Klux Klan line."

"What of it? The Klan's the best thing that ever happened to this country. It's the only thing that keeps the niggers and Reds from taking over completely. God help us all if the Klan ever goes under, and you can quote me on that. Oh, miss, you really do need a lesson." He leaned close and gave her a lecherous wink. "Come up to the statehouse and I'll show you how laws are made."

She smelled the sour alcohol on his breath. He reached for her hand but she stepped back as Eaker's wife drifted close. "Draw in your claws, darling," Mrs. Eaker said, looking at both of them. She led her husband away, leaving Anna to wander on her own. She felt good. The argument had boosted her confidence, and now she walked through the rooms with no sense of inferiority whatsoever. It hardly looked like the same place she had seen just two weeks ago. Tables had been moved out of hiding, and now lined the walls of one entire room off the main hall. Piled high on the tables were dishes of every kind she could imagine: roast duck, huge slabs of beef, ham smothered in hot fruit sauce, creamed vegetables. From the other room, she heard a spoon striking the side of a glass, as Gail called for attention. Since it was to be an early evening, and especially since many of their distinguished guests had political calls to make later (loud laughter and raucous cheers accompanied this), they should begin eating. From her corner, Anna watched the people load their plates with gluttonous ease, as if they expected nothing less from life. She thought of her own pantry and found it hard to believe that such luxury existed and that, at least for tonight, she was part of it.

But it left her with a strange lack of appetite, and she stood still and watched a while longer. Like a passing parade they came before her, the men distinguished and reasonable-looking, their women decked out in silks and beads of the latest style. The women drank and smoked along with the men. Occasionally she heard swearing above the noise, followed by peals of female laughter. One elderly man arrived wearing a coonskin coat, and people flocked around him with roars of laughter. Gail cranked up a phonograph and people danced to the music of "Hindustan" and "I'll Say She Does." Some stared drunkenly into space and snapped their fingers to the beat of the music. A group of women passed, all wearing thin sleeveless dresses. They were talking about birth control, and there wasn't a wedding ring among them. They cocked their eyes at her as they passed, then burst into laughter as soon as Anna was out of earshot.

Men came past, talking politics and Klan candidates and the day's vote. The polls had closed, and the men drifted toward Senator Philip Owens' den, where a telephone was ringing and two radios had been set up at opposite walls. Anna followed the tide across the hall. She saw Mrs. Eaker hurry out, holding a dress drenched with punch, and thought *good for somebody*. In the den, Senator Owens had grabbed up the phone and two men wearing jazzy suits and polka-dotted bow ties had strapped the earphones of the radio sets over their heads. Owens hung up the phone and shouted, "Morley's taken an early lead!" A roar rattled the room. Two men behind Owens' desk had propped up a blackboard, with various races chalked in white boundaries. Within minutes the smoke had turned the air blue, and Anna couldn't see across the room to read the changing totals. One of the men was complaining loudly that his wireless wasn't working, and his brother was getting all the good news. Owens helped him adjust the crystal and he moved his slider until he got something. It was just a station in Kansas City, where the only interesting race on the air was for President.

She sank into a chair, dizzy from the heat and smoke. After a while Gail found her, and led her away to the drawing room, where most of the ladies had segregated themselves. "Don't you think of leaving," Gail said, clutching her hand. "My God, if you leave me alone with these Kluxers I'll go crazy. Come on, get something to eat." She grabbed up a plate, piled it high with everything and stuffed it into Anna's hands. Someone grabbed her shoulder and she disappeared again, leaving Anna alone in a corner, nibbling delicately and watching the women. The flutter of feminine voices washed over her, and she found herself listening to half a dozen broken conversations, focusing on one, then tuning out and finding another. Sex seemed to be the only topic of the day. Ladies long oppressed and sheltered now burst with curiosity and nerve. One tiny blond told of visiting her boyfriend's estate, sitting on bedroom floors, and smoking opium far into the night. And soon this room became as smoky as the den, the voices as loud, the air as close.

The food was superb, and she saw that she had eaten most of what Gail had put on her plate. For the first time she even ate the tiny morsels of ham, loving the rich salty taste of it. She put down her plate, as she had her drink, with vague feelings of guilt. She almost expected to see her dead father, challenging her out of the blue pall of smoke.

Laughter bubbled like the wine. Somewhere a cork popped and Gail came in with a foaming champagne bottle. More laughter, more cheers. The cheers mixed with a husky male roar form the den, where good things were happening for the Republican Party. Someone called for music and the phonograph went up. Chanting began: *We want O-wens! We want O-wens!* Gail, by then weaving and bobbing, clutching the wall for support, called for the old man's coonskin. It was passed up with great laughter and cheering. Gail hoisted herself up onto the nearest table and shouted, "Let's hear it for college boys!" More shrieks, laughs, and a sprinkle of rah-rahs from a far corner. She rolled down her stockings to riotous laughs, and the ladies began to catcall as she showed a square of white thigh. Someone put "Charleston" on the phonograph and turned the volume all the way up. Even drunk, Gail was the best dancer in the room, crossing her knees so fast that Anna got dizzy watching.

Now the blond woman kicked her shoes off and joined Gail on the table, to more whistling and cheering. Gail slipped and almost fell, spilling a bottle of champagne across the floor. Someone began to boo and Gail made a gesture with her hand that calmed everyone down. "Here, help me up," she said. "It's time to check on the boys and see what's going with this goddamned election." She disappeared and Anna closed her eyes. She felt lost in space and time. Cool air poured in from the garden, and beyond the trees she could see dim lights in the house where Bonfils had lived. She opened her eyes and Gail was back, hitting her glass with a spoon. "Listen, everybody, attention! Here's the guest of honor if ever there was one. He's just arrived fresh from running the world, and stopped by for a few moments on his way to Governor Morley's side. Ladies, meet the fellow who really runs this state, the boy genius of politics. Mr. William Brown."

Anna blinked and tried to see his face. Gail gave a bow and a sweep of her arm toward her guest. "The third," she said, almost reverently.

9

He was there for less than a minute, but his eyes hardly left her face. She felt the blood rush to her cheeks and managed to look at his lapel, where a tiny state pin was clasped. He said a few words, which she missed, because all she was thinking was how little his voice had changed. Then he was gone, vanishing across the hall to be with the men. She gathered up her coat and worked her way toward the front door, but her chauffeur had gone on another errand and wasn't due back for half an hour. She thanked Gail, promised to return, and waited outside.

People pushed past her going both ways. Inside another eruption shook the windows. Colorado was choosing a new governor, the age of the Ku Klux Klan had fully dawned, and she really didn't care. The Willie Brown thing had shaken her up, like the sudden appearance of a phantom, dredged up from a long-lost dream. She had actually been in the same room with him, just a few minutes ago. Now she could barely remember his face. It came to her in fragments. His face was thicker, if anything, more handsome, and his hair was slightly darker. His shoulders had filled out. He had that scar over his lip, which added worldliness to that boyish charm and kept him from appearing fragile or glossy. She drew a clearer picture from their brief passing in the Coal Building months ago than she could from this party, which already seemed like a distant fantasy.

She heard a noise and suddenly he was there, coming up behind her from the patio. She couldn't see him, didn't turn around, but at the first sound of his footsteps she knew he had found her. "It's Anna, isn't it?" The voice sounded distantly boyish, soft, kind. "Anna Kohl?"

"Yes." She turned and looked him in the face. "How have you been, William?" She had to reach far down for the words, and they tried to slip away even as she brought them up.

"Good. Fine. Yourself?"

"Lately I've been doing well, thank you."

"I saw you when I came in. And that other time, a few months back. Wasn't that you in my office building?"

"Yes. I was looking for an attorney," she lied.

"Nothing serious, I hope."

"Oh, no. Everything's fine now."

He waited for what seemed like a long time. "I've thought about you since that day. You know, the way people think of old friends. So when I saw you here tonight, I hoped we'd get a chance to talk. I had to go pay my respects to the men—you know how these things are— and I'd have been very disappointed if you'd left. One of the ladies told me she thought you were still here, waiting for the chauffeur to take you home."

"Yes."

"I have a driver. I'd be glad to take you home."

"Thank you, no, I couldn't do that."

"No, of course not. I wouldn't want to embarrass you. Still, if it gets much later you must let me send you home, even if you won't allow me the privilege of riding along."

She didn't say anything.

"Are you married?"

"Oh, yes."

"Yes, of course." But he didn't ask who her husband was, or where he was. "You haven't changed much."

"Well, you always were a flatterer." A soft laugh, the laugh of a flirting schoolgirl, tried to wriggle out of her throat. She swallowed hard and snuffed it.

"That's no flattery, just the truth. Do you mind if I wait with you?"

She did mind and she didn't. She didn't know what she thought. "People inside will miss you."

"That doesn't matter. And anyway, they'll only miss me for a moment. Only then because someone will tell them to. It's really not important, and one thing I've learned in the past ten years is never worry about anything that's not important."

"You've learned a lot in the past ten years, it seems to me."

"Oh?"

"I read the papers."

"Now it's my turn to be flattered. Or is it?"

"If you're flattered by things like fame, then your life will be a happy one."

He laughed. "You haven't changed at all."

"I feel changed. I feel a million miles away from the girl I was."

Another pause, another long silence. He said, "If you read the papers, then you know I'm divorced."

"Yes."

"Twice."

"Yes."

"I've never had a happy marriage."

"Some people never do."

"I hope you're happy."

"Very much so."

"That's grand. I'm truly glad for you."

Still he didn't ask about her husband. She said, "My husband is a printer. He had to work tonight."

He didn't react to that at all. After a while he said, "When I saw you that day in my office building, I wanted to tell you something. I tried to catch you but you'd disappeared into the crowd."

"Well, sir, now you have my undivided attention."

"It's something that's been on my mind all these years."

"Really, there's nothing to be said about that."

"It's been like a thorn in my conscience."

"It shouldn't be. What's done is done. Let it lie."

"I'm sorry. That's really all I wanted to say. After all this time, what else is there?"

"Nothing."

"I am sorry. Sometimes we do foolish things when we're young. That's the only excuse I can give you now. It's a cross I've had to carry. Maybe telling you will make it easier."

"I hope so," she said, and she did.

"Can I ask about the child?"

"Now you are embarrassing me."

"Then I won't carry it any farther."

"The child . . . has been raised . . . as my brother. I guess you've got a right to know that."

"I've got no rights at all, other than what you want to give me."

"I'm sorry. It's just that in our house this . . . thing . . . has been unspeakable for so long. It's hard for me to talk about it."

"I can understand that. And I can see how uncomfortable this is for you. So I'll leave now. Just let me say one more thing before I go. If you read the papers, you must know that I'm not poor anymore. I'm not bragging, but I worked hard and I've made some strides."

"I never doubted you would, did I?"

"No. Everyone else in all my life thought my background would hold me down. In fact, being raised in the poor section was the best thing that ever happened to me. It got my back up. But here's the point. I feel an obligation."

"Not to me, for heaven's sake."

"To you and . . . good grief, I almost said *it*. I'm sorry, I don't even know . . ."

"It was a boy. Is."

He nodded.

"His name is Gabriel."

"Gabriel. He took your parents' name?"

"Yes."

"Gabriel Kohl." He turned the name over on his tongue, getting used to the feel of it. "Anyway, what I was getting at . . ."

"We don't need any help," she said shortly.

"All right, fine. God knows you've gotten along without me all these years. Just remember I offered."

Gail's chauffeur arrived. Willie Brown stepped out into the driveway and opened the back door, holding it for her. The car glided down the long drive into the street. She looked over her shoulder and found him standing at the edge of the sidewalk, just under the two gaslights. He was staring after her.

The chauffeur's voice startled her. "That's a bad apple, miss."

"Beg pardon?"

"That man you were talking to. He's a bad one."

"He doesn't seem so bad."

"That's what they all think. Take my word, miss. I used to work for him."

"Is this part of your job, giving advice to passengers?"

"No ma'am."

"What do you think Mrs. Owens would do if she knew what you just said?"

"I know what she'd do, miss. That's why I've had so many jobs the past few years. I can't seem to keep quiet about people like Mr. William Brown the third."

"You'd better try. Jobs are getting harder to get."

The clock in the hall said one-thirty as she let herself in. David lay awake in their bed, his hands clasped behind his head. She undressed quickly and slipped in beside him. They lay side by side without touching or talking for a long time, and after a while he did touch her hand, just the little finger, rubbing it softly with his own.

"Sorry I'm so late."

"It's okay. How was it?"

"Interesting. I wish you'd been there. Have you been home long?"

"Since ten."

"I'm sorry. I should have been here when you came in. You should have come over."

"You know how I am at things like that. Besides, I didn't feel like celebrating tonight."

"The election, you mean?"

"The older I get the harder people are to take. I can't say I'm surprised, and yet in a way I am. Right now the bloody Klan is out there winning this whole state. Governor, House seats, seat on the Supreme Court. And I lie here and I ask myself, how can people be so stupid?"

"Let me cheer you up." She touched him on his bare skin, moving her hand below his navel. But he covered her hand with his own.

"Would you mind? It's hard for me when I feel like this."

"Of course." She took her hand away and sat on the edge of the bed, brushing her hair. "It was a freak vote," she said at last. "That's all it was, people voting their fears. Years from now people will look back and call it a thing of the times."

"Like they say now about the Inquisition," David said. "That lasted five hundred years. It was a thing of the times too, but that didn't make it any easier on the generations of people who lived through it. Maybe I'm overreacting. I hope I am. But all day I've had this cold fear that won't go away. We really ought to think about Alaska again."

"Ah, Davie . . ."

"One thing's for sure. Living in Colorado will be worse than living in hell from now on."

10

She was typing a letter for Mr. Roberts, her boss at the *Post,* when Willie Brown arrived. In daylight, the split in his lip stood out more, and somehow he looked smaller than she remembered. When she saw him coming across the office, she lowered her eyes in the old way and tried to look busy. He came straight toward her, and her hands began to tremble. She forced her face up, her eyes to a level with his.

"Well, sir, what brings you here?"

"I wanted to see what you look like in daylight. If you're the way I remember you. And please, don't call me sir."

"I look older. Much the worse for wear, I'm afraid."

"Not at all."

"Please, is there something you want?"

"After you left that night, I realized I couldn't let it go like that. I want to talk."

"That's not possible."

"Why not?"

"Because I'm working," she said with irritation. "I can't just drop everything and talk."

"Then have lunch with me. What I have to say to you is strictly on the up and up." He picked up the letters she had typed and looked at them. "You do very nice work."

"I can't talk to you, I can't meet you for lunch. That's unthinkable. It surprises me that you'd even suggest it. Would you please leave? I'm sorry to put it like that, but you don't give me much choice." In a frantic whisper, she said, "William, please, I can't afford to lose this job!"

"You won't. I know John Roberts personally, and I can promise you he won't fire you. Here, I'll prove it." He walked across the office and disappeared into a glass-enclosed room. A moment later he returned with John Roberts.

Roberts nodded to her. "Mrs. Waldo. If Mr. Brown wants to talk to you, you can use my office. I'll be gone most of the morning." He went to the coatrack, took down his coat, and disappeared.

298

"Now, what could be simpler than that?" Willie Brown said.

"Such power, Mr. Brown. Such influence."

"Please." He stood aside and motioned with his hands. She let him show her into Roberts' office. It was a small room that fronted Champa Street. There was one desk and one chair. Willie Brown held the chair for her but she refused it.

"I don't want to talk about this," she said. "My husband has no idea what happened between us."

"That's exactly how it'll stay as far as I'm concerned."

"Just talking about this makes me very uncomfortable. You must see how embarrassing this is for me."

"Sure I do. I wouldn't put you through it if I didn't honestly feel that what I've got to say is more important than your embarrassment. Anna, I don't take that lightly."

"Then say it and let's have this over with."

"First let me say this. I tried to let it go the way we left it at Gail Owens' party. I really did. But there's just no way . . ."

"Please!"

"All right. I've come here to offer you a job."

"What!"

"A far better life than you've been able to have these past few years."

"What do you know about my life, now or any other time?"

"I've done some checking."

"You *checked* on me?"

"My motives were honorable, I promise you."

"I don't care what motives you had."

"Let me just tell you. Then if you're still mad, all right, I won't blame you. All I know is that there are some things—debts, if you want to call them that—that words alone don't erase."

"How many times must I tell you? You don't owe us anything."

"There are no strings attached . . ."

"It doesn't matter. It's out of the question."

"A job in my company, as confidential secretary to one of my people."

"William! Now stop it."

"One hundred dollars a week."

She drew in her breath. "You must be joking."

He waited. When she didn't respond, he said, "One hundred a week, paid every Wednesday afternoon."

"No secretary is worth money like that."

"You are."

She looked at him coldly. "Why? Because I can type fast? Oh, no, you could find a dozen girls to do as well, at one-third the salary. Strip away all the gloss and there's just one answer. It's because of what happened between us, and that's all it is. There's nothing professional about this, it's strictly personal and I won't have it. I just can't get involved with you again."

"You won't be involved with me. Not in any way. In the first place, you'll be working on the sixth floor of the Coal Building, for a man I hardly ever see. You won't see any more of me there than you see of Bonfils here. So that's no problem, and your other argument is simply not true. I need people like you. You've got something I know and respect, and I'm not talking about secretarial skills. Those things can be learned. What can't be learned are honesty and integrity, and I know you and I know you've got that. Do you know what it means to be a confidential secretary?"

"I think so."

"It means doing your work and keeping your mouth shut outside the office. It means having loyalty to people who are good to you, and you've always had that. I should know, better than anyone."

He let the words settle between them, then said, "You know what happened in the elections. It had special significance for me. Things are starting to happen in my life, things you wouldn't dream of. I can't even begin telling you . . ."

"Oh, I think I know."

He smiled. "You couldn't possibly."

"You're playing politics with the Ku Klux Klan."

That stopped him cold, for perhaps ten seconds. Then he said, "Long ago I learned that if you see an evil coming, if it's truly inevitable and powerful enough, your best hope is to climb aboard and go with it, till you can get enough power within it to make change."

"I don't believe you."

"Then you tell me what else works. Today this state is completely Klan-dominated. By the time Morley's sworn in, nobody in city or state government will be able to do anything without checking with the Klan first. At this moment there's just one voice at a high level that's even whispering moderation. They're crazy with power after that vote. They think they're going to rule the world. And who do you think that one voice is?"

She didn't say anything. Willie Brown crossed to the window and looked down into the street. "People like you, your family, your friends. All the people who live over there. You think you know what persecution is? You people will never have another full night's sleep once this new administration gets rolling. Unless you're working for me."

"I told you. It's out of the question."

"You haven't heard the rest of it. One hundred a week. An end to Klan harassment. Oh, yes, I know what you're going through. My people, when they check someone out, are very thorough. An end to all that. And one more thing. A scholarship in the bank for Gabriel. Ten thousand dollars, to see that he has the money when he's ready for college."

"Ten . . ."

"I know it sounds like a lot of money to you. It's nothing. A drop in the hat. In fact, that part stands, whether you take my job offer or not. A scholarship for Gabriel. My son."

"*Don't* call him that."

"All right. Whatever you want. We can go down to the bank today and transfer the money. Nobody ever has to know but you and me. You can tell him it's a legacy from his father."

"He'll think it's from . . . my father."

"I know what he'll think and I don't care. I promise you I'll never try to see him or get close to him in any way. I just want to know he's taken care of."

"He is!" she said heatedly. But the hostility in her eyes was gone, replaced by tenderness. "William, I simply can't."

"Are you going to let silly pride interfere with your child's welfare? Come on, you're bigger than that. This is something I want to do. I *will* do it, either now or after he's eighteen."

She didn't say anything. She dabbed at her eyes.

"One final thing," Willie Brown said. "A job for your husband. A good job, with dignity and self-respect."

"Davie? What could he possibly do for you?"

"I didn't say the job will be with us. I just think he may suddenly start finding things easier. I have a hunch things will start falling his way."

She shook her head. But she didn't say no.

That night, walking to catch her trolley, she wondered how she would explain things to David. She couldn't shake the feeling that, like Faust, she had just made a pact with the devil.

11

Early that morning, David and Gabriel had come to an understanding. The time had come: David would talk to Anna tonight. It was an area of her privacy that he had never invaded, and the prospect filled him with dread. Now he saw that Gabriel was right, that postponing it had only increased the difficulty. He would simply tell her, in bed tonight. First, that he knew. When she had absorbed the shock of that—that Gabriel knew. That the only difference it made to either of them was to make them love her more. That the boy desperately wanted what they alone could give him. Something more, that he hadn't even told Gabriel yet. David would adopt the boy, and yes, he still had Alaska on his mind.

He felt a growing sense of urgency with the changing seasons. Gabriel had deepened his involvement with a street gang. Jewish punks, who roamed the streets looking for lone Gentiles. They called themselves the Anti-Klan and took their revenge on the sons of known Klansmen.

That night after dinner, when he and Anna had washed and cleared away the dishes, they climbed the stairs to that sacred bedroom and sealed out the world. She stood at the window, fingering the buttons of her dress and looking down into the dark street. Suddenly a thought struck her and she looked across the room at him.

"Davie, it's Friday night and the Klan hasn't come."

"I noticed. Maybe their leader's dead."

"Wishful thinking, love." It was a signal from Willie Brown, a sign of his power. She was sure of it.

She drew the shade and stepped out of her dress. In a moment he joined her in bed and turned off the light.

"Davie? Can we talk a bit first?"

"That's what I was hoping."

"Good." She nestled against him and he engulfed her with his arm. Her voice was light, almost false, as she said, "The strangest thing happened today, love. An old friend came by the *Post* and offered me a job."

Five minutes later he lay stunned and quiet, his hopes for an easy go shattered. The specter of this Willie Brown, this man he had never seen, loomed beside the bed, clutching at them, dragging them apart. Now what would his words mean to her? Would they seem more accusation than kindness, more suspicious than hopeful? Would she see his words as the unspoken accusation that she had taken the job only to be near her old lover?

"Davie? What do you think?"

"I think what I always think. That you should do what strikes you best."

That was his way. Play it out slowly, see where it was taking them. Let her find herself, and see that this road was not their salvation, but was full of peril. Then maybe he could tell her that he'd known all along, but had trusted her enough to let her do it her way. He did trust her, absolutely. He did. She was the one sure bet in his life.

In the morning, Gabriel glared at him over the breakfast table. "You promised. You promised and then you lost your nerve."

David got up and squeezed the boy's arm. "Come on, let's go to work. I'll tell you a few things on the way to town."

CHAPTER
FIVE

1

"My dear?"

"Yes, Papa."

"I'm here now."

"I see, Papa."

"You've been in my thoughts constantly."

"I know that, Papa."

"I can't tell you how much it hurt me to have to bring you here."

"I think I know, Papa."

"You simply left me no choice."

"I'm sorry, Papa."

"The doctor says you've made great strides in recent weeks."

"Yes."

"And our nasty little problem seems to be under control now."

"Yes, Papa."

"It's all over now. I think you can understand why I did what I did."

"Yes, Papa."

"You know at last that what I did, I did out of love. All this nonsense is in the past."

"Yes, Papa."

"Doctor?"

The doctor came close. "As I told you, your daughter has shown fine progress in the past few months. Her hostility is gone, she works well with the staff and with other patients. I think she's ready to leave anytime, in your care."

"Did you hear that, my dear?"

"Yes, Papa."

"Do you want to come home, my dear?"

"Yes, Papa."

"The children have missed you."

"I've missed them too."

"Orrin?"

"Yes, sir."

"Help Miss Nell to the car. We're going home."

Going home. The words were as strange as the tongue of the Chinese washwoman who worked Mondays at the hospital. Stranger yet to see countryside moving past her window, to know that the people she saw weren't controlled by barred windows and men in white. People crossing the street, sloshing through the first snow, shoveling out drives and walks. It had been snowing the day they had brought her here: early snow; heavy, wet autumn snow. So a year had passed.

Orrin and her father sat immovable while the world had changed. Now there were no horses at all on the streets. Roads were being paved for automobiles; plankings and boardwalks were being ripped up and cement sidewalks put down in their place. Styles had changed. They drove past a lovely old country estate and she saw two women, obviously sisters, climbing into a car with two young men. Hem lengths had reached the knee, and dresses were tighter. She would have to throw out all her old dresses.

Houses were going up too; country living was becoming popular. She saw families dressed in beautiful, rich clothes and she thought, *it must be Sunday*. Some Sunday in November, 1924. Your typical early winter day in Denver, with snow melting and kids out rolling in it. She put down her window and enjoyed the slight sting of it on her cheeks. Gregory Clement turned his head. "You'd better keep your window up. We wouldn't want you to catch cold." She said "Yes, Papa," and rolled it up.

She didn't argue anymore. She knew better now. All that time she had worked for the vote, and what had it done for her? People could still walk in and have their grown daughters committed to institutions, on nothing more than their say-so. Tradition and money talked a language of their own, and money talked the loudest language of all. How many rich men had committed wives or unruly daughters for sheer personal expedience and self-interest? Take Mrs. Miranda James, forty-five, once obviously beautiful but now losing her looks. Her husband had found himself a young flapper and wanted her out of the way. Had anyone seen this phantom woman? No, of course not, he'd been too careful for that. So it had been noted, persecution complex probably: suspects people of conspiring against her. Combined with her old record—nervous breakdown at fifteen, another two years later, rebellious childhood, unstable first marriage, loud and violent behavior since her commitment—it was enough. Anyone would be convinced. In all the world, only Miranda James and Nell Clement Hastings knew. *She's no crazier than I am. What in God's name is she doing here?* And still the doctor stands there, writing, writing, writing, until Miranda snaps, leaps from the bed, and goes for his eyes. *Give me that pen, you goddamn idiot!* And another entry appears on her chart.

Violent. Homicidal.

At least Nell had never fallen into that trap. Not since the first week.

Gregory Clement had turned in his seat and was looking at her with a crooked smile. "You'll notice a change in the boys. They're much better behaved now. All it took was a firm hand."

"You always did know best about things like that, Papa."

His eyes were hard as he looked for any trace of sarcasm. She smiled sweetly. She looked away and found the beady eyes of Orrin in the glass.

The car was skirting the fringes of southeast Denver. Across the snowswept plains she could see the flat red buildings downtown. Trees and shrub-lined drives floated past: the last reds and browns of autumn, clinging desperately in the cool breeze.

Streets appeared. Their street. How different it looked, how old and established. She had last seen Tom here, late one night, parked on this street. Perhaps she resented him most of all. He should have found her. Big-time reporter. He should have tracked her down in a day. But the days had passed, and even that hope had begun to fade. One spring morning she had realized, quite suddenly, that he wasn't coming. Not today, not ever. If Gregory Clement chose to leave her here, then here she would remain, until one of them died.

The thought was terrifying. With his heart condition, what if the old man died without telling anyone where she was? She thought of drawing his attention, slashing her wrist with the top of a tin can she had stolen from the kitchen and hidden under her bed. That would only get her written up as a potential suicide. No, she must do nothing to get in their charts. Must cooperate, smile, curtsy. Say *Yes, doctor* and *No, doctor* and *I'm fine, doctor* and *How are you this morning, sir? Isn't it a lovely day?* Help with Miranda when she becomes unruly. Make the bed. Mop the goddamn floor without being asked. Mop up the vomit and somehow hold down your own. Never throw up where they can see you because that, as much as the screaming and cursing, is thought to indicate resistance and hostility.

Much later, when she was briefly left alone in the doctor's office, she stared at the telephone and thought of Tom's exchange. She didn't even try to call. She didn't know what she would say to him.

"Papa?"

He turned again in his seat. "Yes, my dear?"

"Have you heard . . . do you know . . . what's become of my husband?"

He surprised her. His eyes were kind, almost understanding. "He's gone, my dear. He's nothing for you to worry about, ever again."

"But where's he gone?"

"No one knows. He seems to have left Denver."

"Did he know . . . about me?"

"Of course."

"He knew where I was?"

"Oh, yes. He came to the house that Saturday. I told him myself. We had a terrible row. But this is so unpleasant. Let's talk about something else."

"What happened? You said you had a terrible row."

"It was mostly about the children. I finally had to threaten to bring in the police. I told him if he wanted custody he'd have to take us to court. He never even tried, so I assume it wasn't that important to him. I don't even like to talk about it. It was very unpleasant."

"Then he just left? And he never came back?"

"No."

"But what became of him?"

"I told you, no one knows. All we know is that he left his apartment and is no longer working for that abominable newspaper."

"He quit his job?"

The old man frowned, and all the kindness drained from his face. "I've told you that's all I know, now let this be the end of it. Say good riddance to bad business and let it be finished. I don't want to hear that man's name spoken again. Is that quite clear?"

"Yes, Papa."

The estate rose out of the snow, lonely and forbidding. Orrin unlocked the gate and eased the car through, then got out and locked up again.

A black Studebaker was parked near the front door. As the Packard came up the long horseshoe drive, a woman came to the front door. "That's Mrs. Johnson," Gregory Clement said. "She's taking care of the boys."

He paid the woman and dismissed her. Inside, the house was cold. The upstairs and back wings were still closed off, and no sounds at all came from the boys' room. Gregory Clement crossed the hall and opened the door. From the hall she saw Paul, sitting on his bed, doing nothing. Michael sat at a desk, reading a book. They were *so* quiet. She came to the door. For perhaps thirty seconds she stood watching them. Paul seemed to be staring right at her, as if he could see, but his face never changed expression. Both looked so stiff and formal. They wore starched shirts and neckties. Their shoes were shined. Their hair was brushed shiny and neatly combed. She came into the room and Michael stirred at the sound. He looked up and saw her, and his eyes went beyond her to where Gregory Clement stood. He didn't move. She tried to smile and made a bad job of it. "Well," she said, her voice husky. "Do you have a kiss for your mommy?"

Paul blinked and cocked his head. Still Michael didn't move. Nell came in and got down on her knees near Paul. She held him against her, then motioned to Michael and hugged him with her free hand. She tried to laugh, and a moment later didn't know if she was laughing or crying. "Would you look at me now?" She sniffed and dabbed at her nose. "How've you been?"

Neither of them spoke. Paul's lower lip trembled.

"Your mother asked how you've been," Gregory Clement said from the doorway.

"We've been fine, Mother," Michael said.

"Good," said Paul.

"Did you behave yourselves for Grandfather while I've been away?"

"Yes ma'am."

"What's this? You know you don't call me ma'am."

"I taught them that," Gregory Clement said. "There's nothing wrong with respect for your elders. You get precious little from children of this generation."

"Yes. Well, I'll see you boys in a little while, after I freshen up. We'll have us a nice long talk."

"I'm looking forward to that," the old man said. "Just the four of us, around the fire. Just like old times."

She got up and went into the hall. He followed her to her room. "You'll find it just as you left it," he said. "I want you to be comfortable. If there's anything you need, tell me and I'll arrange it."

"There's one thing I'd love. Tomorrow when the stores open I'd like to go window shopping. All by myself I'd like to walk with people on Sixteenth Street and look in windows."

"Ah, I think not. Not just yet. You've still got some adjusting to do, then we'll see."

"Yes, Papa. Whatever you say."

Shutting her door and closing him out was a blessing. Like teaching herself not to cry, not to vomit, not to swear or lash out, she now tried to teach herself love. What he had done to her—*for* her—he had done in love. She tried to believe that, but it wasn't working. And she felt then something very close to hysteria. Like picking up something, a poker, a bookend, a paperweight, and fighting each time her father or Orrin came near her. It was foolish. There were better ways, and more time to explore them later.

She sat at her mirror. A quick look brought tears to her eyes. It was the first time she had seen herself in a year. That place had left its mark for everyone to see. Two years ago, at thirty, she had still looked twenty-five. She had been proud of her young looks. Gone forever were the days when she could pass for twenty-five. She was clearly in her thirties now, perhaps to a stranger even in her late thirties. She might even pass for forty. She had lost that much ground in a year. Lines had begun around her eyes. She saw graying hair and rummaged frantically through her drawer for scissors. Unable to find them, she pulled at each strand until she saw no more. She enjoyed the luxury of her hairbrush for fifteen minutes. Twenty. She lost track of time. After a year of regimentation, she had no schedule.

The luxuries around her, the things she had once taken so for granted now seemed part of rich, extravagant living. She felt like a visitor. The act of taking a bubble bath was such a delight that she thought she might soak forever. Soak away the weeks and months, and afterward she rubbed cold cream into her face and arms and dared take another look in the glass.

Better.

She brushed out her hair again, stroking it until the roots hurt. She shaved her legs. The hair under her arms had grown long and wiry and she had to cut it slowly, inch by inch. Patients weren't allowed to use razors. Or think. Or breathe.

Talk between two or more of them was, if it went on for more than a minute, construed as plotting. The only time they were expected to talk was with the doctor. They had long daily sessions, when the doctor probed their hidden thoughts, asking questions that were pointed and embarrassing. Modesty was out the window; privacy was a right, to be earned by giving the doctor their total cooperation. She thought the doctor was a bit bent himself. He claimed to have studied under Freud in Vienna, but she doubted it. He believed that every act had some sexual motivation. They would be talking about her mother, and suddenly the doctor would ask, "When you think of her, do you sometimes feel sexually stimulated?" At first she replied indignantly. "Of course not. Do you?" Later she learned to answer everything with a simple yes or no. "This man Orrin. You seem to have very strong feelings toward him." *Yes. I hate him.* "That's what you say, and I don't doubt that you yourself believe it. But your hatred is a mask for something else." *What else?* "You tell me." *I can't imagine.* "Desire, perhaps?" *No sir, not a chance.* "You think not?" *It's the most ridiculous thing I've ever heard.* "Then you tell me, what do you desire in a man?"

Later Miranda told her that the doctor was a bad man, that he was sleeping with two of the patients on their ward now. "What he was probing for was to find out how you feel about him." In the darkness Miranda came and sat on Nell's bed. "Don't let him get to you. Don't give him anything. There are better ways of beating this goddamn place. Let me show you."

Miranda slipped down to her knees and touched Nell's leg. With her tongue she made a long wet line above the kneecap.

"Let me show you."

Nell lay back.

Back . . . and touched the silk pillow in her father's house.

In the waning afternoon she walked through the snow behind the house, far back into the trees where the ground sloped down toward the creek. She walked along the fence, aware that he watched her from one of the dark windows. She went innocently, but her eyes missed nothing.

She was tired by the time she came around front. She went straight to the guardhouse, coming upon Orrin so quickly that she startled him. He had been sitting against the outer door, propped there on a wooden chair. He sat up straight and the chair flopped down. She turned away without a word and started up the long drive to the house.

"Miss Nell?"

She stopped, but she wouldn't turn. She wouldn't dignify his presence with a look.

"I want to tell you something."

When he didn't speak again, she turned and looked at him.

"It's nothing much. It won't matter to you. But I wanted to say I'm sorry."

"Sorry for what? What have you got to be sorry about?"

"I thought what happened to you . . . well, it was . . ."

"Yes?"

"It was . . . obscene. Miss."

"Why, Orrin, you *dare* question my father's judgment?" She smiled at him, but the smile, like her voice, was cold.

"It'd cost me my job if he found out I said it. So maybe you've got something on me at last, hey, miss? Use it or not; I don't care. All you'd have to do is tell him."

"Then I will tell him."

"I don't care anymore, miss, and that's the truth." Then he said something that bothered her. "You're very much like your mother." At the garden she looked back. He was still there, watching after her.

That evening the four of them sat quietly beside the fire. The boys didn't talk at all, and at last Gregory Clement sent them off to bed. They had a good-night toddy, father and daughter, and he talked about the days when her mother was alive. He was like a man talking to himself. They went to bed at nine by the clock. She didn't tell him about Orrin.

A few weeks later, Gregory Clement took the boys to St. Louis on the train. It was another of those arbitrary decisions that had once infuriated her, but now she welcomed having the house to herself. That morning, with her father and the boys out of the house for less than an hour, she put on some streetclothes and worked herself up for battle. She took a butcher knife from its rack in the kitchen and hid it in the folds of her dress.

She went outside and started across the dead garden. Let it start or end here, she thought, clutching the wooden handle: If he tries to stop me, I will kill him. But as she approached the guardhouse, she saw that the gate was wide-open. Orrin sat unmoving, except for his hands, which whacked away at a stick with a pocket knife. She drew even with him and he looked up. Still, he didn't move. Something in his eyes tugged at her heart, and for an instant she had the insane urge to cradle his head and mother him. She thought it probable that no one ever had.

She walked on through, to the street. That afternoon she found work, as a maid in a rich man's home on Grant Street. It was tedious, degrading work. Each night after dark she returned to the estate; each morning she left just as the sun was rising. Orrin never tried to stop her. At the end of the week, she moved out of the estate and found a room on the fringe of the lowers, near Larimer Street. It was small and had bugs, but it was all she could afford. And finally it was all right. It was better than all right. It was almost good.

The old man returned the following week. She was called to the telephone by the lady of the house, who directed her to the telephone with disapproving eyes. Employers didn't like hired help to take calls during the workday. She was surprised to hear Orrin's voice when she picked up the earpiece. "He's back, miss. Thought you should know. He's in a stormy temper and I may be out of a job. But I thought you should know, he'll be coming for you soon."

He came a few hours later. She saw the Packard stop outside and drew in her breath. Orrin sat behind the wheel, waiting while Gregory Clement came up the walk. He was shown into the drawing room by the lady of the house, who gave Nell her second disapproving look of the day.

When they were left alone, the old man smiled. "It's good to see you've not lost your spirit. Now take off that silly apron and come along home."

She didn't move.

"Come along now; we'll forget this happened."

She didn't say anything.

"Do you know how easy it would be for me to have you discharged from this position?"

"Oh, yes," she said. "Yes, I know that."

"Then come, let's go home. This is silly."

She didn't move.

"Why must you always force me to do ugly things?"

"Go ahead," she said defiantly. "Have me fired."

"And if I do, what will you do then?"

"You'll find out."

"Is that a threat? Are you *threatening* me?"

"I'm telling you." Her voice trembled now; she couldn't help it. "I will never . . . spend . . . another night . . . under your roof."

"That remains to be seen." An ugly light had come into his eyes. "I could remind you that there are worse places to sleep."

"No. Not for me."

"That remains to be seen," he said again. "Have you forgotten so soon?"

"I'll never forget."

His eyes, drifting across the room, found the telephone.

"Call them if you want," she said. "If you put me away, I'll escape. If you have me fired, I'll find another job. If I can't, I'll beg for pennies on the street. And if I can't do that—well, there are other ways for a woman to get along." A flush of red came to her cheeks, but she made her eyes hold still on his.

"Now you are being insane."

"Well, I've had a lot of practice at that this year, haven't I, Father? I promise you, I'm absolutely serious. I'll die before I go back with you. If it comes down to that or nothing, I'll kill myself."

He looked at her while the long seconds ticked away on the mantelpiece clock. When he spoke again, his voice was hostile, but

311

there was a tiredness there that she hadn't heard before. "You'll never get the boys. You're both unfit parents."

"Fine," she said. "You may have them."

His face registered shock, then bewilderment. And suddenly there was nothing more to be said between them. Later she thought about what she had given up. Like any other combatant, she had learned when to retreat and gather her forces. When she was ready, she would go after her boys. Then Gregory Clement would learn how she could fight.

2

The new governor of Colorado was sworn in and gave his inaugural address at the city auditorium in mid-January, 1925. The huge chamber was decorated with bunting streamers of red, white, and blue, and there were flowers and an orchestra. At a press table not far from the governor's feet, six reporters sat recording his words for posterity. Not far from the press table sat another reporter, watching, though without much interest. Politics wasn't her game, and if you asked her now what she was doing here, she'd have had to tell you, honestly, that she didn't know. It was her day off, and in all the world nothing felt better than to be completely anonymous. A simple observer, with no responsibility to the story or the public. Not to have to make something out of nothing was the best feeling she'd get today. It mattered little that what the governor was saying was sure front-page. The thirst for big by-lines had gone.

She didn't like politics, and yet she listened carefully to what the man was saying. She wondered how much of it had been written by John Galen Locke, and as Morley droned on, she thought she could actually pick out the parts. A proposal to repeal the law authorizing state examiners. A move to abolish the Juvenile Court. Opposition to the proposed public defender act. Crime, Morley said, "should be dealt with energetically and relentlessly. In my judgment nothing is so well calculated to promote crime as a spineless enforcement of our criminal laws, and the pains and penalties that should be visited on all offenders alike. When the taxpayer is called upon to provide lawyers to defend as well as prosecute violators of law, it may next be urged that tools with which crimes may be the better committed be furnished at the expense of the state." But the most obvious segment of Klan doctrine was Morley's proposal to eliminate from the Prohibition law the exemption allowing the use of wine for sacramental purposes. "Incredible," she said out loud.

When the man was finished, the audience sang the National Anthem, and the new governor began receiving people on the auditorium stage. Reporters moved out, some to telephones in the lobby. Marvel moved out into the street and walked southeast, toward the statehouse. It was after noon when she arrived. The statehouse boys came in hot on her heels: half a dozen wide-brimmed hats and bow ties rushed past her into the press room, and the frantic sounds of typewriters and telephones erupted out of the quiet. The man from the *News* came in and gave her a cold stare. She moved out of his desk and took a chair near the door. She felt as if people were watching the back of her head, and she turned in time to see the man from the *Post* cut his eyes back to the telephone and the note pad on the table before him.

What else was new? She had never been accepted in this town, not by any of them. They were all cliquish, especially the political beat men, locked away in their autonomous little world. They shared tips, shared sources, and sometimes even shared stories. If there was less dignity in that kind of coverage, there was also less risk. They were threatened by anyone who didn't belong. Anyone who didn't play their game, anyone who refused to gang-cover events, was a subject of suspicion and hostility. No one but old political hacks worked there, and when Marvel Millette showed up unexpectedly, people looked at her and wondered what the hell she was working on. When she left, she knew, there would be talk and questions. The man from the *News* might even place an angry call to city desk, demanding to know what she was doing and why she was here. The City Hall man had done that only last month, when she turned up suddenly in his territory and wouldn't say why. She had told him to go to hell.

She could have told them all that it was her day off, that she was simply here to meet Malloy for lunch. But no, let them wonder; she wouldn't dream of spoiling their fun. What wasn't so clear was why she had traipsed all the way downtown to hear a load of political drivel that she could have predicted without even leaving her apartment. The proceedings had bored her to tears, and the funny part was, she had known they would, even as she was dressing for the trip downtown. Was she that hard-up for things to do in her free time, or was she just becoming one of those newspaper dames she read about in stories? She had to admit it, there was some of that. She had joined the brigade of the cynical, the hard, and the dubious. A very large percent of everything was bullshit, and she simply had no patience with it. She knew something else: She was very certain of her own ability to see through things and people. It was her gift, and she always followed her hunches, without exception, even if an encyclopedia told her to forget it.

This time her hunch had been wrong. There it was, then, the real reason she had gone to the auditorium. Him. Yes, that other him. *Nolo contendere.* She had had a hunch he might be here, even after all these months. Standing in the far back corners of the auditorium, listening, because the Ku Klux Klan and its governor meant something special to him, as they did to her. But he hadn't come and the event was over; Malloy was here to take her to lunch and that was the end of it. Malloy had just come up from the House chamber, where the first wave of administration bills was hitting the floor even before Morley had gone to his desk. She waited while he called the *Post* and dictated a sidebar, then they left together, the stares of the statehouse men hot on her back.

He took her to a restaurant on Seventeenth Street, an expensive place she knew he couldn't afford. They ordered lunches that made them feel extravagant and a little giddy: shrimp cocktail and prime rib, with New York style cheesecake for dessert. With the tip, the tab had to be at least three dollars.

He asked if she had heard him dictating.

"Some of it," she said. "I heard the same thing down at Morley's speech."

"What were you doing down there?"

"Slumming, dear. It's a hobby of mine. Anyway, from what you were phoning in, I gathered the Klan's wasted no time."

"The first bill out was to eliminate the Civil Service board and put it under one man, answerable to the guv. Same thing's going down in the Senate. Young's put in bills abolishing all kinds of state boards and bureaus. There's a rumor that Eaker is studying the constitutionality of putting armed guards at the stateline and stopping anybody from coming in who doesn't have natural citizenship."

"Umm." She sipped her coffee. "Pardon me, Mickey, I was almost about to say something ugly. This is really a very fine lunch. Sometime you'll have to let me do something nice for you."

He gave her a sly look. "Any time."

"I wasn't thinking of anything that nice. It's a good lunch, but in the long run that wouldn't be nice. And it wouldn't be fair." She put her head on her propped-up hands and gazed at him across the table. "You know, Mickey, you're a damned good guy. I'd really hate to hurt you."

"Marvel, I'll take you any way I can get you. Even as a friend, if that's how you want it."

"That's how it is."

She had to hand it to Malloy. He never wore his hurt on his sleeve. After a moment, she said, "How about a matinee, my treat? Do you know what's playing?"

"We could walk long the lowers, see if anything looks good.

Speaking of the lowers, Jesus, you'll never guess who I saw yesterday."

She shrugged.

"Tom Hastings."

Her eyes opened wide. "You're kidding."

"Swear to God. Panhandling, can you believe that?"

"Where?"

"In an alley near the old Burlington Hotel on Larimer Street. I almost didn't place him. He had on baggy, patchy clothes, like maybe he'd stolen them out of a mission somewhere. Had a two-week beard on his face. I started to reach for my wallet. I mean, Jesus, you got to help an old reporter out. But he stepped back in the alley and when I went in after him he was gone."

"You're sure it was him?"

"Sure I'm sure. I couldn't have made a mistake like that. Hell, Marvel, I sat right across from the man for two years. Isn't that incredible?"

She nodded.

"Brother, when you come down, you sure come all the way." Malloy called for the tab. "I'd hate to think of any friend of mine living in those old hotels. Those guys kill each other for a drink. It's their lifeblood."

They walked northeast, toward Curtis Street and the long row of movie palaces. But now the gaiety was gone, and Malloy was too wise in the ways of the girl not to notice. She stopped at the corner of Seventeenth and California and looked at him with sad eyes.

"What's wrong? Was it something I said?"

"It's got nothing to do with you," she said. "It's a headache, Mickey, that's all it is. It came on me suddenly, while we were sitting there. Do me a favor, don't press me on it." She leaned over on tiptoes and kissed him. "You're a hell of a good guy, Mickey. Thanks for the lunch. I'll make it up."

Without another word she walked away. For a few minutes she wandered aimlessly, her mind troubled. Then, like a skipper with a fixed compass, she struck out to the northeast. She crossed Curtis Street and found herself at the edge of the lowers. Two bums sat on the sidewalk and watched her from across the street. A wind came up, blowing newspapers across the trolley tracks. She moved slowly up the street, shivering. She knew exactly now why she had come out on a chilly day in January to hear the Klan governor. Him again. And Malloy, bless his poor soul, had found him for her.

CHAPTER SIX

1

Newton and Pike had gone. One morning David opened the front door, stepped out into the cold pre-dawn air, and the truck was not there. As always, his alarm had gone off at three, but this morning she had kept him in bed, holding him there playfully, then not having to hold him, finally pushing him toward the bedroom door. By the time he'd come down, Gabriel had gone off without him.

He arrived at the warehouse where he worked just in time. When the truck failed to arrive on the second day, he grew bolder and went to work by a more direct route. On the third morning he walked right out his front door, and by the end of the week he was coming and going as he chose, like any other free man.

It gave him more time for his family, and time to find a better job. Now he was working in the Wentworth Paint and Glass Shop, where Richard Watson had been driven out of his job just six months before.

316

David did the heavy work. He took barrels of broken glass to the dump, made heavy deliveries, unloaded trucks, and rotated the paint stock. His pay had increased by fifty percent, and it was all the same brute labor. Later he would reflect that it was simply the difference between working for people who were civilized, and working for people who weren't.

At home Anna was her eternal self, and the days, like her, were unchanging and unchangeable. Nothing ended and nothing began. Even the weather was monotonous, and that never happened to Denver in January. Anna was happy. Abe at least was quiet. Even Teresa had perked up with the sudden shot of money. Only Gabriel was hostile and impatient, and in that too there was no change.

Willie Brown, his unseen enemy, had ended their long nightmare, exactly as promised.

In every respect her job was perfect. She worked regular hours, came home at five-thirty, and was never asked to stay after quitting time. There was no nonsense. David's suspicion of Willie Brown and his motives began to fade. Once he asked her, in a very casual manner, what she thought of her boss. "I never see him," she said. "He told me I wouldn't and I haven't." It seemed proof enough, if he needed any proof, that what had happened between Anna and Willie Brown had been a fling of childhood, that both had grown infinitely beyond it. People grow and learn, and feelings change.

He had only to look at his lovely wife to know the truth of that. Fifteen months ago a recluse, she was now doing a professional job, was helping her mother run the house and still found time to read three books a week. Her world now had vistas and horizons that she was just beginning to explore. It made him proud and a little afraid. He felt what Jessie must have felt, even if she couldn't articulate it, as she watched him drift away from her. Fear. Uncertainty. The sure knowledge that someone very close has private feelings that you can never share. And jealousy—yes, a little of that too. It was what he had wanted for her, what he still wanted. Her response was what made her continually exciting and challenging to him.

He never knew what to expect from her. On his forty-second birthday, he came home to find the house decorated and a huge cake with a candle for each year perched on the table. She had taken off an afternoon to do it. Anna brought out the presents. There was something from each of them, but the most precious thing to him was the day itself. It was his first birthday party ever. He opened Anna's present last. It was a plaque, hand-carved, and the letters said DAVID WALDO'S PRINT SHOP. "We'll hang it on the wall, over the bed," she said. "It'll remind us every day what we're working for."

She had another surprise for him later, in bed. When he came to her, she was already undressed beside him. She had never initiated sex, but now she tossed back the quilt and rolled over him, guiding him with her hands, moving her hips against his. He awoke in the early morning and found her gone. When he went downstairs he got his third surprise. She was sitting in a chair by the window, reading the second volume of *Das Kapital*. On a table beside her lay Darwin's *The Origin of Species*.

She looked up, a bit sheepish. "I thought maybe later, when you get your group going again, you might want to talk about some of this. Thought I might read it and surprise you."

He smiled tenderly, full of love. "What do you think?"

"A lot of it's nonsense."

He sat facing her and they argued until the sun came up.

Her biggest surprise came in mid-February. Promptly at five-thirty she burst into the lower hallway with a shriek. She ran up the stairs and into their room, shouting, "Davie, my God, we're going to Washington!" She threw off her wrap and flung herself at his feet. "A whole entourage, the entire office! Everyone's going!"

"What on earth for?"

"To meet the President!"

"You're not serious."

"Everyone in our section, husbands and wives. You, me, everybody! Mr. Brown is so excited he's taking a whole group of us on his private train. There'll be three cars hooked on just for married people. Can you believe this?"

"Slow down and tell me about it."

"It's a special invitation from the White House. Republican governors and important people from states throughout the Midwest. Governor Morley can't go . . ."

"So Willie Brown is going instead."

Her hands were trembling with excitement as he helped her up.

"Do you know," she said, "that outside our honeymoon trip, I've never been out of Denver? And now we're going to Washington."

"Are you telling me he's closing up the whole Mountain States Coal Company just to take people on a lark?"

"*Selected* people, dear. My boss, heads of other departments, and their wives. This is what being a confidential secretary means; I told you that. There'll be work to do all week long, on the train and in D.C. When it's done, you'll be there."

"Well, Anna, there's more to consider than just picking up and taking off. I've got a job too."

"But that's . . ."

"It's what? Not very important maybe . . ."

"I didn't say that."

"Not as important as a trip to Washington to meet the President . . ."

"Oh, David!"

"Listen, I'm not scolding you. I admit this in an important thing."

"Well, then?"

"Well, then, fine, except I can't afford to lose my job now."

"John Wentworth would let you off."

"John Wentworth would fire me right now. Anna, he's a decent man, but he's got a business to run. He pays me to be there. How long is this trip supposed to take?"

"Two weeks."

"It's out of the question. There's simply no way I could get off for two weeks."

"Then quit. You'll find another job."

He smiled patiently. "How soon we forget. Do you remember what hell I went through trying to get this one?"

"Things are different now. Are you going to go through life afraid to take a chance just because we had it hard once?"

"I'll take a chance when I can afford it. Right now I've still got a struggle on my hands just getting up the mortgage on this house every month."

"All right, then." She sighed and looked away toward the wall. "I guess I knew it all along. You're right, it's just common sense. I knew we couldn't afford it. Still . . ."

"Sure, you wanted it." He rubbed her shoulders. "We'll get caught up and I'll take you to D.C."

"To meet the President, love?"

"You're kidding yourself, Anna. There's no way Coolidge will have fifteen executives and their staffs from each state to a White House dinner."

"Of course not. I never said that. Mr. Brown will go to the dinner alone. But he did agree to meet the staff briefly on the White House lawn."

David looked at her. "I'm sorry. What else can I say?"

That night he lay awake, thinking. He thought about politics and how it had begun to touch his life. Morley wouldn't go to Washington: he was too flagrant a Klansman. Morley *couldn't* go, because John Galen Locke had told him not to. In his place would go the flamboyant William Brown, the fire-eater from the plains, who could be brash or quiet and who knew with unfailing instinct which to be. Morley must be stewing in his own juice. So must Locke. Locke would give back his medical degree, if he'd ever had one, for a trip to the White House, but there was no way Calvin Coolidge could receive so notorious a Klan chief. So Locke had looked at his roster and up popped Willie Brown III. For Willie Brown it would be a triumph on a major scale. He was a crown prince at the door of national politics, and people with that much to lose didn't risk it fooling with other men's wives.

That thought calmed him, and by morning he had worked through the rough territory of an idea. Before they went down to breakfast, he sat on the bed and put it into motion. "You know," he said, "just because I can't go doesn't mean you should stay home."

She was doing her hair. In the mirror her eyes met his, and her hand froze in midair. "Go without you? Don't be silly love. Of course, there is a chaperone. But it still wouldn't be proper, would it?"

"I don't see why not."

She shook her head.

"Well, you think about it, make the decision yourself. Whatever you decide's fine with me."

It was done. He had said it and there would be no taking it back. Tonight there would be bitter words between Teresa and Anna: arguments over decency and propriety, counter-arguments of ladies' coaches and chaperones, counter-counter-arguments, bickering. Later he would draw Teresa aside and calm her fears. Anna would be fine: He was absolutely certain of it, otherwise he'd never let her go.

Still later, after she'd gone, David would tell Teresa and Abe what had come to him in the long night, and what they must do. Anna herself had given him the key. She had handed him that one wedge that would pry open all their locked doors, that would let him say at last what he had to say and bring Gabriel back into the family.

Late that night, when everyone else had gone to bed, David sat in the living room waiting for Gabriel. The boy came in at midnight. His shirt was torn and there were red stains down the front. His nose was crusted over and he had the beginnings of a black eye. He brushed past toward the stairs, but David said, "Wait a minute, Gabie. We need to talk."

"Not tonight."

"Yes, tonight."

The boy turned and looked at him. "Has something happened?"

"Yes. Wash your face and meet me outside in the garden."

They walked far back, to the edge of the garden. "Your mother is going away for a few weeks," David said. "She's going to Washington for her job. When she comes back, the first night she's back, I'll talk to her."

"I've heard that before."

"When I talk to her, I want certain things to have been done. We'll talk to Teresa and Abe together, the day your mother leaves. At the same time I'll get the wheels moving for an adoption procedure. When she gets back I want all the legal groundwork to be finished. I want this to be as painless as buying a house, you understand that? Anna will have to cosign the papers, there'll have to be a court hearing, and you'll be ours. As far as Anna's concerned, I want it to be like stepping off one treadmill onto another."

He took the boy's arm. "There are some things you need to do. I'm counting on you to be an adult and act with some sense and responsibility. There's bound to be a change in her attitude toward you. You might not know what to make of it. She might seem distant, maybe even shy. If she needs time, you give her that. You've already had time, so give her the same chance to get used to it. She won't feel like a mother, maybe not for weeks or months. Whatever she does, it won't have anything to do with you. That's what you have to remember, all the time. What she'll say are the words society expects her to say. Don't show any resentment if she doesn't seem to take to it right away. It'll take time and love. You understand what I'm saying?"

Gabriel nodded.

"Good. There's more. I don't want to live here anymore. I want us all to move, far away."

"Where?"

"Alaska. Canada, maybe. That may be the toughest part of all, prying your mother and Teresa away from here. Starting a new life is always scary. They've got roots here, attachments to places and things. What they don't realize is that their roots have already been torn out. They're already displaced, they've got nothing left here but harassment and heartache. Teresa will be especially tough. She still thinks Tom might come back. But we're going away."

"Jesus Christ," Gabriel said.

"There's just one more thing. Now that we've decided to do this, you'll be responsible to me. Do you understand what that means?"

"I'm not sure."

"Let's be sure. First of all, it means that your days with this anti-Klan gang are over. No more gangfighting, no more late nights, and if you don't believe that, you'll find me a lot more unreasonable than Teresa is. If I'm going to have trouble with you, let's know it now, before we get too far along."

Gabriel looked up at him. "I don't want to leave Denver."

David hugged the boy's head against him. "Neither do I, son. Maybe someday the world will come to its senses. Maybe then we can come back."

2

Willie Brown had promised a seven o'clock departure, and latecomers could cry and wave good-bye as the train pulled out. Promptly at six-forty his car arrived at Union Station and was hooked onto the caravan train. Willie Brown got out and moved among his people to growing applause. He wore his three-piece suit and a distinguished felt hat. He waved and smiled, then mounted a small box that had been erected near Track 1 and gave a short talk. From their vantage point under the rainshed, David and Anna couldn't hear what he was saying. They were too busy saying good-bye. She promised to write every night. He kissed her on the head and held her against him while Willie Brown finished his talk. There was more cheering and applause. "I'd better go, Davie, people are starting to board." She squeezed his fingers. He tried to smile but didn't quite mean it, and in those last few moments his eyes were on Willie Brown. The man seemed troubled and nervous as he scanned the faces of his people. Then he saw Anna, walking toward the train, and the troubled look disappeared. David didn't like that. He didn't like the way Willie Brown bounced along now like a boy at the beginning of a summer vacation. Willie Brown leaped up the steps of his train and disappeared inside. David still hadn't moved out of the rainshed. He saw Anna, standing on the fringe of a group of ladies. She looked tiny and vulnerable. He wished he could change his mind and call her back.

A gray-haired woman about Teresa's age was talking to the ladies. It was as Anna had said, very professional, very proper. The ladies began to board. They were in the car nearest the engine, separated from Brown's car by the length of the train. David moved down toward the track, walking bare-headed in the cold air. At the platform, Anna turned and gave him a final wave. His heart sank. He didn't want her gone from him, with Willie Brown or anyone, for any length of time at all. She smiled and her excitement filled the gap between them, then she disappeared into the train. He walked along, hoping for a glimpse of her in a window, but there was nothing. She was gone, and in all the life he had spent alone, David Waldo never felt more alone.

At precisely seven o'clock the train began to move. David stood on the brown earth just east of Union Station and watched it pass. Smoke poured from the stack as the train struggled to build speed. Ahead the plains stretched out forever. He felt like a man after a war, handing over his town to a conquering enemy. He was torturing himself for nothing. The thing was done. He headed west across the valley, for his talk with Abe and Teresa.

He hoped he was doing the right thing. He believed he was, but you could never be sure. When she came home and faced a new world of change, this would help her through it. She would look back on her trip to Washington with Willie Brown III, and she would know that it had been the greatest possible expression of his faith in her.

3

For ten hours she saw nothing but sagebrush and silos. No textbook could have prepared her for the vastness of the great American prairie. Her workday was short. Once during the morning she had been summoned to one of the rear cars, where her boss dictated some short letters. All the letters had been political, to cronies and contacts of Willie Brown. None was related to the coal business. She did not see Willie Brown at all. They left her alone through the long afternoon and she did not leave her compartment. On her first trip alone, she was content to sit by her window and watch the landscape that never changed, even if the people did remind her of characters on some stage, in a sad, wordless play.

Most of the women had to share compartments, but she had drawn the last odd one and had it all to herself. There had been the one work break, which had lasted three hours. She had found her compartment equipped with a typing stand, a typewriter, and lavish amounts of bond. In a desk drawer were letterheads of Mountain States Coal and the personal stationery of Maxwell Koth, her boss. She was expected to know by the nature of the letter which to use, and did. Now in the last hour of the afternoon she watched suburban Kansas City roll past her window and thought how much it looked like Denver. It brought on her first touch of homesickness.

But that vanished in the next hour, when everyone was summoned to the dining car for the evening meal. Unlike lunch, which had been catch-as-catch-can, the dinner was elaborate and communal. Its intimacy made her, for the first time, uncomfortable. Willie Brown sat at the head of a long table, his most trusted friends and aides along his right side, each man separated by a lady. Perhaps it had just worked out that way, but Anna was seated at the far end of the table, facing Willie Brown, as a hostess might face her husband at a banquet. She had taken her place when she realized that her chair too was special: It was high and thronelike, matching his. She thought she detected an undercurrent at the table, something moving silently among the ladies, passed by their eyes. No one spoke. Waiters brought their appetizers, delicious shrimp and red sauce, and that was followed by clear red champagne. Willie Brown stood and lifted his glass.

"Ladies and gentlemen, to all of you," he said. "Thank you, for all working so hard this past year."

There was a rustle as they sipped, and Willie Brown offered a toast to the future. He looked at Anna and raised his glass. Another rustle of clothes: everyone drank, then a burst of talk, laughter and some uneasy applause. The meal was grand. Afterward there was brandy and a touch of crème de menthe for the ladies. Those closest to the head of the table caught Willie Brown's ear and there was much political talk. It lasted for a short while, then abruptly Willie Brown retired. In her compartment, Anna wrote a long letter to David, telling him about her day. She told him about the trip, making it as exciting as she felt it, and closed with a brief description of the dinner. She didn't tell him about the feeling she had got from the ladies, or about being seated at the foot of the table.

Dinner the next night was a copy of the first. Everyone sat in assigned places, Anna in the plush velvet chair at the foot of the table while Willie Brown sat in its mate, laughed gaily, proposed a toast, and chatted with his cronies. Only the menu was changed. The meal was pheasant; the most incredible food she had ever tasted. Now she was even more aware of her changing status. It made her self-conscious to the point of embarrassment. No one spoke to her. It was almost as if she had been placed inside glass and propped up at the end of the table like a fern or artificial tree. They had been on the rails thirty-six hours and Willie Brown had yet to speak to her. But his eyes found hers at odd intervals. Sometimes she would look up and find those blue eyes on her face even as he was talking to someone else.

When they were in eastern Virginia she sealed a second letter to David and placed it near the first, still unmailed. Towns flashed past, one after another. She was keyed-up, tense. But surprisingly, when she went to bed, she slept at once, and deeply.

4

Washington was different than she had expected. It seemed smaller, its streets less crowded, and there were no skyscrapers at all. It was a city of wide streets and square, squat government buildings. Everything seemed to lead downtown, to the Capitol, to the White House, and twice that afternoon she walked the perimeter of the White House grounds, staring at the upper-floor windows where the President did his work. There was little traffic. Even for a Sunday the streets were clear and there was street-side parking right across from the White House.

She stayed for a long time at the Lincoln Memorial, awed by the immense president sitting inside. She went up close to the statue and stared into Lincoln's face. She didn't know how long she had been there when she heard the footsteps behind her. When she turned, Willie Brown stood about twenty yards away.

He was alone. He came closer, his face in semi-shadow, the open street to his back. When he was very close, he stopped and looked at her.

"Is it an accident that we end up in the same place at the same time?" She laughed uneasily, knowing it was no accident.

He said as much. She heard the word *no,* disembodied, floating, originating nowhere.

"You followed me here?"

"Yes."

"May I ask why?"

"You know why."

"William . . . "

"Don't say anything. I don't want to hear it."

"You've got to hear it, whether you want to or not."

"Why? Is it wrong for a man to talk with a woman who works for him?"

"Here and now, under the circumstances, of course it's wrong. You made me a promise."

"I'm taking my promise back."

"William, don't joke."

"All right, I tried to keep it. Didn't I try? How many times in the last six weeks have you seen me? You can count them on one hand. How many words have I said to you? Half a dozen? Eight? Eight words in a month's time."

"That's exactly how I want to keep it."

"Do you really now?"

"What a question! Of course I do. What do you take me for?"

"A very, very lovely woman who's made some bad decisions that she's now trying desperately to live with. I've kicked myself a thousand times for what I did to you. I've paid for it, though I don't expect you to understand that."

"We went all through this. You said you wouldn't bring it up again."

"I can't help it. It still preys on my mind, all the time. I can't help thinking that if things had been just a little different . . ."

"Then you wouldn't be who you are. You'd be working in a gas station on West Colfax somewhere."

"Oh, no." He smiled. "Not me."

"Anyway, it was a pretty clear-cut choice, as you saw it. I'm sure it was the right one. And it's past, over and done with so long ago that there's not even a trace of hurt left."

"I don't believe you."

"William . . ."

"Otherwise why come to my office that day? Why stand in the foyer reading the directory?"

"I told you."

"Ah, Anna, no more nonsense, please. No more lies. You came in because you knew it was my building."

She felt her cheeks burn at the truth of it, and she fell back to the false front, to primness. "You flatter yourself, sir."

"Then tell me, what was the lawyer's name?"

"What lawyer?"

"The lawyer you came to see in my building?"

She didn't say anything.

"Anna, there are no lawyers in that building."

"Is that why you came here after me, to embarrass me and shame me?"

"If it's the only way to crack through that iron shell, then yes, I'll use anything I can get."

"That part of you hasn't changed, has it?"

He sighed, then did a curious thing. He took off his coat and sat on the cold floor. When he spoke again his voice was soft, like Gabriel's would be in a few years. "On the train, in the dining car, didn't you enjoy that, Anna? Didn't it make you feel special, better than the rest of them?"

"I love my husband. It's true. I don't care what you believe."

"A lie, Anna, a lie so plain everybody on the train knows it."

"That's your fault. Anything those people think is your doing, not mine. You arranged the chairs in the dining car. Didn't you do that?"

"I had it done."

"Now I've had enough. I won't listen to any more of this. I'm going back to the train, and if you try to stop me or bother me in any way, I'll catch the next train out of here." She brushed past him, walked a few steps, stopped and turned. He hadn't moved. He was still sitting on the floor, his back to her. "This trip has been a mistake," she said. "This job, everything, a mistake. I said no secretary is worth what you're paying me and I was right, wasn't I? There was always more to it than what you said."

"There's always been more between you and me," he said loudly, looking up at Lincoln's feet.

"Good-bye, William. You have my resignation. When we get to Denver I'll put it in writing if you like."

326

"You're making a mistake."

"Yes. I'm good at that."

She walked away, leaving him alone among the strangers coming in. He looked small and almost humble as he sat at Lincoln's feet.

5

She didn't see him again until Wednesday night. She mailed her two letters and wrote a third, and that night she stayed in her compartment and tried to read a book. When dinner was served, she didn't go. Her thoughts drifted along the whole eighteen years since she had first seen him, that sunny day in 1907 at Cheltenham School. From that day to this, no week had passed that she hadn't thought of him. Shame and anger can be almost pleasant emotions if that's all you have left. Now she had pride. She was proud of her performance in the Lincoln Memorial, and she thought about it and denied that fourth emotion he had tried to wring out of her. That was nothing to be proud of. It was her dark side, the devil she had carried inside her for more years than she wanted to remember. That was the side that said yes, she had enjoyed the feel of him even when he was hurting her, and she would do it again if things were different. Consequences be damned, she would do it, and pay the price.

At least she had that under control. She had demonstrated that, both to Willie and herself. She would not be coaxed or bullied, and that was the end of it. Monday night she decided to confront the devil again, and went to the dining car for dinner. She took a chair in the middle, deliberately defying the seating pattern. It was a wasted effort; Willie Brown did not come out for dinner. On Tuesday morning, even before she was dressed, a messenger came to her door bearing a startling handwritten card on a silver tray.

President and Mrs. Coolidge
Request Your Presence
At A Dinner,
March 11, 1925
The White House

She was stunned. She looked at the man, but his face told her nothing. "There must be some mistake," she said. "Who were you looking for?"

"Mrs. Anna Waldo?"

"Yes, but this is a mistake."

"I don't know about that, ma'am. I'm just to deliver it." He bowed and backed away. Immediately Miss Berger, the gray-haired office manager who was in charge of the ladies, burst into the room. "So," she said, looking at the card. "Do you have any clothes?"

"Not for something like that! Miss Berger, it's got to be a mistake."

"It's no mistake."

"They might mean somebody across town for all we know."

"Come, now, let's stop this fussing. We'll have to work to get you ready in time."

Anna was horrified. "I can't go. I won't!"

"You can't turn down an invitation from the White House, dearie. Nobody does that. *No*-body. You do that and you bring disgrace to us all. You think about that while I size you up." She took a tape measure out of some mysterious bulging pocket. "Trust me."

Anna felt the tape on her back. "I don't believe it."

"Whether you believe it or not doesn't matter," Miss Berger said. "You probably still won't quite believe it years from now, when you tell your grandchildren about it. Now come on, look alive. Throw back your shoulders."

Miss Berger's fingers worked along her arms and hips, then the old woman whisked out and left her alone. Thirty minutes later a man came in, led by Miss Berger, carrying a dozen boxes of shoes. They sat her near the window and the man kneeled at her feet, trying various sizes and styles until Miss Berger nodded her head. "That pair. It's exactly right. It will go with the dress. How does it feel?"

"Tight," Anna said.

As if on cue, the dress arrived. It was a beautiful formal of floor length. "The President likes colorful things, Mrs. Waldo," Miss Berger said. "That's just one of the facts we've unearthed about him in the past few minutes. Beads. Trinkets. Loud colors. Mrs. Coolidge must have a terrible time. Here—stand up for your fitting. Did you have anything planned for this afternoon?"

"I was going to see the Capitol."

"You will have lunch with me, here in this room." To the shoe man, she said, "The same style, please, one size larger." Then, turning back to Anna, "When we get the dress right, we'll have you tutored on protocol."

"Really, Miss Berger."

"Oh, don't look so wounded. It's no reflection on your manners. They're quite fine for us, but there are ways things are done at the White House. Very particular ways, which you will learn."

Miss Berger held up the dress. Anna thought it was stunning. She took it gently and slipped behind the screen to put it on. Miss Berger came around and helped her with the back. Then she knocked on the door and two tailors appeared. Miss Berger, who seemed to be a competent tailor in her own right, made most of the final decisions. When she was satisfied she dismissed the tailors to the corridor, and again pushed Anna behind the screen to take off the dress. It disappeared down the hallway, into waiting hands. It almost hurt her to see it go, and she wondered what would happen to the beautiful dress on Thursday, when her adventure in the White House was finished. She wondered how expensive it was, and if she might possibly buy it, and if David would mind too much.

Miss Berger, reading her thoughts, said, "The dress is yours to keep. You can show it to your grandchildren when you tell them about it."

"I couldn't. It's too much."

"Be happy, child. Dear God, you look terrified. I'll leave you alone, to collect yourself. One hour. Time for you to get your bath and relax a bit. When I come back we'll have a nice leisurely lunch together, with no talk of what's to come. This afternoon you'll meet your tutor. In the morning the dress will be delivered, and if I know anything it'll have to go back for another adjustment. Then we'll all go to the White House for our tour. If we're lucky, you'll meet the President and his wife on the lawn. When we come back here, you'll take an afternoon nap. That's your program, Mrs. Waldo, everything I can think of to have you at your best tomorrow night. Do you have any questions?"

"You have it well planned. So well that it makes me wonder."

"Wonder what, child?"

"How long have you known about it? Miss Berger, you want me to believe you got that dress here thirty minutes after the invitation came?"

"The dress came with us from Denver."

"I see."

Her tutor was a slender, moustached man named Scott Hamilton. He arrived, as Miss Berger had promised, at exactly two o'clock. Hamilton took off his gloves and made himself at home in the chair opposite her. He tried to make her feel at ease; they talked for perhaps fifteen minutes about Denver and her life there. Then he told her what he proposed to do. He would run through the chain of etiquette for all formal dinners, which was generally followed at the White House and which, he was sure, she already understood.

Then he would touch upon matters peculiar to the White House. He talked quickly and smoothly, with a voice like velvet. He covered the rule book in twenty minutes: how to accept various dishes and beverages; selection and placement of the guest of honor; the arrangement of cards, by which the male guests would receive the

329

names of the ladies they would escort up to dinner; the juggling of people to avoid having two ladies seated together; the announcements of who goes to the dining room in what order, when it is done, and how to carry oneself. Hamilton told her what to do when dinner was announced and how to know when the hostess was turning the table. He told her what to do when the table was turned, how to open a new stream of conversation with a new partner, almost without breaking stride. He impressed her with the point that she was obligated to talk with the people on both sides, and she should be alert for the moment when the hostess turned the table. She began to be afraid. He saw her doubt, and he smiled. It was simple. They would run through it again.

"Please," she said. "Slowly."

There was so much to learn that she wanted to take notes. Dishes, of course, were never passed from hand to hand, as they always were at home. People were served everything. The hostess would decide when the table was to be vacated, then the ladies would take the arms of their gentlemen partners and allow themselves to be escorted to a drawing room, where liqueurs and cigarettes were served on silver trays. It seemed to her that Hamilton placed much emphasis on the manners of the lady of honor. She would sit on the President's right. She would be the first to take her leave, signifying as she stood that the evening had ended. Punctuality was a cardinal rule. The President's invitation was for eight o'clock, so Anna and her escort should arrive in the White House Blue Room not later than seven fifty-five, and should take their places at the foot of the stairs. Guests would be arranged in order of importance. She should address the President as "Mister President," his wife as "Mrs. Coolidge." No one should ever sit while either the President or Mrs. Coolidge were standing. No one should leave the room, for any reason, while the President still occupied it. She wondered about going to the bath-room, and wished for the first time that her tutor had been a woman. It wasn't a question she could ask the proper Mr. Scott Hamilton.

Hamilton smiled again. His voice was gentle. "Would you like me to run through it one more time?"

She nodded.

When he had gone, she sat for a few minutes with Miss Berger talking about The Event. "Mr. Hamilton is effective, don't you think?"

"Very," Anna said. "I wish I'd had another hour with him."

"I anticipated that, so I asked him back tomorrow, just after we return from our White House tour. You can have another long talk, just like today."

"It's all so much to remember."

"But it must be remembered, Mrs. Waldo. It's very important, especially for the lady of honor. Yes, you will be on the President's right, Mrs. Waldo. He will escort you to the table."

6

She dressed as plainly as possible for the White House tour Wednesday, but even as the group prepared to go by bus into the city, she detected the changing attitudes of the women around her. None of them had ever been close to her, but now there was a distance that hadn't been there before. They seemed nervous and tense in her presence. It took her a while to work through it, and the answer came suddenly, with a jolt. They were afraid of her, and there could be just one reason for that. *They think we're lovers.* She could see it in their faces as she passed them, and the thought, once she was past the initial shock, fascinated her. It was the first time she had ever known the sensation of power. She had never had it, not even over her own growing son. Truly, she believed, she had never wanted it. Now it might have amused her as, coming suddenly upon a group of them in the dining car, they stepped aside for her. It might have amused her if there'd been an ounce of truth behind it. If she'd been that kind of woman.

But it fascinated her enough that she put it to the test. She sent for Ernestina Hammond and asked her to run an errand. "Ernestina, would you mail this for me? I'm going to be busy all day." It was something she wouldn't have asked, as recently as yesterday. But Ernestina clutched it and held it against her breast. "Glad to, Mrs. Waldo. I'll run out now and see that it gets in the mail. Anything else I can do while I'm out?"

Anna, suddenly embarrassed at her own arrogance, said, "No, thank you, I have no right to ask."

"Please! I'll be happy to do anything I can."

"That's kind of you, Ernestina. You don't mind if I call you by your first name?"

"I'm delighted, Mrs. Waldo."

"Anna, please."

"Anything else I can do, please ask." She turned and rushed out of the room.

She looked at herself in her glass. Was she really that formidable? In another minute, Ernestina Hammond would have been kissing her feet.

But they weren't all that way. Now, as they went through the White House, she caught glares of hostility, suspicion, and open hatred. She followed them out onto the lawn, to await the President and his wife. Coolidge came out almost at once. He was a thin man, with sandy-colored hair, hawk eyes, and a tight, wiry mouth. Mrs. Coolidge, leading a raccoon on a chain, came a few steps behind her husband. The women stood in a line and the President and Mrs. Coolidge came along and shook each hand. The President was abrupt, his wife warmer and more generous with her time. Coolidge seemed to be in a hurry to get back inside. He pumped each hand once, tried to smile, then pulled himself along to the next hand. He shook Anna's hand exactly as he had all the others, giving no indication that he recognized her name or knew that, in a few hours, she was to be his lady of honor. It took Mrs. Coolidge perhaps another two minutes to reach her. When Mrs. Coolidge arrived at the end of the line, she took Anna's hand in both of hers and smiled directly into her eyes. "I'm so glad you could come," she said. "I look forward to seeing you tonight."

Back at the train, she fidgeted until Scott Hamilton arrived. Her second session with the protocol man was a disaster, for she had forgotten everything he had told her the day before. Again he went through it twice. Then the dress arrived, and the final adjustments that Miss Berger had ordered were completed. The tailors stood in the hall and waited while she tried it on. It fit perfectly.

"And now, Mrs. Waldo, it's bedtime for you," Miss Berger said. "I want you to sleep for two solid hours, till I come back and wake you up." She drew the curtains and plunged the room into twilight. Anna lay on the bed, but sleep didn't come easily. She kept staring at the closet, where the dress was, and thinking about tonight. She thought about the White House and people looking up to her, Ernestina Hammond's reverence, the hatred of the others. She thought about power. People who hold power over others, just by being who they are or by association with those who have it. Finally she thought, as she drifted into sleep, that the woman who married Willie Brown would have to be very wise and humble, to avoid having it all go to her head.

She awoke to footsteps and fading daylight, as Miss Berger came in and opened the curtains. "I figured you might have trouble getting off," Miss Berger said, "so I let you sleep an extra hour. Now it's time to get up. It's almost nightfall. Time to go."

7

Pennsylvania Avenue, all along the route to the White House, was glittering with streetlights and cars. By contrast, the White House and the grounds around it looked dark and unusually quiet in the spring night. It looked almost as if no one was home. Then she saw the lighting, brighter as you came close, and she realized that what was happening here tonight undoubtedly happened every night in the week. For kings and queens, for presidents and their wives, for heads of state and political powers, but never for the wife of a Denver printer. Their chauffeur, who went about his business as silently as Calvin Coolidge tended his, maneuvered the limousine to the front gates, stopped for the guard, and glided up the long drive to the White House. Anna was hardly aware of Willie Brown in the seat beside her. Now, as the car came to a stop, he looked at her and said, "Relax, you'll do just fine." A uniformed Negro stepped up and opened the door, and she was ushered into a lobby with a shiny marble floor. For a panicky moment she lost track of her escort. Was she supposed to walk ahead or follow him? Was she to take his arm? He saved her by appearing at her side, taking her arm and leading her across the lobby. She decided to follow his lead in everything, watching the ladies of the other men as they arrived and took their places. She would do what they did, and everything would work out.

An usher met them in the middle of the lobby. He was a white man, and his eyes were kind. "Some of the others have already gone up, sir," he said to Willie Brown. "I'll take you up now, if you wish." They went up in an elevator, and the man talked to them while they rode. "Mrs. Waldo, of course, will sit on the President's right. The President will escort her." Willie Brown nodded. The door opened and they walked into the Blue Room, a huge chamber with a long flight of stairs that disappeared into the upper rooms. Two couples were standing near the stairs talking. They were introduced by the usher, who bowed slightly and departed. She forgot their names at once. One, she knew, was a governor; the other, she thought, had been introduced as a businessman. Both were much older than Willie Brown, the governor and his lady both in their mid-fifties. Willie Brown chatted with them as equals. Such poise for one so young, such influence that his companion would walk in to dinner tonight on the arm of the President. Or was it that at all? Did they spin some big roulette wheel, and had her number come up? Or had the other ladies perhaps been of equal social rank, with nothing to distinguish them? To Anna, that sounded more logical. She had been chosen lady of honor because she ranked not at all, because she didn't belong here, let alone sitting beside the President. Perhaps it was all some cruel joke. But they didn't play jokes like that at the White House.

More people arrived. No one seemed to know the others, and somehow that helped. They came in a bunch, and slowly began to form a circle. She and Willie Brown were at the head of the circle, nearest the stairs. The room went quiet as a shuffle was heard at the top of the stairs. A small group of uniformed men came down, and she remembered the words of Scott Hamilton. These were the President's naval and military aides. It was exactly eight o'clock. The Coolidges appeared, the President on the left, his face its usual mask. At the bottom the military aides began presenting Coolidge to his guests. He took her hand and, without smiling, said he was happy to have her. She bowed her head, so slightly, and said, "Thank you, Mr. President." Coolidge moved on to Willie Brown. The exchange between them sounded stiff, polite, and formal; not at all like the talk of men who know each other even slightly. She thought then that the workings of this White House dinner would remain one of the great mysteries of her life. She might never really know how she had come to be here, and how she had been given the spot of honor. Mrs. Coolidge was before her and the instant was gone. The first lady was wearing a pale blue dress that complimented her own. Again she took Anna's hand, and her smile was one of friendship and affection. "So glad you could come." She greeted Willie Brown briefly, as the President had, and moved on down the line. By the time Anna had caught her breath, Coolidge had toured the room and had arrived again at the head of the circle. Her agony began anew, as the President offered his arm. She took it, certain of her clumsiness. There was a correct way to walk to dinner with a President, and yet she could remember none of it now as they moved toward the dining room. She knew that every woman's eyes were on her, critically and enviously. Watching this bumbling, lame cow.

Behind her, Mrs. Coolidge brought Willie Brown to the table. Anna sat on the President's right and conversation flowed one-way along the length of the table. All the ladies talked to the men on their left as the servants brought the soup and fish. She remembered that the talk was controlled by the ladies, that she was expected to carry on with the President of the United States until Mrs. Coolidge saw fit to turn the flow the other way. She looked up and met Coolidge's eyes. He seemed cold and distant, and more than a little bored. His mouth was set in that half-mean expression he put on for all public appearances and photographs. The man was impenetrable. He gave her no kindness or warmth, no reassurance whatever. She struggled with and rejected a dozen possibilities for small talk, but they all seemed superficial and idiotic addressed to the President. *How are things, Mr. President?* How could she be expected to understand any answer he might give? *Mrs. Coolidge looks lovely tonight.* Ladies' chatter. *What a wonderful party!* He would think of her as a giddy child, rendered speechless by even the slightest spectacle. At last, driven almost to collapse by her own relentless nerves, she said, "Have you ever been to Colorado, Mr. President?"

He looked at her and, like the master politician who suspects traps in even the simplest question, considered his answer. Finally he said, "Yes," and her terror began to drain away. Nothing frightened her so much as his silence; now he would talk, the ice would break, and they would be fine. But he didn't talk. She waited for elaboration that never came. He tasted his soup and the others began eating too. Anna could hear Mrs. Coolidge chatting away with Willie Brown, and across the table the governor's wife was laughing softly at something the businessman had said. Coolidge never talked much. That was his reputation. Their eyes met and she thought he looked almost shy, a person out of his element, thrown into a spotlight that was too big, that made him look smaller than he really was. His silence, his coolness, were all part of the masquerade. If she kept that in mind, it eased her tension and helped her along. He was just a man, a wandering Jew who had come to her mother's table. What would she say to him?

"I trust the weather wasn't too cold for you?"

He looked at her, not understanding. Almost a minute had passed since she had asked him about Colorado.

"In Colorado," she said. "But I guess you're used to the cold, coming from . . ." For a horrible instant her mind went blank. She wanted to say Maine, but instinct warned her. Instead, with only the briefest pause, she said, "Pardon me, New England."

Again, he took his own time answering. "In Massachusetts we get our share."

"I'm sure." She looked at her plate. "This is certainly lovely china, Mr. President."

"It's the Roosevelt china," he said at once.

"And the silver." Her spoon was simply embossed, with the lettering *The President's House.*

She tried again. "You must be full of optimism, Mr. President."

He looked at her suspiciously. "Why do you say that?"

"Because of your huge mandate last fall, and because the country is doing so well."

"Business keeps the country moving. The economy is growing every day."

She dropped her spoon. She looked at the President helplessly, wondering if it was proper for her to pick it up. But a servant appeared at once with a new one.

"My husband is a student of economics," she said. "He fears the boom will end suddenly and send the country into a depression."

"The country has survived depressions," Coolidge said. "Many times." He regarded her with that long, icy look. "Naturally such talk has reached my ears. A great many economists have predicted it; at least some have. But my own economic advisors disagree."

335

"And you agree with them."

"If I didn't, we'd be pursuing a different course. No, Mrs. Waldo, I don't subscribe to scare talk. In good times, people are always looking for the turn of the coin. People always expect the worst."

"Still, Mr. President, the good times can't be expected to last forever."

He looked truly surprised. "Why not?"

"They never do."

Now she thought she saw interest in his eyes, and perhaps a shadow of self-doubt. Basically, she thought, he is an insecure man, probably wondering, as I am, what he's doing here. Even after two years, Calvin Coolidge hadn't become accustomed to White House tradition. He had the thirst for the office that all politicians have, but it was laced with a hatred of the routine and pretension. He was a simple man, elevated beyond his abilities or desires. If that could be true, the dropping of a spoon had no significance at all. The way to talk, the thousand and one forms of address, the proper way to hold a gentleman's arm—all these things fused and evaporated. Anna Kohl Waldo and Calvin Coolidge had no names. They were in Denver, in her mother's house on Osceola Street. They were on Willie Brown's train, about to be served in the dining car. They were anywhere.

It helped her move past her fear. She left it with the soup bowls as the waiters cleared their table. She took the full force of the Coolidge eyes as he said, "They never have, you mean. It doesn't mean they never can."

"That's a tall order, though, isn't it, Mr. President? Nothing lasts forever."

Her tone teased him slightly. She felt bolder, more daring. Again Coolidge waited a long time. Again those suspicious eyes explored her face.

"I don't think it's unreasonable," he said. "With proper political leadership, I fail to see why the economy can't go on improving, year by year."

"Maybe the key is, as you said, proper political leadership."

"Meaning politicians who leave the business community to its business and don't try to meddle in affairs that don't suit them."

"And assuming that the leaders who come after you will continue to subscribe to those views."

Coolidge shifted. He looked vaguely uncomfortable, caught perhaps in a political conversation he hadn't expected from his lady of honor. Anna wondered if she had gone too far, whether one was supposed to talk politics at all at the President's table. "We can talk about something else if you'd prefer, Mr. President. I understand you're having a musicale after dinner."

"Not at all," Coolidge said. "I mean, yes, we're having a musicale, but getting back to what you were saying, I fail to see why Republicans can't run the country indefinitely. People will elect us as long as times are good. Times will be good as long as we do a good job. If Mr. Dawes followed me in office, well, I think his views are pretty much in accord with mine."

She was elated. She decided to challenge him again. "Even if that happens, sir, don't you think there should be some checks on business? Even at its best the business community can sometimes be cruel. In the working conditions it provides for its people. In factories and mills. Child labor . . ."

"All right, I agree with you to this extent: We've got to protect the children. The rest of it's up to free adults. That's the principle this country runs on. People don't like where they work, they quit and find somewhere else. People who have it hard today do so at their own choice."

The waiter brought their fish. She waited until they had been served, then said, "I see what you mean, but there are times when circumstances take the choice out of our hands."

"That's what the communists would have you believe."

"Well, Mr. President, I'm no communist . . ."

"Of course not. I didn't mean to imply . . ."

"But I do know of many cases personally. My own husband has been entrenched in the factories of this country. In his younger days."

"Mrs. Waldo, you say factories as if it's a national conspiracy. As if we, as a people, have deliberately conspired to bring it about."

"It doesn't matter, Mr. President. The result is the same in either case."

"Do you really believe that?"

"I do, sir. I truly do."

Coolidge didn't return her smile. He said, "Any man out of a job today is doing exactly what he wants to do. That's what I believe. Any man entrenched, as you say it, in the factories of this country is free to seek his fortune elsewhere. Let me throw the example of your husband back at you. You were quick to point out that his life in the factories happened some time ago, in his youth. I conclude from that he had the gumption and wherewithal to move on to better things. Am I correct?"

"Well, yes, you are . . ."

"So you see, no one is a prisoner in America. The business community does what it has to for its workers. No more, no less. Which is just as it should be. Conditions in the factories are what they are because that's how the people want them. When the people are ready for change, they'll make change. You see?"

"Yes, Mr. President, only sometimes people in the working classes are hesitant to speak out. They're slower yet in resorting to activist methods."

"And of course I wouldn't counsel them to. I don't think strikes and violence solve anything, Mrs. Waldo. In the long run they only create more strife and ill-will than they solve."

She paused for a few bites of food, and to catch her breath. She had broken every one of Scott Hamilton's rules and was going on her own instinct and poise. She had captured the President's interest. Perhaps it was just the fascination of a political enemy, for he must know by now that she was that. She felt him watching her while they ate, his eyes sweeping the table but always coming back to her. Finally she flattered herself, for she had seen that look in other men and knew what it meant. He was interested in her as a person: beyond that, as a woman. From that moment her confidence was unshakable. Spoons and forks be damned. She looked at Coolidge and said, "Don't you believe, Mr. President, that there are times when even violence is justified?"

"For what end?"

"For the right to live in peace and quiet, to make a living the best way you know how."

"The Constitution guarantees you that right, Mrs. Waldo. No one needs violence to obtain something that's theirs already."

"There are people who do unconstitutional things, Mr. President. Do them with impunity. Some of them are the same people we've entrusted to uphold our laws. Believe me, Mr. President, what I'm telling you is true."

"Then these people should be prosecuted and punished, removed from office. Assuming that what you say is true and can be proven, of course. No offense intended, Mrs. Waldo, but sometimes we confuse emotions with facts."

"These are facts, Mr. President. Take the Ku Klux Klan as an example. In my town, Denver, probably fifty percent of the police force are Klansmen."

Coolidge took a long time responding to that. He nibbled at his fish, his face as bland as before. "Tell me something, Mrs. Waldo. How did you happen to be here, with Mr. Brown?"

"We're old friends, Mr. President. We've known each other since childhood."

"You also seem to be political opposites."

"I wouldn't be surprised, sir."

His brow wrinkled. "My position on the Ku Klux Klan is and has been that it's entitled to exist, just like any other organization. The fact that a man is in the Klan doesn't preclude his being a policeman. But if Klansmen or policemen resort to unlawful methods, they must be exposed and punished, just like any other person would be."

"What if they're public officials, Mr. President? Mayors. Governors."

"Especially then, Mrs. Waldo. The laws of this country must be obeyed."

His political guard had gone up again. There was a stir from the other side of the table and she realized, a bit late, that Mrs. Coolidge had turned the talk. She looked away from the President and found herself in conversation with a man from Indiana whose official position, if he had one, she never did get straight. By the time the entrée had arrived, she had the notion that he was, like Willie Brown, a political strategist, only much older and more dogmatic. Despite his age and ability with words, she sensed that his real accomplishments had not matched those of Willie Brown, and his lady had had to sit on the President's left and wait her turn for talk. Anna talked with one ear on the President, and she learned two things that amazed her. The Indiana woman never did penetrate the Coolidge cool. She chatted endlessly about trivial, boring matters and in reply got only periodic grunts from the President. Anna felt smug, very pleased with herself. She thought it had been a long time since Coolidge had shared that many words with any woman over dinner.

The second thing she learned surprised her even more. After a few moments, she was able to split her concentration with no loss of comprehension whatever. She was able to carry on with the gentleman from Indiana and listen to the President and Mrs. Indiana without ever losing track of either conversation. In a third corner of her mind, she was able to sift parts of both conversations, adding her own reactions. It would have been a grand ability for a politician's wife. By the time dinner was finished and the ladies had retired from the table, she could look at them with the same critical eye she had imagined focused on herself earlier. All of them came up short. They knew their manners, they had read Emily Post, but without exception they were as shallow as the pond in the White House garden.

She was relieved when the social hour was done, and the men mixed with the ladies again. The President and his wife went to the East Room for the violin musicale, and as soon as they were seated the guests began to file in behind them. She sat beside Coolidge, with Willie Brown beside her, the couple from Indiana next, and the seating order progressing as it had in the dining room. She didn't hear any of the musicale. Her mind was full of the things she had seen and done. The violinist finished abruptly and the evening was over. She felt Scott Hamilton whispering in her ear, knew that the time for leave-taking had come, and that the duty was hers. She asked for her wrap and was sent away warmly by Mrs. Coolidge. At the door, the President took her hand, and told her he was glad that she had come.

He said he hoped they might meet again, and seemed to mean it. Then they were outside, it was over, and somehow she had survived. She had done her bit for the political career of Willie Brown III. Somehow she had impressed the President of the United States.

She was aware that Willie Brown watched her, but she kept her eyes on the White House until it disappeared past the side of the car. Then she settled back against the seat and closed her eyes.

"You were fabulous," he said.

Strangely, his words irritated her. Somehow telling her seemed to diminish the accomplishment. She didn't need him for that anymore. She sat up and looked at him, wondering if she needed him for anything.

"Just great," he said, and now she saw in his face the first hint of uncertainty she had ever seen there. He was like a man groping with something he only half understood.

"I had a few missteps," she said.

"But you came through it fine. The kinds of things you're talking about are just trimmings. They're the things you learn. It's the things you can't learn that are important. Instinct. Common sense. The ability to read people. You drew the old man out and everybody at the table knew it. What did you two have to talk about for so long?"

Without opening her eyes, she smiled, "The weather, William. What else?"

8

Now the rhythmic wheels were bringing her home. The train swayed gently through Virginia, and all the magic of the journey was gone. She had dined with the President, and that fact overshadowed everything that had happened since her marriage. She had peeped into the palace and had found there just people. Calvin Coolidge was a product of circumstances, no better or brighter than her husband if put to any real test. She saw now the full scope of what David had tried to tell her, the need for constant growth, intellectual stimulation, and learning. A dozen times she left her seat and walked to the closet where the blue dress hung. It would always be her fountain of youth, her most cherished keepsake. Any lapse of self-assurance would dissolve with just a look. She had been someone, even if only for an evening. The dress was hers. Of course she would keep it. Who else was entitled to it?

She knew that, in the short span of twenty-four hours, her life had changed. Everything from her distant past had been boxed and sealed in her mind, put away on some emotional shelf like the toys she had once taken to bed. That part of her life, at long last, was finished. Her night with the President had done something else. It had increased her appreciation for the simple things, heightened her contempt for gloss. She had nothing left to prove, at least to herself, so she felt she could live any way she chose. She would not be a secretary for Willie Brown or anyone. She thought she might open a bookstore. A place where writers and artists might gather and talk. Perhaps the new print shop could also be a bookstore. Possibly they could be developed side by side, in one of those Capitol Hill duplexes, with nooks and skylights and a basement for old books. She would run the store while he worked his trade. And maybe on certain nights, if people felt like hearing it, if the mood was right, she would show them her blue dress and tell them about the night she ate with Calvin Coolidge.

She looked out at Virginia, impatient for the journey to end. In a moment of pure joy, she thought she might even find the words at last to tell David about Gabriel. And wouldn't that be something?

She had stayed in her compartment all morning, seeing no one. Someone had sent her a breakfast tray, and now as the green landscape became brown and the trees thinned out, she got lunch the same way. No one brought her dinner, but she did not stir. She thought of the scene in the dining room, with the empty chair opposite him, and she smiled. It was a sweet sensation, to have taken all the nonsense she would ever have to take from him. Poetic justice.

Dusk came, and still she didn't eat. She thought she might sit here for the entire two days, without eating anything. But just after eight o'clock she heard a soft knock on her door. Before she could get up, Willie Brown opened it and let himself in. He stood framed in the red of the dying sun. She made no move toward the curtain.

"We seem to have changed directions," she said.

"Oh?"

"Yes, we're going north now, aren't we? Is there a reason for that?"

"Right. The east-west track is being repaired. We've been routed to Indianapolis."

"That's a bore. I'm anxious to get home."

He didn't question that, as he might have done only yesterday. He nodded and seemed to accept it. "It'll just add a few extra hours to the trip," he said. He sat across from her and leaned over his knees. "Do you mind?"

"I wish you wouldn't."

"I wanted to ask why you embarrassed me tonight. Why you didn't come in to dinner."

"Because it would have embarrassed *me* to have done it."

"I wanted to toast your success with the President."

"I'm sorry." She let a moment lapse, then said, "Last night will always be a cherished memory for me. I'm grateful to you for that."

"I don't want your goddamned gratitude!"

"Then I'm sorry for you, because it's all I have."

He shook his head in disbelief. "You simply can't be serious. What happened last night was just the tip of the iceberg. It was only the beginning. There can be a thousand nights like last night."

"Not for me, I'm afraid."

"Yes, for you. You just say the word and it's all for you."

"I'm sorry."

He sighed and pulled himself out of his chair. "You're really serious," he said. "You really mean it."

She almost laughed at him. "Yes. I really do."

"You'd go back to that beggar in his dirty print shop . . ."

She covered her ears. "I won't listen to that. If you're going to talk like that, get out of my room."

"You forget, it's my train."

Trees flicked past, breaking the last of the sunlight into a million tiny fires on his face. In another few minutes it would be dark.

"All right, I'll go. I'll leave you alone. There are a few more things, and I'll ask you to listen, and after that I'll leave you. You won't ever have to see me again. There'll be a time, not too long from now, when you could be living in that house. You think about that. The dinner parties could be your dinner parties. The china, the silver, the servants, all yours. I've never said that to anybody. In politics it's not something you're supposed to talk about. It's not proper to look at high office until you're ready for it. But I've always known it. Always. It's all I ever wanted, even in the sixth grade at Cheltenham School, I damn well knew it. I've gone after it with a single purpose, and I've never lost sight of it even for a minute. I know it'll happen. I know it. Do you doubt me?"

"I've never doubted that you'll do everything you want to do."

"When it happens, it'll mean nothing unless you're there. You're what makes it worth getting. I've wanted to say that for ten years. More."

"William, I'm truly sorry you feel that way. What else can I say?"

"You were so beautiful at the White House."

"Thank you."

"You were like an uncut jewel."

She did laugh then. "That's an uncut compliment if ever I heard one."

"It's the highest compliment I give. Alongside you, the others were like paste and glass."

342

She smiled, tenderly now, the way a schoolteacher does at a student who has fallen in love with her. "You'll find someone, William."

"Right," he said. "Of course you're right. I told you what I thought and that's that. That's how life is. Have a glass of wine with me."

"No."

"One glass. Call it the toast we missed tonight. Here—I brought the bottle with me."

She saw it for the first time, perched on the edge of the table.

"Let me toast your happiness," he said. "To you and your lucky husband."

"How can I refuse such a generous offer? Thank you, William."

The wine was very dry, almost bitter. She took another sip and looked out at a passing town. When she turned back to him, he had finished his. "Bottoms up," he said. "Time for me to go."

She drank the rest quickly and gave him her glass. His eyes were cold now. He turned and left the compartment without saying good night, and she sat back in her chair, closed her eyes, and breathed deeply.

She was vaguely aware of time passing, of a floating sensation. She heard noises and thought she must be dreaming. There were people moving in the hall outside her compartment: bumps and voices of people getting off the train. They must have reached Denver. She turned on her side and opened her eyes, but saw only the darkness of her room. There was a sudden lurch and the train was moving again, slowly, like maneuverings in a train yard. She closed her eyes, and when she opened them later—she didn't know how much later—it was still dark and the train was absolutely still. There were no sounds beyond her own breathing, which was heavy and forced.

She tried to stand, but couldn't. She collapsed on her bed, and had just enough strength to kick off her shoes. She knew then what he had done. He had put something in her drink. He had poisoned her, and she was too tired to fight it off.

Sunlight streamed in through the window. She was still on her bed, exactly where she'd fallen. The closet door stood open, revealing the blue dress, still in place on its hanger. No sound reached her ears and there was no movement. The train stood still, and only by concentrating very hard could she hear the faraway sound of a prairie wind.

When she did look out, she saw plains, vast and unending. The wind stirred the tops of the grass and occasionally a tumbleweed rolled past on an eternal journey.

Nothing, as far as she could see.

She went into the hall. The compartment across the way was open, its closets and bureaus empty. It looked as if no one had used it for months.

She walked to the end of the car, went out to the platform, and climbed down the iron steps to the ground. The sun was harsh on her eyes. She shaded them with her hand.

Her car was standing alone on a siding, in the middle of nowhere.

9

She sat on the iron steps until a new wave of sickness came over her. She retched and staggered away from the train. In a small arroyo about twenty yards away, she threw up violently, her sides heaving until nothing but air came up. She sank back in the brown grass, shading her eyes from the sun, until the nausea went away. She returned to the train with a clearer head. She could walk now, and her mind had begun to work again. She didn't know where she was, what day it was, what time of day, how far Denver was. She didn't know which way Denver was. The sun lay off to her right, about a quarter of the way down in the sky. That would make it late morning, but only if the train had been left pointing north. Otherwise it would be early afternoon. The terrain looked like eastern Colorado: dry, brown, and desolate. She thought for a while that this was his farewell to her, his final gesture of contempt. Denver and the Rockies might be over the next rise. Later in the afternoon she walked up and took a look. Ahead was more of the same: rolling brown land with parched patches of billowing grass.

A chill came over the plains as the afternoon waned. The wind had picked up, and whipped furiously around her car. She went back to the compartment and sat near the window, just as if nothing had happened. She would wait him out. She knew he hadn't just left her here; he would have something else in mind. She might have walked, but she had no idea which way to go, and her shoes were fragile and dressy. So she would sit and wait, and the hours went, and gradually her physical hurt was replaced by mental fatigue. The headache went and the hunger came; the anger went, to be replaced by a growing fear.

At dusk she heard a noise: the sounds of an approaching train. She sat absolutely still. This was where he would find her, sitting calmly in her chair. She wouldn't even mention it to him, wouldn't say a word, but she would take no food or drink, and wouldn't sleep again until she was home with her husband. But the train didn't even slow down: It came roaring down upon her car and its lighted windows flicked across the empty corridor. The caboose whipped by, and she jumped up and ran to the rear platform. "Stop!" she screamed, but there was no one to hear. The caboose was just disappearing beyond the ridge.

She looked around for something that might make a sign. At last she made a flag with part of her petticoat. She attached it to a stick with pine, went outside, and draped it off the rear platform.

There were no lights on the train now, so she had to use an oil lamp. She turned up the wick and propped it behind her head. For a time she stood in the half-light, cocking her head, listening. She thought she heard a noise, someone moving just outside the train. She went along the dark corridor to the platform and stood just inside the door, listening to the night sounds of the prairie.

She heard the cry of a coyote. Or was it a wolf? She closed the door and hurried back to her compartment, closed that door and propped a chair against it.

It must have been twenty minutes later when he came for her. She heard him first outside. She cracked open her window and put her face against the screen, but saw no one. The footsteps continued, around the car to the rear platform. She heard him climb onto the train and push the door open, and the sounds came closer as he groped his way along the hall. He pushed the door, toppling the chair over into the room.

He was still wearing the suit, but his white shirt was open at the neck and his tie was gone. His hair was rumpled, as if he'd just done a lot of hard physical work. Even in the poor light she could see that the front of his pants were dirty. He looked strange, standing there without the trappings of his wealth. She strived for calm. Her voice must not tremble. She looked him in the eyes and said, "Where did you come from?"

"I've been here all along."

"Where are we?" she said softly.

"Canada."

She nodded slowly. "I see."

"Would you like to know why we're here?"

"If it's not too much trouble."

He smiled. "We're taking the scenic route home. The others just couldn't wait to get back to work, but you and I, I thought, deserved a bit more than that. After all, they didn't have the strain of entertaining a president." He same inside and sat in a chair near the door. As he did, his coat parted and she saw a gun, clutched against his belt in a small holster.

"William," she said. "Have you gone mad?"

"I don't think so. If I am, then you're responsible. You Kohls. All of you, Your father. Your big brother. All of you."

"I don't understand that."

"Such simplicity, so much love. You people never needed anybody but yourselves, did you? It must be nice, growing up in a self-contained world like that."

She smiled. "And all along I thought we envied your world."

"Let me tell you something about my world, Anna. People who know us both tell me I inherited my political instincts from my mother. She knew what a disaster getting involved with a Jew would be. And that's why we're here, out in the middle of the Canadian prairie, fifty miles from any town. It's been like two giant magnets pulling me in opposite directions, and it's been tearing me apart. And now I can't help thinking, maybe this is my last real chance to break that pull and do something *I* want to do. Just once. Can you understand that? It's the first thing I thought of the day my mother died, years ago."

"William, you've got to forget this."

"I will *not* forget it." He slammed his hand down on the table, so hard it frightened her. "Don't you tell me what I'll forget."

"I'm married to someone else."

"So was I, twice, so I'm well aware of the fragile nature of marriage. Oh, don't tell me about it, I wrote the book on marriage. I had two horrible marriages arranged for me, so I know about that."

He didn't say anything for a while. He took the gun out of his belt and placed it on the table, then took off his coat and folded it neatly across the back of the chair. "My mother almost died when I got that second divorce. She thought it'd ruin me politically. I don't think it'll hurt, do you?" He paused. "In all my life I've only been afraid of two people. One was my mother. You know who the other one was, Anna? Your big brother."

"Thomas?"

"The man's insane, a maniac. You really didn't know what your brother did to me, did you? That he damn near killed me? It's not really the kind of thing he'd tell you, is it? It might upset that perfect little world you Kohls have created for yourselves."

"I don't know what you're talking about."

"I'm talking about the night he dragged me out of a party and covered me with garbage." He pointed to the split in his lip. "And I'm talking about this."

"Thomas did that?"

"Oh, yes. So I've carried the memory of more than one of you all these years."

"People don't brood about things like that."

"*Some* people don't. And some never forget. I'm one of those people, Anna. I never forget an old love or an old enemy."

They had reached a stalemate. He stared at her and she fidgeted nervously. Finally she said, "We don't seem to be getting anywhere. What do you plan to do?"

"Talk."

"Don't you think everything's been said?"

"Not as long as you're evading me."

She clasped her hands, which had begun to tremble. Suddenly there was something very ominous about Willie Brown III. It went beyond what he had done, to the heart of what he was. Until that moment, even seeing the gun, she had never really felt unsafe. He wasn't simply willful. He was mad. Still holding her own hands tightly, she sat forward and spoke in a soft, even voice. "William, do you have any idea how much trouble this can cause you?"

"I think so. You know I never do anything without knowing exactly what the consequences are. And this is a risk I'm willing to take."

"It's a big risk, William. One your mother might call dumb."

He laughed at that. "My mother would use language a great deal stronger than that. But she's dead, so that's one piece of it I don't have to worry about."

"You'd give up everything, go to jail."

"I doubt that."

Silence stretched between them. At last she said, "You really think you're above the law, don't you? You think you can do anything you want with me and get away with it."

"In Colorado that happens to be true."

"I thought you said we were in Canada."

He smiled. "Maybe we are. Would you really do that, Anna? Send me to jail?"

"If I had to. Or we can forget this ever happened. Bring the train back and let's go home. It doesn't have to go past this."

"That's where you're wrong. Now that it's started, it has to go to the end."

His words chilled her. "What does that mean?"

"What do you think it means? You think about it for a few minutes. Think about the incredible job it was for me to get us here. The strings I pulled, the pieces I had to fit together. When you think that through, you'll know I won't forget it. We'll play it out, see what happens. That's the only way I know how to play the game."

He was gone for a while, leaving her alone through the early night. After a while she heard some sporadic shooting. She turned out the lamp and tried to see what was happening, but the night was cloudy and the prairie was black. In her compartment the darkness was perfect, as black as black ever is. She felt reality slipping away, and now she was truly afraid. If he turned suicidal, what might he do to her?

347

She had read such things in literature, and occasionally a real case popped up in the *Denver Post*. The papers called it a lovers' death pact, but who could say what had really happened? Where was the coroner so skilled who could uncover the emotional story, could reconstruct the words said between them, the looks given, the feelings that still lay buried? If Willie Brown was insane, if he should shoot her and then kill himself, what verdict would the police render? It would all come out: their teenage romance, the story of Gabriel, their second meeting more than a decade later. It would make what Thomas called a good read. And who could deny it? Certainly not the people on the train. They were convinced, every last one of them, that she had left the train with Willie Brown willingly. He would become the victim, she the seductress, and what records there were would substantiate that. The records at the Crittendon Home, the report from Willie Brown's detectives, her own work records, showing her willingness to work for him. Her inflated salary: *Why had she been paid so much money?* Her eagerness to take this trip, while her husband remained at home. Such was the melodrama that ran through her mind in the two hours that he was gone. Each time he shot, she put her hands against the glass and peered out. Each time she saw only darkness. His final volley erupted just outside her window. A moment later she heard his feet in the corridor, heard him open the door, felt his presence. "Light the lamp," he said. When she didn't move, he came into the compartment and lit it. "I think I shot a wolf," he said. "A big dog of some kind. Maybe a coyote."

She just sat and stared at him, waiting for his next move. He put the gun on the table and took off his coat. Then he began unbuttoning his shirt.

"What do you think you're doing?"

"The one last thing that'll take us back to the old days. The way it was. What I should have done three years ago, the day my mother died." He came toward her. "Oh, you lovely goddamn Jew."

10

She lay in bed, too numb to move. Under the covers she wore nothing. The remains of her dress lay beside the bed. Her skin felt raw and clammy, hot to touch. She stared at the ceiling with dull eyes. Her hair was matted against her head. Across the hall, in the companion compartment, she could hear him moving around, freshening up. He had poured a pail of water, and she could hear him splashing his face.

She hadn't moved from the bed in eighteen hours. He had been brutal, as though having to rape her had been the final insult. She had fought violently the first time, and the second. After that she just lay senselessly, like a slab of dead meat, and tried to turn her mind away from what was happening. She had not resisted him after that. She had lost track of the hours, knew only that they were actually in Nebraska. He had told her that. That and another thing: This afternoon the train was coming for them. They were going home.

Determination was her only companion through the long day that followed. Not to move. Not to talk. Not to look at him unless he forced her. Determination. That way the sin was all his. All of it. She would be his accomplice only if she gave him anything. And the hours would pass, and he would come like now, and it would begin again.

He came in again. He was smiling at her, his tender smile. Loving, full of remorse, yet faintly teasing, as if he still couldn't take her attitude seriously. He sat near the door and began to talk. He told her she had begun to come around; her willpower was dissolving. He had felt, in the midst of his own joy, her convulsive spasm. Her fingers had tightened around his and a soft moaning sound had come from her throat. She didn't believe him, but it gave her guilt anyway. He came around and sat with her, tenderly stroking her stiff hair. She tried not to cringe, not to give even that. He touched her cheek. "Poor Anna," he said. "The battle is over and she doesn't even know it. Without me you'll always be a common Jewish peasant. You'll be nothing. A wife to nothing. Mother of nothing. Jewish trash in the midst of Jewish trash. One of those who picks up after others. The people who roam the earth, persecuted by the majority. Isn't that how it is, Anna? Jews have never been wanted by anyone, anywhere. Only me. I want you. Jesus Holy Christ, I can't get enough of you. I want you so much I'd take in the whole Jewish race if I could." He dropped his clothes and turned down the blanket, rolled over, and covered her body with his. God, she thought, I must be foul, not to have stirred from this bed in so long. But he didn't seem to notice. She thought of home, and Gabriel, and finally of David. How many hours had she and David spent like this, doing this? Delightful hours, delightful, alone in bed. Davie. It was simply Davie. She was home in her bed with Davie. And suddenly, without knowing how it had happened or how she had weakened, she began to come to orgasm.

She tried to hold still, but it spread across her, engulfing her. Her legs stiffened. She gasped and grabbed his hand. With her free arm she clutched him, pushed him away, clutched him again. She squeezed his hand, as involuntarily as her heartbeat, as natural as a breath of air. Her back arched up from the bed and she screamed, not from ecstasy, for already that was over and fading, but with the sheer stark horror of it. He closed his eyes and came against her, filling her with himself.

They lay there for a long time. He rose slowly, touched her hair, leaned over to kiss the corner of her mouth. Proof that in victory he could still be tender. When he had gone, she was barely aware that he had left the room. She lay still and listened to the sounds of the wind, and in a little while she heard him moving around in the compartment across the hall. There were water sounds, the sounds of his hands in it, of it splashing in his face. A low grunt; his weight on the springs of the bed as he sat and let his emotions unwind. He was still on that mental high that always accompanies a good fight. She waited, and a few moments later he moved out of the compartment and into the adjacent bathroom. She threw back the covers and slipped into her bathrobe. She felt muggy and wet, slimy all over. She hurried across to his compartment and found what she wanted in less than a minute. His gun, tucked in among his clothes in the top drawer. It was a small revolver, requiring only that she cock the hammer and pull the trigger. Yes, it was loaded. With her thumb she cocked back the hammer and sent a bullet through the floor.

He burst into the room. She had cocked it again and now had it pointed at his belly. He tried to smile, but one look in her eyes froze it on his face. Her hand trembled. Her finger twitched on the trigger. For a full minute they stood like that, separated by the width of the room. Then, so slowly that she couldn't be sure he had moved, he began to ease toward her.

"Anna . . . give me the gun."

"No!" She thrust the barrel toward him, still trembling, her finger touching the cold steel trigger.

Uncertainty spread across his face. "Anna . . . that gun has a hair trigger. It's nothing to fool with. Now come on." He took another step. "My God, Anna, you couldn't shoot me."

The gun wavered. Tears had come, blurring her vision. If he had moved then he would have had her, for she was blind. He had won again. She couldn't shoot, couldn't even shoot him. In that instant he must have seen it too. He leaped toward her, but before he could touch her, she had turned the gun up at her own head.

"Anna!"

His scream was the last thing she heard. Her finger twitched, then tightened as she squeezed the trigger.

CHAPTER
SEVEN

It was a big story in Denver. All four papers carried it on their front pages. If Harry Tammen had been alive, it would have been blazed across the front of the *Denver Post* in blood-red type. Strangely, Bonfils exercised rare taste. It ran across eight columns of Page One, in black type. There was no red ink anywhere on the front page that day.

All the papers gave the official police version of what had happened on the train. The woman, Anna Waldo, thirty-one years old, had put a gun to her head and shot herself. She had lingered in a coma for two days while the train zigzagged across the plains of western Nebraska and Wyoming. Still unexplained were the strange actions of William Brown, who had ordered the engineer to reverse himself several times in an apparently meaningless journey to nowhere. Once, at a water stop, the engineer reported hearing Brown's voice, pleading with the woman to marry him. Marry him and he'd take her home, get her the help she needed. The man remembered those precise words, but if Mrs. Waldo had answered, it had been too faint to hear. In Denver she had been rushed to a nearby hospital, where she was pronounced in very grave condition. It had taken her a long time to die.

It was officially a Nebraska case, but when Willie Brown returned to Omaha for his preliminary hearing, reporters and photographers from all four Denver dailies followed him up. They heard him tell the judge that Mrs. Waldo had never gotten over their childhood romance, which had produced one child. The child had been raised as her brother. Brown said he had given the woman a job, and had taken her to dine with the President. They had resumed their affair, and she wanted to end her marriage to David Waldo and marry him. The hearing ended, the case was continued, and still no one knew how the car had come to be uncoupled from the rest of the train and left alone in Nebraska.

Willie Brown came home from Omaha, stepped down into Union Station, and was greeted by a small group of his people. As he passed through the tiny crowd, he came face-to-face with David Waldo. David Waldo raised his hand and a woman screamed. In his hand was a pistol, bought in a Larimer Street pawnshop the night before. He shot Willie Brown once between the eyes, then dropped the gun and vanished into the throng of stunned people.

An hour later police arrested David Waldo at his home on Osceola Street. He was sitting in his living room, staring into a cold fireplace. He offered no resistance, and was taken at once to the city jail, where he was booked for murder. The arresting officer was Lieutenant Virgil Joseph Moran.

End of Book Two

BOOK THREE

BOOK
OF
MARVEL

CHAPTER
ONE

1

They call this skid row: a ten-block area of lower downtown, where fifty-year-old flophouses that had once been grand hotels stood crumbling in the sun. In newspaper lingo, the lowers. You can find the same street in Chicago or San Francisco, the liquor stores with plate windows barred against the night, the fifty-cent rooms, the pawnshops, the whorehouses. Here, men fought for the food they ate, for the cheap wine they drank, for the right to sleep out of the snow, on a roach-infested piece of floor that someone else had paid for. They came to Denver under trains, riding the rods in during the warm months of July and August. They camped in tree groves near the railroad yards, leaving behind piles of bottles and bean cans. Some of them left with the first snow. Those who stayed looked for shelter inside, in the hotels along the lowers. They camped under dark staircases, sat through the night four-deep in shower stalls, flopped

354

and slept wherever there was a bare space. There were men who would kill for a bottle of watered whiskey.

It was a savage place, a place where a whore walking alone was fair game, not for her flesh but for what she had in her purse. Where glass is broken in the night and men scuffle in a deadly dance behind a neighborhood bar. Where the answer is quick and the scream is brief, as though life itself isn't worth the effort.

A savage world, the world of the lowers. The new world of Tom Hastings.

People called him Hasty down here. He sat alone in the dark, the bottle clutched tight in his fist. It was still half-full, the first good whiskey he had had in a week. Between then and now there had been plenty of bad. He knew some of it had been made with denatured alcohol. After a while you reached the point where, just by putting a drop on your tongue, you could tell good whiskey from bad. Little it mattered: You always drank it anyway, and hoped tomorrow's would be better. In the old days he had heard some bad stories of whiskey poisoning, and was almost afraid to drink out of any bottle without a label. People said you could go blind. There were newspaper stories of whole parties being poisoned on bootleg gin. Now he drank anything that had even the suggestion of alcohol. After that first greedy gulp, it didn't matter what it was. If it was good whiskey, you appreciated it all the more. If it was bad, as the old saying about sex went, it was still pretty good.

He was staying at the Silvercliff, a ramshackle place in the heart of the lowers. It was owned by a Japanese–Hawaiian family named Taketa, and was managed by the eldest son, Jon. Taketa had been his best source of human interest material when he'd been covering the lowers for the *Post* years ago. Taketa ran a store across from the Silvercliff, which had decayed year by year until it was now the city's worst flophouse. The Silvercliff had gotten so bad that even Taketa didn't go there. He had given Tom an old army cot and permission to use one of the rooms, and in return Tom collected his weekly rents. Three dollars a week, payable in advance. He dunned those who paid late, threw out those who didn't pay at all. Once a room was bought and paid for, what they did with it was none of his business. They could sleep twelve to a room for all he cared, as long as somebody was responsible for the rent next Friday. He knew Taketa didn't care either. Two or three times a week, to help keep him on his feet, Taketa gave him a dinner of old bread and thin stew.

Taketa liked to drink too. He was lively as hell for a Jap. Tom had never met an Oriental quite like Taketa. Usually they were such solemn bastards. But Taketa was cheerful and full of interesting talk. He had a fierce loyalty to his family. Talking about it made Tom think of *his* family. He looked at Taketa's telephone and thought about trying the old man's estate, just to see if they were there. He thought about Golden, and the night Paul had gotten Havana on his wireless, and he'd think, *Jesus, I really should call, let the kids at least know their old man's alive.* He would do that. Pull himself together, starting tomorrow morning. Wash up and go back to Capitol Hill, see if Georgeann had saved any of his things. Put on some clothes and catch the trolley for west Denver. Eat dinner tomorrow night with Anna and David. Take a week and dry out, never touch another goddamn drop as long as he lived. When he felt good about himself again, he'd put on his best coat and hat, tie his tie, slip into his good boots, and take himself a little walk downtown. Confidence was what counted in this game. Walk into the *Post* and give Bonfils one chance to hire him back, and if he didn't know a good thing when it walked right up to him, so be it. There were three other papers in this town, and half a dozen press agencies. But that afternoon he'd seen Malloy, passing the alley behind the hotel, and he knew it wasn't that simple. And now, looking up at Taketa's smiling face, he said, "Christ, Jon, I really need a drink." And Taketa poured generously from his bottle of good Canadian bourbon, because it had been a good day for him. His daughter had gotten married off and was off his hands forever. When Tom left, Taketa gave him the bottle.

He had been sitting on the floor of his room, nursing it for two hours.

He heard a noise outside his door, the sound of several men walking. Whoever it was had stopped just outside his door. His groping fingers found the cork, pushed it into the bottle, and tucked the bottle behind him in a corner. He felt around on the floor until he found his stick.

It was heavy, cut from a green elm tree. He always slept with it close by and had never had to use it. For perhaps a minute he heard nothing. Then came a soft knock on his door. He didn't move, hardly breathed. Again the knock, this time louder. One man spoke in Spanish and the doorknob turned. He heard the click of a tool, a jimmy against wood, and he got to his feet slowly as the wood split and the door swung in.

Three of them stood in the dim hallway. He had never seen any of them. The one nearest the door peered in, then moved inside.

"That's far enough, pilgrim," Tom said.

"Just a little whiskey, friend." The voice had a soft texture, lulling, and a slight Mexican accent. The three of them came in and began to fan out in the dark.

"I said that's far enough."

"Just a drink from your bottle. One drink and we'll go away."

"Not too likely, Mexican."

It was over in less than a minute. The three men backed him into the corner. The bottle crouched between his legs like a frightened child. He heard the snap of a switchblade, saw the gleam, and met the man as he lunged. He swung the stick at the black face, feeling the crunch as it smashed the nose flat. The man dropped at his feet and Tom finished him off with a kick in the ribs. It was like letting the air out of a balloon.

The others hung back, suddenly wary. Tom pushed the fallen one with his foot. "Get him out of here. Come on, pick him up before I give you a taste of it too. Next time watch whose room you break into."

They were gone. He went to the door and tried to fasten it shut, but the wood was split and it hung open limply. He went back to the corner for his bottle, sat there, dropped his stick, drew the cork, and took a long drink. He felt good. He was still a fighter, still had some of the old juice left. The teachings of Shaughnessy were still with him. He had met three of them head-on and had sent them crawling back to the gutter.

He could still do things. He could still go home. He could walk out of here, tomorrow if he wanted to. Any time. He still had the stuff. Any time at all.

Sometime during the night he got up. His spleen felt raw, ready to burst. He used his stick as a crutch and staggered down the hall toward the bathroom. Six or eight drunks were always sleeping there, huddled together on the floor, or in a shower stall that hadn't been used for showers in so long its walls were caked with mud. He pulled at the door, and as it opened a thin hand grabbed his shirt. He was jerked into the bathroom, got a quick glimpse of black eyes and olive skin, a face with a pencil-point moustache, then the door slammed behind him, sealing him in darkness. He felt the knife slice through his shirt, felt the bite as the blade slipped in. The man twisted the blade and ripped it up, and Tom felt the sticky wetness on his shirt. The hands grabbed him again and pushed him against the wall. He sank slowly to the floor.

"Die, gringo sonovabitch."

They left him there. He groaned and stretched out. His whole side had been ripped open, and a large slab of flesh hung there against him. He couldn't see, couldn't reach the hall, couldn't possibly make it down the stairs to the street. All he could do was pack the wound and hope to stop the blood until someone came by. Someone who might care enough to call the cops.

He found a scrap of rag, a scrap of paper. He felt across the floor and found a foot. He pulled closer, worked up the man's body until he reached the shirt. He tore at it until he had pulled off a piece. Then he packed it into the wound, rolled over and lay on it, hoping the pressure would stop the blood. It might be days before Taketa would cross the street to see what had happened to him.

He closed his eyes. Daylight came and he was aware of the men getting up around him. Shadows moved over him, out the door into the hall. Sunlight poured in through the tiny window above the toilet. The door opened and in the hallway he saw a pair of feet. Women's shoes, silk stockings. He looked up. When he saw who it was, he knew for sure that he had died and gone to hell.

2

She had been looking for him for months. Several times a week she came out at first light, sifting through the lowers for an hour before work. The night the *Post* hit the streets with the story of his sister's death, Marvel hit the streets too. She walked the lowers and went into dim hotels where vagrants watched her with hungry eyes. She walked through the Silvercliff, stopped people in halls, asked questions. No one knew anything. At least they weren't telling her.

She had been assigned to cover the Brown-Waldo case on an ongoing basis, to dig beneath what police said and sift out the facts. Everyone in town knew Brown was lying: the only question left was how much the court would let him get away with. The fine details of that train ride still lay hidden, bringing up a dark stench that only a newspaperman could smell. So they passed it to Marvel. Her heart wasn't in it, but she was on the train to Omaha with that contingent of Denver press when Willie Brown had his first day in court.

Willie Brown left immediately after the hearing, brushing past the press with a grim "No comment," and no one had been able to get near him. She went to his hotel and was kept away by two bodyguards. Everywhere he went he was escorted by police. The trip home was a nightmare: unseasonably hot and stuffy; the train had run out of ice two hours out of Denver. Brown rode home in his private car (the death car, the reporters called it) and he arrived in Denver at least two hours ahead of the train bearing the press. He was promptly gunned down by the victim's husband, and the whole mess leaped onto page one again.

The morning after the Brown shooting, the *News* had it all, in a blazing front-page display with three action pictures as its centerpiece. Above the story was the 72-point headline BROWN GUNNED DOWN AT UNION STATION. Beneath it, in the style of the time, a series of rapidly diminishing subheads. DIES AT ONCE OF BULLET IN BRAIN.

HUSBAND OF MRS. WALDO ARRESTED AT WEST DENVER HOME. ANAR-
CHIST GIVES UP WITHOUT A STRUGGLE. CONFESSES AND WILL PLEAD
GUILTY. But with those pictures, you didn't need words. In a break
photographers wait a lifetime for, the *News* man had been taking
Brown's picture at the precise instant when David Waldo rose out of
the crowd to confront him. The first picture showed Brown's reaction:
terror, raw and gut-deep. The middle picture showed Willie Brown,
already dead, toppling backward, hands over his face. The third shot
showed both Brown, crumpled in a heap, and David Waldo, walking
calmly away. Inside was more art: police arresting Waldo on Osceola
Street, and a long shot of Waldo being removed from the police car at
city jail. All things considered, a hell of a piece of journalism. The
story ran under the joint by-line of two police reporters; she had been
miles away on the press train. She didn't care. Could it be that she
was losing her taste for limelight? The job didn't seem to matter as
much as it once did, and beats had become hollow, temporary
victories, gone in a day. Could this be the beginning of what *he* had
felt, as he sank into his big slump? Were there really only two
alternatives in this game? Were you either a fire-eater, hated by the
mob, or a mindless dolt who took the pablum, stirred it around, and
fed it to your readers with a baby spoon? In her own case, she knew,
there was another factor. She now had something outside the
business competing for her attention. She had the search.

Two months had passed since his sister's death, and he had not
turned up. She made periodic checks with his mother, but they
hadn't heard from him either. She covered David Waldo's trial,
freeing the court reporter for the routine. It wasn't much of a trial,
didn't take much of her time. Waldo pleaded guilty. His voice was flat
and even as he said the word. And District Judge Rube Henry,
appointed to the bench just this year by the new governor of Colorado,
had cleared his throat and calmly read the sentence. Death by
hanging, to be carried out by the warden of the Colorado State
Penitentiary, sometime during the week of June eighth.

It was less than three weeks away. Rube Henry, the old redneck
from the south, had hung his first man as a District Court judge.

They shackled David Waldo and led him away. He looked at her as
he came past, and she saw him smile. His eyes were old and tired,
and she thought she saw relief there. Here was a man who wanted to
die, who had seen too much of life and was ready for something else.
She went home that night and brooded over a cold pork chop.

In the morning she started the search again. Now she had a new
angle; something so obvious that she cursed herself for not thinking
of it sooner. Malloy had given it to her that first day, in the restaurant
on Seventeenth Street, and she'd been too blind to see it. *Those men*

will kill each other for a drink. It's their lifeblood. She called city desk and reported in sick. Then she dressed and went to the *Post* morgue, where a dollar brought her a copy of his mugshot. She hit the lowers again, stopping people on the street. Many had seen him. They knew him as Hasty. She told them she had ten dollars for the man who found him. Finally a half-dead bum, speaking a brogue she only half understood, led her to the Silvercliff Hotel, along the upper corridor to the bathroom at the end. She looked inside and almost passed out from the stench.

3

The first night he slept in her bed, while she took the roll-away in the living room. She had passed him off as a brother, down on his luck, to the doctor who had come to sew up his wound. The doctor prescribed red meat and pills, which she ordered by telephone. He insisted on complete bedrest for a week, and a program of sound nutrition to ward off the effects of too much bad whiskey. She started him on a cup of thick beef soup. He was still too weak to sit up, so she propped pillows around him and spoon-fed him. He had still not spoken, but his eyes followed her constantly, with looks of doubt and disbelief.

She didn't care whether he talked or not. When the doctor left, she put the light out and sat beside him until he was asleep. She sat there and listened to his heavy breathing. She was mixed up with conflicting feelings. *How can I tell him what he means to me?* How could she tell herself? She honestly wasn't sure. At that moment she felt a whole range of emotions: disgust, revulsion, pity, affection. Hostility. Respect. All were woven through her in apparently equal doses. She could call any of those emotions to the surface just by thinking of whatever it was about him that made her feel them. He was a drunk. She had hated drunks since those dim days with her father on the farm. It was perhaps her strongest emotion: that, and an esteem of powerful writing that was almost reverence. Here he was, representing both elements. She could forget all his drunkenness if he would just sit up on the bed and write her something. One small piece, as powerful as the yellowing Mary Wolfe clipping, which she still kept pressed away between the pages of a book. If he would do that for her, and tell her it was hers, she might make a career of pulling him out of bars and tacky hotels.

Looking at him now, she had to realize that he might never write anything again. Beneath the beard his cheeks were sunken and

360

hollow. His temples were gray. He looked ten years older than the last time she'd seen him. Maybe it was true, maybe people did lose their stuff. She knew from experience that alcohol brought on brain rot. It had done that to her father, made him something weak and subhuman.

It had taken an artist to do what Tom had done with Mary Wolfe. Tell the story in the most objective way possible, subjectively, from every viewpoint. Write it like a piece of fiction, a short story of a dozen conflicting characters. Only these characters were real, their names written in the police record, their tragedy splashed across every front page. Somehow, in his relentless probing, he had even managed to make her feel sorry for the killer. Hate and compassion, so neatly blended that, predictably, the editors didn't understand it. They had played his piece inside, using the dry report of a beat man on page one. Later they understood, when everyone told them how great it had been. When wires picked it up verbatim and carried it coast-to-coast. When four years later Will Rogers mentioned it in his *New York Times* column, calling it a classic. *Oh, my friend, if the stupid Pulitzer committee had been around then, how different your life might be today.* But no, they'd probably have missed it too.

Prizes in themselves meant little. They gave the writer freedom from editorial oppression, but usually too late. By the time the prizes came, the slender thread was broken. It hurt her to admit it, but the thing about him that mattered most to her might be gone now. Perhaps he couldn't have written the Mary Wolfe piece in any other year but that one.

4

His eyes were open, fixed on her. She had been dreaming of the Locke papers, only in her dream things had worked out differently. She had baited him, teased him, and then at the last moment she'd given him the file and let him write it while his juices were flowing. The *Post* had printed it; it had made a national splash. Just like Mary Wolfe. She had fallen asleep in the chair, watching over him, sometime in the early morning.

His eyes were clear, but the flesh around them was red and tired. His cheeks, so hollow and gaunt last night, now looked swollen, as if he'd taken a beating along with the knifing. His first words were half-muffled, like a man eating cotton. "I need a drink," he said. She felt his head with the back of her hand. He told her again that he needed a drink. She went into the kitchen and put on some bacon. When she came back to the bedroom, he had turned on his side and was looking at the window.

"Please," he said. "Turn it off. Whatever it is, whatever you're cooking. You must be trying to make me puke."

"Not much danger of that. You've hardly got anything inside you to throw up." She sat on the bed, facing him. "I'll take my chances."

"Look, I really do need a drink."

"I'm sorry. I never keep any."

His face became hostile. "Sorry," he said with contempt. "You're not sorry. Lying bitch. Lying goddamn bitch."

"It's just a half-lie. I'm sorry you feel bad. I wish I had something that would help you."

"Only one thing helps me. Jesus Christ, my head."

They stayed still for a minute, watching the blue sky beyond the window.

"How'd you find me?"

"It wasn't easy. Sometime I'll tell you."

"Why'd you bother? Never mind, I think I know. Your victory is complete, as you can damn well see."

"It's not my victory. Is that what you think of me?"

"Miss, these days I try not to think of you at all. I try not to think of any of that old stuff. The goddamn world and all its booby traps. Who needs it?"

If you only knew, she thought. The biggest booby traps are just ahead. Maybe he did know. If he didn't, he was in for a shock.

"All those months," she said. "Did you keep in touch with people?"

"What people?"

"Your family."

He didn't say anything. She went to the window and drew the curtains all the way back, letting the sunlight flood across the room. She turned and faced him, and tried to tell him then. But the words wouldn't come. "Tell me what it was like, dropping out of the world," she said lightly. "Did you ever see any newspapers?"

"Are you kidding? I'll tell you something. I didn't miss newspapers one goddamn bit. If all the newspapers in this country closed up tomorrow, that'd be fine with me."

They looked at each other.

She said. "There are some things I have to tell you."

"What things?"

She took a deep breath, and sat beside him again. Good things first. "First of all, you have a job offer. I talked with Sidney Whipple at the *Express* last week. He'd take you on anytime you wanted to walk in and see him."

362

"That's a pretty small paper."

"Maybe."

"But beggars can't be choosers, right?"

"It's a good paper. For my money, the best in town. Whipple's the only editor in town who's taken this Klan stuff seriously. He's got one man covering the Klan full-time and could use another. I don't know about you, but I find that kind of challenging."

"Then *you* go to work for him."

"He didn't offer me a job. But he remembers you, some of the stuff you did at the *Post*. The Mary Wolfe—"

"Sure, everybody remembers the goddamn Mary Wolfe piece. I could make a career rewriting that one story."

"Whipple's also interested in your Klan stuff."

"All right, I'll think about it. What else? You said there was more?"

The silence stretched between them. At last he said, "My father. That's it. Sammy's dead."

"Yes."

"Oh, boy." He covered his face with his hand, then let his fingers run up through his hair. "How long?"

"I don't know exactly. Some months now."

"That's just great. I bet my mom thinks I'm swell."

She let him lie there, absorbing it. It all had to come now; there could be no dribbling it out to him in tiny doses. He had to have it all, to get past it if he could. "There's more yet," she said.

His eyes met hers and she began to tell him. Slowly, while she was talking, his eyes grew dull and his face went numb. It was like a gaslight being slowly turned off.

When he spoke again, his voice too had died; the tones were flat and without life. "Tell Whipple I just don't care anymore, would you tell him that for me? Everybody I know is either gone away or dead."

She reached out to him, to touch his hand, but he drew away. "You have more to live for than you think, my friend. You still have a wife and children. A mother. A brother. And your brother-in-law."

"Not David. Not for long."

You think about it. Think about the living, Tom, and when I get back we'll talk about it."

She walked out and left him there with all the elements of his own destruction. It was a three-story drop from her window into a stone courtyard. Her razor lay open on the bathroom sink. In the kitchen a few feet away was the stove, and gas. She had left it all so open, so obvious; so clear, she hoped, that she was betting on him.

She went to the Roman Catholic Cathedral at Colfax and Logan. The priest talked about the sins of the flesh, but she barely heard him. Afterward, she hurried home nervously. His bed was empty. She called his name, but there was no answer. She went into the kitchen and heard the sound of water running in the bathroom. She knocked on the door.

When he opened it, she saw that he had bathed and shaved. He wore only his dirty, matted pants.

"I'll need some clothes," he said. "Maybe a little cash."

"It's Sunday, but I'll see what I can do." She put on her hat and moved to the door.

"I'll pay you back."

"I know you will."

"And the money won't go for booze. I promise you that. I'm finished with all that."

"I'm glad."

She opened the door, but stopped as he said her name. "Marvel," he said. It was the first time he had said it. She tried to smile at him, but they both choked up, and he closed the bathroom door between them. She thought his face in those few seconds was the saddest face she had ever seen.

CHAPTER
TWO

1

He slept in her bed again, and in the morning she changed the
dressing on his wound. She called in sick again, fixed his breakfast,
remade the bed. They didn't talk yet about David. He seemed to be
handling things one at a time. His side was stiff and crusted over, but
he insisted on moving. Lying there on his back, he said, was driving
him crazy.

They walked to the lot where he had left his Model T. She called a
wrecker and had the car towed to a neighborhood garage, where two
tires were replaced and a battery installed. She paid the bill. By noon
they were rolling across the viaduct into west Denver. She didn't push
him, just sat with him and let him find his own way back. They were
in his old neighborhood now, and he still had a few shocks coming.
The building where Sammy Kohl's store had been was his first. It was
boarded up tight, and the NO TRESPASSING sign hung by one nail. He

365

just stared at it as they went past. A few blocks away, they came to the burned remains of David Waldo's print shop. He stopped across the street and looked at it for a long time. He asked her what had happened and she told him as much as she knew.

They pushed on into Osceola Street, and the last of his little shocks. He parked on the dirt street, across from the house, and knew at once that it was empty. A sign stuck into the front lawn said FOR SALE, and had the bank's name printed beneath it. The house had a look of desperation about it, as if its people had taken flight suddenly and without warning. The trim still stood out sharply in the noonday sun, but the windows had been broken, and glass was scattered across the porch, down the front steps, and into the street. He got out, crossed the street, climbed the steps. The front door stood open and he went into what had been the living room. It looked different. Ashes from the fireplace were scattered across the front-room floor. There were signs of hobos: wadded papers, a few beer cans, stains on the brick where the dirty bastards had stood and pissed against the fireplace. He visited each room in its turn, knowing he would never stand inside this house again. He was closing a book of his life.

He went into the room Teresa and Sammy had shared for twenty-five years. Into the bathroom with its hideaway staircase to the attic. Into Anna's room. He walked across the threshold slowly, and stood for a moment like an intruder. In her closet he found the framed picture of Aimee Semple McPherson, virtually untouched, and a few pieces of paper from her scrapbook. He left them there. They were cuttings of an incident he didn't understand, and they meant nothing to him. Stories from the *Post* about some woman he'd never heard of, a Mrs. Reynolds, who had died of heart failure eighteeen years ago.

He drove away without looking back. Beside him, Marvel said, "You've come through the worst of it now. I think it's uphill from here."

They were on Speer Boulevard, headed southeast. He had been heading toward Gregory Clement's estate. But at Colorado Boulevard he turned north. He had other business now, other things to clear up. "My mom and brother," he said. "My sister's kid. Do you know where they are?"

"You're going the right way. Just keep driving, I'll direct you."

2

The road led straight out of Denver to the north. The car overheated, and they had to stop at a gas station for water. He wondered what his mother was doing in the country. They had gone more than ten miles, and were up in the endless stretches of farmland near Brighton. Near Henderson, she pointed to a tree-lined road, and he stopped outside it, unable for a moment to understand where he was. "The poor farm," he said at last.

He jerked the car into gear and raced along the dirt road. Soon they came to a cluster of buildings, some barracks-style with screened and unscreened porches. Beyond the buildings lay another hundred acres of plowed fields.

They found the office and again she waited while he went in. A girl told him that Mrs. Teresa Hastings Kohl could be found in a wooden building straight ahead. "I'll have to ask somebody to go in and tell her you're here."

"Can't I just go in?"

She shook her head. "It's the TB ward."

He waited on the porch while a young man went in for Teresa. The man came back and told him that his mother was dressing and would be out shortly. It must have been ten minutes later when she came. Suddenly she was old. She had brushed her hair back but now the breeze caught it and swirled it around her face. Tears stood out on her face as if they'd been painted there. She tried to talk, but coughed instead. He went to her and she hugged him around his neck. "Everything's fine now," she said. "Now I've got both my boys back."

She didn't ask where he'd been. For a while they didn't say anything. She held his hands and they sat on chairs side by side in the breeze.

"Where's Abe?"

"He's over in another building. Over that way."

He looked toward the cluster of buildings but couldn't see them. For a moment he couldn't see anything beyond his own arm. He dried his eyes on his sleeve and said, "This is my fault. It's all my fault."

"Sometimes things happen," Teresa said. "If you've got to blame somebody, blame the Klan. They started out to break us and they did it."

"They wouldn't have if I'd been more of a man."

"That kind of talk gets you nothing. What's past is gone. It's what happens now that counts."

"I would have come back sooner. If I'd just known what was happening. I only heard yesterday about Anna."

Teresa looked him in the eye and said, "I don't let anybody talk to me about that. We have to look ahead."

"I'll get you out of here. You've got my word on that."

"This place is okay. Really, it's not half-bad. We could be worse off back in the city. Look around you. We got shade trees and the food's not bad. There's a doctor who tries to help Abe. That can't be all bad, can it? Nothing hurts us anymore, except maybe our pride. But you get older, and you learn how little that means."

"It means a lot to me."

She touched his hair. He gripped her hand in both of his.

"Ma, wouldn't you like it to be like it was?"

"It can't."

"I know, not exactly. I mean living in a house of your own with a fence and a garden. A garden out back. Maybe a swing under the trees. Someplace where you can sit and swing. Feel the breeze, watch the sailboats on the lake."

"I've got all that here, except the lake, and I don't miss that any. Tell you the truth, son, the old neighborhood was getting me down. It never was the same after the Howes left. And the Klan every weekend. I don't think I could live with that again."

"We'll find us another neighborhood."

"If that's what you want, then it's what I want too. You keep dreaming about it. That's what dreams are for, young people like you."

He asked her about Gabriel.

"That poor child, God only knows where he is now. Last time I saw him was the day police came for David. He's probably living on the street, with that gang of kids. I pray for him every night, and still it don't give me no peace. I can't tell you what this thing's done to him. If there's one thing I'd like . . ."

"I'll find him for you."

"Yes, promise me that. There's something you can do for me. Bring him here so I can talk to him."

"I promise."

"And Thomas?"

"Yeah, Ma?"

"Don't take too long."

They sat there for a time, the old lady in the chair, the man on the floor at her feet. After a while he said, "Maybe I'd better go over and see Abe."

"That would be nice. Tell him I'll be over in a while."

He got to his feet and went to the edge of the porch.

"Take it easy with Abe, son," Teresa said. "He don't talk much these days. Don't press him too hard. If he don't feel like talking, just sit with him and you talk. Don't ask him a lot of questions."

He nodded.

"See if you can cheer him up. Whatever you do, don't talk about the old days. Abe's not strong like you and me. You've got to remember that. One more thing, and maybe it'll help you understand Abe a little better. He got a letter last week from Julia. They settled in Idaho, a little town forty miles from Twin Falls. Imagine that, Jacob Howe with his feeling about cars, driving all that way. It's a farm community, lots of horses and mules yet, lots of harnesses to mend. Jacob's business has been good. The people are nice folk. And there's no Klan."

"I'm glad Jacob found what he wanted."

"Peace and quiet, son, same things we all want. Just to be left alone to raise our kids and live our lives. If I was younger and healthier, I'd go to Idaho myself. It sounds like heaven on this earth."

"People make places sound better than they are, Ma. Places are the same all over."

"It was the right move for the Howes. Right in a lot of ways." She was quiet for a long time, then she said, "Julia got married. Late last year, at Christmastime. Her letter was kind, and it was the only honest thing she could do. She'd been putting it off and putting it off. It's a lovely letter, Thomas, kind of a fond farewell to all of us. That's better than having him sit there at that window, always waiting for the time when she might come back. Now he knows, she won't be coming back. He'll have to live with it, go on with life. In the long run it was a kind letter."

"You always did like Julia."

"I understand her better now. She's not like you and me, not as strong as we are. She couldn't be expected to live out her life with a cripple. What happened to Abe wasn't her fault, and she tried hard all those years after the war. Nobody could have done more for him than she did. The trouble was somewhere inside Abe himself. He came back changed. He lived for the times when Julia would come, then he smothered her. Wanted her there with him twenty-four hours a day. No girl could handle that, especially a lovely young thing like Julia. Did I tell you, she's expecting her first child this summer. She'll call him Abraham."

"Please, Ma. No more about Julia, okay?"

"I just wanted you to understand. Abe's ours by blood, and so is Gabriel. They're partly your responsibility now. You didn't ask for it, but you might say you inherited it. God knows it's the only thing you'll inherit. A pretty sad legacy from the Kohls to you, but there it is. You're the last one left now. It's up to you. If you want to turn your back on it, you can walk out of here and go back wherever you've been all these months. I won't blame you if you do."

He found Abe sitting alone in a great empty room, four buildings down. He sat in his wheelchair, outlined in the sunlight of a window in the far wall. Tom crossed the room, and the hollow echo of his footsteps bounced off the walls. Tom drew up a chair on Abe's blind side and they sat there without talking. Abe's eyepatch was off, lying in his lap near a handwritten paper that must have been Julia's letter. The empty socket was riveted to Tom's face, accusing more viciously than the most ruthless eye. Abe made no attempt to cover it. His hair was totally gone in front now, his hands trembled, and he needed a shave. Tom sat with him for a long time, perhaps fifteen minutes, and in all that time nothing brotherly passed between them. By the time he got back to the car his shirt was damp and his own hands were shaking. He asked Marvel to drive, but finally he couldn't even turn the crank. A handyman passing by cranked it for them. He felt like he'd lived a lifetime in an hour. All he wanted now was a drink and a cool place to lie down.

3

The only drink he got was a pitcher of iced tea, which she stirred up for dinner. All the time he was drinking it, he thought of booze.

They talked into the night. She had an uncanny sense of priorities: what should come first, what to do next, and next, and after that. She kept him busy throughout the evening. First she gave him her clips of David's arrest and trial. It hadn't been much of a trial: a guilty plea and, a few weeks later, a sentence. He was amazed that Rube Henry was now a District Court judge, and had been allowed to preside at David's trial. He wondered if the judge still had the scars on his hand, where Marvel had stuck him with her hatpin.

David's lawyer had been appointed by the court. His name was Walter Jakes. Tom had never heard of him, but the name had a haunting familiarity, as though he should have. Jakes hadn't put on any defense. His client had done it, shot Willie Brown through the head in view of two dozen witnesses and a *Rocky Mountain News* photographer. The only thing to do was make the plea and hope for the mercy of the court. And as he had finished the clips, darkness had come to Denver and he could hear Marvel setting the table in the

kitchen. She had cooked a steak, smothered in onions and surrounded by potatoes. More iced tea to drink, apple pie for dessert. He
had forgotten how good food like that could be. They sat at the
window and looked into the alley behind her apartment building, and
she let him eat in peace. They ate by candlelight. He was digesting
the trial along with his food, and after supper she made him start on
the lawbook she had borrowed from the *News* editorial department.
Then came their first brainstorming session, over pie and coffee. She
said, "It's a strange law, don't you think?"

"You mean the secrecy bit."

"Yeah, don't you think that's strange?"

"I don't know." He looked up at her. "I'm sorry. I've got a thing
about executions."

"Well, look at it again. The warden is the one who decides exactly
when a prisoner is hung. All the court says is that it's to be sometime
the week of June eighth. It's the warden's baby after that, and it's
done in absolute secrecy, without any press or public."

"All right, what are you getting at?"

"I don't think we can figure on anything later than sunrise on the
eighth, do you? They'll want to get it over with. I think they'll do it
right away."

"What's today?"

"May 25."

"Two weeks from today, then."

"Unless we can get it stayed."

"Do you have any ideas?"

"A few. My problem is I don't understand all the laws. Appealing to
the court is an obvious waste of time. A plea to the governor is out. It
looks to me like the only chance is an appeal to the State Supreme
Court. Try to offer evidence that the trial was improper. What if we
could prove that both Judge Rube Henry and Walter Jakes are
members of the Ku Klux Klan?"

"The judge . . ."

"And the defense lawyer. It might not be enough," she said. "The
Klan would have to become an issue in the trial. We'd have to link
Brown in too."

"He's in. I remember his name from the Locke file."

"You're sure?"

"Absolutely. Brown and I go back to childhood. His name was the
first one I saw. And I remember seeing Henry's too."

"And I'm pretty sure I remember Jakes. It still might not be
enough. Just because the three are in the Klan doesn't automatically
mean a conspiracy."

"What else could it mean?"

"I'm just telling you what the court might say. Maybe we don't have to prove a conspiracy to get it stayed, maybe just the possibility of one. I don't know. Damn, I wish I knew more law."

"It would help if you did. Those bastards on the Supreme Court are pretty arbitrary in what they hear."

"I know it. That's what's scary. I covered a murder trial here last year. Lawyer was convinced his client was innocent, but there was no way they were going to let him off. I've never forgotten what he said to me the night that boy died. Some terrible things have been done in this state in the name of justice. That's what he said. It's something you remember at a time like this."

"It doesn't help much. You got any more ideas?"

"Well, what if we got a jury roster?"

"What jury? I thought he gave a plea?"

"There was a jury list for this trial. There was a list drawn up, and people waiting to be called from it. If we could get it and check the names against the Locke papers . . ." She let the thought trail away, and looked at him over the candle's flame. "You do still have them?"

"The pictures? Last time I saw they were in my apartment on Gilpin Street. I had them all in that big cardboard box, pushed away in a corner. Everything was there, my notes, the pictures, Goodwin's negatives. I thought I'd never need them again."

"All right." She let it settle between them. "Tell me exactly what happened the night you decided to leave civilization."

"I didn't decide, it just happened. I'd lost my job. My wife and kids were gone. I'd been turned down for a job at the *News*. I guess I just drifted into it. Christ, I don't know how it happened. Don't look at me like that, I really don't."

"It might be important."

"You're asking me to remember something that happened months ago, in the middle of a drunk."

"Stop trying so hard to alibi and think."

"I went home from the *News*. I remember I'd just seen Eddie Day about a job. He wanted to hire me. In fact, I thought I had the job. I remember Eddie telling me how great I was, then he came in and said no dice. Somebody up front had killed it. I could tell from the way he talked. I was feeling mighty damned low. I went home and started drinking. Next thing I knew I was at Taketa's place."

"And you never went back to your apartment again?"

"Not as far as I know. When you're drunk, sometimes it's hard to tell."

"Yes, I know. What's the name of the man who owns the place?"

"Harvey Settle."

"Do you think he might have saved your things for you?"

"I doubt it. And anyway, he's in the Klan." .

"Oh, that's great."

"I guess anything's possible. He might have kept them in the storeroom in the basement."

"Did he know you're a reporter?"

"Sure. Once he tried to hustle me to join the Klan. Told me I'd be surprised to know how many of my friends were members."

"Then he'd have looked through your stuff. They don't miss chances like that."

"Yeah, then what?"

"Does your apartment have an incinerator?"

They stared at each other across the table. The flickering candle danced between them. Her eyes were grim, intense. He looked up, coming out of a thought, and sucked in his breath.

"You thought of something?" she said.

"Something else, yes. A very long shot." He looked out into the alley. "There was a maid there. We got to be . . . pretty close friends. She might have saved my stuff. Her name was Georgeann."

4

Tuesday morning. She called in sick again, had a third cup of coffee, and thought it through. He had given her a short list of lawyers' names, people he knew, people friends had told him about. Lawyers who had spoken against the Ku Klux Klan, no matter how long ago. She had added a few names of her own, and now typed up a final listing on her old Underwood in the bedroom.

She would begin with that, would spend her day interviewing them and checking them out. She had set a deadline in her mind, and the deadline for the lawyer was sunset tonight. By then they would have to have their lawyer, with no second guesses and no looking back. There simply wasn't time.

He would spend his morning chasing the box of photographs. They would meet for lunch, in a tiny café off the beaten paths, where they wouldn't be seen by anyone they knew. Quickly she gathered her notes and left him a note on the kitchen table. *Have to run, see you at noon.* She signed it *M*, clipped it to a ten-dollar bill, put it under a milk bottle, and slipped out of the apartment.

He was twenty minutes late for their lunch. She had ordered a sandwich and was eating it when he arrived. He came in looking haggard and dried out, a picture of defeat. She motioned to a waiter.

He gulped the water that the waiter brought him. "Nothing to eat, thanks."

"Bring him one of these," she said. "Without the cheese." The waiter moved away and she looked at him over the table. "Bad morning?"

"Frustrating as hell. I waited around the building hoping she'd come in. She's the maid there."

"So you said." She bullied him with her eyes.

"So the maid came and it wasn't her. This girl didn't even know her."

She shrugged. "Happens all the time. People move on. She should be easy to trace."

"That's just it. I know she's easy to trace, if I'd just use my goddamn head. I seem to have lost something up here."

"It's just stiff from lack of use. It'll come back."

"I don't seem to be able to anticipate stuff anymore. I can't seem to find those shortcuts."

"Would you please stop feeling sorry for yourself and tell me what happened? I'm sorry, but we just don't have the time."

"I chased Harvey Settle all damn morning. Nobody seemed to know who the hell he really was or where he worked."

"But you finally caught up with him."

"He's a vice president in one of the downtown department stores. Typical man on the way up. To hear everybody say it, a helluva guy. It's like he leads two lives."

"A lot of them do that. Go on."

"He got in the Chamber this year. Belongs to clubs, gives to charities, has a home in the southeast . . ."

"And runs a Capitol Hill whorehouse on the side. Look, I know the type. What I want to know is what he said."

"Said he didn't have any idea what happened to my stuff. The maids had orders to keep all belongings of derelict tenants downstairs for one month, then chuck it. He agreed to let me look downstairs, which I'll do first thing this afternoon. But don't hold your breath. This is the dumbest thing I've ever pulled."

The waiter brought his sandwich. He attacked it between gulps of water. "You won't believe this, but he hit me up for back rent, right there in his office. It was like Jekyll and Hyde. One minute he's a downtowner, neat and respectable, the next he's some Klan landlord dunning me for money. I had to give him the ten."

"Ah."

"I'm sorry. It'll teach you not to give me money. At least it didn't go for booze."

"All right, what about this, uh, maid? What's her name?"

"Settle doesn't know what happened to her. She got arrested about two months after I left and he hasn't seen her since."

She finished her own lunch, drank daintily from the water glass, and pushed her plate aside. "This girl. Did she like you?"

"I guess so."

"Well, was it anything special between you?"

"Why do you want to know that?"

"Come on, answer, I'm working on something. Look, I don't care what you did with her. Let me put it another way. If this girl *really* liked you, that's where you'll find your papers. If they still exist."

"You think so?"

"I only know what I'd do. If Settle ever had them, they're long gone now anyway. I think the girl's your best bet. So how about shifting gears this afternoon? I'll keep after the lawyers, you go after the girl. Get down to the cop shop, get the sheet on her, and find out what she was arrested for. See if you can track her through the sheet, get a line on her address that way."

"All right, I wasn't born yesterday. You don't have to draw me a goddamn blueprint. How'd you do?"

"I saw three people this morning. Two were zeros, the other wasn't interested. Two others wouldn't even talk to me when I told them what the case was. Nobody wants a case that's already been lost once, unless there's a lot of money up front, and everybody in town seems to be running for some kind of office. Damn lawyers." She pushed back her chair and got up. "Undaunted, I go forth again. See you tonight."

He hated the thought of going into the police station. The place was full of people he knew, and there would be talk and embarrassing questions. But he went straight to records without seeing anybody, and the girl behind the cage was new. He used his press card and got the sheet on Georgeann Johanssen, saw her last known address as an apartment house on Elm Street in Park Hill. He looked deeper into the record. She had been picked up soliciting near Fourteenth and York, in something that sounded very much like a police trap. It was her only arrest. The case had gone before Judge Rubin Henry of Denver District Court, and wasn't it a small world? She'd been found guilty, but Judge Henry had amended the charges to a misdemeanor, reduced the sentence, and granted probation, subject to her continued contact with the court and good behavior in the future.

Continued contact. The rotten old bastard, he could just imagine. Once a lecher . . .

Her house was of brick, perhaps thirty years old. He knocked, but no one came. He tried again, then sat on the steps to wait.

Shadows lengthened along the street. A block away, a trolley stopped on Seventeenth. Soon he saw a woman and two children trudging up from the trolley stop. She had had her hair cut. The little girl at her side was her daughter, no question of that, but the boy's looks were mixed, darker, as though the father had been Mexican or perhaps an Indian. They came slowly, and she didn't see him until she unhooked the gate and turned into the walk. She jumped back, momentarily startled, and in the purple light it took her a while to recognize him. She came closer. "Tomas?" That old friendly smile spread across her face and she made a tiny gesture with her hands. The children clutched shyly at her skirts, peeping out. They came closer, and he saw that the dress she wore was expensive, the bonnet gay and springlike. She looked prim and pretty. Every inch a lady.

She reached out to him. "My Godt! Where dit you go to?"

Her English had improved. He wondered if she had been taking lessons.

"Just dropped off the edge of the world for a while," he said. "You look good."

She smiled, but a nervousness had come over her. "I'm doing goot. Not like der oldt place."

He got to his feet, holding her hand. She still hadn't invited him in.

"Ve shouldt talk sometimes, Tomas. Not tonight. Something else tonight. You understand?"

"Sure, Georgeann."

"I talk goot English now. Ve couldt talk now too, instead of yust der utter." She laughed.

"Affairs of the heart."

She laughed again. "I remember."

"I know you've got things to do . . ."

"Yah, I be, how you say it, running late."

"I was wondering if you kept any of my stuff."

"Some tings. Few tings, not much. Stuff Mr. Settle trows in trash."

"Is it handy, where I could get at it?"

"Yah, sure. Tomorrow."

"Tonight, Georgeann."

"Tomas, please. No time ternight."

"It's important to me. Real important, Georgeann."

They went inside. A clock on the mantel showed six thirty. "Too much to do tonight, Tomas. Got ter vash, get in der tub, get der kids vashed and into bed."

"Just point me the right way, then make like I'm not even here."

She looked at the clock. "You got ter be gone by seven latest."

"I promise."

She led him to a narrow set of wooden steps that led down into the basement. "Most good stuff's gone. Mr. Settle sold all yer clothes. Took der typewriter."

The basement had no lights. She gave him a kerosene lantern and followed him down, pointing the way around old furniture and stacks of blankets. Finally she settled on a stack of boxes in the corner. "Some mine, some other peoples. Now please hurry, Tomas, please. Remember, seven o'clock."

He began unloading the boxes, piling them at random on the cement floor. He came to one he knew and opened it. It was full of papers, some typed, some in his handwriting, and on top was a paper that said *For Nell, who* . . . That presumptuous book dedication, as unfinished as the book itself, as sad to him now as an old love song. He put it aside, and moved on to the next one. He held his breath and opened the flap, and there it was. Harvey Settle had had it in his hands and had been too dumb to know it. He blessed Georgeann; she had won a place in his heart for all time. He put the box with the other one, then searched the pile through to the floor. That was all of it: one man's life wrapped up in two cardboard boxes. Two men's lives. Yes, he had almost forgotten that David's life was in there too.

He held the lantern in his teeth, gathered up the boxes in both arms, and struggled up the stairs. He heard water splashing and the muffled cries of a child. Georgeann's voice, soft and soothing, came to him through the open bathroom door. He wanted to go in and put his arms around her neck one last time. But the clock showed him that he had already broken his promise: it was a quarter after seven. Outside a car door slammed. He left the lantern, still burning, on the kitchen table, and stood in the hall watching her wash her babies. Then he heard the sound of heavy feet on the front porch steps. As he slipped out into the back alley, he wondered who it was.

The question haunted him for an hour, all the way to Marvel's place. By the time he arrived, he thought he knew.

CHAPTER THREE

1

The day had gone and she had missed her deadline. She had seen five lawyers and none had worked out. Three who had been highest on her list of anti-Klan prospects weren't interested. A fourth would be out of town. A fifth was interested only after discovering that her bank balance, a healthy figure derived some years ago from the sale of her father's farm, was equal to the job. A money-grubber, plain and simple.

Now she sat in an office at Potter, Yates, & Evans, listening to Warren Potter talk in that smooth, easy way he had, hearing the words she had waited all day to hear. Potter was all charm. He was a gray-haired gentleman of fifty-five, spectacled, with a large red nose. He was neither a money-grubber nor aloof, and the sensational elements of the case seemed to intrigue him far less than its human elements. His politics, from their viewpoint, seemed to be in the right

378

place. He never crusaded against the Ku Klux Klan, but in her days as fill-in court reporter she had seen him defend several cases of little people against the system. He seemed quick and able, tenacious in protecting his client's rights. Why, then, did she distrust him?

He had heard her out without interrupting, then told her what she already knew: that far too much time had elapsed, that the wheels of justice were turning even now toward their court-directed conclusion, that David Waldo's appeal should have been filed weeks ago. The Supreme Court, even if there were time to present it at that level, might well turn it back without comment. The best they could hope for at this late date was a brief stay, until the new evidence could be weighed. There would have to be much documentation, but yes, *if* the possibility of a conspiracy could be laid before the court, and *if* they could do this in time, and *if* the high court could be satisfied that they had proceeded properly, *if* the court itself wasn't packed with Klansmen, *if* they could get a transcript of what had transpired in Judge Henry's court, *if* the transcript could be certified (which might be more of a problem than she had thought, since even the clerks in the District Court were in the Klan)—if all these things could be done on time they might catch the court's ear. Potter was concerned over how the documents had been obtained, but since they weren't being used in a criminal case against anyone named within them, he held the hope that the court would at least look at them.

She thanked Potter for his time and said she would call him in the morning. When she saw Potter again she wanted Tom to be there. That night she carried home a heavy burden, doubting her judgment for the first time in many years. The spirit of David Waldo seemed to be walking with her, though she had seen the man just twice and had never spoken to him. It had become suddenly important, beyond all her understanding, that she make no mistakes.

Darkness had come when she arrived home. She found only a cold, empty flat, and she thought that was a bad sign. It meant he was having trouble. He was running into dead-end streets, getting nowhere. He was still out on the streets, digging.

She wouldn't think about that. She turned up the radiator and went into the bathroom to draw her bath. Her city editor called. They had been trying to reach her all day. She said she had been to a doctor, wasn't able to keep anything down, and hoped to be back at work by Thursday. The *News* had a job for her. She took notes while the man talked, and rang off just before the tub overflowed. She undressed and eased herself with a weary gasp into the hot water.

He came in about five minutes later. She heard him open the door with her spare key, then he began shuffling through some papers in the living room. He called her name and she muttered a response, too tired to answer him. Tom walked past on his way to the bedroom, then came back, as much at home as if he'd always lived there. It was the first time, in spite of what they said about her at work, that any man had shared her apartment. But he was different to her and always had been. Finally, at long last, she had to admit it. He had mixed up her life, had made it so much better and worse, so much more interesting. He'd filled it, by his long absence, with stretches of unbearable boredom and had ruined it for good men like Malloy. And the insane part of it was, there was nothing between them. They hadn't touched since that first day, when she pulled him out of that hotel and helped him into the back seat of a cab. When they exchanged things—money, the spare key, plates over the dinner table—they did it carefully, so their hands wouldn't touch. Like two juveniles on a first date. She sank in water to her neck and thought, I really need to get away from him. He was becoming a bad influence. She thought about the West Coast, and about Chicago. Chicago was really exciting, next to Denver the most riotous newspaper town in the country. But she saw the lie in that too: She wouldn't go to Chicago or the Coast, wouldn't go anywhere as long as he was here. What, then, was this feeling she had for him? It wasn't love; she had been in love and knew what that felt like. It wasn't sex. She seldom thought of him that way. But that was another lie, because whatever it was, it sure as hell wasn't platonic. She just seldom thought of sex, wouldn't allow herself to worry about it. That was a weakness she couldn't afford in a job dominated by men. But when she did, it was often him that she saw beside her.

Something about him awed and frightened her. Even in weakness he was somehow bigger than she could ever be. She knew that one move from him would change things between them for good. A word out of place, laughter, a chance meeting of their hands across the table, maybe even a sudden emotion unrelated to themselves. Anything that made him see her as a woman instead of a ballbreaking newspaper broad. When it happened, if it happened, she would have to fight herself to keep from stepping back into that goddamned newspaper shell. She'd have to play straight with him, at least that one time, and see where it was going.

She was suddenly hungry. She stepped out of the tub, clutched her robe around her, opened the door, and got the biggest shock of the year.

He was sitting on the sofa, and Goodwin's pictures were scattered across the floor at his feet.

"Happy birthday," he said.

"Oh, my God."

He picked up one picture and held it up to the light. "Mr. Walter Jakes," he said calmly. "Defense lawyer."

380

"No!" She leaned against the wall, then sank slowly to the floor. She dipped her hands into the mound of precious paper, loving the feel of it. They looked at each other and laughed.

The moment had come and she had let it pass. She had seen it at least once in her mind: the sudden victory, drawing them into a bear hug of joy, the bear hug becoming something else, then something else as his hands found her breasts and her hair and her smooth skin. But they didn't hug or dance for joy. A kind of numbing elation washed over them, and they sat sifting through the prints and putting them into some kind of sequence. They ate in silence, a time of quiet, sobering for both of them.

After a while she said, "Tomorrow we've got to decide on a lawyer. There's one you need to meet. He's the only one I could find today. I told him we'd let him know tomorrow, but I'd like to meet with a few others first."

"What's wrong with this one?"

"Nothing. Just say I'd like your judgment, unhampered by mine."

He nodded. "If we do get a lawyer, it's pretty well out of our hands. I mean, it's up to him then. There's nothing else we can do."

"I don't see anything."

"Then I'll go see Whipple."

"Really?"

"Man's got to start somewhere." He thought for a minute. "And I'm going to Canon City, to see David. I've got to do that. What about you?"

"Go back to work before they fire me."

"Well, I'll be able to get out of your hair, get my own place, as soon as I get my first week's pay."

"No hurry. None at all."

"Too bad we won't be on the same paper. We work pretty well together."

"They're assigning me to cover the rest of it," she said. "That means I'll be there, all through the week of the eighth, till it's over. Unless we can get it stopped. It's an assignment I can do without," she said. "Maybe if I tell them how I've been working on it, they'll let me out of it."

"Maybe they'll fire you, too."

"Yeah," she said. "And maybe I don't give a damn." She took a deep breath. "We'll be running a series on the death penalty, starting the Sunday before and running through the week. I've got to review every damned case since the law was changed, so yeah, I'll be busy."

They sat there with the big box of pictures between them. Every so often Tom would reach in and touch them. He looked at her and she thought, for one terrible instant, that he might touch her then. She looked away and sought refuge in her work.

"Did you know Colorado once abolished the death penalty? They reinstated it twenty-five years ago. Some colored kid killed a girl near Limon and the people were so outraged because there wasn't any death penalty that they lynched him. Can you believe it, they burned him at the stake with every paper in Denver covering it. They want that for the Sunday piece. It's grisly, but it makes a hell of a lead."

He just looked at her.

"It's the kind of thing you should write," she said. "A lot of powerful material. I hear the clips are unreal."

"Yeah, Marvel, right," he snapped. "It'll make a helluva lead. Real hot copy."

"Oh, come on. You know how I meant it." But her smile vanished. "What's wrong with you?"

"Nothing. I don't know. Maybe I just don't like executions." He picked up the pictures, said good night, and went into the bedroom.

2

Potter had spent a long time looking over the documents, and now it was nearly dusk of the following day. For Marvel it had been a carbon of the first day, a long line of polite refusals, her own growing apprehension, and fear. For the first time in her life she was afraid of making a mistake. Tom had none of her fears, and he was much closer to David Waldo than she would ever be. Still it wouldn't go away.

They sat without a word, watching while Potter rifled through the box, pausing over interesting scraps, then reading through the membership roster with intense interest. "The list isn't complete," Potter said, looking up at them. "It only goes through the letter M."

"It's enough," Tom said.

"Enough to show that Brown was in," Marvel said.

"And Jakes," Tom said.

"And the judge," said Marvel.

Potter nodded. "And some pretty important others. This could make you a lot of trouble."

"I don't care about that," Tom said.

"You're willing to testify how you got them?"

"Damn right."

Potter held the negatives up to the lamp, trying to read them. "Do you know what might be on these?"

"No idea," Tom said. "Maybe the rest of the list. I was sure we'd shot it all."

"We'll have to get them printed," Potter said. "In fact, we'll have to get the whole file copied again, to have a spare set to give the court."

"Just so one of us is there when it's done," she said.

Potter looked at her patiently, giving a little smile. "My dear, you've got to stop being so suspicious. Am I your lawyer or not? That's what you've got to decide. If you're going to work with me, you've got to trust me."

Tom looked at her and nodded.

"Now then," Potter said, "let's talk about the conspiracy angle for a minute. You people being reporters, I'm sure you know what that's about. It's a flower that blooms only in the dark. We need to establish a much closer link between the major parties . . ."

"Isn't this enough?" Marvel said.

"What, that they belong to the Ku Klux Klan? Probably hundreds of people are in the Klan who've never even met each other."

"But," said Tom, "John Galen Locke is the connecting link. He gives all the orders. The people don't have to know each other. Those goddamn judges do just what Locke says."

"Then we have to prove that. Not necessarily that he *did* give such an order, but just that he might have. Just the fact that he has that power might be enough. We'll do as you say, get the jury roster for that day, compare it with the Klan list as far as it goes. The problem with stuff like that is how do you prove it?" Potter said. "If we could do it, it would start a riot downtown. Every judge in Denver would have to disqualify himself, and there'd have to be a visiting judge brought in. We could subpoena Hayes, then Locke, and get the originals of these files . . ."

"Do it!" Marvel said. "I'd love to see that toad on the witness stand."

"It's something to consider later, if and when a re-sentencing date is set. If we can then get a new trial. Our immediate problem isn't proving what Locke and Hayes and Henry might have done. What we're faced with, first of all, is keeping the client alive before he gets ground up in the justice system. Stopping the wheels long enough to work out another strategy. Then we can worry about taking it out of Judge Henry's hands."

"What are the chances of that?"

"Not too bad, actually, if only we can get this damned execution stopped. That's the big problem now. There are channels to go through in cases like this, deadlines to meet in filing motions for appeal. Your friend hasn't met any of them. He just sat there like a man who wants to die. The wheels turn relentlessly in cases like this." He fumbled in his desk and lit his pipe. "Once we *do* get it stayed, then it's a different story. Then we've got more time to prepare, to argue it on a new level. At the very least there were extenuating circumstances which should be part of a case like this. David Waldo should never have been allowed to plead to that charge. It was so clearly a crime of passion. The matter of his wife, of her trip east with this Brown, all those elements should be in the record. And before we go any further, I have to tell you something else. The best you'll get in a case like this is a very long prison term. There doesn't seem to be much question that Waldo actually shot Brown, so don't expect me to walk in and get him off. Have either of you asked the defendant what he thinks of this?"

Tom shook his head. "There hasn't been time."

"Somebody should do that. After that, it's my fight. I think we're in the position of a politician who appeals to a lot of people, but not to elements within his own party. He'll have a tough time getting the nomination, but once past that, he'll sail through the election. That's where we are now, in the middle of the convention fight. If we can get past it, I really think the next step is easier. And I'm willing to try."

Marvel looked at Tom.

"Great," he said.

Potter nodded. "Then it's settled. I suggest you let me keep these documents in my safe. In the morning I'll have them copied for submission to the court."

He reached across the desk and drew the box toward him.

"There's the matter of a fee," Marvel said, still watching the box.

Potter waved her away.

"Seriously," she said.

"There are certain cases that lawyers feel obligated to take on," Potter said. "Whatever you can pay."

"That's very generous of you, Mr. Potter."

"Not at all." He pushed back his chair and stood. "Shall we call it a night?"

They went down the hall alone, and the desolation and doubt settled into her stomach. The elevator came but she didn't get on. She stood in the dark hall until the door closed.

"What's the matter?" Tom said. "You forget something?"

But still she didn't move. "What did you think of him?"

"Potter? He's a fine guy."

"I thought he was a little too fine. I'm probably all wrong anyway." Still she didn't press the call button. "Wait for me," she said. "I'll be right back."

She walked back to Potter's office. The lawyer had turned off his lights but the door remained unlocked. She opened it and saw a thin line of light at the bottom of the inner office. She heard his voice. He was talking with someone on the telephone. She came closer but the voice was a dull drone. Suddenly, instinctively, she wrenched open the door. She and Potter stared at each other across a cluttered desktop, and in that instant each seemed to know that here was a blood enemy. The documents were scattered across the desk. Potter had been reading them to someone on the telephone.

"I'll have to call you back," Potter said, and hung up the phone. He looked up at Marvel. "Was there something else?"

"Yes." She came across the room and reached for the cardboard box but Potter's fingers tightened around it.

"My friend is in the hall," she said. "Shall I call him?"

Slowly he released it. His face made itself over into the old mask. He was friendly again. "You're making a mistake," he said. "I don't know what you're thinking . . ."

"I think you do, Mr. Potter. Oh, yes, I think you know."

She lifted the box from his hands and walked out with it. At the elevator she said, "Potter's a Klansman. Let's get out of here, quick."

3

They had stopped in a diner south of town, and it was late when they got back to her place. Tom, still shaken by their near mistake, clutched the Locke papers against him all through dinner, and now carried them with him to bed. He slept less than an hour, waking suddenly without any apparent reason. He sat on the bed and listened. Soon he heard footsteps, a creaking of boards in the other room.

He crossed the kitchen and went into the front room. There were no lights anywhere in the apartment. He saw the roll-away bed, still unused, standing folded in a corner. He called her name and she answered from the blackness of the heavy drapes over the window. He moved toward her until his hand found her bare arm.

"What's the matter?"

"Somebody down in the alley," she said. "I knew we shouldn't have come back here tonight." She pointed down between the trees. "Look carefully, right over there between the trees and the garage. You can just make it out."

He squinted and saw the dim outline of a pickup truck, about twenty yards from his car.

"There are two of them," she said. "Two men. They walked all around the backyard. They were mighty interested in your car. One of them opened the door and looked in, then they went back and sat in the cab of the truck. They've been there ever since. Look, one of them just lit a cigarette."

"Like they're sitting there waiting for something. I wonder what."

"Maybe they want to make sure we're asleep."

They stood watching the alley, and for a long time nothing happened. But she was still tense. They waited some more. "Potter told them, I'd bet my life on it," she said. "We shouldn't have come back here tonight. That son of a bitch told them, and now they've come to get the papers."

The door of the pickup opened and a heavyset man got out. He tossed a burning cigarette into the deep grass near Tom's car and stood looking up at the apartment. The other man got out and came around, and the two stood leaning on the fender, talking.

"They'll be coming in a minute," she said. "We'd better think fast."

The men had moved away from the truck and were crossing the backyard. At the house they split up, the heavy one going around toward the front. She raised the window slightly and they heard the soft sounds of feet on the iron fire escape. "Check the front door," she said. "Make sure it's locked."

She stood absolutely still, peering down the black staircase that hugged the back of the building. A moment later the man appeared, climbing steadily past the second floor toward her window. She moved across the room and joined Tom at the front door. Three floors below, the stairs creaked as the big man started up.

He motioned her back into the apartment, slipped inside, and locked the door. Outside the moon came out, and a face appeared at the window. "Don't move," Tom said. He slipped along the wall in the dark. "Just stay where you are."

She had already begun moving the other way, where her hat lay on the living room coffee table. The man lifted the window and her fingers found the hatpin as he stepped into the room.

He turned on a pen light, holding the beam ahead of him as he walked toward the front door. He moved the beam from side to side, along the kitchen baseboard, and stopped cold as the light touched Tom's feet.

There was a time—perhaps only a second, perhaps as long as five—when nobody knew what to do. Tom moved first. He leaped at the man, spun him around, and gripped him under the throat. They fell back against the wall, swinging at each other blindly. Marvel leaped into the fight, grabbed the wrong man, and rammed her hatpin into Tom's leg. "Get back, Goddammit!" he shouted. By then she had the man around the waist and was pulling him down to the floor. He struck at her with his fist and she plunged the pin full-length into the soft flesh under the ribcage.

He let out a scream that must have carried to the statehouse. "Nate! Nate! Godamighty, they're killin' me! Oh, Jesus Christ, hurry!" They heard feet running up the stairs, the rattle of the doorknob, then a thump as Nate hit the door with his shoulder. Marvel wrapped her arms around the man's head, smothering his mouth. They rolled over and again Marvel was on top. She braced herself against the writing table, and her free hand found the steel case for the Underwood. She gripped the handle and swung it hard against the man's head. He went limp, groaned, and rolled over on his back. "My God, Tom, I think I've killed him." He pushed her toward the window, scooping up the Locke papers with one arm, and they crawled out onto the fire escape just as Nate came crashing in through the door.

They slammed down the iron steps and ran across the yard. She jumped behind the wheel and he began to crank. The car sputtered and died. Now the two men had come through the window, the big one taking five steps at a time. Tom turned the crank again. It slipped out of his hand. Again. He felt his wound tear open. Nate leaped the last few steps, rolled over on the ground, and came at him on the run. Time for one more try. He wrenched the crank with all his strength and the car started. By then Nate was upon him. He jerked the crank out of its socket and brought the pointed end up into Nate's ribs. He heard the man grunt, "Son of a bitch," and saw him slip back to the ground. Nate sat there, holding a broken rib, and Tom stepped close and dropped him flat with the crank. Nate rolled over and Tom hit him again, sending him face-first in the dirt.

He whirled around, but the smaller man had stopped his charge halfway across the yard and was standing there watching. Tom eased sideways, toward the door of the Model T. The man didn't move. Nate groaned and rolled over on his back.

A few seconds later they were gone, roaring out of the alley toward Sixth Avenue. He turned to look back, and felt the blood soaking through his shirt.

"He's getting up," he said. "I should have bashed his brains out."

"They'll be after us. They won't stop."

He zigzagged toward Sixth Avenue, keeping on the dirt streets of the quiet residential areas. He drove without lights. In a while he turned off the motor and they coasted to a stop. They sat under the trees outside a huge mansion on Marion Street. They heard the truck race past on Sixth, stop, backtrack, and move on. There was a faint series of backfires, far away, perhaps as far as ten blocks, then nothing.

"We'll have to keep moving," she said. "We're like sitting ducks here."

"Yeah."

"Maybe we should head out of town. Cheyenne maybe, or Colorado Springs. The main thing is protecting these papers. Get us a locker somewhere, then we can come back and try again."

"I don't even trust the banks in this town," he said. "That goddamn Potter. You sure called that right."

"We've got to be very sure of what we do from now on. I'm not sure how we should go about things. All I know is I'm getting very nervous sitting here."

"Then let's move."

He got out and cranked. He eased the car across Sixth, down the quiet blocks to Speer Boulevard. He doubled back up to Eighth, turned west, and opened the throttle. The car clattered along the washboard road, leaving a telltale trail of dust behind them. Soon they hit the paved stretch, and occasional streetlights whipped past. They burst out of Capitol Hill and saw the downtown lights to the right. Broadway flashed by, and the streetlights became regular. They saw cars going north and south, and a trolley passed. They turned into Speer again, and went west along Colfax toward the concrete road to Golden and the mountains beyond.

"We could go to my folks' old house," he said. "Pull the car around back where the garden was. Nobody'd see it. We could stay there in one of the back rooms till dawn."

Cheltenham School, dark and gaunt, rose out of the gloom on the right, and suddenly they bumped off the pavement and were in the old neighborhood. Again the darkness seemed to envelop them, and again that old warning alarm went off in her head. "Something's not right," she said. They had just passed Sammy Kohl's old store, and the burned-out shell of David's print shop looked like a ghost rising up to warn them. "Don't ask me what, but something's wrong. Keep going." She made it sound like an order.

He had slowed the car to half speed.

"Keep going!" she said, louder. "Don't stop and don't turn in, whatever you do."

They whisked past Osceola Street. Ahead of them Colfax was empty. She looked back through the glass and saw a car turn out of Osceola Street and fall in behind them.

"Oh, my God," she said.

He glanced back. "Just a car. It might be nothing. Can you see it?"

"I don't know what it is. Let's turn in here and drive around the lake."

He turned into Quitman Street and approached the hospital from the southeast. The moonlight shimmered on the lake and a light wind rippled the surface. She looked back through the glass.

"They're there. Somebody is. Too far back for me to see them."

They had crossed Seventeenth and had turned into the winding dirt road that skirted the lake when the light flashed behind them and the wail of a siren drifted across the water.

"Cops," he said.

"Don't stop. Jesus, don't even think of stopping. Open it up. My God, don't stop for anybody!"

He pulled the throttle and the car clattered over bumps, trembling violently. "She won't take much of this!" he shouted. But the police car stayed behind them, neither gaining nor losing. He headed uphill, into one of the dark residential streets north of Denver. Here the houses were sparse, there were no streetlights, and the streets were all rough and upaved. He cut between blocks, turned west, then north, but the police car stayed with them, about a block behind, like a cowboy herding a calf to the slaughterhouse.

The residential area petered out, the houses trickled away, and they climbed that last long hill that looked back on Denver. The radiator boiled over and the engine made a deep rumbling sound as they cleared the top and started down. They were on a narrow dirt road leading into the hills, already well past the city limit. Soon the road became a rutted trail, full of holes and sharp turns and then rocks. He hit a rock and felt a tire go. The car swerved, still running at top throttle, leaped a ditch, and plunged down a ravine, landing in a hole at the bottom with a loud snap.

Marvel was stunned. Her head hit the corner bar of the windshield, and for a full minute her eyes wouldn't focus. She saw the lights from the police car and heard the hissing of the radiator. Sounds of scuffling feet came closer as men scrambled down and surrounded the car. The door jerked open. She felt hands on her arms, around her waist, and under her breast. They were lifting her out. She saw a blue coat, a badge, a gun, and a sheathed billyclub. She saw Tom climbing out, his middle soaked with blood and his hands empty.

"Moran," he said. "A little out of your jurisdiction tonight, aren't you?"

"Get him down from there, boys," the cop said.

"Are we arrested?" Marvel said.

"I'll tell you about it downtown," the cop said. He looked at his men. "One of you get their . . . things . . . out of the car. We wouldn't want them to lose anything."

But they didn't go downtown. They went south to Thirty-eighth, then east. No one spoke. Tom was placed between two cops in the back seat, and the cardboard box lay with its flaps closed on his lap. Marvel shared the front seat with the driver. They kept going due east, and soon they were out of town again. They were on the plains; the lights of Denver had dwindled and disappeared over a ridge. The prairie looked like an ocean in the moonlight.

Tumbleweeds blew across in front of the car, and as they went farther east the wind picked up. Bits of sagebrush pelted the windows and swirls of dust danced in front of them. They climbed another long hill and looked down at the South Platte River, twisting its way across the plains to Nebraska. The driver began to brake, looking ahead for a turnoff. He found it a moment later, turned in and followed the river. Moran leaned against his door and looked at Tom. "Hastings, I'm going to give you some time to think over what happened tonight."

"Maybe you'd better tell me, then. What did happen?"

"It's a long walk back to Denver. You'll likely have all night long to think about it. When you get there, come down to headquarters and tell me what you've decided. If I like what you say, maybe I'll forget about the man you almost killed back at Miss Millette's place tonight. Maybe we'll overlook the attempted murder, and the reckless driving, and eluding the police. Because we're good guys, Hastings, and because we want to keep our good relations with the press."

"Don't do it," Marvel said. "Make him take us downtown and book us."

The car was crawling along now. On both sides of the rutted road, bushes and dwarfed trees grew down close, scratching the doors and windows. They came out into a clearing, perhaps a hundred yards across, which sloped down to the edge of the river. The driver pulled down to the water and stopped.

"This is where you get off, Hastings," Moran said. "We'll see you in the morning."

"Me too," Marvel said. "If he goes, I go."

"Oh no, we've got a special treat in store for you. A personal police escort home, right to your doorstep."

"Keep your goddamned escort."

"Modern womanhood never stops amazing me, " Moran said. "What you women won't go through for your men. The thing I can't understand is the men you choose. Losers. Like you, Miss Millette. And your sister, Hastings. Lovely girl. Tragic, what happened to her. You two," he said to the uniformed cops, "help Hastings out of the car."

Marvel pushed the door open and tried to leap out, but Moran grabbed her around the neck and jerked her back against the seat. The two cops had pulled the other door open and one had gripped Tom by his belt, pulling him out in the dust. He tried to kick, but one of the cops billied him. He sagged into the dirt. Somewhere in the back of his mind, he heard Marvel curse, heard Moran cry out in pain, then felt the shoes of the cop, hard against his ribs. He heard footsteps all around him, felt his arms being raised, and the box of documents tucked under it. "Don't forget these," Moran said softly. "You've taken such good care of them. It'd be a shame to lose them now."

390

4

In a way it had been like a bad binge on cheap wine. He had been only partly unconscious, and then for only a short time. He rolled over and sat up, and the faint hum of Moran's car could still be heard beyond the rise. A bank of dark clouds was drifting over the moon, and the wind had slacked off to a gentle summer breeze. He took the Locke file under his arm and walked the thirty yards to the bank of the South Platte, kneeling there and splashing water on his face.

He remembered Moran's parting words, like the echo of an old dream. It made no sense to him, but he looked inside the box, saw that all the papers were there, and again tucked the box under his arm. He estimated the walk to town at four hours, maybe five, unless he got lucky and snagged a ride. But he didn't move yet. He sat by the river and thought about it. There was a purpose in Moran's madness, he was sure of it. He might do better to stay off the road, to wade across the Platte and hike back overland. But hiking the plains at night without a flash could be fatal. Already the moon was partly gone, and now, as if in warning, another cloud drifted in like a storm front was blowing in. He would have to feel his way, even staying on the road, and now his five hours looked more like seven.

He walked along the riverbank, taking measure of the clearing for the first time. It was a sandspit, with alternating stretches of sand and rock, reaching along the river for perhaps two hundred yards. As he came close to the end he saw something that brought him up short. It was a bulky object, looming over him like some giant with out-stretched arms. It was black on black, bigger than big, ominous and threatening. He moved closer, to be sure, and the wind brought a smell of kerosene. In that moment he understood why Moran had said what he'd said, why he had been left here and what was about to happen.

They seemed to materialize out of the dark. He was standing in a circle of silent, hooded men. He looked around him. They were strung out on the north bank of the Platte too, perhaps twenty strong there, watching, waiting. In another moment the chant began.

> Klakom, Klukom
> Koken, Klikom
> Panther, Anther
> Hokum, Sibla
> Bunko, Piffel
> Siffel, Ribla

A man came toward him, stopping under the cross. He repeated the chant and made a sign with his fingers in the sky. More Klansmen appeared on foot, walking in from the dark plains. He heard a horn blow, and far across the plains he saw cars coming. A torch appeared, touching the ground near the cross, and the clearing erupted into brilliant white light.

The first of the cars pulled into the clearing with their lights on, forming a tight circle around the ceremony. Horns blew nonstop. A great cheer went up and the chanting resumed. The wind sucked the flames high in a swirling funnel, like a cyclone of fire. It made the dark white, made the sheets stand out against the black, the eyeslits in the hoods stand out against the white. He felt naked before them. They hated him without knowing him, they were people he had never seen. Garage mechanics, plumbers, clerks in stores where Nell had done her shopping. Church people, out for a blood feast. He wondered if the redneck judge was there, and the cops, and the lawyers. His backbone stiffened and he faced the cross, still holding the Locke file tight against his chest.

Someone brought up twelve folding chairs and set them up in two rows. A larger chair was placed farther out in the clearing, facing the twelve. He was to go before a kangaroo court. The twelve men came forward and took their places, and the chanting dropped off and a great silence came over the clearing. All he could hear, for a full minute, was the sound of the fire, whipped by the wind. Now came the judge, a huge man with the sign of the Klan sewn into his sheet.

"The defendant will face the bench."

He didn't move.

"The bailiffs will escort the defendant to the bench."

Two men came down, took him roughly by each arm, spun him around, and pushed him down at the judge's feet. They gripped him again and hauled him to his feet. He was staring into those two black eyeholes, and he could see the fire reflected in the man's eyes. "You are charged with being an enemy of the people. You are charged with undermining the ideals of the United States, trying to corrupt the morals of its people through subversive newspaper articles and through covert actions outside the newspaper business. You are charged with being a communist sympathizer. How do you plead?"

He said nothing. The judge waited for a long time, until one of the arms crumbled and fell from the cross and the color of the sheets went from white to orange. "Let the defendant's silence be accepted as a plea of guilty," he said. "The accused wishes to put on no defense for his overt and covert acts of the past year. I shall cast your fate to the jury."

They stood, twelve as one. He thought they had been rehearsing their roles for a very long time.

"What say you?" said the judge.

392

"Death," they said in one voice.

"The jury has decided that death is your punishment. We will poll the jury."

Then the twelve, individually, and in order, repeated the word, shouting it at him across the clearing.

Death . . .

Death . . .

Death . . .

Still he didn't move. His face didn't change in any way. When the last man had pronounced his sentence, the judge motioned with his hand and they sat. The second arm fell from the cross in a shower of sparks and ashes, and two Klansmen began building it up as a bonfire. The judge, facing the fire, had taken a leatherbound book from a briefcase. He read to himself for a long time, and when he looked up, his eyes met Tom's.

"These are grievous crimes," the judge said. "The court deems the sentence fair and adequate. Is there anything you wish to say before the court accepts or rejects the decision of the jury?"

He just stared at the man.

"The court construes from your silence that you do not challenge either the findings or the sentence of this court. We will pass judgment now."

The crowd moved in expectantly. It was as if everyone had drawn breath at the same time, and all were leaning forward on the balls of their feet. The judge closed the book and looked at Tom.

"It is not the wish of this court to be unduly harsh. Nor can we condone or excuse subversive, un-American behavior. With that in mind, the court commutes the death sentence and pronounces judgment thus: The defendant will be tied to a whipping post, said post to be erected on this spot, here and now. He will be flogged twenty-five times with the cat-o'-nine-tails, and will then be tarred and feathered as befits a scoundrel and a knave. The defendant will further be banished from this community forever, remembering that the death sentence may be reinstated at any time, and heeding the court's warning that, should he return, the original judgment may be carried out." He took a long step toward Tom and the orange glow was bright against his hood. "Take heed of this, mister. Do not take it lightly. The Klan is not to be played with."

Having no gavel, he clapped his hands. The mob swarmed in, surrounding them. Tom was pushed one way, then another, pushed from hand to hand, punched, and finally pushed into the sand near the riverbank. He saw the judge standing over him. "The bailiffs will confiscate the documents stolen by the defendant and will relegate them to the flames while the defendant watches." And again the angry men were upon him, tearing the box loose, grabbing him by the hair and arms and propelling him across the clearing on his knees. He heard the curses and laughter of the mob, saw a hood lift briefly and felt spit on his cheek. The arms pushed him so close to the bonfire that he felt his eyebrows singe.

"The defendant will taste the dust of the earth," the judge said, "and will walk like the serpent, on his belly, as long as he shares the presence of true men."

The two men pushed him face-first into the earth, splitting open his lip and breaking a tooth. One stood over him, a booted foot in the small of his back, while the other held his hair, forcing him to watch while the judge destroyed the documents. The judge fed the papers to the bonfire one at a time. Then came the truck, with its hideous stink of hot tar. He heard the hammers at work, driving the whipping posts into the ground, and the boot was lifted from his back and again hands were upon him, dragging him through the dirt to the place where the truck waited. His shirt was ripped off, his arms lashed tight against each post. He felt the presence behind him as one of them uncoiled the cat. The knotted leather tongues fell against his back. It didn't hurt, not until the fourth stroke. The eighth broke through his skin and the twelfth fell on open, bloodied flesh. By the end he could only be sure he had survived and had faced them like a man. He had not cried out once.

Now the pickup truck backed down to the whipping posts and he heard the top being lifted from the tar vat. The first smear went right on his open wound. The judge smeared it across his back with a stiff wire brush. He writhed and groaned, and passed out.

He was conscious off and on during the tarring. They did his back, then his feet and legs, his arms, and even his face. They smeared it through his hair and around his eyes. The feathers hit like a powder puff, and a great cheer went up from a hundred voices. He was pushed back into the dirt and left there.

Marvel came for him about two hours later. He was still lying where they had left him. He hurt too much to move. He lay on his side, staring at the embers of the fire, feeling the heat of the rising sun on his back and wondering how long it would take him to die. He heard the car and a voice calling his name. She rushed to him, called, "Over here!" and a moment later a black man wearing a taxi driver's hat appeared beside her.

"Klan work," the man said.

"Here, get his feet."

"Klan done that. See that fire, where they burn the cross? I don't truck with no Klan work."

"Get over here." Her voice had its most biting, dangerous edge. "Get his feet and help me get him to your car or you'll have something a lot worse than Klan on your back. I mean now! Let's move."

CHAPTER FOUR

1

He went to Canon City by train. A hat covered the pink patches of scalp where skin had come off with the tar. His face, like his head, was patchy. Alternating splotches of pink and white were broken by bruises and cuts. He wore a coat in spite of the warm weather, for his back wouldn't stand sunlight. It burned like blazes even through two layers of clothes.

She had fussed and worried over him, and her biggest worry had been the strain of the trip on his back. He had survived it like he survived everything else, and had arrived at the east wall of the state penitentiary. He walked slowly and used a stick to help him. Somehow his leg had gotten hurt; he couldn't remember how, but his left leg hurt in both joints, knee and ankle.

He knew the gate man from those days long ago when he had covered pen news for the *Post*, but the man didn't recognize him until he had given his name.

He knew most of the people who worked in the prison. In the old days he had taken the time to walk around and talk to people. He had brought smokes to screws and prisoners, and most of them knew him by his first name. He knew the warden well. Perhaps that was why he was granted this last-minute interview. He had connections with the warden; that, and the fact that David Waldo—told that Tom Hastings wanted to see him—had fashioned it as something of a last request. Here was family come to call; the only family David Waldo had on this earth, the last friendly face he would see. Tom ate with the warden, in a private part of the dining room, segregated from the prisoners. The warden sat on his right, ringed by his assistants and a few favored guests.

"Never thought I'd see you up here under these circumstances," the warden said when they had eaten. "Hangings are nasty business."

"Yes. I wouldn't want your job." Tom searched for the words, then said, "When are you going to do it?"

"Was gonna this morning. I mean, why drag it out? Then you called, so we'll have to postpone it."

"Till when?"

"You know I can't tell you that. The whole process is supposed to be a secret."

"You've told me before. It never got out then."

"That was different. You didn't have a personal stake in those cases."

"As far as you and me are concerned, this case is just like any other."

The warden thought for a moment, then said, "Noon tomorrow, then. Why drag it out? That's always my position in anything like this. Nobody enjoys stuff like this, not if he's normal. It's just part of the job. Get it over and done with, that's what I say. It's what you'd say too if you were sittin' in my chair."

"I'm sure it is."

"Just so we have one thing straight," the warden said. "And listen, Hastings, this has got to be your honor-bound word. I know you're back in the newspaper game again."

"Word travels fast. Hell, warden, I didn't finish my first piece till late last night. It probably won't even make the paper till tomorrow. How'd you find out so fast?"

"No matter. Like you said, word travels fast."

"All right, you tell me the rules and I'll follow 'em. My word on that."

"The only rule is this. You're here at the request of the prisoner, not as a representative of the press. There'll be no stories on any of this, nothing on anything he might tell you. Understood?"

396

"Absolutely. I'm here on my own."

"Then let's go find your man."

He was led outside, up along the outer wall past the death house. Inside, he heard the trap spring with a dull thump. The infernal machine. It had been attacked by humane groups for years; he himself had run a campaign against it in the *Post* three years ago. It was a sling with a noose in one end, bent over double to fit the head of the condemned. When the trigger tripped, the noose tightened around the prisoner's neck and the man was jerked off the floor. In theory the neck would be snapped at once. But good theory was bad practice, and the machine seldom worked. Usually the men died hard, thrashing about for long minutes while being slowly strangled. One man had been hanged three times before the machine did its job.

They went into another building and he was left alone in a tiny room containing only a bare table and two chairs. A moment later two guards escorted David Waldo to the door, unlocked it, nudged him inside, and left them alone.

David was thinner than he remembered. His beard was gone. Tom sat straight in the chair, keeping his back off the rest. He didn't try to get up as David came in. They didn't shake hands. For a long time they didn't speak. David circled the table and took a seat facing him. "I won't ask how you've been," he said. "I can see these months haven't been easy."

"I've been on a bender."

"I guess we all knew that. I tried looking for you a couple of times, then finally decided you'd find us when you wanted to."

"That was a smart decision. Is there anything I can do?"

David nodded. "Maybe we can talk a while. That's what I really want, just to talk a little. There's one thing you can do for me, and I'll tell you what it is when you leave. I want it to be the last thing you hear from me. The last words you remember. But since you're here and you've got some time, let's talk about some other things. Things I always wanted to write, but never had the talent. You've got the talent but never had the urge. Maybe I can help you with that, give you that urge to write that book you've always wanted to write."

"Ah, Davie. Christ, everybody thinks I'm a writer just because I know a few clever turns of a phrase. I'm just a goddamn hack reporter."

"Still, it's there, isn't it? That itch. That urge."

"Sure. I started a novel once. About ten pages in, I fell into the old trap all newspapermen fall into when they try to write books. I saw that I just couldn't get it up for three hundred pages. We're so used to writing on that goddamn deadline. It's all that matters after a while, and when it's not there anymore, you're lost. Then there's the form.

Five hundred words, no more, and forty minutes to do it in. So you sit down to write something real and nothing happens. You've got all this blank paper and a subject bigger than all outdoors. Like justice, for Christ's sake. How the hell do you write about that? So nothing comes. You start losing yourself in your work, you start working long hours to make up for the fact that you can't write, then you justify not writing by the long hours you keep. Then you start drinking."

David reached across the table and took Tom's arm. "You've always had such grand instincts. You just know things I'd take days to ferret out in my mind. *That's* what makes a writer, that kind of instinct. I'm going to tell you something a great writer told me once, and I hope you'll listen and do something with it. This is word for word, as best I can remember it. Let it flow. Flow is everything. Don't worry about form, and don't worry when it's bad. Keep it going, because movement is the breath of life. It can be very bad and still have life, and in those early stages of work that's all that matters. Don't fuss over it, don't be too much a grammarian. That's all there is, just getting it down somehow. That's what I never could do, never stop fussing, picking at it. I picked my own stuff to death even before it was out of the typewriter. My stuff was always stillborn. It had no life. The words were always so precise, with every comma in place and every word selected for its most exact usage. Even after London told me, I couldn't stop it. I couldn't write out a grocery list without making sure all the words were spelled right. That's the way I am, and I can't help it or change it any more than you can help being the way you are. That's why I never wrote my book." David released his arm and sat back. "Would you listen to me a while longer?"

"Sure I will."

"I might ramble, but I want to tell you some things. Maybe someday you'll be able to use them."

The sun was low over the prison wall when he had finished. He had told his life the way he remembered it. He talked about Jessie and the fire, the Chicago days, the endless talks with Jack London, and London's own special rage against society. He talked about the Palmer raids, the sweatshops, the relentless harassment of people like Moran. At the end of the day he was exhausted and his voice was weak. So Tom talked a while. He told David about Ethan, and Preston Porter, and Shaughnessy. "It's all there, brother," David said. "All the stuff that books are made of. Take some of yours and some of mine. Put in everything you know and feel. Read some of London's stuff. Some of it's so badly written, but it has a majesty and power that doesn't depend on anything but heart. You do that and you'll find out what you were put on this earth for. Just say you'll try."

"I will. I'll try."

"Listen, they'll be coming up soon to bring me down to dinner. So we'd better get on to that last thing before you have to go."

"I think I know what it is. Mom already made me promise."

"No, promise me, Tom. This is one thing that's got to be between you and me." David looked down at his hands. "We get so caught up in our own passions that we don't stop and consider what effect our actions might have. All I could think of was what I'd lost, and revenge. It wasn't until I'd been arrested and thrown in a cell that I thought about the kid and what might happen to him. That's the one thing that makes me wish I'd done it differently. I'd lost every reason I had for wanting to live. It never occurred to me that there were other reasons, until it was too late."

"I'll find him, Davie, you can rest easy on that."

He drew in his breath. "Good. I feel better knowing that. You always did have good skills at finding people, didn't you, Tom?"

"That's what they tell me."

"Then I guess this is it." David stood and pushed his chair back. He reached out his hand and Tom clasped it around the wrist. "I'm glad I know you," David said. "I wish I'd known you earlier."

He knocked on the door. A moment later the guard opened it, stood aside, and waited for him. David gave Tom a long look and then he was gone. Tom went to the hall and watched until they disappeared down the staircase.

He left the prison about fifteen minutes later, hobbling out through the front gate without looking back. It wasn't until later, rocking back toward Denver in the train, that he thought about what David had said. He arrived at Marvel's at ten o'clock and went straight to the other box he'd found at Georgeann's. He shuffled through his notes, making fresh ones in the margins. At one o'clock she brought him some fresh coffee.

He seemed aware of her for the first time. "I thought you'd be down at the pen."

"I told them to find somebody else. It's the first time I ever refused an assignment."

"Have you heard from Whipple today? Is he going to run the story?"

She shrugged. "We'll know tomorrow." She came and sat beside him. "It's almost over now, isn't it? You've come through it all and you're ready to start again."

"You think so?"

"Well, almost. There's still the matter of your wife."

"It's like walking into a saw. I must have thought about it fifty times this week. Just getting in my car and going over there. I can't seem to do it."

"Maybe this will help." She went to the coffee table and came back with that night's *Post.* "This came while you were down at Canon City."

Spread across three columns of the front page, just below the fold, was the headline LOCAL TYCOON FELLED BY STROKE. Beneath it, a series of decks. GREGORY F. CLEMENT, WIDELY KNOWN DENVER BUSINESSMAN, COLLAPSES AT HIS HOME. CONDITION THOUGHT BY DOCTORS TO BE CRITICAL.

"Simplifies things, doesn't it?" Marvel said.

"Not for me. But you're right, it does end the stalemate. I guess I'll be driving out there in the morning."

2

The gate was open, and the guardhouse stood empty in the morning sun. If there had been arrangements to make, she had made them, and again the place was peaceful and quiet. The house looked different; its paint was fresh and new, and the grounds had been neglected for some time. There were no summer flowers along the horseshoe drive, in the garden or in the pots near the door. The old man's green Packard stood under the trees, like a faithful pet awaiting the master who would never come again. Still walking with pain, he climbed the sloping steps to the front door, gripped the knocker, and struck it against the door. She opened the door inward, swinging it like a child, with both hands. She was wearing an old green dress, prewar, that came to her ankles. It was the one she had always loved at home, the one she'd worn the night Harding had died. Its colors were faded now, the material thin. She blinked when she saw him, as if she couldn't quite place the face. Then she clutched at her throat and said, "Thomas! Oh, my God!" She turned and fled, leaving the door open behind her.

He was standing on the threshold of the Clement home, looking into a spectacular living room. He had never seen the inside of the house. He came closer, stepping across into the dim hall. The living room stretched away to his right, running down the entire length of the house. There were sofas and a grand piano and a fireplace containing enough bricks to build a house of normal construction. Everything was of fine wood. Spruce. Walnut. Mahogany. In an immense dining room he saw displays of silver and china and cut glass. Any of them would have taken his month's salary. Finally he returned to the living room and took his place on one of the sofas. They seemed to be arranged in ascending orders of intimacy. There was a cluster of fine furniture near the far end of the room, at the

400

fireplace. An intermediate layer of soft chairs stood at mid-room. A final set stood near the door, for waiting visitors. How like the old man, to let everyone know just where he stood. Tom sat nearest the door. He knew it might be quite a while before she returned.

He realized too that the room represented money. All the money in the world. The trinkets in this room alone were worth enough to build a house, to bring Abe and Teresa back from the living dead, to take some time off and find the kid. She had everything here.

He saw the liquor cabinet.

It was set into the wall behind the piano, a deep cabinet with leaded glass doors. Inside were perhaps thirty bottles of the finest Canadian and imported whiskies. Bourbons. Scotches. Brandies. Enough good booze to last a week. He took down a bottle of brandy and uncorked it, swishing the dark liquid around under his nose. He heard her footsteps on the staircase, and quickly replaced it. He was standing before the piano when she came in. His first thought was, *Christ, how she had aged.* He wondered what she saw in him.

"You'll excuse me if I don't take off my hat and glasses," he said. "I had an accident."

"Your hair . . ."

"It's gone for now. We had to shave it off. Sometime I'll tell you about it. It'll grow back." He came closer, so he could see her better. The sun came in through the open drapes, lighting up the doorway where she stood. She came into the room, found a place on the sofa nearest the door, and sat. He sat in a chair about ten feet away.

"I've been ill, too," she said. "It shows, I'm afraid."

He saw that in the hour she had been upstairs, she had done something to her hair. The gray he'd noticed was gone, but so was that natural hue he had always loved. Her eyes were different, too. For a moment she looked strange, out of place in her own house. "Where've you been keeping yourself?" she said.

"I've been on a binge. Six months. Eight. I don't know how long. But I'm okay now."

"I'm glad." She looked away from him, toward the fireplace. "Would you like to move down to the other end of the room? There's more light."

It was her way of taking that first step, inviting him down to the intimate side of the room. She seemed somehow stronger than he expected; she spoke with greater ease and self-assurance than he remembered. But he refused her offer. "I need less light, not more. It hurts my eyes. How are the kids?"

"They're fine. I sent them away for a few days, until I could get things worked out." She paused. "So. You must have seen the paper. About my father. And that brought you, ah, out of it?"

"I've been out of it for some time. Hearing about my sister did that."

"Anna? What about her?"

"She died."

"Really? How sad. She was so young. I had no idea."

"It was in all the papers."

"I never see the papers anymore." She moved her hands down to her lap and clasped them there. "Was her death an accident?"

"She killed herself."

"Dear God, how dreadful! Your poor family. Your father must be devastated."

"He's dead too."

She waited for a moment, for the embarrassment to go away. When she next spoke, it was as if nothing had been said. She didn't refer to his family again.

"So. You've put this . . . problem . . . behind you."

"I thought I had. But just before you came in, I was seriously thinking of rifling your father's liquor cabinet. All I can tell you is I haven't had a drop in almost a month. Who knows what'll happen tomorrow?"

"Thomas . . ." She pouted, the way she had always done while scolding the boys. It irritated him.

"Nothing's changed at all, has it?" he said. "Look at us. Look, that's what I mean. A year passes and we sit here like we'd seen each other only yesterday. All the same problems are right where they were."

"Oh, I don't know. It depends on how you look at it, I guess. In fact, there may be a few new ones. Why didn't you come for me?"

"Was that what I was supposed to do, play your little game? Do you really think either one of us would have gained anything if I'd chased you to St. Louis?"

"What about St. Louis? I don't understand."

But she had begun to understand. She sighed and let her hands fall to her sides. "My father again, no doubt. And all that time, all those months, you thought I was in St. Louis."

"What was I supposed to think? I even got letters from you."

She shook her head. "Amazing. Simply incredible. If it matters, I'll tell you where I was. Does it matter, now?"

Before he could answer, she swallowed hard and put her pride on the block. She leaned forward and reached out to him. It was like trying to reach across an infinite gulf, to pull back years and laughter, places and feelings that had once mattered to both of them. Things that still mattered: feelings that were, she could see in his face, still alive. She felt obligated to play it out, to probe all the cracks. It had to be explicit between them, with no lingering threads. Only then would she be free enough to look ahead.

"I still love you," she said. "I think we can still have a life together."

402

But that was too strong. Again, the past had risen up to blunt the present. She softened it. "At least it's possible. Don't you think so?"

"I really don't see how. Do you?"

Her hand dangled before him, but he wouldn't help her. He didn't move, and after a while she let her arm drop. They sat for the longest time, saying nothing, probing with their eyes. And just as she had understood about her father, so she suddenly understood about Tom. After ten years, she knew him well. She wanted him and yet she didn't; she wanted to move ahead and at the same time cling to the past. The tenderness attracted her by its warmth and repelled her with its traps. It was still there between them, if that was what love was, but that old worship born of total dependence had eroded at the foundations. That house was coming down, at long last. Now she was impatient, as he must have been, for it to be finished and done with, one way or the other. She pushed it quickly to its turning point.

"I guess I always wanted too much of what you had to keep."

"I had to be away from you before I could even start understanding that. It wasn't your fault, but I was writing again before I was on my own a month. Just little things, unimportant stuff, but it was selling and paying my rent. That was the part of me you never could stand. The writer part."

The gulf had widened. She felt a final surge of desperation, and tried to cast her last lifeline into the past.

"That's all over now."

"It's just getting started," he said.

"Whatever you want to do. We can work it out."

"There's one more thing. It might not work out so easily."

"Tell me."

He just looked at her.

"Ah," she said. "I should have known. Another woman."

He didn't say anything.

"One of your Capitol Hill whores, no doubt. You're surprised I know about that. You and your whore Georgeann. You and that Alice Wilder. I always knew about that." She spoke with all the old bitterness, then pulled herself up short. Now, in the last intimacy that would pass between them, there was no place for that. Again she reached out to him, touching his cheek. "It's all right, Tom. It really is all right."

"This isn't like that."

"Of course it isn't. I know it isn't." She smiled at him. "You see? See how easy I am to get along with? You work it out. Handle it any way you want, only do me a favor. Don't tell me about it please. When you've got it settled in your mind, come back and tell me what you've decided. I'll be here."

•   •   •

She stood at the open door and watched him walk away. Her eyes never left his back. She watched him crank the Ford, as she'd done so many countless times, and drive away from her. When he was gone, she went slowly up the stairs.

Her father had collapsed only yesterday, and already she had begun to make over the house. She had moved her things from the tiny bedroom downstairs into her old room on the second floor. She had opened the back wings of the house and had walked halls dusty from two years of neglect. Now she drew up close to the window and stared out at the lawn and the pool and the trees beyond. Down there, just below her window, Tom had had his first meeting with Gregory Clement, and her mother had spilled a drink. Her children had spent much of their last two years on that lawn. And yesterday her father had rushed there, his face purple with rage, to confront her as she came to reclaim her boys. He had known it even before she had. She had been on her own for months, and now she had grown beyond them all. As she faced him down on the lawn, he must have seen it in her eyes. He had started to threaten, but almost in mid-sentence it became a whine. He was an old, pitiful man. Then he was begging her. He clutched at her dress, but never made it. His right arm curled into a tiny knot of bone as the stroke gripped him and brought him to her feet. The last thing she heard from were the words, "My dear . . . help me."

In a real way, she supposed, she had killed him. She could feel no guilt about that; she wouldn't carry that cross, not even for a day. Still, he was her father. There was blood between them and she would try to treat him kindly. If he didn't die, she would visit him in the hospital and help him spend the hours. She would read to him on summer afternoons, and tell him about the world that used to be.

She heard a noise. Footsteps came up on the front porch. She ran down the long staircase. Her first thought was that Tom had come back. But Orrin stood before her, a weathered suitcase in one hand.

"I'm all packed, miss. I'll be leaving now."

"I see. You'll want references?"

"As it pleases you, miss."

"Come in."

She led him into her father's den. She sat at the desk, took a piece of the old man's stationery, and wrote out two short sentences. *To whom it may concern: The bearer of this letter, one Orrin James, has been in our family employ for more than thirty years. His work has always been conscientious and admirable.* She signed it *Nell Clement Hastings,* wrote in the date, and gave it to him.

At the front door, he said, "I wish I could stay a bit, miss. This place

404

has been my home so long, it brings a lump to my throat to be leaving here. But of course it's out of the question, miss. I understand that. Still, young lady like yourself, you'll be needing some help running this big place. Somehow it feels wrong, leaving you alone like this. The old master wouldn't like it, I imagine."

"I imagine not."

"I wouldn't mind staying on, miss. Just for a few days, till you get your mind settled and decide what you want to do. Stay in the cottage, watch over the gate, do the odds and ends that always need doing around a big place like this. I don't suppose you'd be receptive to anything like that, would you, miss? Just out of loyalty to your family? You wouldn't need to pay me anything."

"That's very admirable, Orrin."

"You'd hardly see me at all, miss. Unless, of course, you needed something. Just anything at all you needed."

"All right," she said. "Yes, you may stay on. We'll talk about it later this afternoon, work out just what your duties would be. Come up around four and we'll talk then."

"Thank you, miss." He picked his way down from the porch and went slowly back to his cottage.

3

Tom walked across town. He had left the glasses and the stick, and it felt good to be walking in the sun again. The day was young and so was he. He had nothing to do, wasn't expected at the *Express* until early next week. But he had given them the one story in advance, and now he felt the need to see it in print. That old ego, churning his blood around as he got closer. He crossed Sherman Street and walked up the hill to the statehouse. It was a long climb to the press room. As he turned into the hall, he saw it in his mind. It would be just like the old days; there would be copies of the paper everywhere, his piece in every hand. Hastings the great was back with a bang. But when he arrived, no one was there. He remembered that there was a press conference in Morley's office. The governor had appointed John Galen Locke head of the state militia, and the flak was coming down. He crossed the room, disappointed to see that there were no papers anywhere. Then he heard the tapping of a typewriter. He moved into the back room and saw Barney Gallagher, sitting at the *Express* desk, pounding out something. Gallagher looked up and saw him. He ripped the page out of the typewriter, wadded it up and threw it away.

"Hello, hotshot," Gallagher said. "Long as we work for the same outfit again, I was gonna leave you a note. Instead I'll tell you. That was one helluva goddamn story you got up for today's paper."

He let out his breath. "They used it."

"Used it? Jesus Christ, I guess. You got every son of a bitch in town after your throat. You should hear the bastards. I hear the phones down at the office haven't stopped ringing since the paper hit the streets. Somebody shot out all the windows this morning, and old Whipple's in seventh heaven."

"Where is it? Where's the paper, Barney? Christ, I've got to see it."

"Not around here, you won't. Every copy we had's been gobbled up and carted off an hour ago. I doubt if you'll find one anywhere in town." Gallagher looked at him, and Tom thought he saw admiration there. "When you come back, you really do it right. Don't bother looking through the trash for the paper. It's a waste of time. If you want to read something, try this. It just came out too."

Gallagher tossed a small, home-printed newspaper, about six pages thick, on the table beside him. Under the logo he saw the words, OFFICIAL PUBLICATION OF THE KU KLUX KLAN; under that, a picture of himself. The caption read AN ENEMY OF THE PEOPLE.

"They don't waste time, those pricks," Gallagher said. "They must have had a tip it was coming. Seriously, Hastings, if I were you I'd go on a long trip somewhere. I think I'd let this be my swan song in Denver."

"In a pig's eye. See you around, Barney."

"I hope so, hotshot."

He went downstairs. The governor's office was packed with press, but he didn't stop. He went out of the rotunda and across the street. Downtown he found the newsboys, swarms of lean and hungry urchins. They came through the streets screaming the headlines of the *Post, News,* and *Times.* It took him a long time to find a kid with the *Express.* He had only two left. Tom called him from across the street and asked him to hold it up, folded so he could see it. There they were, every name he and Marvel could remember between them, each laid out in 18-point type. All the car dealers and the judges and the politicians and cops, the dime store owners, the reporters, the lawyers. The whole front page was nothing but names, laid out under a screaming banner that read KLAN MEMBERS REVEALED.

Even from across the street, even with his bad eyes, he could read it. He ran across and bought it, took it to the courthouse and sat on the bench reading it. Far away the clock at City Hall began tolling the noon hour. He read every name, every word of the story, three times. By the time he was finished, the bell was tolling twelve thirty.

The afternoon drained away, and night came to Denver. Still he walked the streets, too restless to sit, too full of turmoil to go home. He brushed past people he had never seen, and watched their faces as they hurried through life. All the world was a deadline. He walked past Miller's and didn't stop, watched from a corner as Alice Wilder and Arthur McCantless left the *Post* together. He walked north, into the throngs on Curtis Street, where Mabel Normand was making a comeback, and had dinner alone in a place on Arapahoe Street.

A few blocks away, Gabriel came out for the night. Across town, Nell Clement Hastings took a sleeping pill, closed her eyes, and slept without nightmares. John Galen Locke turned a key on Glenarm Place and walked into the cool evening air, to be escorted in his scarlet Pierce Arrow to a dinner party with the governor. Bonfils finished his work and went home to Humboldt Street, to a dark and empty house. And Marvel Millette sat at her table, wondering when and if her man was coming home.

AUTHOR'S NOTE

Denver is a work of fiction, based on fact. Thanks are due the authors of three books on early Denver journalism. Bonfils' affair with Mrs. Madge Reynolds was first described in Gene Fowler's *Timber Line*. Denver historian Bob Perkin described the raucous press room at the old City Hall in *The First Hundred Years*. And Bill Hosokawa, author of *Thunder In The Rockies: The Incredible Denver Post*, has the dubious distinction of providing half the inspiration by giving a talk about the old days, which this writer was privileged to hear. Thanks also to George Ernsberger, for excellence in editing.

There was no Tom Hastings, no David Waldo, no West Colfax family known as the Kohls. Marvel Millette is a composite of the most daring female reporters of her era. Gene Fowler, Calvin Coolidge, and Aimee Semple McPherson are obvious historical personages. The depiction of Bonfils and Tammen, and the kind of newspaper they ran, is, I believe, accurate and fair. Reporters did pick locks, jimmy windows, steal evidence, and rustle booze from Prohibition Squad storerooms. The scene when Bonfils tries to tempt Anna through the hedge was taken from life, though, as Caroline Bancroft tells it, it happened quite differently than I have it here. The scene when Goodwin and Fowler and Tom go to the morgue for a picture of a corpse was also inspired by life—not fifty years ago, but less than ten. Thanks to Patrick A. McGuire, fellow scribe, for that.

John Galen Locke really was Colorado's Grand Dragon. The Ku Klux Klan did take over the state, and for two years held the government in a stranglehold. Ben Stapleton and Clarence Morley were real Denver politicians. Stapleton shook off his Klan ties and served more than 20 years in office. Morley lasted two years as governor and in 1935 was convicted in a mail fraud case. Judge Rube Henry is fictitious, but the situation in the Denver courts is not. Locke did pack juries, rig cases, and dictate appointments. The "thirteenth juror" rape case happened approximately as described, with the same results.

There was no meeting of Klansmen in Grand Junction, but the people who comprise it in the book did live, and held the positions they hold there. The split between various Klan groups was deep and bitter, the feuding between Stephenson and Evans leading ultimately to a break. Stephenson, whose hunger for national power knew no limits, raped his secretary on a train ride not wholly dissimilar to the one in the book. She took poison and died three weeks later. He went to prison for life.

Locke eventually was deposed in Colorado. He died in 1935. William Brown III has no counterpart that I know of in Colorado politics. Senator Patterson did own the *News*, and his fight with Bonfils happened as related in the book. Sidney Whipple lived, and his *Denver Express* was the only paper in town with the guts to consistently buck the Klan.

Bonfils died in 1933, a deathbed Catholic. The *Post* did run a school for newsboys, teaching them to fight, but it wasn't at Limon and wasn't run by anyone named Shaughnessy. A final footnote from history is the lynching of Preston Porter on the plains near Limon in November, 1900. The girl, Louise Frost, was raped and murdered and, with all Denver papers covering the event, her father lit the fire that burned Porter alive. Naturally, Tom's speculation about the murder, and the guilt he feels because of his stepbrother Ethan, are my own inventions.

The *Denver Post* is still the top newspaper in its region. Today the *News* is its only competition. The *Times* and *Express* have long since vanished from the scene. A Woolworth store stands where the old *Post* stood, but the Bonfils legend, *O justice, when expelled from other habitations, make this thy dwelling place,* is still displayed over the front door of the new building, at Fifteenth and California Streets.

John Dunning
Denver, Colorado

Made in the USA
Coppell, TX
02 March 2021